Helena Hunting

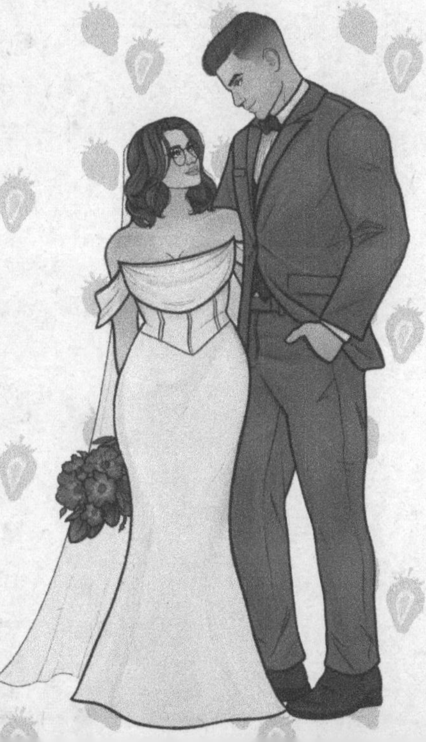

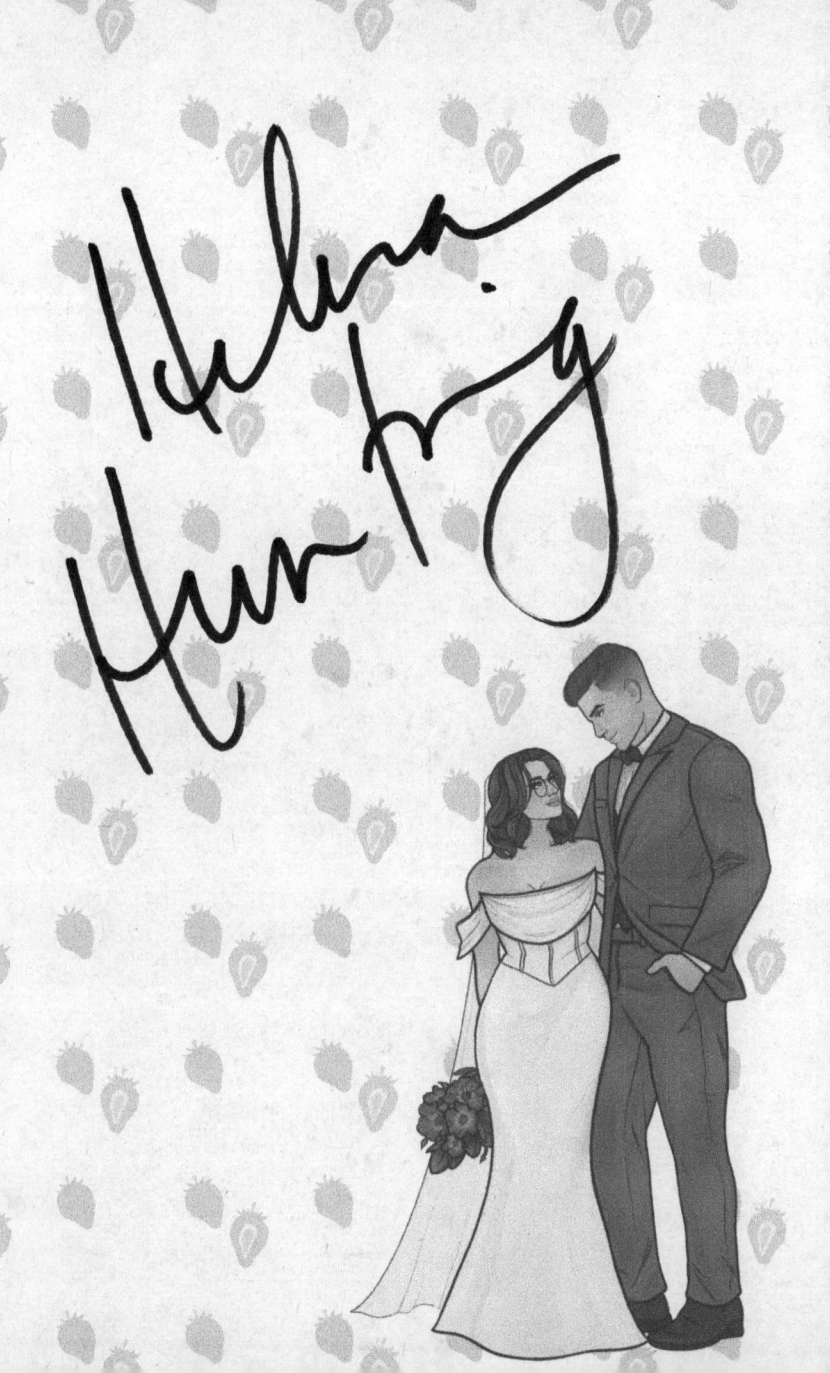

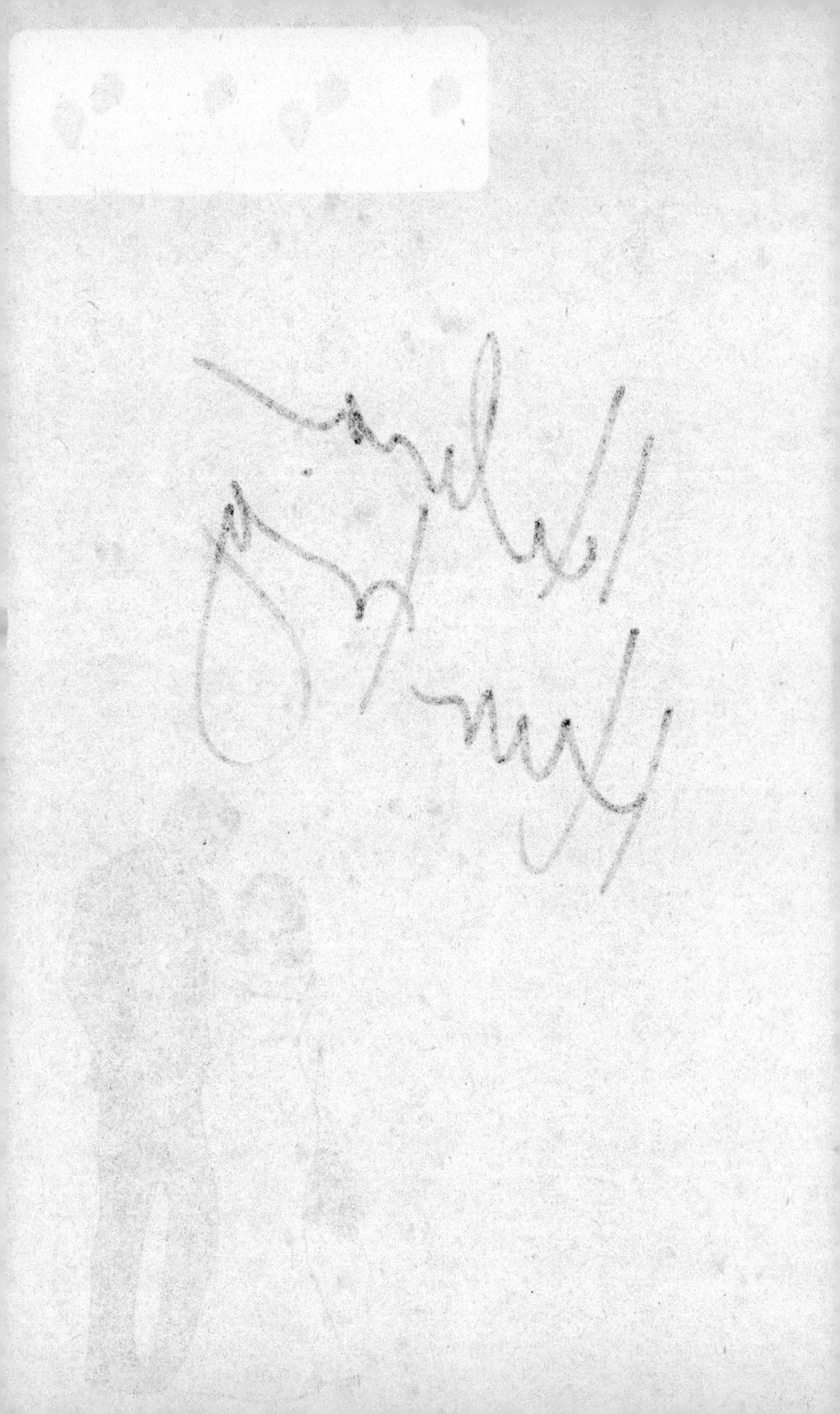

IF YOU *Claim* ME

NEW YORK TIMES BESTSELLING AUTHOR
HELENA HUNTING

IF YOU *Claim* ME CAST

CONNOR GRACE
TERROR ENFORCER
WHOLLY DEVOTED TO HIS MEMS

SIBLINGS
ISABELLE & PORTIA

PARENTS
DUNCAN & COURTNEY

MILDRED REFORMER
(DRED, DARLING, LITTLE MENACE)
BEST FRIEND TO FLIP

SIBLINGS
NONE

PARENTS
DECEASED

TEAMMATES
CURRENT & FORMER

TRISTAN STILES
HUSBAND TO RIX
BEST FRIEND TO FLIP
SIBLINGS: NATE AND BRODY

QUINN ROMERO
TERROR ENFORCER

FLIP MADDEN
BROTHER TO RIX
BEST FRIEND TO DRED

HOLLIS HENDRIX
BEST FRIEND TO RONAN
BOYFRIEND TO AURORA

DALLAS BRIGHT
BEST FRIEND TO ASH
ENGAGED TO HEMI

KELLAN RYKER
TERROR GOALIE

ASHISH PALANIAPPA
HUSBAND TO SHILPA (TEAM LAWYER)
BEST FRIEND TO DALLAS

BADASS BABE BRIGADE

LEXI FORREST-HAMMER
(LEXI)
MARRIED TO RONAN
TERROR ASSISTANT COACH
SISTERS: FEE & CALLIE

HEMI REDDI-GRINST
(HEMI, WILLS, HONEY)
BEST FRIEND TO SHILPA
ENGAGED TO DALLAS BRIGHT

SHILPA PALANIAPPA
(SHILPS)
BEST FRIEND TO HEMI
MARRIED TO ASHISH PALANIAPPA

PEGGY AURORA HAMMERSTEIN
(PEGGY, AURORA, BUMMER, PRINCESS)
DAUGHTER TO RONAN HAMMERSTEIN
GIRLFRIEND TO HOLLIS HENDRIX

TALLULAH VANDER ZEE
(TALLY/TALLS)
DAUGHTER OF TERROR COACH
ATTENDS TILTON UNIVERSITY

BEATRIX MADDEN
(RIX, BEAT, BEA)
SISTER TO FLIP MADDEN
ENGAGED TO TRISTAN STILES

RONAN FORREST-HAMMER
FORMER TERROR GOALIE
MARRIED TO LEXI

ESSIE LOVELOCK
ESS, SWEETHEART
RIX'S BEST FRIEND
GIRLFRIEND TO NATE STILES

Copyright © 2025 Helena Hunting
All rights reserved
Published by Helena Hunting
Cover Design by Hang Le
Cover Illustration by @rosiesfables
Developmental Edit by Becca Mysoor Fairy Plotmother
Editing by Jessica Royer Ocken
And
Erica Russikoff of Erica Edits
Proofing by Julia Griffis
Amanda of Drafthouse Editorial Services
Sarah at All Encompassing Books

If You Claim Me is a work of fiction. Names, characters, places, and incidents are all products of the author's twisted imagination and are used fictitiously. Any resemblance to actual events, locales, or persons, living or dead, is entirely coincidental.

Except as permitted under the US Copyright Act of 1976, no part of this publication may be reproduced, distributed or transmitted in any form by any means, or stored in a database or retrieval system, without the prior written permission of the author.

Produced by the Inkfluence

ACKNOWLEDGMENTS

Husband and kidlet, I adore you. You inspire me every day and I'm so grateful for your love.

Deb, how have we been at this for so long? Thank you for always coming along for the ride.

Becca, thank you for making this journey such a joy.

Kimberly, thank you for finding an amazing home for the audio at Dreamscape.

Sarah, your organizational skills are legendary and I'm so grateful for you.

Victoria, thank you for sharing your creative energy with me, and for always sending the reminder texts.

Alpha-Betas your feedback is so greatly appreciated, thank you for being on my team.

BBB, thank you for sharing your creativity with me!

Catherine, Natasha, and Tricia, your kindness and wonderful energy are such a source of inspiration, thank you for your friendship.

Jessica, Erica, Amanda, Julia, and Sarah, thank you so much for working on this project with me. I couldn't do this without you.

Kate and Rae, thank you for being graphic gurus. Your incredible talent never ceases to amaze me.

Beavers, thank you for giving me a safe place to land, and for always being excited about what's next.

Kat & Krystin, your friendship means the world to me. Thank you for pulling me away from the keyboard to live life.

Readers, bloggers, bookstagrammers and booktokers, thank you for sharing your love of romance and happily ever afters.

For the ones with the hardest shells and the softest hearts.

CHAPTER 1
DRED

FRAUD.
 I am a fraud.
 I have committed fraud.
 The word keeps slicing at me—unraveling my fragile ecosystem, poisoning it.
 A panic spiral I don't have time for is heading my way. If I was at home, I could succumb, let the anxiety wash over me and drag me down. But I'm at work, and my shift at the library doesn't end for several more hours. I slip my finger under the hair tie around my wrist and pull it away from my skin, letting it snap back into place.
 I repeat the action a dozen times, fighting to contain the panic before it can turn into a prickly weed and wrap me in its unrelenting, thorny hug.
 The paper in my hands taunts me as I will the words and numbers to change, but they remain the same. I owe $105,300.27 in back rent (with interest) to the new apartment manager. I should have realized the rent I was paying was far too cheap for the building I was living in, but I didn't question it, and now here I am—because my name is the same as my late grandmother's, and until the management company changed, they

continued to charge me what she'd been paying. Now I've made the leap to current market value and have to fill in the five-year gap I created.

I stop snapping the hair tie before I break the skin, fold the letter, and slide it back into my purse. Looking up, I grasp the edge of the sink, meeting my distressed gaze in the reflection. "You do not have time for a breakdown," I say aloud. "Put it on hold. You can lose it when you get home. But you cannot do it here. You will figure a way out of this. You always do."

I hope I'm right.

I take a deep breath, put my feelings on lock, and step out into the hall. I have five minutes left on my break, enough time to make tea. And then the after-school crowd arrives, which means my favorite twins Victor and Everly will grace me with their vibrant energy—which I could use right about now. They live at the group home a couple of blocks away, and I adore them.

Except as I turn toward the staff lounge, I run smack into a very solid chest. Warm hands wrap around my shoulders to steady me, sending an unexpected jolt through my body. I recognize the cologne immediately. I frown as I look up and am met with a closeup of the very chiseled jaw of Connor Grace.

He's irritatingly attractive, and his presence is wholly disarming.

Also, we're making physical contact, and my body enters haywire-mode as a result—like I wasn't already distressed.

Connor's piercing, steel gray eyes are locked on me, and his full lips tug down at the corners, as though the world is an irritant he's forced to endure.

I know two versions of the man standing before me.

The first is the archenemy of my best friend, Flip Madden—that Connor is a Terror enforcer with a nasty reputation on the ice and professional hockey's favorite villain.

The second Connor is the pro hockey player who attends his

coach's younger sister's practices and games because she's his number one fan, and he's hers.

These are vastly different sides of the same man. The latter is a glimmering ruby of kindness I want to tuck in my pocket like a treasure.

For the past year, Connor has taken up space in the seat next to mine at Callie's games on a nearly weekly basis. We both love that little girl.

New panic takes hold. *Callie.* "What are you doing here? Is Callie okay? Is Lexi?"

Lexi Forrest-Hammer is Connor's pregnant coach and my best friend.

"Lexi is fine. So is Callie." He drops his hands from my shoulders. "I've been looking for you."

His tone makes it sound like it's my fault he couldn't find me. Like he wasted precious time, and I should feel bad about it.

Looks like our shitty moods match.

"Well, here I am. What do you want? I'm on break." *For three more minutes.*

He rubs the back of his neck. "I need Meems's books."

"Who?"

"Meems. My grandmother. I need her books."

I ignore the soft feeling that blooms in my chest at the adorable nickname this hard-edged, posh-as-fuck man has for his grandmother.

I have so many new questions. Like, why am I the person he's sought out? Also, he and his family are billionaires. Why in the world would he need books from the library for his grandma when she can probably afford to buy every bookstore in the city?

I link my arms behind my back so I can snap my hair tie a few times. I'm still fighting my panic spiral. "The world doesn't revolve around you and your needs, Connor."

"Oh, I'm highly aware." His steely eyes stay fixed on me, full of secrets and sadness. "My needs are generally at the bottom of everyone's list. But my world revolves around Meems, and right now she needs what you have."

Is this emotional manipulation? Connor knows how soft I am for Lexi's sisters. Maybe he's exploiting that for his Meems. My natural reaction is to dig my heels in. "So my world is supposed to revolve around her now, too?"

The harsh slant of his brow softens slightly, despite my sharp words. "Meems has an appointment in less than an hour. I've been looking for you for twenty minutes already, and I'm supposed to meet her at the doctor's office. I just need her books."

I cross my arms, frustrated by his pretty face and his entitlement. "Why is your lack of time management my problem to solve, Connor?" I have my own crap to deal with, but my compulsion to fix problems wants to win this battle. Which is so damn annoying.

Dorothea, the ancient and unfortunately unfriendly head librarian who has worked here longer than the world has been turning, rounds the corner. The lines in her face deepen. "Mildred! You are not allowed to bring nonemployee guests into the staff room! Tell your boyfriend he can visit you in your off-hours."

"He's not my boyfriend, and I didn't invite him back here." I take Connor by the elbow and ignore the warmth that travels through my arm at the contact. "I'll just show him out."

"Your break is over in one minute!" she calls after me.

"She seems fun," Connor mutters.

"You have no idea." I usher him through the door and steer him out from behind the counter, putting much needed space between us. "How did you even get back there?"

"I walked through that door." He points to the one clearly labeled *Employees Only* with a long, perfectly manicured finger.

He pulls a list out of his pocket and holds it in front of me. I snatch it from him. The handwriting is familiar. "Please explain."

Because I don't have the mental or emotional bandwidth to decode this mystery on my own.

"That's Meems's—my grandmother's—list. She comes here every Wednesday to return her books and take out new ones. I'm here to pick them up." He crosses his thick arms over his thick chest and stares down at me with expectation and irritation. "She said you would have them ready for her."

From the little I know about Connor, his grandmother is one of the only members of his family who supports his career. "I'll need to look her up. Is Meems her real name?"

"No, it's Lucy Drake. Do you have the books or not?"

The dots connect. *Oooohhhhh.* I know that name well. In all the months he's been sitting next to me at Callie's games, Connor has never once mentioned his family. Although, when we attend Callie's hockey games, Connor is focused on cheering for Callie and makes the most limited of small talk. But he always sits beside me. Every time. And he's stiff and awkward with me and sweet as a gooey marshmallow with Callie.

Of course this means I find him endlessly fascinating.

And this new information only ups that intrigue. "Lucy Drake is your grandmother?"

"Isn't that what I just said?" his voice drips with impatience.

"Why doesn't she go by Grace?"

"Because it's less recognizable."

"Right." Another wave of panic hits, and I reflexively snap my hair tie half a dozen times. "Why isn't Lucy here? What kind of appointment does she have?"

His jaw tics, and his eyes flash. "She's been unwell. As I said, she has a doctor's appointment. I'm her errand boy, hence my request for her books."

"How ill? Is she okay?" Lucy is one of my favorite library patrons. I look forward to her weekly visits. She's always dressed like she's ready for Sunday service, which makes sense now that I know she's richer than God. I always reserve one of my breaks for when she comes in.

Connor purses his lips, like offering personal information is painful. "She's felt better. May I please have the damn books?"

"They're not ready yet. She doesn't usually come until later in the afternoon, and I'm waiting on one to be returned. It should be here before the end of my shift."

He runs a hand through his hair, his discontent shifting. "She needs the books. I can't disappoint her."

His swell of anxiety softens the edges of my own, like my body is trying to neutralize it. I know that Lucy reads in the morning and in the evening before bed. It's part of her routine, and I understand how hard it can be to lose that. "I can bring them to her tonight. I'm off around six."

His shrewd gaze doesn't leave my face as his tongue drags across his delightfully plush bottom lip. He seems to be assessing my level of honesty.

I'm not used to seeing Connor off the ice or outside of the arena. This version is in distress and out of his element. Like a cheetah who has escaped its enclosure, he's exotic, beautiful, and potentially lethal. Despite knowing how much Flip despises him, my girl parts appreciate Connor's hotness, which feels like a betrayal to my best friend.

Connor holds out his hand. "Give me the list."

I pass it back to him, unsure where we're going with this.

He pulls a pen from his pocket and scrawls something on the back. "This is her address, and this is my phone number. Message when you're on the way. You'll bring the books?"

"I promise." Like I need this hot, entitled douchebag wreaking havoc on my ovaries two days in a row with his furrowed brow and expectations. But curiosity has gotten the better of me. Also, I want to see for myself that Lucy really is okay.

He passes me back the paper. "You better mean it."

"I won't let Lucy down."

CHAPTER 2
DRED

I'm clearly in full-on denial mode about the impending loss of my home. This explains why I'm standing outside the Grace mansion while my life is at risk of falling apart. Also, I'm horribly curious, and I need to know who Lucy is outside of our library encounters. In addition, I'm unreasonably eager to peel back another of Connor's layers. And finally, being here means a delay in dealing with the shitstorm of my life, if and when I choose to acknowledge it.

I focus my attention on the property around me. *This is next-level.* I know this for sure, though I can barely make out the house's peaked roofline and turrets—the place has freaking *turrets*—through the perfectly manicured gardens obscuring my view. Victor and Everly would be so impressed. Maybe I can sneak a few photos.

The grounds are protected by a ten-foot wrought-iron fence. I stand in front of the ornate gates like a peasant hoping to gain favor with the queen. It's not far off the mark. Lucy is important, at least to Connor. And me.

I press the intercom button. A man who is not Connor answers. "Grace Manor, how may I be of assistance?"

"Hi, uh, I'm Dred—Mildred Reformer." It seems more appropriate to use my given name over my preferred nickname. "I'm from the Toronto Central Library. I'm here with Lucy's books." It sounds utterly preposterous.

"Oh wonderful!" His voice lilts up. "She's expecting you. I'll meet you at the front door."

I glance up at the camera trained on me. "Sure thing."

The gates open. As soon as there's enough room, I slip through. It's another five-minute walk up the winding interlock driveway. I take pictures of the gardens lining either side. When the house—mansion—comes into view, it's like something straight out of a fairy tale.

I don't have a chance to sneak another photo, because a man dressed in a full suit is waiting in the open door for me as I huff my way up the steps. His gray brow furrows as he looks past me to where a Rolls-Royce and another expensive car are parked.

"Were you dropped off, Ms. Reformer?"

"No, I took the bus."

His frown deepens. "I would have come down to pick you up."

"It's a nice night, and the gardens are beautiful." I point to my feet. "Besides, these work just fine."

He makes a sound and steps back, ushering me inside. "Come in. I'll fetch Mr. Grace."

"Sure." I feel like I've stepped into the pages of some kind of period novel with the butler who uses words like *fetch*.

He rushes off. I stand in the massive foyer, taking in the sheer opulence. It feels more like a museum than somewhere a person should live. The ceilings must be twelve feet high, and the trim itself is a work of art. The whole room is. The floors are tiled in an intricate mosaic design. Each recessed wall panel tells a story with custom wallpaper. In the middle of the room is a table with scenes carved into the perimeter. A massive vase of fresh flowers sits in the center.

I knew Connor's family was rich, but it hadn't really computed that they were *this* wealthy until now. It's difficult to process. And I understand a little better why my best friend Flip, who attended the same hockey camp as Connor when they were teens, has harbored such deep loathing for him all these years. Flip has fought for every step he's taken up the financial ladder, whereas it seems Connor has always sat at the top.

This also reframes my feelings about Connor's place in the hockey world. He plays not because he needs the paycheck, but because he loves the sport. And the world has twisted him into someone to regard with disdain and disapproval.

Except Callie doesn't. She sees something else. Something good. I'm pretty sure Lexi sees it too.

Footfalls pull my gaze toward the arched doorway, and my stomach twists. Angry, guarded, covered in art, Connor Grace's broad shoulders are rolled back, brows a dark slash, beautiful face a mask of stunning arrogance. And based on our interaction earlier today, he's just as fragile as the rest of us.

"Cedrick said you took public transit here," Connor snaps by way of greeting.

"Uh, yeah. I came straight from work." It was the most logical option. Going home first so I could drive Betty, my beater of a car, which sometimes chooses not to start, would have been a waste of time.

"I would have had a car pick you up." His brow furrows, which seems to be his standard expression.

"The bus was already going past this street anyway." I fully expect him to take the books and send me on my way.

He tilts his head. "Does your best friend know you're here?"

"Of course not." Flip would have insisted on driving me and acting as my bodyguard.

Connor's nostrils flare. He spins around, motioning for me to follow him as he strides down the hall. "Meems is waiting for you, and apparently she's very fucking excited."

"That makes one of you," I mutter.

Connor isn't particularly chatty at Callie's hockey games, but he's not typically this brusque, either. I can't decide if it's the change of location or the people involved causing it.

I try to take in the details in the woodwork as I follow Connor through the expansive mansion, but the guy has long legs, and he's in quite the hurry to get to Meems. *Or away from me.* He's wound tight, body tense, hands flexing and releasing with each step. It's like he's uncomfortable with my presence, but these are the instructions he's been given. For someone who is often pegged as *not* a team player, he seems able to put his own needs aside for the sake of others when it matters.

I follow him up a huge spiral staircase, trying—and failing—not to stare at his ass. In my defense, it's fucking spectacular. He turns right and stops at the first door.

His eyes find mine, flaring briefly with unease as he taps the door with a single knuckle. "Meems? Can I come in?"

"Of course!" she calls.

He opens the door. "I brought you your librarian." Connor steps aside and motions for me to go ahead of him.

"And I have your books," I add as I move past him.

Connor watches me, like he's cataloging my reactions.

The space has cathedral ceilings, ornate woodwork, lush carpets, and high-backed chairs that make it feel like it belongs in another era. But it's the tiny spitfire of a woman seated regally in a deep green velvet chair that inspires a shocking wave of relief and puts a smile on my face.

Lucy grips both arms of the chair and pushes to stand.

Connor rushes across the room to help her. "You're supposed to be resting."

She brushes away his offer of assistance. "Resting is all I've done for the past week." She turns her bright smile on me. "Dred, I'm so thrilled you're here."

"I'm glad I could come see you." And put to rest my churning worry that she would be too ill to handle a visit. "You have a beautiful home."

"My late husband liked grand things, may he rest in peace." She makes the sign of the cross, then reaches for me.

I curve my hand gently around hers, feeling her grandson's eyes on me. "Connor told me you've been sick. Are you feeling better?" I scan her face; she looks tired, and smaller than I remember, but I can't decide if it's because this space is huge, or if she's shrunk since I last saw her.

"I'm fine. Just old, and little things are bigger when you get to be my age." She squeezes my hand. "Come sit." She nods to the chair across from her. "Connor, dear, please have Cedrick bring us tea, will you?"

He tucks a hand in his pocket. "It's already on the way."

"Of course it is." She smiles up at him with clear adoration.

A gentle grin tugs the corner of his mouth, as though this small praise is a gift he cherishes. Someone loves Connor Grace, and based on his behavior today, he loves her back just as fiercely. This is the other person Connor is soft for. Hard, angry, baleful Connor is sweet for Callie and his Meems. The dichotomy is dangerously alluring.

Beyond the tattoos hidden under his long-sleeved shirt, the aggressive ice play, and the I-don't-fucking-care attitude is a man who cares very, very much. So much that he invited me inside his world for the person who means more to him than his privacy.

Meems smiles impishly. "Now that you've visited Dred at the library, you can ask her on a date."

I'm glad the tea hasn't arrived yet, because I would have sprayed it all over Lucy. As it is, I nearly choke on my spit.

Connor jumps in before I can splutter out a response, his cheeks flushing pink as he rubs the back of his neck. "Meems, don't meddle."

"I've told him all about you." Meems winks.

"You're not playing matchmaker," Connor grumbles.

Lucy makes a clucking sound. "You need a partner before I pass to the other side."

"Well, it looks like you'll have to live forever then, since that's unlikely to happen," he grumbles while inspecting his fingernails. It sounds more like a plea than defiance.

Every time she visits the library, Lucy talks about how wonderful her grandson is. I hadn't realized until now that she's never mentioned his name, or what he does for a living. But she's always promised to bring him with her one day so she could introduce us. How ironic that he happens to be my best friend's most-loathed teammate.

A woman arrives carrying a tray with a silver tea set, and a man follows with a tray of food. They pour tea, then leave with a bow.

This feels a lot like *The Twilight Zone*.

I pull the new books out, passing them to Lucy.

Her eyes light up. "Is this the one with the highland warriors who travel back in time?"

"It is. It came back this afternoon. It's very steamy." I wink. "I think you'll love it."

"I'm sure I will."

"I'm sure I won't," Connor mutters.

"It's educational, dear," Lucy quips.

"You mean it's embarrassing," he counters.

"Connor reads to me at night sometimes," Meems explains.

I bite back a smile. I would pay good money to see broody Connor reading spicy romance to his posh grandma. "Some of them have audiobooks," I offer.

"Meems enjoys my discomfort," Connor replies dryly.

"And Connor pretends to hate the books, but he never says no to reading them," Lucy stage-whispers.

My heart squeezes at the fond smile that softens both their faces. This is the kind of familial love I've never had, and I'm shockingly, painfully jealous. Even the Terror's villain is beloved by someone.

Lucy's eyes light up. "Tell me all the juicy library gossip. How are those saucy twins? Did Victor get the A he was hoping for on his English essay? Is Everly staying out of trouble?"

"Who are Victor and Everly?" Connor asks, like he can't help but involve himself in the conversation. This is probably the most I've heard him speak at any given time.

"They're teens who live in the group home a few blocks from the library. They're my favorites," I explain before I turn back to Lucy. "Victor got his A, which isn't a surprise, and Everly made it through last week without losing any privileges."

This is part of our weekly routine. I always take a break when Lucy arrives, and we sit in the coffee shop, drinking weak brew while I fill her in on the library gossip before we talk books. She's endlessly interested in the community programs I've developed.

Connor moves to sit in one of the empty chairs. He says nothing, just listens and observes.

I share the previous week's adventures, and we discuss last week's books before I tell her about the new ones I brought while we finish our tea.

I set my empty cup on the table. "I should probably head home so you can have your evening."

"Would you mind reading me a chapter before you go? Connor tends to skip the spicy parts," she whispers.

"Your heart is too important to tax with excessive spice, Meems," Connor replies.

I steal a glance at him and smile at the blush coloring his cheeks. "Sure, I can read to you. Would you like me to start with the highland warriors?"

"Oh please. They sound fun."

"So fun." I settle in and do my best to ignore the feel of Connor's eyes on me as I read. Lucy is fast asleep by the end of the first chapter.

I tuck her book ribbon between the pages. "Will she be out long?"

"She might be done for the evening. I'll move her to her bed if she doesn't wake up." Connor carefully adjusts the footrest and reclines the chair, tucking a pillow by her cheek so she doesn't get a neck crick. He kisses her temple and guides me out of the room.

I take one last look at her before I go. I adore Lucy. We've grown close—closer than I realized maybe. Our time together always feels special, and it fills a selfish need for a maternal connection.

Our conversations have mostly revolved around books, the library programs, and sometimes her late husband. Occasionally, we've veered into personal pieces of our lives, but neither of us has ever spoken of our connection to the Terror. I'm intensely protective of my friendship with Flip, just like she's protective of her grandson.

I wait until Connor and I are halfway down the hall before I ask the question that's been eating at me. "How did Lucy's appointment go today?"

He stops just before we reach the stairs and turns to me. "She needs surgery."

"What kind?"

"The kind that could keep her here for another decade." He rubs his bottom lip with his manicured fingers. "But right now she's not strong enough to survive it, and the doctor is concerned she might never be."

Pain lances my heart. "What does that mean?"

His jaw tics, but his eyes remain on mine. "She needs a heart valve replacement. If she can't have the surgery, I could lose her inside a year."

The truth is sandpaper rubbed across raw skin. There's an answer to his problem, a way to keep Lucy here, but it's out of reach. That's almost more than I can bear. Maybe because my world is falling apart, and I already stand to lose so much if I can't figure out what to do about my apartment. Maybe because I sense how devastated Connor is by the prospect. Maybe because I've come to see Lucy like the grandmother I never had.

I reach out and cover his wide palm with mine, his fingers flex, but he doesn't pull away. "I'm so sorry." Emotions rain down on me, and tears well up—for making my emotions his to deal with, for his pain, for my own.

He looks at me strangely. "You didn't make her heart weak."

I withdraw my hand and rummage in my bag for a tissue, still on the verge of tears. This is his loss, not mine. *Then why does it hurt so much?*

"I should go." I finally find the tissue I was looking for, but with it comes a piece of paper.

It unfolds as it flutters to the ground, and Connor scoops it up before I can. His brows pull together as he scans the document—the one from my landlord.

"You're in trouble." It's a statement, not a question.

I grab the letter and stuff it back in my purse. "It's a misunderstanding. I'll figure it out." I rush down the spiral staircase, wishing a fairy godmother would appear, wave her magic wand, and fix my problem.

It seems all gifts come with a price.

CHAPTER 3
CONNOR

I connected the dots a while ago that Meems's favorite librarian was the woman I sit next to at Callie's games. But I kept that to myself until recently, mostly because it meant I had an unguarded, unfiltered view of Mildred through my grandmother's eyes.

My palms dampen as I enter the arena. I keep trying to shove Mildred back into the neat little box labeled *my enemy's best friend who I sit beside at Callie's games*, but yesterday she stepped out of it, and now I can't get it closed.

Because on top of how sweet she is with Callie, I saw the way she was with Meems. They care for each other, and I witnessed how much it hurt Mildred to find out I could lose Meems—that *we* could lose her.

I watched Flip at practice today for signs of stress. Mildred is his best friend—maybe more, but I've never seen evidence to prove that. He was his usual self at practice, focused, no signs of worry, no compulsive phone checking in the locker room. Which begs the question: Does he know she's in trouble? And if not, why?

The kids are already on the ice and Callie is in net. I scan the seats and spot Mildred, my heart rate spiking as I head in her direction. She's sitting in the front row, wearing a team toque, bundled in a winter jacket. There's a smile on her beautiful face as she adjusts her glasses. She hasn't noticed me yet. Neither have the team moms a few rows back.

"He's usually here by now," one of the moms says as I enter hearing range.

"Maybe he's not coming."

"Here's hoping. He's such a bad influence on these kids."

"Right? When isn't he mouthing off on the ice?"

"Or getting into fights. Did you see the most recent article? Apparently the head coach is worried about the season without Hammerstein."

"I heard he was the only one who could keep Grace in check," another mom agrees.

I'm used to this kind of chatter. I'm always the bad guy, always the team problem. And I feed into it. Why shouldn't I? The hockey world always needs a villain, and I'm the perfect candidate. Rich family, entitled, bought my place in the pros according to the media, and an asshole on the ice. And off it. Might as well give the people what they want and live up to my reputation.

Mildred never treats me like the bad guy, though, even if her best friend, one of my teammates, hates me. It's one of the many reasons I find her fascinating.

I reach the front row, and the moms who were openly shit-talking me drop their voices to a whisper. Anticipation makes my skin prickle as I slip into the seat beside Mildred. She smells like books and strawberries and vanilla.

Her shoulder-length brown hair is tucked under her cap, her glasses need to be cleaned, her nose is pink, and so are her cheeks. She looks every bit the librarian she is.

Mildred glances at me and then over her shoulder before refocusing on the ice. "They'd probably shut their mouths if they saw you with your Meems."

"Doesn't make me less of a dick on the ice." I steal a peek at her, admiring the slight smile that quirks the corner of her mouth before shifting my eyes to the rink.

"No, but it is eye-opening." She tugs at the hair elastic on her wrist. "How is Lucy?"

"In love with you."

That faint smile grows. "Tell her it goes both ways."

"She wants me to invite you for dinner." Meems couldn't stop talking about Mildred and how amazing she is. And beautiful. I agree, but pursuing her might elevate my villain status to new, deplorable heights.

Mildred's eyes find mine. Chocolate brown, full of secrets and questions. "Is she feeling better?"

I nod. "She's getting her strength back." Which means I won't have a reason to visit Mildred at the library, or ask her to bring books to Meems again. But if she accepted an invitation to dinner...

She turns to look at me. "How long have you known I'm her librarian?"

"A while. You never told her about your connection to the Terror." Hearing about Mildred through Meems's eyes showed me another side of the woman seated next to me. I didn't want to ruin it. Or connect the dots Meems and Mildred hadn't.

"Neither did she," Mildred notes. "It didn't seem relevant. It's more a posturing thing, isn't it? Talking about our affiliation to someone we perceive as famous, so we seem important. I'm here because Lexi is one of my closest friends, and Callie and I have a special bond, just like you." She tips her chin up. "If you didn't care about Callie and what she thinks, you would have given those moms more reasons to shit-talk you." She turns her attention back to the ice.

She's not wrong. I don't want Callie to see me the way everyone else does.

Callie saves a shot on net. Mildred and I rise at the same time to whistle and cheer.

"What's a while?" Mildred asks.

"Pardon?"

"You said you've known I'm Lucy's librarian for a while, but you were rather vague."

"Does it matter?" I run my hands down my thighs. When I realized it was Mildred Meems met with every week, I started asking about those library trips so I could learn more about her. She develops community programs, she devours romance books, and she loves sourdough bread and strawberry shortcake. It made me feel like I know her, like we share a common bond because we care about the same people.

Mildred hums and returns to her seat.

We sit in silence, watching the game, cheering every time Callie stops a shot on net.

As the final minutes count down, I ask the question I've been pondering since last night. "What's going on with your apartment?"

Her posture stiffens, and she throws my words back at me. "Does it matter?"

"If you're in trouble—"

"Please, let's not." Her eyes are hard and soft at the same time, pain mixing with anger.

"But you—"

"I can't talk about this right now." She motions to Callie on the ice. "That little girl is my family, so are Lexi and Flip and the rest of the crew. They're my whole world, Connor. Losing my apartment means I could lose everything. Again. Like I always do. So please, let it go. It already hurts. There's no need to pour salt on the wound."

The final buzzer sounds, and the kids file off the ice.

Callie rushes over in her bulky goalie equipment and throws her arms around me. "Did you see my shutout?"

"I sure did! You were awesome on the ice tonight. Good job protecting the net. I'm so proud of you."

"Thanks!" She beams up at me. "I feel like I play better when you're here. You're my good luck charm."

"I feel the same way when you come to my games." I wink, stepping back to let Mildred have her moment.

I find her eyes on me, lips curved in a pretty smile.

I come to Callie's games because I care, but it's also nice to feel like I'm important to someone other than Meems.

And I like sitting beside Mildred.

After yesterday, that's increased exponentially.

Callie goes to the locker room, and the coach stops to talk to Mildred. I want to wait, to walk her out, to ask her questions, but I won't push. She smiles and waves as I pass.

For a moment, I wish I was the good guy and not the villain.

Or maybe with Mildred, I don't have to choose.

Maybe I could be both.

CHAPTER 4
DRED

"What are you doing here?" Standing in the hall outside my apartment is Connor Grace. Dark hair perfectly styled, steel eyes trained on me. He's wearing black boots, dark-wash denim, and a long-sleeved black shirt, despite the warm weather. Under that shirt he is a canvas covered in beautiful art. I know because I saw it when we were in Aruba for his teammate Tristan's wedding this summer, though mostly from a distance.

He looks gorgeous as usual, but discordant with his surroundings. Every time I see him outside of the arena, he seems out of place. Though he fits at least a little better in Lucy's home, amidst the opulence and grandeur.

I glance over his shoulder to the closed door across the hall, where Flip lives.

"I need to talk to you," Connor states flatly, but he still manages to infuse the sentence with certainty and insistence. His gaze drops to Dewey, tucked into the crook of my elbow. "What the heck is that?"

"Dewey, my pet hedgehog." I pull Connor inside my apartment, quickly closing the door.

I have enough bullshit going on in my life without him and

Flip punching each other out in the hall. Also, I'm terrified that something happened between Callie's hockey game last night and now, and Lucy has met an untimely end. But Connor doesn't look destroyed, and I have a feeling losing her would ruin him. Worse, based on the way my heart is thrumming in my chest, it will ruin me too.

Still, I ask the question, just to be sure. "Is Lucy okay?"

"For now." That's a painful truth.

He stuffs his hands in his pockets, but they only stay there for a second before he laces his fingers behind his neck. Connor glances around my apartment. Not with judgment, but with interest, maybe—like he's trying to see me in the things I surround myself with. Which to be honest, is mostly old books and board games.

The apartment is a mausoleum to the life my grandmother left behind. I kept everything she had when I took over the lease after she passed, seeking some kind of connection to my history other than our shared name. It was the one gift she gave me, along with a letter explaining why she stayed out of my life.

"Let me put Dewey away." I cross to his hedgehog condo and gently set him inside before turning back to Connor. "What do you need to talk to me about?" I cross my arms, then drop them to my sides, then cross them again. Looks like we're both fidgety. "Can I get you something to drink?" I move to the kitchen, which is all of three steps away, and shove my head in the fridge. I need something to do with my hands that doesn't involve wringing them.

I have water, a single can of no-name lemon-lime soda, strawberry cordial, and two ultra-light beers.

I grab the beers. Whatever the reason, Connor being here can't be good.

I uncap them both and pass him one, then chug half my own and grimace because I dislike the taste of beer immensely. I only have it because Flip left them here for our game nights.

Connor sets his beer on the table. "Please show me the letter that fell out of your purse when you were at Meems's the other night."

This again? "Why?"

"Because I want to read the entire thing."

"You already know the gist. Why do you need to read the whole thing?" *And why are you suddenly so interested in me?*

"Because I do."

"And that's supposed to be enough of a reason?"

He blinks at me.

I blink back. But I'm too intrigued by his sudden appearance at my apartment to refuse. So I fish it out of my purse and hand it over. I took it to a lawyer today. Apparently, it's legit. That was an expensive and shitty conversation.

Connor scans it with an unnervingly attractive furrowed brow. He's brutally handsome. His steel eyes lift. "Who else knows about this?"

"No one." *Yet.* I considered telling Lexi because her dad is a fancy New York lawyer, but she's married to Roman, and he's tight with Flip. While I won't hide it from Flip forever, I want to be sure of the scope of the problem first. And ideally also have a solution.

Connor employs his mind-reading skills. "Why haven't you asked Flip for help?"

I roll the beer bottle between my hands. "I won't do that."

Connor's brow pulls together. "You don't think he would help you?"

"He would insist on it, and I won't ask."

Curiosity shifts his features, changing the harsh landscape to soft questioning. "Why not?"

"Because it would change our relationship, and I don't want that for either of us."

"Do you love him?"

God, he's blunt. "Yes. Like family, but I'm not *in love* with him."

Connor isn't the first or last person to ask this. All our friends have believed it to be true at some point. So I'll just be clear. "There has never and will never be anything romantic between us. He's too important to me, and I won't ask for his help on this, and that's all I'm going to say about that."

Flip has been used by enough people in his life. I won't unbalance our friendship by having him step in and fix this for me. My love for him and the health of our relationship is too essential. And Connor is the last person I would choose to confide in about any of that.

Still, he nods, seeming satisfied, and rubs his chin. "You care about my Meems."

That's a hard right. It takes me a moment to catch up. "Uh, yes. She's been coming to the library for a long time."

"You have lunch with her every week."

"I do," I confirm.

He cants his head, eyes locked on mine. "Do you love her like family, too?"

I bite my lips together. Admitting this feels like a trap.

My expression must tell him what he needs to know, because he hums, nods, and stares down at me with serious, calculating eyes. "I have a proposition for you."

"That sounds ominous." And like there are strings attached. As it seems there always are.

"It's not ideal, but it will solve your problem. However, it will also create a few new ones."

"Isn't that always the way?" One person's win is another's loss.

"Basically, yeah." He crosses his arms. "My Meems adores you."

It melts my ovaries every time this perpetually broody man refers to his posh grandmother as *Meems*. I nod. "We've already established that I adore her back. I'm not seeing how that solves my problem."

He releases a tense breath, jaw flexing as his gaze shifts to the right. "Without the surgery, she has at most a year, maybe a bit more, if she's very careful. But her immune system is struggling to the point that the flu could take her out right now."

My stomach sinks. "She's that immunocompromised?" How can she come to the library when it's often full of germ-infested, adorable kids?

He nods.

"I'm so sorry." I want to offer comfort in the form of a hug, but Connor doesn't strike me as very hug receptive. Besides, every time I touch him, my body goes haywire.

"You don't have anything to be sorry for. You didn't do this to her body." He rolls his shoulders back, like this next part is uncomfortable. "She wants to see me married and settled before she passes. She's been fairly relentless about me pursuing you. If you become my wife, it would make her happy, and it would solve your financial problems."

"How would marrying you solve my financial problems?"

"My family has a lot of money."

Shock makes me feel weightless for a moment. He's serious, though. His intent is written all over his handsome, remote face. "But...until yesterday you didn't even really speak to me unless you had to. We don't even like each other?" The second half comes out as a question. Sure, I'm fascinated by him, and I find him attractive, but that's a far cry from wanting to marry him.

"I don't dislike you." He looks anywhere but me and swallows.

His phrasing seems intentional. Protective. "Not disliking me is not the same as liking me," I point out.

He shifts from foot to foot. "I enjoy sitting beside you at Callie's games."

"In silence," I note.

"It's often better when I don't speak."

This is a man who is used to being hated. By everyone—except his Meems and his number-one fan, who's a nine-year-old orphan.

"I'll hire the best lawyer in the city to handle this for you."

He holds up the letter from my landlord. "I will cover the legal costs and the rent owed on the apartment, and for every month we're together, starting thirty days from our engagement forward, I'll pay you a quarter of a million dollars. When Meems passes"—he makes the sign of the cross—"we'll annul the marriage, and you'll be free to live your life."

The proposal itself leaves me reeling. But more than that, the end of Meems is a heartbreaking thought.

If I agree to this, I could leave the relationship with three million dollars. I'll never struggle financially again.

"What's the catch?" Other than all my friends will wonder whether I've lost my mind, and my best friend might murder my future husband. *Am I really considering this?*

Connor frowns. "You'll be married to me for an undetermined number of months. It could be a handful, or it could be more than a year if something miraculous happens. You'll also have to meet my family, who loathe me almost as much as my teammates. That's the catch, and it's a pretty big one."

Geez, this guy really can't stand himself. He's so rigid—prepared to either be laughed at or negotiate the terms of this business venture. Because that's what it is. He's offering me financial stability in exchange for his grandmother's happiness. She would be my Meems, too. She would be *my* family. *Having her for a grandma is almost worth it on its own.* This offer tells me more about Connor as a human being than maybe he realizes. Under the gruff, cold exterior is a man with a very soft, very fragile heart.

"You said annul."

"That's correct."

"So no consummating the marriage." *Why are parts of my body that have no business being excited tingling?*

He clears his throat and looks away uncomfortably. "You would be under no contractual obligation to do so. Although there may be occasions when you'll have to kiss me," he warns.

"Like the wedding."

He nods. "Like the wedding."

"I assume you have some kind of legal and binding contract?"

Connor doesn't seem like the kind of man who would come to the table unprepared.

He pulls an envelope out of his pocket. "You should read it over."

I take a seat at the kitchen table and read the contract through twice while Connor stands with his arms crossed, wearing an expression of impassive indifference. But his thumbs tap restlessly against his biceps, belying his nerves.

"If you agree, the plan would be to have a short engagement," he adds.

"Won't Meems be suspicious?" My friends sure will.

He glances away, toward my bookshelves. "I may have mentioned Callie's games."

"You mean that we sit beside each other?"

He dips his chin.

I wait for him to elaborate, but apparently I'm supposed to draw my own conclusions. Like somehow our attending Callie's games has made us realize we're in love? But maybe his sitting beside me every time is a bigger deal than I've realized. I assumed he had ill intentions at first, but then...he just kept sitting there, just kept being sweet with Callie and not a dick to me.

And now here we are.

If I agree to marry him, I keep not only my apartment, but the found family I've worked so hard to foster. I won't have to move out of the city so I can afford cheaper rent.

Flip will be pissed that it's Connor. But he'll get over it. He loves me like a sister. He knows what it's like to always worry about making ends meet. And he'll understand why I didn't let him come to the rescue.

I reach behind me and pluck a pen from the mug on the shelf.

"You'll have to pretend to like me," he warns balefully.

"You'll have to make my Meems believe that we're real." He makes this sound like an impossible feat.

"I know." I press the end of the pen, and the point appears.

"You'll have to move in with me," he adds. "You'll have to live with me for the duration of our marriage."

Is he trying to dissuade me now? "I understand. I'm doing this for me and Meems, in that order."

He nods his approval. "Good."

I hover the pen over the line with my name typed underneath. It feels like giving a blood oath. But this is the way out of the mess I'm in—probably the only way without making it my best friend's problem. It's a contract. Just a job with a deadline, an excellent payday, and the most amazing grandmother in the world. Besides, Connor is gone half the year.

I sign my name and date the papers before I have a chance to second-guess myself.

Connor leans in and does the same. "I'll have it filed and send you a copy." He folds the contract and tucks it into his pocket. Then he pulls out a small velvet box.

He doesn't drop to one knee, and I don't expect him to. This isn't a love match. We're doing it because we love the same person, and this union gives us both something we need. He flips the lid open. Inside is the most stunning engagement ring I've ever seen. I hope it isn't a family heirloom.

Wordlessly he extends a hand, and I place mine in his palm. Tingles shoot up my arm, and warmth courses through my veins at the contact. Marriage has never been on my radar. Romantic love isn't something I'm well-versed in. All love is scary, but the kind where you give your heart, body, *and* soul to another person has always seemed too precarious a thing to want for someone as broken as me.

But this isn't love. This is a business arrangement. We're helping each other, and that's it.

Still, my heart stutters as he gently slides the ring onto my finger.

IF YOU CLAIM ME

I meet his gaze, and sadness flickers there for a moment before his expression goes carefully blank. "You're stuck in this nightmare with me now." A small, rueful smile tugs the corner of his mouth. "It will probably get worse before it gets better, but I appreciate you doing this for Meems."

CHAPTER 5
CONNOR

"I should go." I've accomplished what I set out to. I thought it would be harder—that she might laugh at the audacity. I was fully prepared to offer half a million a month to sweeten the deal, but apparently the idea of being married to me isn't quite as reprehensible as I'd expected.

And now Meems's ring is on Mildred's finger. A perfect fit. It looks good there—like it belongs, despite Mildred being used to a modest life.

She'll be my very own Cinderella, complete with evil in-laws.

Meems will be thrilled, and that's the goal. I need her to believe I'm settled, and I won't spend the rest of my life alone—that someone other than her can love me.

Mildred pushes her chair back and stands. "What happens now?"

I ruin your life for the next year. "I'll take this letter to my lawyer and have him dig into it." I slip the document from her landlord into my pocket, alongside the contract. "But I'll be able to get it all straightened out."

She blinks up at me, her beautiful, guileless, wide eyes searching mine. "I mean with us. Now that we're engaged."

Oh. "We'll have to make an announcement, but you can leave that to me." I'll make this as painless as possible for her. The parts I can, anyway. "After the announcement, we can negotiate timelines."

"What will you say to Meems?" she asks.

"That we've been spending time together for months."

"And you think that'll be enough?" She tugs at the hair tie on her wrist, then folds her hands behind her back.

"Yes. She wanted me to ask you out and here we are." I'm confident Meems will be easy to persuade.

"A date is a little different than an engagement."

"I can be very persuasive," I assure her. "Especially when it comes to Meems."

She looks like she's on the verge of panic, and I can't have her changing her mind. Not now. Not when Meems's happiness, and maybe even her life, is on the line. A full heart has a better chance at survival than a half-empty one.

I need to get out of here before she asks for the papers back. "I'll call when I have an update," I assure Mildred.

I leave her standing in her tiny, run-down kitchen and step into the hall.

As if I've somehow summoned him, the door to the right swings open and Flip, the Terror's golden boy, appears. In the eyes of the team and the media, he can do no wrong. He's like Teflon. Bad things slide right off him.

The easy smile drops from his face and appears on mine. It's almost a conditioned response for me to derive joy from his misery. Flip has always had all the things I want: a family who adores him, friends who support him, a team that's always backed him, a best friend who lights up everyone's world. And even if it's only temporary, this special piece of his world is now mine.

I shouldn't be an asshole, but I can't help myself. Besides, it's what everyone expects.

"What are you doing with Dred?" He crosses the short distance and grabs me by the collar, shoving me against the wall.

"I told you to leave her alone."

My smile widens. He's aware that we both attend Callie's games. Maybe he even knows I sit beside her. Every time I so much as say hello to Mildred when she's with her girl squad, Flip gives me another warning. This is how it's been between us since our Hockey Academy days. Flip is the phoenix who rose from the ashes of poverty and struggle. I'm the spoiled, rich brat whose family bought him a pro hockey career. The joke's on Flip, though, because my family never for a minute believed I was talented enough to make it. They expected me to come home with my tail between my legs. Even my teammates expected me to fail, yet here I am, a constant thorn in Flip's side.

He doesn't realize that he's the knife shoved between my ribs.

He has always had everyone's allegiance, and I've always been on the outside. Nothing has changed since I joined the Terror. I'm forever the outcast, the problem that can't be solved.

"I asked you a fucking question." Flip pushes into my personal space, his nose an inch from mine. "What are you doing with Dred?"

"That's my business, not yours." I goad him and hope he takes a swing. I deserve a split lip and black eye for what I've just done to his best friend.

The door behind me opens.

"For fuck's sake." Mildred sighs and tries to push her way between us. She gives me a look that reeks of disappointment. "Let Connor go, Flip."

I arch a brow. "Yes, Flip, let me go."

"You're not helping," Mildred snaps.

"I'm not trying to."

Her nails scratch my skin as she pries his hand from my collar.

"What is this asshole doing in your apartment, Dred?" Flip's anger is usurped by another emotion—maybe betrayal, or hurt.

For a moment I regret pushing his buttons. Mildred's already stuck with me for the foreseeable future. Straining the relationships that are important to her, my fiancée, is not in my best interest. I need her happy and compliant, not angry and defensive.

Flip grabs her hand, eyes wide with shock and horror. "What the fuck?"

I wish I could revel in the glee of knocking him off-kilter, but he's touching what's mine and raising his voice, and I won't have it.

I settle a palm on Mildred's shoulder. I've recently discovered that it's startlingly soothing to touch her. "Stop yelling at my fiancée," I warn through gritted teeth.

"Just throw gasoline on the fire, why don't you?" Mildred mutters with an eye roll.

"The fuck?" Flip looks like his head is about to explode.

The elevator doors slide open, and half my team and their significant others fill the hall. Their timing couldn't be more perfect.

I turn to look at all of them. "Mildred and I are engaged."

CHAPTER 6
DRED

Connor's timing could not be worse. My friends pile out of the elevator as he makes this announcement. Rix is carrying a churro cheesecake, and her husband, Tristan, has a cooler, also likely full of delicious things made by Rix.

Dallas and Hemi, Lexi and Roman, Hollis and Hammer, Essie and Nate, and Tally all wear matching confused expressions. Only Ash and Shilpa are missing, but Shilpa just had a baby, so the Palaniappas get a pass on fajita night. The men of the group are current and recently former Terror hockey teammates—except for Nate, who is one of Tristan's younger brothers—and the women are my Babe Brigade. They're the only real family I've ever had, and I'm about to drop a significant bomb on them. Here's hoping they can handle it.

"Am I high? Did Connor just say you and he are *engaged*?" Rix's eyes are saucers.

"The fuck, man?" Hollis shoots daggers at Connor with his eyeballs. "When are people going to stop stepping on my damn toes?"

Hammer squeezes his arm and whispers something to him. Probably reassurance. He's been waiting to pop the question while everyone around him gets married.

IF YOU CLAIM ME

"This is a joke, right?" Flip looks like he's on the verge of something not good.

"It's not a joke." Connor looks Flip dead in the eye as he leans down and kisses my cheek.

His lips are soft and warm, fingers flexing gently on my shoulder. I'm annoyed at the thrill that shoots down my spine. I give him what I hope is a scathing look. "Can't resist lighting the match, can you?"

"Just playing my part, darling." He winks. "I'll be in touch."

And with that, he slips past everyone and disappears into the elevator, leaving me to deal with my very confused friends. Fucking Connor Grace. Why can't he be the nice guy who sits next to me at Callie's hockey games? I take a deep breath. *He's fixing your life*, I remind myself. *You probably should have asked him to stay.* And needle Flip? Not a great idea.

It seemed like a fantastic idea in the moment, but how the hell am I going to explain this?

"I think we should move this into Flip's apartment," Rix suggests. The *before he blows a gasket in the hallway* is implied.

Lexi slips between the others to join me, worry etched on her pretty face as she threads her arm through mine. She's pregnant and showing and still acting as a barrier between me and Flip and everyone else. Aside from Flip, Lexi is my best friend.

She's married to Roman Forrest-Hammer, formerly Hammerstein, the Terror's recently retired goalie. Lexi understands loss. She became the legal guardian to her sisters Callie and Fee when her mother and stepdad were killed in a boating accident a couple of years ago.

"Is everything okay?" she asks.

I nod. "I'll explain."

We file into Flip's apartment. He's already pacing with his hands in his hair. "How long has this been going on? How can you be engaged to that assclown? Why would you commit yourself to someone like *that*?" He spins to face me. "Why him?"

Flip knows me better than anyone. Of course he's upset.

Before I can respond, he fires another question at me. "Is this some kind of revenge plan on his part?"

I cross my arms. That Connor's world and mine overlap should be wildly implausible, but I'm still a little offended. "Because he obviously can't be truly in love with me, is that what you mean?"

"He doesn't deserve you!" Flip shouts. "He's malicious. He always has been! He's going after the people I care about!"

If that were really true, it wouldn't be me Connor went after, it would be Tally. But Flip isn't ready to pull himself out of Denial River yet.

"Are you saying I'm not strong enough to stand up for myself in the face of coercion?" I press.

He continues to pace the room. "Have you lost your mind?"

"Aside from the sandwich incident, he's actually a decent guy," Nate says.

"Don't take his fucking side!" Flip snaps.

Tally steps in front of him and places a hand on his chest. "This isn't helping."

I sigh. I expected a meltdown. But Flip is already in a spiral, so I need to recalculate. He's not reasonable enough to be given the truth and hear it. And beyond that... "You know what? I don't owe you or anyone an explanation. Not everything is about you, Flip."

He spins around, and his anger melts as his face changes to a mask of guilt and regret. I've said this exact thing to him before —when his sister, Rix, and his best friend, Tristan, were hate-turned-love fucking behind his back.

His choices had made it difficult for them to be honest with him. And his reaction now is doing the same for me. We stare at each other, our friends gathered around us, not taking sides, not judging, ready to step in if they're needed. *God, I love these people.* They're more than enough reason to go through with marrying Connor. Besides, I've already signed the paperwork, and I have a feeling getting out of it would cost more money I don't have. Connor doesn't seem like the type to half-ass something like this.

Flip raises his hands. "You're right. I'm sorry. I'm just... I'm shocked. I didn't see this coming. At all."

"I don't think any of us did," Hemi, the head of Terror PR and one of the Babes, adds.

I seriously hope I haven't made her season impossible with this new development. Flip and Connor were at least civil at the end of last season. Fingers crossed they don't go back to fighting in the locker room over their teenage stupidity—or this.

"I know." I glance around the room. "Connor and I both go to Callie's games." It's true, even if it has little to do with why I'm in this position.

"So you've been secretly dating each other?" Flip asks, the hurt in his voice slicing through me.

Lying will just make this more difficult, so I carefully step around the truth. "We know each other better than any of you realize." Maybe even better than he and I could have known. "Connor and I have our reasons for getting engaged."

"This sounds like a business transaction, not a marriage," Flip says.

I can barely meet his forlorn gaze. Flip has deep convictions about love and marriage and what it all means. "I need you to set aside your personal feelings about all of this and just... support me, okay?"

"Are you in trouble?"

"No." *Not anymore, provided Connor follows through.* I get the sense he isn't someone who doesn't keep his word.

"So you're not in danger?" Flip presses.

"No. I'm not in danger."

"And this isn't coercion on his part?"

"You know I wouldn't let that happen." I've been forced into enough corners in my life. This one I can confidently navigate without falling on knives.

Flip nods slowly, shoulders deflating as he exhales a heavy breath. "This is something you want?"

"It's the right thing to do," I reply.

"You didn't answer the question," Flip presses.

"It's what I want. He has a big heart. You've seen him with Callie." None of it is a lie.

"He's stepped up for us in the past." Tristan wraps his arm around Rix's shoulder. "In Aruba he took care of the hotel situation."

"He took care of a lot more than that," Nate mutters, but I think I'm the only one who catches it.

Essie hugs Nate's arm and kisses his bicep.

I ran into Connor on the beach in Aruba after the wedding. He seemed particularly despondent, even with his bottle of expensive champagne and the pretty view. I didn't push then, even though I wanted to.

Flip turns back to me. "If you ask me to support you, I'll support you, no matter what. But if he fucks you over in any way, I'll end him."

I smile up at my best friend, grateful and sad. "I know you will." I can't tell him why I've made this choice. He'll want to fix it, and I won't risk it changing our friendship. Everyone in this room is too important.

I just hope Connor doesn't give Flip another reason to hate him, for the health of his team and our friendship.

After a long look, Flip hugs me. "If you let me, I will always have your back, Dred."

"I know," I say, muffled by his chest. "Thank you. I promise this is the right decision for me."

"I need a drink," Flip announces. The guys follow him into the kitchen.

The girls converge on me.

"Are you pregnant?" Rix asks.

"No. I'm not pregnant." And I don't have plans to consummate the relationship even though I find Connor wildly attractive.

"Are you going to tell us what's going on?" Hemi, who is usually the boss of us, asks gently.

"Eventually, yes."

"But not right now?" Hammer clarifies.

"Not right now, no."

"Have you secretly been in love?" Tally asks hopefully.

With Connor? No. But his grandmother is another story. "It's a complicated situation. I promise all of you I want this, and that eventually, I will explain it all, but for now, I just really need you to be on my side."

"Okay. We can do that," Lexi pipes in.

The rest of the girls nod their agreement. This group has been through it over the past few years, from Hemi's on-ice engagement to Lexi marrying the team goalie last season. We always have each other's backs.

"He really is a good person," Essie whispers.

I smile, even as that makes me wonder what she knows that other people don't.

"Whatever you need, we're in this with you," Rix promises.

I nod. I want to believe I won't end up with a broken heart, but I don't know if that's possible—not because I'll fall for Connor, but because I already love Meems.

The guys return with drinks and stare expectantly at us.

I need to diffuse the tension and take the attention off me, otherwise I might crack under the pressure. "How are we feeling about this years prospects?"

"Pretty sure Brody will be a top pick when they call him up," Roman says, bless his heart. He's on my side because I was on his when he and Lexi planned a shotgun wedding last season to save her career.

Brody Stiles is Tristan's younger brother. He's currently in college, but destined for the pros.

"He was magic this summer at the Academy," Hollis agrees.

Tristan nods. "He'll be a better player than me."

While they come out to talk hockey in the living room, the Babes move to the kitchen to unpack the contents of Tristan and Rix's cooler, setting up for fajita night.

"We should also discuss the fundraising gala for the library. We have two location options, and I've already secured some incredible silent auction items," Hemi says.

The library where I work is my other current love. "I can't tell you how much I appreciate you and your willingness to help out with this," I tell her. "I feel like your idea of a gala and Dorothea's are not the same, and as a result, our profit margin will be substantially higher this year."

Hemi nods. "Yeah, the Legion hall is cute for a stag and doe, but not the best if you're trying to raise funds for programming."

We toss around some ideas for the evening as we set the table.

"My contribution to dinner is still in my fridge at my place," I tell the girls when we've finished. "I'll be right back."

"I'll come with you," Lexi offers.

She follows me across the hall, waiting until the door closes before she asks, "Is your life in danger?"

"No."

"Did the two of you fall for each other at Callie's hockey games?" Despite me already answering this, she seems hopeful.

He's not a one-dimensional dick, but that's not the same as being in love. "Also no, but I'm aware that aside from the way he plays hockey and the way the media portrays him, he's a good guy."

"He sits beside you every time."

"He does," I agree. "And I definitely find him irritatingly attractive."

"He's not my type, but he's a good-looking man," Lexi agrees.

"Yeah."

We both nod.

"Do you know what Nate's comment was about?" Lexi asks.

"You caught that, too?" I rub my bottom lip. "I just know Connor came to the rescue with the accommodations at Rix and Tristan's wedding. If something else happened, I wasn't told about it."

"Me neither." She props her hip against the counter. "So are you going to fill me in on whatever is going on here?"

"If I tell you, it has to stay between us."

She rubs her baby belly. "As long as your life isn't in danger, I can agree to that."

I explain what happened, including the letter from the landlord, how I went to a lawyer for legal advice—it was the most expensive hour of my life—and Connor's proposition this afternoon, including my relationship with his Meems and her health.

"So this is a business transaction." She shakes her head. "Flip would help you out of this. So would Roman and I."

"I know, but you also know I can't accept that from either of you," I reply. "It changes relationships. This is my best way out of the hole I'm in, Lexi."

"There are other ways out that don't include marrying Connor, though." She tips her head. "So why did you really agree?"

It's my turn to sigh. "I love his grandmother."

Her eyes widen. "But enough to marry him? I'm not trying to be difficult," she assures me. "I just want to understand. Tell me how it sounds to you."

"Like I've lost my mind." I play with the ring on my finger. "All these months I've been sitting next to him, watching him show up for Callie. And then I saw him with Lucy and it just... hit this place inside me. He's broken, Lexi. Like me."

"You're not broken, Dred."

I take my friend's hand. "I am, though. The things I went through as a child shaped me in a way that means I don't always fit with the rest of the world."

Spending my first three years being raised by drug addicts who were always looking for the next fix was damaging in ways

I can't explain. I spent three days in a house with two overdosed parents before the police came knocking. The memories of that time are only fragments, but with time and age I've been able to fit them together like a puzzle I never want to finish. And they made me who I am.

"You fit with us," Lexi says.

"I know." My bottom lip trembles. "I'm so grateful for this family. I love all of you, but I don't know if I can ever fall in love the way others can. All Connor wants is to make his Meems happy, and I needed a way out of this situation that wasn't asking the people I love to save me. So like I said, he and I both get what we want out of this. Being financially indebted to the people I rely on for emotional support is..." I shake my head. "Not something I can do. Asking friends for money unbalances the relationship, and Connor isn't my friend." He's an ally, and there's a difference.

"So you're marrying him." She sounds concerned, not upset.

"For a finite amount of time, to make his Meems happy. He loves her so much, Lexi. She's the only one in his family who seems to support him." I try to hear the words through her ears, but it's impossible to separate myself from this situation. I know in my heart this was the right call for me. Not ideal, but the best option for the circumstances. Honestly, when I give myself a moment to reflect, it's kind of miraculous.

"Isn't there another way around this that doesn't include becoming his wife, even if it's supposed to be temporary?"

I shrug. "I'm not sure, but I've already signed a contract, and I can't imagine Connor's lawyers would leave loopholes. I'm at peace with my decision."

"It's a tricky position to put yourself in," Lexi whispers.

"I can handle it."

"I just wish you didn't have to." She sighs and hugs me, hands settling on my shoulders as she steps back. "But I'll be here to support you, however you need me."

"Thank you."

IF YOU CLAIM ME

My phone buzzes with a new message from my fiancé.

CONNOR
Engagement party: Saturday, 2pm. Don't worry about attire. I'll take care of everything, including your transportation.

GRACE HOTELS HEIR ANNOUNCES ENGAGEMENT

CONNOR GRACE, HEIR TO THE GRACE HOTELS DYNASTY ENGAGED TO LIBRARIAN MILDRED REFORMER

Connor Grace, son of Duncan and Courtney Grace, older brother to Portia and Isabelle, and grandson to Lucy Grace (née Drake) has announced his engagement to local librarian Mildred Reformer, daughter of Gary and Judy Reformer, both deceased. Connor is heir to the Grace Hotels dynasty. He has a degree in economics from Harvard University.

Grace currently plays professional hockey for the Toronto Terror after an unexpected trade last year. A long-standing feud between him and the Terror's popular center, Phillip "Flip" Madden, made for a tumultuous season. However, the Terror rallied and made it to the playoffs, though they did not secure a Cup win. It is highly debated whether Grace and Madden's discord is in part responsible. Grace has a long-standing history of bad behavior on the ice and holds the record for penalty minutes with the league. It is unclear whether he intends to join the family hotel business upon the conclusion of his hockey career.

Mildred Reformer graduated with honors from Tilton University with a BA in library science. She also has a master's in library science from Tilton and a PhD in the same. Sources report that Mildred spent her childhood in the foster-care system and has been described by former teachers as "bright, but reserved." Her estranged grandmother and last remaining relative died five years ago.

According to our sources, Connor and Mildred were introduced through mutual friends, and Grace is intent on continuing their whirlwind romance with a short engagement. "I plan to marry Mildred as soon as possible," he told *The Toronto Daily*.

CHAPTER 7
DRED

"Thank you for making this presentable." I motion to my face as Essie dusts my cheeks with setting powder.

"You don't need makeup to be pretty, Dred," Flip notes from his spot on my couch.

I glance over at him. Dewey walks across his shoulder and sticks his nose in his ear. Flip doesn't even flinch. He may not love who I'm marrying, but he's determined to be involved in every part of the process.

"What he said." Essie hugs me. "You're stunning. I'll see you in a couple of hours."

The fact that she and Nate live two floors down makes it convenient for her to jump in as my makeup artist. When she's gathered her things, I close the door behind her and turn back to Lexi and Flip. "This whole engagement party/meet-the-family thing is intense."

"We'll be there to support you the whole time," Flip assures me, gently scratching Dewey's head.

"I know. Thank you."

Lexi glances at the clock over the stove. "We should get you into your dress. Your car will be here soon."

"You're right. Let's do this."

The engagement party is being held at Connor's parents' house. I assume it's also a mansion. I wish it was being held at Lucy's. At least then it would be a little familiar. And Lucy already likes me.

I leave Lexi and Flip in the living room and walk down the hall to my bedroom. The dress is laid out on my bed. It was delivered yesterday, along with shoes, a clutch, and undergarments. How Connor knows my size in everything is a question mark, but it's the most beautiful dress I've ever seen.

I strip out of my joggers and T-shirt and step into the buttery soft fabric. I zip it as far as I can, running my hands over my hips. I tried it on yesterday and was surprised at how perfectly it fits. It hugs my curves in all the right places and is my favorite color.

I tug at the hair tie on my wrist out of habit and wince as it snaps back into place. My skin is bruised and raw from the incessant snapping over the past few days. When I was a teen, the habit became a replacement for more dangerous methods of dealing with my anxiety. Normally I have it under control. But this situation is far from normal. I'm engaged—to a man who "doesn't dislike" me and has agreed to pay me a quarter of a million dollars for every month we're together. Yeah, it's pretty fucked up. I quickly slide several mismatched bracelets over my wrist to cover the damage. Then I return to the living room.

Flip's eyes widen. "Wow, that dress is... You look great."

Lexi nods her approval. "It looked good on the hanger, but on you it's..." She makes a chef's-kiss gesture.

"I can't fathom what it cost," I admit.

"Just remember that his family are billionaires, so dropping ten grand on a dress isn't something they think twice about," Lexi says.

"Do you really think it cost that much?" I'm sure my horror is written all over my face. "Betty is worth half that."

"Your car is a trooper." Flip deposits Dewey back in his enclosure.

"She is," I agree. "God, I'm nervous." When I signed the contract, I was in full panic mode, terrified to lose everything. And now I'm terrified by what's ahead of me. I know Connor loves his Meems and has a soft spot for Callie. But he's antagonistic and used to being hated. I really don't know who I'm committing myself to for the next year. *I've survived so much worse, though.*

"It's in Connor's best interest to take care of you and make sure you're comfortable and happy," Flip says.

He doesn't know the half of it, but in terms of the health of his team, he has a point.

"He's obviously trying with the dress." I just wish I was better prepared. In the week leading up to the party, Connor has texted updates, but we haven't spent any time together because our schedules didn't allow either of us to make Callie's practices or games.

My phone pings with a message.

> CONNOR
>
> The car is there to pick you up. It's a Rolls-Royce. Cedrick is the driver, you met him when you brought over the books. He'll alert me when you arrive, and I will come to collect you. See you soon.

I send back a thumbs-up and slide my phone into my clutch. "It's go time."

"Let's get you to your engagement party." Lexi and Flip take the elevator to the lobby with me. Lexi snaps a couple of photos in front of the garden before they walk me to the waiting car.

"Connor isn't picking you up himself?" Flip's brow furrows with disapproval. "I would have driven you if I'd known that."

"Ms. Reformer, it's lovely to see you again," Cedrick says jovially.

"Hi, Cedrick. It's nice to see you, too." I introduce him to Flip and Lexi.

"Mr. Grace's coach and teammate." He nods. "It's wonderful to meet you both. Will you be joining Ms. Reformer?" He holds open the door for me.

"We're just her escorts to the car," Lexi explains.

"I'll see you soon." I hug them both, then climb into the back seat.

Flip is still frowning as we drive away.

We haven't been on the road for more than a minute before my phone pings with a new message in my Babe Brigade chat.

I open it to find a photo of me, shared by Lexi.

> **LEXI**
> Check out the hot librarian.
>
> **TALLY**
> Ooooh!!!! You are so pretty in that dress! Cannot wait to see you!
>
> **HEMI**
> So this is happening! •• You are stunning! See you soon, you 🤍
>
> **RIX**
> You are smokin' hot!
>
> **SHILPA**
> You look incredible.
>
> **HAMMER**
> That dress is Ah-mazing!
>
> **ESSIE**
> I need to know who the designer is!
>
> **DRED**
> It's not a belated April fool's prank. I'm glad I don't look as nervous as I feel.

While they don't know the actual truth, at least it's not a complete charade. I didn't envy Rix when the whole thing with Tristan finally blew up. Flip was beside himself when he found out, but so much of it had to do with his own issues and how his past actions made him feel.

It was just as challenging for Hollis and Hammer, and then Lexi and Roman last season. They tried so hard to stay on the right side of the line, but it's clear they were meant for each other. At least it's only Connor's family and Meems that we have to convince that we're madly in love.

Lexi sends me a private message.

> **LEXI**
> You've got this. Just be yourself, and if they can't see how amazing you are, fuck them.

I hug my phone.
It buzzes against my chest.
I look back at the screen.

> **FLIP**
> I hope Connor knows how lucky he is.
>
> I've got your back, forever and always, okay?

> **DRED**
> I know. And I'll always have yours.

> **FLIP**
> Family for life.

How many times did I wish for a foster brother like him? There were so many new families. I remember every last one, even though there should be too many to count. Twenty-six times I moved into a new place.

The fear had nearly eaten me alive the first two times I was dropped off at another unfamiliar house. All I knew was hunger, loneliness, and parents who loved their drugs more than me.

I'd been so certain it would be a repeat of the home they'd taken me out of—that these people would end up as blue-tinged mannequins, silent, staring into the endless forever, and the cycle would repeat.

It would be years before I had a true sense of what stability meant. Too many years. By then I was irreparably broken. Pieces missing, holes carved in my heart and my soul.

Every kid that comes into foster care has endured some horrible trauma. They don't take kids away unless the situation is dire, or in my case, unless both parents OD'd and there were no relatives to take me.

I shut down those memories. They're unhelpful and the last thing I should focus on. I wonder how different Connor really is from me. Sure, he grew up in a home with two parents and endless money, but it doesn't mean he was loved or cared for by the people who brought him into this world.

On the drive over, I review the photos Connor sent me this week with details about his family members. His parents are Duncan and Courtney. Duncan is Lucy's only son. Connor also has two younger sisters, Portia and Isabelle. Portia's husband, Bryson, and Isabelle's husband, Julian, both work for Connor's father at Grace Hotels, as do his sisters, although in less prominent positions.

Half an hour later, I arrive at the Bridle Path, a very exclusive neighborhood in Toronto full of mansions. Every yard is manicured, with beautiful flowers blooming in picture-perfect gardens and driveways full of flashy cars. Interestingly, his parents' house isn't far from Lucy's.

Cedrick pulls down the long, winding driveway. It's nothing like Lucy's house, which feels like it belongs to every princess ever born. This mansion is modern and sterile, with straight lines and little personality.

With each glimpse into Connor's life, I peel back another layer. A picture starts to form. The fighter on the ice, the enforcer, the man who needles people until they crack and end up in the penalty box along with him. He's good at pushing buttons and garnering reactions. Then there was the determined man who presented me with an offer, a way out of my situation. But as soon as I accepted it—gratefully!—he began apologizing for what I was about to endure.

What new things will I learn today?

Cedrick announces our arrival and exits the vehicle as Connor comes down the front steps. The tension in his shoulders seems to melt as Cedrick opens the passenger door, unveiling me.

Was he worried I wouldn't come? That I would change my mind? My heart skips a couple of beats as I take him in.

He's ungodly gorgeous, which is infuriatingly typical, and impeccably dressed.

His suit isn't black, or navy, or gray. It's the same deep teal as his hockey jersey, and it matches my jeweled clutch and my shoes.

Of course he would color coordinate us.

Connor steps in and extends his hand. I take it because it feels rude not to. And I'm increasingly intrigued by the way it feels when he touches me. Heat shoots through my fingers and up my arm, spinning through my body as I carefully step out of the car.

His gaze moves over me on a slow sweep. "I wasn't sure if I could make you look less like a librarian." He nods his approval. "This was the right dress for you."

I look up at his irksomely handsome face. "Was that an insult decorated with a compliment?"

"I'm used to your cardigans." A hint of a smile tugs at the corner of his mouth. "Can you see without the glasses?"

I bat my lashes. "Fuck you, Connor."

"I don't believe you want that from me." He gazes down, untouchably aloof. "But I'd be happy to amend our contract and add that to our arrangement. Sort of like a bonus?"

I smile up at him. "Please fuck *yourself*."

"Why, when everyone else is so much better at it?" he quips darkly.

I reach up and press my palm to his cheek. His eyes flare in surprise. "Stand down, Connor. Just because you're everyone else's villain doesn't mean you need to be mine, too."

His expression shifts and almost softens, if just for a moment. "I thought you'd change your mind and run."

"I considered it."

"Smart woman. But that contract is thorough, so you're mine now, for better and definitely for worse." He holds out his arm, and I link mine with his.

"What's the story we're telling your parents?"

"That I fell for you at Callie's hockey games," he says smoothly, fingers brushing the line of bracelets on my wrist. "Don't worry, I won't let them eat you alive."

"That's your job, then?" I press.

"Again, not part of the contract, but I'm happy to make amendments to suit your needs, darling."

With that, he guides me up the steps and into the lion's den.

CHAPTER 8
CONNOR

I blame the idiot shit that's coming out of my mouth on the fact that Mildred looks incredible in the dress I picked for her, she smells like vanilla and strawberries, and it's discombobulating. Beautiful, smart, sassy, and slightly broken—she's all my favorite things.

Despite her signing on the dotted line, I still feel bad for what she's about to endure. But she agreed to the terms, and that means tolerating events with my family for the foreseeable future. Once the engagement party and the wedding are behind us, we can avoid my parents for the most part. Although, it will be nice to have someone to attend these gatherings with, even if she's only here because she has to be.

"Wow. This house is…" The crease in her brow and the pucker in her lips gives away her distaste. It's the opposite of her awestruck expression when she dropped off the books last week at Meems's.

"Monochromatic?" I supply.

"*Sterile* is the word that popped into my head, but yes, that's accurate," Mildred murmurs.

I cough to cover a laugh.

She glances up at me with a small smile.

55

I bend until my lips are at her ear. "My mother thinks her decorator is a revolutionary." I hate everything about this house. Although that has more to do with childhood memories than the lack of personality or color.

Her grip on my arm tightens. "I'm nervous."

I turn to face her, my hand sliding up the inside of her arm to cup her elbow. "You have every right to be. Just pretend you like me enough to be my wife, and if that's a challenge, remember that every month you endure with me has a fat paycheck at the end, and this afternoon will only last a few hours."

She narrows her beautiful eyes. "That was an exceptionally shitty pep talk, Connor."

"It wasn't meant to be a pep talk." Money aside, I'm the clear winner in this unfortunate arrangement. I smile tightly. "It was a reminder and a reality check. Just stay by my side, and you'll be fine."

She shakes her head. "You don't have to fight me like you do everyone else, Connor. We're on the same team here."

"Remember you said that after you meet my parents." I guide Mildred to the living room, which is a white box with white furniture, leading to a white deck with more white furniture.

"It's like walking into a blizzard. Why are your parents so opposed to color?" Mildred asks.

"It's a reflection of their personalities," I deadpan.

"By that logic, your house will be an homage to dark horses?"

I gaze down at her. "You'll find out when you move in with me."

"Can't wait," she mutters.

I chuckle. "You're cute when you lie."

She turns her head, bringing our lips mere inches apart. Her eyes spark with mirth. "And you're pretty even when you're being an asshole."

I laugh. She's so full of fire, something my family can't and won't appreciate. She's perfect. "I think I'll enjoy having you as my wife."

Her expression remains placid. "Currently that makes one of us, but you have lots of time to change my mind."

"Mm... I'm doubtful that will happen." I roll my shoulders back. "Shall we get this over with?"

"The sooner the better."

I cover her hand with mine as we enter the living room. In part to keep her from bolting, but also to ground me.

"Did I miss the sad beige children memo?" Mildred runs a hand over her hip as she looks around.

I nearly choke on a laugh.

"We're a little ostentatious for this crowd, Connor."

"We're supposed to be the center of attention, darling."

"Well, mission accomplished, I guess."

"Meems is on our team, too, though." I nod in her direction.

She stands out among my family in her bright teal, floor-length, sequined gown. The rest of the men wear black suits and their partners pale, neutral-tone dresses.

A lovely, authentic smile curves the corner of Mildred's pretty mouth. "God, I love her so much."

"That's how I locked you into this with me," I murmur.

Mildred's devastation matched my own at the possibility that Meems's life might be cut short. I should feel remorse for using that against her, but I don't. Mildred exudes the same warmth and light as Meems, and making her my fiancée gives me more opportunities to be close to her. I'm hopeful more time with Meems will make up for the nightmare that is being married to me.

Meems swats my brother-in-law's hand away when he tries to help her out of the high-backed white chair. "I'm old, not made of glass."

Mildred releases my arm and steps away from me. I instantly want to draw her back to my side.

But Meems is already pulling her in for a hug—and not the

kind my family is so fond of, barely making physical contact, air-kissing each other's cheeks. No, Meems wraps her thin arms around Mildred and squeezes her tightly while Mildred carefully folds her in, like she's precious. I swallow the discomfort that comes from watching people share genuine affection.

Meems whispers something to Mildred that makes her toss her head back and laugh. It's carefree, and pretty, and loud, drawing the attention of the hyenas.

I move in again, wanting to protect my future bride as my brothers-in-law's judging gazes lock on Mildred. My sisters, Portia and Isabelle, stand on either side of their husbands, wearing matching curious expressions. I've never introduced them to a girlfriend, so the fact that I suddenly have a fiancée has raised some questions. But they're easy enough to explain away since I always have been and always will be the outsider.

"You're just so beautiful." Meems holds both of Mildred's hands in hers and turns to me, her approval clear in her smile. "You picked the most perfect dress for Dred."

"You picked this dress?" Mildred asks.

"Meems had the final say," I explain.

"He took me shopping earlier in the week," she adds.

"Well, aren't you the sweetest," Mildred says, her earlier sarcasm missing in her tone.

"You two are adorable." Meems is beaming.

My youngest sister is the first to break rank from the family huddle. Isabelle approaches, wearing a nervous smile. She is the epitome of the perfect daughter. She married Julian, the son of one of my father's business associates. Julian works for my father and enjoys all the perks of marrying into a family with billions of dollars, including my trophy-wife sister who never disappoints my parents.

I accept Isabelle's air kisses as she places a hand on my shoulder and whispers, "Mother will be displeased with your suit choice."

"I'm sure she'll believe I picked it just to be difficult." I picked it so I would match my bride-to-be and Meems, since we're our own little team. "Where are our parents, anyway?"

"They had to take a call. They'll be back soon, I'm sure. Are you trying to be difficult?"

"When am I not?"

She rolls her eyes to the ceiling and taps her chin. "I'm trying to recall a moment, but having difficulty," she rebuts.

"At least I'm consistent." I've always been the one who doesn't fall in line. It made things tumultuous growing up. I was forever causing problems, and my sisters were the standard I could never live up to. My mother was perpetually keeping the peace, trying to make me into something I could never be—compliant, easy, the perfect, dutiful son.

"I don't know why you always have to push their buttons." Isabelle sighs.

"I don't know why you don't."

She shakes her head. "It's not just your own life you make harder, Connor."

A wave of guilt washes over me. I'm sure she's been on the receiving end of our mother's wrath since I announced my engagement. It's bad enough that I play professional hockey for a living. Now I'm marrying someone outside the approved social circle. My father will likely be angry, which puts pressure on my mother, who downloads it to my sisters, whose husbands must deal with their stress. It's a vicious, depressing cycle, and in the end it's always the same. No one understands me, and I'm the problem with no solution.

Arguing with my sister won't make today better for either of us. "Let me introduce you to my fiancée. I think you'll love her."

She side-eyes me. "She'd have to be a sass machine to handle you."

"Isn't that the truth." I skim the back of Mildred's arm to get her attention.

She turns with a warm smile. "You must be Connor's sister. Isabelle, right?"

Isabelle's face lights up in a matching smile. "Yes! That's right."

"Connor has such wonderful things to say about you," Mildred lies smoothly.

"Really?" Isabelle's surprise sucks, but we're not all that close.

"Absolutely! It's so nice to meet you!" Mildred's voice pitches up, and she pulls my sister in for a hug.

Isabelle once again looks surprised, but she gently pats Mildred's back and gives me a quizzical smile.

"It's nice to meet you too, Mildred," Izzy says once they part.

"You can just call me Dred."

Isabelle's eyebrows rise. "Dred?"

"It's what my friends call me."

"Oh, right. That's cute." She takes Mildred's hands in hers and glances between us, like she's trying to fit us together. "It's just so nice that Connor has finally brought someone home."

"Izzy," I warn.

"What do you mean?" Mildred asks.

"Well, he's never brought anyone to meet us before." Isabelle pats my arm. "He's always been so private."

"I wonder why," I grumble.

Mildred hugs my arm. "Obviously you were waiting for the perfect woman to come along, and it was me."

I smirk down at her. "Obviously."

Isabelle grins. "I like her."

"Me, too." It's not a lie. I enjoy Mildred more than I should.

The Terror begin to arrive, bringing the stuffy down several notches. Though most of them are here to support Mildred, not me, I'm thankful they showed up. Having the people she cares about here to insulate her will make this manageable.

Lexi and Roman make their way over to us, Callie trailing behind, flanked by her sister, Fee, and Tally, the Terror head coach's daughter. Both Fee and Tally attend Tilton, a local university.

Callie does not look excited to be here. She's half-hidden behind her sister.

Lexi gives Mildred a hug.

"Everything okay with Callie?" Mildred asks.

"She'll be fine." Lexi's smile is knowing.

I drop to my knee. Last year it would have put me at eye level with Callie, but she's grown, so now I have to look up. "How's my favorite future pro goalie?"

She shrugs, and her bottom lip trembles.

"It's okay, Callie," Roman says.

She spins and throws her arms around Roman's waist. He's become like a father to her—not a replacement for the one she lost in a boating accident a couple of years ago, but someone who fills that hole in her young heart.

"She okay, Coach?" I ask Lexi.

Roman crouches, then brushes away Callie's tears as they have a whispered conversation.

Lexi drops her voice. "She had a little crush, and she's sad about it."

I frown. "A crush? On who?"

"On you," Mildred says gently. "Did you not realize that?"

"I thought I was her favorite player."

"You are." She squeezes my arm. "She's not the only one who likes the bad boys."

I gaze down at her. "Only the baddest, apparently."

Callie holds Roman's hand and stays tucked into his side as she approaches.

I drop to my knee again. "Got a lot of big feelings today?"

She nods.

"Want a hug?"

She shrugs.

"You mad at me?"

Another shrug.

"I'm not going to take Mildred away from you," I assure her.

"But you're marrying her," she whispers.

61

I nod. "I am."

"Because you're in love with her?" Callie whispers.

"We're very important to each other." It's not a lie. "But you're very important to me, too."

Her lips pull to the side, and she fidgets with the friendship bracelet on her wrist. "Did you only come to my games because of Dred?"

My cold, mostly dead heart cracks. "I came to see my number one fan. And so did Mildred. But it gave us a chance to get to know each other." Again, it's not untrue. "She's hard not to like."

"She is," Callie agrees.

I open my arms.

She wraps hers around my neck and whispers, "Roman says you're too old for me, anyway."

I laugh. "I think that's true."

Callie hugs Mildred, and then she reattaches herself to Roman.

More of my fiancée's friends congratulate us. Mildred visibly relaxes once she's surrounded by her Babes. I envy her easy friendships and the way people rally around her. Mildred is exactly what the Grace family needs. They just don't know it yet.

More than once I catch my brothers-in-law casting judgmental glares at Mildred's friends. I swirl the ice in my scotch—I needed something strong to get through this—as Julian and Bryson finally decide to acknowledge me.

"Connor." Julian tips his glass.

"Julian." *Fuckhead*. I lift my own glass in reply. "Bryson."

"Your sisters seem to like your girlfriend," Julian observes.

"You mean my fiancée."

"Mm... It's a little strange that this is the first time we've met her," Bryson adds.

"She comes to my games all the time." Again, it's not untrue.

"So she spends a lot of time with these guys."

"If you're referring to my teammates, then yes."

"Doesn't that concern you? Your girlfriend being such good friends with a bunch of hockey players?"

"I'm a hockey player," I remind them.

"Yeah, but you come from better stock," Julian says snidely, tipping his chin toward my friends.

"I can see the allure." Bryson claps me on the shoulder and tsks. "But marrying down?"

"Better than sucking my father's dick all day every day," I say through a dark smile.

Julian chokes on an ice cube.

"Connor, I hope you're behaving yourself." Mother appears at my side, looking a little frazzled, but still perfectly put together. She doesn't try to touch me.

"Just talking about how nice it is to be rich and entitled." I scan the room, searching for my bride-to-be. She catches my gaze, head tipping slightly.

"Connor," Mother chastises.

I wish I'd devised a signal so Mildred knew when to stay put. Unfortunately, my focus was not where it should have been leading up to today. Mildred abandons the safety of her friends and heads for me.

And of course, because this day isn't enough of a shitstorm, my father moves to stand beside my mother.

Mildred steps right into the viper pit.

I extend my hand when she's close enough, and she slips her warm, soft palm in mine. I bring her hand to my lips, immediately comforted by her presence and the contact. I wrap a protective arm around her waist and pull her to my side.

"Darling, I'd like you to meet my parents. This is my mother, Courtney, and my father, Duncan."

"It's such an honor to meet both of you," she says warmly. "Thank you so much for hosting our engagement party."

"I thought it was a good way to ensure we'd meet you before the big day," Mother says. "Connor can be quite secretive when it comes to his significant others."

"I haven't been secretive. They just haven't been significant enough to introduce," I correct.

Mildred accepts air hugs and kisses from them.

There's a slightly pregnant pause as everyone waits for me to introduce my brothers-in-law.

Julian steps forward. "Connor's forgotten his manners, apparently. I'm Julian, Isabelle's husband, and this is Bryson."

"Portia's husband, right?" Mildred shakes Bryson's hand, and I want to break it.

"That's right."

"They're both so sweet," Mildred replies.

"They're both very well behaved," Father says, like a clueless fucking idiot.

"They're not dogs. They're grown fucking women," I snap.

"Connor! Your language, please." Mother is already exasperated. "You'd think you were raised in a barn."

"Might have been better for you if that had been the case." I drain the rest of my scotch.

Mildred breaks the tense silence. "I lived in a shed for a couple of months—not quite a barn, but probably similarly unpleasant."

"On purpose?" Julian asks, like the tactless dolt he is. "Were you homeless?"

"At the time I was not unhomed, no." Mildred links her arm with mine and rests her cheek on my bicep.

Today probably constitutes the most physical contact I've had in years that didn't lead to emotionless sex or a hockey fight. It's uncomfortable, but I don't dislike it. Also, does that mean Mildred was unhomed at one point?

Mildred tips her chin up, her smile impish. "I don't think I've told you this story yet. But when I moved from Barrie to Toronto for university, I didn't realize not all 'above the garage' apartments were created equal, so I shared my accommodations with the neighborhood raccoon until I found something a little less… rustic."

"It's unfortunate you didn't have anyone to guide you. You've come so far, haven't you?" Mother's gaze swings my way. "From living in sheds with vermin to being engaged to a hotel heir."

"It has been quite the adventure so far," Mildred agrees smoothly while I bristle at the insinuation.

"I'm sure." Mother nods her agreement. "Connor tells us you're a librarian."

"A professional reader," Julian murmurs into his glass. "What a challenging career."

"Would be for you," I snap.

But Mildred ignores the dig. "That's right. I work at Toronto Central."

"So you're a government employee," Bryson clarifies.

"Um, yes?" Mildred replies.

"The government system has become so bloated," Julian says.

"With so much staff, some of them have to be freeloaders," Father agrees. "In cushy jobs with inflated salaries."

Mildred's eyes widen. "I don't know that I would call my salary inflated or my job cushy, but you obviously have strong feelings about it."

"Well, I just hope your workplace is safe. So many libraries are public spaces that vagrants and the dregs of society abuse," Father explains, like an asshole.

"That's a biased and elitist view," I counter.

"Easy to complain when this elitism affords you your life," Father reminds me.

Which is a joke, because my parents cut me off as soon as I signed my first pro hockey contract. "You have no idea what Mildred's job is. She runs multiple community outreach programs, and much of the work around those happens outside regular hours." I saw the paperwork spread out on her kitchen table. And Meems has told me all about Mildred's work after her library visits. "Mildred gives back to her community every single day, in meaningful ways that take more effort than cutting a check, so maybe do some fact-checking before you insult my fiancée."

"He's so passionate about my work." Mildred squeezes my arm and settles her other hand on my chest, mirth in her eyes. "Everyone is entitled to their opinion, even if it is misinformed. You don't need to start a brawl in my honor. Especially not with your father, or in front of your Meems."

"You're right, darling." I tuck a finger under her chin. "I should save my bad behavior for the bedroom."

Her eyebrow lifts. "I think you mean the ice."

"That's what I said."

"Did you now?" Her smile widens, and her eyes drop to my mouth.

I don't think. I just give in to the overwhelming urge to find out what her lips feel like, dipping to brush my mouth gently over hers.

The shot of desire that zips through my veins isn't unexpected.

But the spark that flickers between us is.

If I'm not careful, it could ignite and burn us both.

CHAPTER 9
DRED

Our server drops off all seventeen of Flip's appetizers. When we eat out, he basically orders one of everything, and I pick and choose what I want while he demolishes the rest.

It's Monday afternoon—two days post engagement party—and Flip asked to take me for lunch. Mostly I think he wants to debrief, and maybe pry for information.

"So that was some engagement party," he says once the server has left us.

"It sure was." I haven't been able to stop thinking about the way Connor's mouth felt on mine. Or his comment about saving his bad behavior for the bedroom, and whether he honestly didn't realize that's what he'd said. Was he playing with me? Regardless, that innocent brush of lips has been living rent-free in my head for the past two days.

"His sisters told me you're the first woman Grace has ever brought home."

"They may have mentioned that." Both of them. More than once.

"His parents are a little…stiff," he hedges, feeling me out.

"They are definitely less easygoing than we are," I agree.

He digs in to a plate of nachos. "His Meems is cool, though."

67

"I adore her." My smile is genuine.

"She adores you—and Grace."

"He has a first name."

"Yeah, right. Sorry." He runs a hand through his hair. "Meeting his family sort of puts things in perspective."

I nod my agreement. Until the engagement party, I've only ever seen the media-curated view of Connor's family, but the real thing was eye-opening. I want Flip's thoughts though. "In what sense?"

"He doesn't fit with them." Flip dunks a piece of skewered chicken into peanut sauce. "Like, he's a Grace, but he's not really a part of them."

"No, he's not."

"He's used to being an outsider," Flip muses.

"Yeah. He is." I dip a cold roll into the spicy chili sauce. "I was used to that, too, until you came along and brought the Terror into my life."

He nods slowly. "You know, back at the Hockey Academy, I thought I knew who he was. I mean, the guy had a serious chip on his shoulder, and he hated me before I even breathed in his direction. But I believed his parents had bought his spot there, and I wasn't the only one."

"Imagine always being on the outside of everything—your family, your team, your social circle. Never fitting anywhere. How impossible would it be to believe you could belong?"

Flip tilts his head. "You empathize with him."

"If you take away the financial piece—which I realize is substantial—he and I aren't all that different," I reply.

"Everyone loves you, though."

"Just like everyone loves you," I remind him.

He sighs. "Are you going to tell me why?"

"Eventually, yeah."

"But not now," he presses.

"Not now, no."

"I hate being on the outside of things, especially with you, Dred."

I smile and nod, but say nothing.

"Fuck." He huffs and laughs. "I am Connor right now."

"Except everyone still loves you, and he's still hockey's favorite villain." I reach across the table and squeeze Flip's hand. "Trust my decision-making. I don't do things without a reason, and I don't do things I don't want to. If that wasn't true, I would go out to the *oons*ing bars with you instead of regularly bailing."

"Okay, that's fair."

"I promise I'm doing this for myself, and to safeguard the people I love the most, and I need that to be enough for you right now."

Even in this short time, I realize I've come to feel...duty bound to see this through. Not just because of the money. It's a huge factor, obviously, but I can't stand the thought of stealing Lucy's joy. And I want to show Connor what it's like to be on the inside of something for once.

"Just keep having faith that I'm smart enough to make the right choices for me," I add.

Flip nods. "I do. I guess I just don't love that he's the choice."

"I think it's less about who it is and more that it doesn't align with your personal views on marriage." I'm one of very few people who know Flip's history and what he's been through. The way he drowned himself in nameless, faceless bodies wasn't about sex, or even feeling good, it was a coping mechanism for deep hurt.

"I just want you to be happy," he says.

"I am happy." Until I met Flip, my whole life was about survival. This little side project will enable me to keep on thriving.

"I mean happy and in *love*." He blows out a breath. "Subject change. This is my wound talking, not yours. Tell me what's going on at work. Any exciting new stories?"

"Oh yes! Yesterday we found a couple of kids boning in the

family bathroom." Everly, one of my favorites and the bad girl to her twin's good boy, has a habit of being rather impulsive. "They would have gotten away with it if a desperate mom hadn't come in off the street with a potty-training three-year-old and a baby who'd already unleashed a demon in his diaper."

"Please tell me *you* found them and not Dorothea."

Flip knows all about the battle-axe head librarian. "I found them."

"What'd you do?"

"Explained that they could be charged with public indecency, that bathrooms are not the best place for such activities, and I made them both very uncomfortable when I asked them about birth control and went into details regarding their options."

I also called the group home and requested that Everly come help me with one of the programs I run so she can complete her community service hours, which are a requirement to graduate from high school. They were thrilled and agreeable.

Flip grins. "I bet they were mortified."

This feels better, more like the me-and-Flip I'm used to. "Exceedingly mortified." At least the boy was. Everly was more annoyed than anything.

Once Flip finishes eating his way through his appetizer smorgasbord, he pays for lunch, despite my telling him I can buy my own meal, then hops on the subway with me.

He pulls his ballcap low and moves a discarded newspaper, offering me the inside seat. I slide in and his knee spills into the aisle, along with half the left side of his huge body.

He glances down at the paper. Connor and I stare back at him. I have no idea where they managed to snag that photo, but at least it's not a bad one.

The headline is another story:

Hockey's Most Hated Player Engaged!

"Connor looks like a serial killer," Flip mutters.

I elbow him in the side.

"Not always, but here he does." He grabs the paper and scans the article. "Which I'm sure was intentional with that headline. I can't believe you're in the freaking newspaper."

"Better me than you." I arch a brow and pluck the paper from his hand, tucking it into my purse.

"I haven't had bad press in a while," he says defensively.

"I know." I pat his arm. "I'm proud of you."

He rolls his eyes. "I don't deserve an award for keeping my dick in my pants."

A businessman side-eyes us.

"No, but you do deserve recognition for realizing it was yourself and the people you care about most that you were hurting by making choices that left you feeling hollow."

"Isn't that the truth." He gives me a sad smile. "But I didn't ruin Rix and Tristan's relationship, or my relationship with either of them, so something good came out of all that bad."

"Silver lining, right?"

"I get why Connor feeds into it, though," Flip adds quietly.

"The negativity?" I ask.

"Yeah. After a while, you just start believing everything you read, like it's the sum of who you are as a person, and my past supported that belief, just like Connor's does." He sighs. "We're all wearing masks, aren't we? Hiding the parts we don't want people to see."

"Every single one of us," I agree. Connor wears a mask of indifference, but it's a cover for his soft center.

We reach my stop, and Flip gets off with me.

"I can make it to the library from here just fine," I remind him. "I do it five days a week."

"I know, but you just got engaged to a high-profile hockey player that the media loves to rake over the coals, and his family is stupidly wealthy. I want you to feel safe if someone recognizes you." He runs a hand through his hair and frowns. "I'm actually surprised Grace hasn't hired a bodyguard, or a car to take you to work and back."

"I have a car."

He snorts. "That thing is held together with duct tape and a prayer. It's a small miracle every time the engine turns over."

"Public transit rarely lets me down. I don't need a car service, and I sure as hell don't need a security detail." It would be impossible to go under the radar if that was the case.

Flip arches a brow.

"Seriously, I can handle myself." We reach the doors to the library. "I'll see you tonight for Bananagrams."

"Wouldn't miss it for the world." He hugs me, and I squeeze him back.

I head inside, inhaling the comforting scent of books.

Odette, one of my fellow librarians, pops up, waving a newspaper around in the air. It's different from the one tucked into my purse, but the headline is similar:

Hockey's #1 Villain Is Getting Married!

Until recently, I hadn't paid much attention to the kind of media attention Connor receives. So far what I've noticed has been mostly negative. How impossible would it be not to internalize it?

"Oh my gosh!" Odette mimes screaming—she does this a lot. She checks over her shoulder and whisper-shouts, "I can't believe you're engaged! Can I see the ring?"

I hold out my hand. The rock is stupidly large. I should have left it at home.

Her eyes nearly bug out of her head. "Wow! That is huge! How many carats is it?"

"I actually have no idea." It wasn't a question I thought to ask while I was signing a contract for a quarter of a million a month.

"Dorothea thought you wouldn't show up today," she whispers.

I frown and tuck my purse in my drawer. "Why wouldn't I?"

"Because you're marrying a professional hockey player, and his family are billionaires."

"So I would stop being responsible and disappoint all the people who rely on me for programming?" I gather my books for the reading circle. I'm extremely thankful the mom-and-tots reading program starts in fifteen minutes. And that my favorite twins will be here to help, one of them grudgingly.

Odette frowns. "When you put it that way…"

"Nice to know how highly Dorothea thinks of me." I smile as Everly lopes over to the checkout desk wearing her customary frown, her twin brother trailing behind her like a happy shadow. "You made it."

"I didn't have much of a choice," Everly mumbles. "Thanks for calling the group home."

"You need community hours to graduate," Victor reminds her. "And it was nice of Dred to offer this opportunity."

Seems Victor has no idea why I've forced this torment on his sister.

Everly rolls her eyes. "Why can't you just give me some of yours?"

Victor already has a hundred hours banked.

"Because then you wouldn't have this amazing experience." I pass her the plastic bin of juice boxes and healthy cookies. "Okay, let's go read stories to kids who still poop their pants."

Everly mutters something under her breath about punishments as she and Victor trail after me.

I love the mom-and-tots reading circle. Most of the group are young mothers who can't afford the paid programs. I've made connections with a couple of nurses who make themselves available after the circle for moms with questions.

I put Everly and Victor in charge of handing out the snacks, so she's obligated to speak directly to the young women and look at their adorable, whining children who range in age from six months to three years. Two of them are scream-crying, another one is trying to run away, and the six-month-old just blew out his diaper. As far as making a safe-sex point, I feel like I'm winning.

I take one of the crying babies so the mom can pump while I read—she's leaking through her shirt—and make Everly turn the pages for me. Victor reads all the male parts and varies his voice. Halfway through, Everly takes over the female characters so I can change a diaper.

Everly and Victor help clean up once the moms and tots have left. When Victor excuses himself to the bathroom, I turn to Everly.

"I'm not going to tell you that you're too young to have sex." Even though she is. "But if you want to do adult things, then do them responsibly. Birth control *and* condoms, not one or the other, because a baby is a lifelong commitment."

"It wasn't for my parents," she says sullenly.

I nod. "It wasn't for mine either, but you can break the cycle by making the safe and healthy choice for you and your body."

"I went to the free clinic last week," she admits.

"Good. But you're still joining me for mom-and-tots reading time until your community hours are finished." Sometimes lessons need to be reinforced.

She rolls her eyes. "Fine."

I pass her the remaining snacks and juice boxes. "Your payment in snacks."

Everly and Victor head home, making it open season for my colleagues. I field more questions about my engagement, dodging personal questions about Connor.

At the end of the day, I take the subway home, grab my mail, and head up to my apartment, my heart lurching as I shuffle through the advertisements and find a new one from the property manager. I wait until I'm inside my apartment before I open it.

It's an eviction notice. If I can't backpay the hundred grand in rental adjustments I owe before the end of the month, I'm out of the apartment. That's less than two weeks from now.

"Fuck." I squeeze the bridge of my nose.

Connor said he would take care of it. But this new development is a wrench in the plan. Telling him about it means talking to him, and possibly seeing him. I'm still struggling to put that kiss we shared at the engagement party into a box with a lid that doesn't pop off constantly.

My phone buzzes in my pocket, scaring the shit out of me.

I stuff the letter in my purse—I don't know why, reflex maybe—and dig my phone out.

Obviously Connor has a sixth sense for when I'm thinking about him.

CONNOR
Meems is out of books.

Of course she is.

DRED
I'll bring more by tomorrow. Just send me a list.

He follows it with a photo of a list in her handwriting. I smile. I knew she'd love the highland warriors series.

And tomorrow I can find out just how good Connor is at keeping his word.

CHAPTER 10
CONNOR

Coach Forrest-Hammer stops me on the way to the locker room after practice. "You and Romero were in sync on the ice today."

"We played together at the Hockey Academy." Quinn Romero and I go back as far as I do with Dallas Bright, Tristan Stiles, and unfortunately, Flip Madden.

Lexi shakes her head. "It's about more than history, Grace. You can predict each other's moves. It'll be good for the team this season, and for Ryker."

I don't know what to do with the uncomfortable feeling in my chest. "We have similar playing styles."

"Maybe just accept the compliment," she suggests with a small smile.

"Right." I nod. "Thanks, Coach."

"You seem more settled these days." She walks away before I can respond.

She's Mildred's closest friend in their group, so Lexi has to know this thing between us isn't made of love and promises of forever. But she's not wrong about me being less...on edge. Meems's happiness is the reason for that, though.

I continue down the hall to join the rest of my teammates in the locker room.

So far it seems to be louder and slightly less civilized without Roman and Hollis to balance things out. The rookies look up to Madden, Stiles, Palaniappa, and Bright now. Roman basically functioned as the team dad, and I think they're trying to find their footing around the huge hole his absence has created. Even I feel the loss. Hammerstein was good at creating team cohesion on the ice, and he made me feel like I wasn't a waste of roster space.

Romero's cubby is next to mine—probably Coach Forrest-Hammer's suggestion. He nods at me as I strip off my jersey and sit next to him so I can remove my pads.

"Everything okay?" he asks.

"Yeah. You?"

"S'all right. Big shift from where I was last year," he admits.

Romero coached for the Hockey Academy and played out in Pearl Lake last year.

"There's a lot of pressure coming in all directions. Can't imagine it's easy to block out all the noise." I can relate, even if our situations are vastly different.

"I'm staying off social media for the foreseeable future for sure," he grumbles.

Romero's dad was a legend in the game, but he had a reputation for being a fighter early in his career. Quinn followed in his footsteps, which contributed to him not being picked up sooner. There's some irony that the Terror management added two of the chippiest players in the league to their team in as many seasons.

"It helps for sure. But you have someone to manage that for you?"

"My friend Lovey deals with most of it." The tips of his ears turn red.

Makes me wonder what the deal is with this friend of his.

"That's good. Definitely makes it easier to stay focused when you can avoid the shit talk."

"And all the women in my messages looking for hookups," he mutters.

"Ah, yes, that gets old after a while."

We shower and change into street clothes. Dallas and a few of the other guys invite us to the Watering Hole. I'm pretty sure the invitation is for Romero, not me, but I'm standing right beside him.

"Yeah, I'd love to." Romero's all smiles as he turns to me. "You in?"

"Let me check with Mildred."

"She's at work," Flip offers, then adds, "But you probably already know that."

He's been oddly civil with me, and I don't know how to take it.

"Yeah, we have a date tonight." It's not a complete lie. And anyway, going to the Watering Hole might also give Flip the opportunity to grill me.

CONNOR
What time are you coming with books?

MILDRED
As soon as my shift is over.

CONNOR
Which is when?

MILDRED
I'm sharing my calendar with you. But I'm off in two hours.

That gives me time to check on Meems and make sure she's ready for a visitor.

An email alert pops up with the subject: **Dred Reformer has shared her calendar with you.**

"I have a few things to take care of before I see Mildred, but maybe next time." *Probably not, though. Unless my fiancée is going.*

"Sure thing." Dallas and Quinn give me props as I leave the locker room.

Half an hour later I arrive at Meems's house. Cedrick greets me at the door.

"How's she been today?" I hang my keys in the entry and trade my outdoor shoes for my indoor ones.

His expression is pinched with worry. "Tired, sir. She's been busy."

"Busy with what?"

"Moving her things into the guest quarters."

I frown. "Why would she do that?"

He stares at me. I stare back.

He arches a brow. I arch one back.

"She would like you to move in here with your fiancée."

I poke at my cheek with my tongue. "This is a twenty-two-thousand-square-foot mansion. She doesn't need to move anywhere."

"You try telling her that, sir."

"Fuck, she's stubborn."

"Seems to be a family trait." He clears his throat. "Madame Grace intimated that Ms. Reformer would be visiting this evening."

"Yeah, that's right."

"Will she be taking public transit again, sir?"

I sigh and rub the back of my neck. "Probably, yeah." In hindsight, I should have gone to the Watering Hole and stopped to pick her up on the way home.

"If there's sufficient time, I could retrieve her, sir, if you'd like," Cedrick offers.

"Yeah, actually that would be good." I have no idea how long it takes to get here by bus, but a car would be far more comfortable. "Oh, and there's a bakery close to the library called Just Desserts. Meems loves their lemon cake." I didn't have time to stop when I went to pick up her books last time. "Can you make sure Mildred comes in with you and chooses something for herself?" I start down the hall.

"What about you, sir?" Cedrick calls after me.

"Don't worry about me, but bring back something for the staff."

I find my grandmother in her reading room with Ethel and Norm, who are filling boxes as she directs them. She's wearing a blue dress, with her hair and makeup done like she's ready for Sunday Mass.

I cross my arms and lean against the jamb. "What are you doing?"

"Connor!" Her wide smile drops. "Where's Dred?"

"Her name is Mildred."

"She asked me to call her Dred, so that's what I call her."

"There's nothing dreadful about her," I mutter as I cross the room and fold her into my arms. She feels frailer, smaller. I wish her heart wasn't struggling to keep up. "Can't you manage this sitting down?"

She brushes me off. "I'm fine."

"Your doctor would beg to differ." She's been sleeping more lately, fatiguing quickly.

"I'm not lifting anything. I'm just directing Ethel and Norm."

I arch a brow. "So you're micromanaging."

Ethel coughs to hide her laugh.

"I'm overseeing."

"You're being an overlord. Sit down, please." I guide her to her chair.

"Where is Dred?"

"She's still at work for a little while."

She frowns. "Well, why are you here, then?"

"To limit your overlording." I'm sure the last thing Mildred wants is to be stuck in a car with me during rush-hour traffic. Cedrick is much more pleasant company.

Meems looks unimpressed.

"Cedrick is on his way to get her."

"You will be the one to take her home," she orders.

"Fine. Now please explain what this is all about." I motion to the boxes stacked neatly by the door, then open the box of chocolate digestive cookies and arrange them on a plate, setting it on the table next to my grandmother. They're forever a favorite of hers.

"I don't need all this space," she says.

I sit in the chair across from her. "You also don't need to move *out* of all this space."

"It's too big for me. It's exhausting just getting to the dining room."

"We can move you to the main floor," I suggest.

"The guesthouse is closest to the important rooms I use," she argues. "Besides, you and Dred will need privacy."

"Because twenty-plus-thousand square feet of space doesn't provide enough of that? Besides, you can't give me this house. It's willed to my father," I remind her.

"It's mine to do with what I want, and I want you and Dred to have it. I've already changed the will, so arguing is a moot point."

I grip the arm of the chair, caught somewhere between shock and validation. "Father will not be happy."

Meems shrugs, unbothered. "He has his own mansion that he's perfectly content living in." She glances away before she continues, "And I won't have him and Courtney moving in here and painting everything white, so it looks and feels like Antarctica."

I snort. "Their house has about as much personality as dry toast."

"That's generous." Her expression softens, and she reaches across to take my hand. "I've already gifted a house to your father, and to each of your sisters. It's your turn. Everything you have right now, you've earned on your own."

"My father would argue with that, considering he paid for my degree."

"Your grandfather and I paid for your degree. Your father just likes to hold it over your head because he wants you to feel indebted. I want you to fill this house with the love it deserves, Connor."

I feel like a giant piece of shit for lying to Meems, but this is the happiest she's been in years. Her approval means everything, and I want to preserve it however I can. "If it will make you happy, Mildred and I will move in here."

Currently I live in a penthouse apartment downtown, close to the arena. Moving here will mean more of a commute, but Meems is worth it. I just need Mildred to agree.

"More than you know." She beams, and it feels like a kick in the balls and the best damn thing at the same time.

The doorbell chimes, and I check the cameras, expecting that it's probably a delivery, but Mildred is standing outside the gates, looking less than fresh. "Mildred is here. I'll be right back," I tell Meems.

"I thought Cedrick was picking her up."

"He was. Something must have happened." I pause at the threshold, anxious. "I'd like to speak to Mildred about moving in."

"Of course."

"I'll meet you in the living room," I call as I stride out of the room, stopping in the hall so I can speak to Mildred through the intercom. I thought I would have time, and now she's here, and I have to convince her to move in imminently. It puts me on edge, and makes my jagged edges sharper. "What are you doing here?"

She holds up her bag and points to it, frowning. "I have the books you asked me to bring."

"But you're early."

"My afternoon reading program was canceled, thanks to a

lice outbreak. Everly wasn't all that sad, but Victor was. Not that it matters." She waves a hand in front of her face.

"Who are Everly and Victor?"

"My favorite twins. Are you going to let me in? Or do you need me to grab a coffee somewhere?"

"No, just come up. Or I can drive down to get you." I open the gate.

"Don't drive down. That's ridiculous." As soon as there's enough room to pass, she squeezes through.

I call Cedrick and inform him that Mildred is already here, and that it isn't his fault since I didn't warn her he was coming to pick her up.

"What flavor of cake does Mildred prefer?" he asks.

"Something with strawberries, if they have it."

"I'll do my best, sir."

"Thank you, Cedrick."

I open the door as Mildred climbs the front steps. Her hair is stuck to her temples, her face is red, and she looks halfway to passing out. We're having one of those fun September heat waves. "How far did you walk?"

"A couple of blocks. The bus's AC was broken. I just need five minutes out of the heat and this will calm down." She motions to her pink cheeks as she brushes by me. She drops the bag and shrugs out of her cardigan, leaving her in a pale purple tank top that does a wonderful job of highlighting her ample cleavage, which is typically covered. I can't stop staring. She's beautiful, curvy, and sensuous.

She waves the cardigan like a fan. "I hope my olfactory senses aren't permanently damaged. A group of teenage boys who'd bathed in body spray were sitting next to me."

"I thought you weren't going to be here for at least another hour." *Why am I incapable of having a regular conversation that doesn't include repeating myself?*

"We've been over that."

"Cedrick went to pick you up," I explain.

"Oh shit. Did I miss a text?"

"No. I didn't text you. I just thought... It doesn't matter." I want to bury my face in her neck and lick the salt off her skin. I wonder what kind of touch she likes. What sound would she make if I kissed a path to her tempting mouth? That will never happen because this relationship doesn't involve sex. She's mine, but she'll never really be *mine*. To touch. To claim. "It would be better if you put the cardigan back on." It comes out snappy, which is not what I intended.

"Are the girls offending you?" She arches a brow. "I don't have much control over how loud and proud they are."

I try not to let my gaze shift below her neck. "I didn't mean—"

"Stop while you're ahead, Connor." She slides her arms back through the sleeves and makes intentional eye contact as she fastens buttons and covers her cleavage. "Better?"

"Not really." I preferred the previous view, but telling her that will probably just make her more uncomfortable. "Meems is excited to see you." I motion for her to follow me.

"Hopefully more excited than you."

"We've already established that my getting excited isn't in the contract, and so far you seem opposed to amending it," I quip.

"I can't tell if you're insulting or complimenting me."

"Neither. I was ogling your assets."

She huffs. "You are something else, Connor."

"So I've been told, darling."

Mildred follows me to the living room. She and Meems greet each other with smiles and hugs. Jealousy over their easy connection makes the back of my neck hot. Would she have accepted a hug from me if I offered it instead of acting like a mannerless brat? If she did, would it be solely out of obligation?

They sit beside each other on the couch, and I take the chair across from them, feeling like I always do—on the outside of everything.

"What did you bring me this week?" Meems peeks in the bag.

"Books two and three in the highland warriors series, and this amazing fall-inspired romance because it fits the season," Mildred explains.

I fade into the background as they discuss last week's books.

Eventually Ethel pops in to announce that dinner will be ready in just a few minutes.

"Oh, I should probably go," Mildred says.

"You should stay," I jump in, acting normalish for once. "For dinner."

Meems squeezes her hand. "Please do. Unless you have somewhere else you need to be."

Mildred nods. "I can stay."

I don't know how to read her yet, so I can't be sure this isn't an imposition. But she links arms with Meems, and I lead them to the dining room, tucking Meems's and then Mildred's chair in before I take my own.

The staff bring dinner to the table.

"This looks amazing," Mildred says as Ethel plates her chicken and Norm steps in with the light cream sauce. "Thank you so much."

"I'll be sure to tell the kitchen staff," Ethel replies.

Once they've finished serving, they leave through the back door, returning to the kitchen.

"It's like eating in a restaurant every night, isn't it?" Mildred muses. "But you're friends with the staff."

"Tonight is special with the two of you here." Meems winks, then asks, "I know you've just had the engagement party, but have you given any thought to a date for the wedding?"

Mildred almost loses her hold on her knife but manages to recover. "We talked about a short engagement." She glances at me. "Right, Connor?"

"No point in waiting when we know what we want," I agree.

The sooner we're married, the happier Meems will be, the harder it will be for Mildred to find a way out of this.

"Well, that's wonderful to hear!" Meems dabs at the corners of her mouth with her napkin. "The two of you must be excited to start planning."

"Absolutely," Mildred lies smoothly.

"I know you have wonderful friends who will support you, but if you need someone to step in with motherly advice, I'm always here."

A smile warms my fiancée's face as she reaches across the table. Meems mirrors the movement, and they curve their fingers together. "Thank you, I really appreciate the offer, Lucy."

"Meems. Please call me Meems."

"Thank you, Meems."

We spend the rest of dinner talking about weddings. Then Meems retires to the guesthouse, and I offer to drive Mildred home.

"I still can't believe Meems and I didn't run into each other when we were in Aruba." She settles in the passenger seat of my car, the space filling with her sweet strawberry-and-vanilla scent.

"We had a private villa on the other end of the resort and a staff to prepare meals," I explain. She was also under the weather for the first part of the trip and mostly stayed by the private pool.

"That makes sense." Mildred tugs at the hair tie on her left wrist.

"Is everything okay? You seem tense." Maybe being alone with me in a confined space is the problem.

"I need to talk to you about my apartment."

"What about it?"

"They're evicting me at the end of the month, unless I can come up with the hundred thousand in back rent."

"When did you get this notice?" Her short engagement comment makes more sense now.

"Yesterday."

"Why are you only telling me now?"

"Because I'm only seeing you now to tell you, and this is the first time we've been alone."

"You should have called me last night."

"I'm not sure if you've noticed, but I don't particularly like asking for help." She tugs at the hair tie again.

I do know this about her. "But you're always so willing to offer it."

She shrugs. "It feels good to help people. It feels bad to ask for it."

"Because someone has something they can hold over you?" I supply. That's how I've always felt about my family. The Grace fortune is a carrot dangled.

"Because in my world, favors come with strings, and some of those strings can be tripping hazards." She snaps the hair tie, then crosses her arms. "I can't lose the apartment."

"You won't. I said I would handle it, and I will. I already have my lawyers working on it. Send me a copy of whatever was sent to you, and I'll make it go away." Might as well rip the Band-Aid off. "But also, it would be best if you moved into Meems's house with me as soon as possible."

Her head snaps in my direction. "I'm sorry, what?"

I stay focused on the road. "She's moved into the guest quarters so we can move into the mansion."

"What? I thought I'd be moving in with you after we're married—and into your place, not with Meems."

I sigh. "That plan has been adjusted and expedited. Meems has already gifted my father and my sisters each a home, and she plans to do the same for us. She just told me this today, but it's what she wants, and as you know, my goal is to make her happy. The sooner you move in, the happier she'll be. Besides, it simplifies things if I can manage your landlord while you're not in imminent danger of losing your place to live."

"What about what I want?"

Heat shoots down my spine at her defiant tone. We're

stopped at a light, so I turn to take in her expression. Under that defiance is fear.

"You get the things you want when this marriage ends." I grip the steering wheel and turn back to face the windshield, hating what that will mean.

"You're unbelievable," she murmurs.

"This is what you signed on for, Mildred. You agreed to the terms, and those terms include making Meems happy. This ensures her happiness." I can feel her eyes on me.

"What do you want, Connor?"

"For my grandmother to be happy."

"That's what you want for *her*. What do you want for *you*?"

"That's irrelevant."

"I disagree. I think it's very relevant."

I throw the question back at her. "Well, what do you want?"

"I asked you first."

"I want to watch my father lose his mind when he finds out that house is no longer being left to him." I want him to hurt the way I always do.

"Again, that's not for you."

"Yes, it is." I hate how easily she seems to see through me. "It's no different than you wanting the financial stability this union provides. Do I need to remind you that it's the only reason you said yes, Mildred? It has nothing to do with your feelings about me."

"It does have a lot to do with my feelings about Meems, though, which happen to be connected to you. And honestly, Connor, I don't know what kind of feelings to have about you. You are clearly loyal to the bone, but you're not giving me much to work with. If we have to spend the next year together, God willing"—she tugs at the hair tie again—"don't you think we should at least try being friends?"

"I don't want to be friends." I want to kiss her again. I want her to smile at me the way she smiles at Meems. I want her to reach across the table for my hand. I want to get close to her and feel her body against mine. I want to know who she is behind closed doors. But I definitely don't want to be *friends* with her.

She crosses her arms. "Wow. You are a fucking asshole."

That presses a wound that's already split wide today. "This shouldn't be new information."

"You're really setting yourself up for the Dick of the Month award, Connor."

"Really looking forward to my Dick of the Year trophy when this is all over," I counter. *Fuck.* Everything out of my mouth is the wrong thing to say. I can't afford to have her hate me on top of everything else, but I can't stop the thorns from pricking her either.

I stop at the light and turn to her again. "You knew what I was like when you agreed to this."

"Who are you?" she snaps.

"Your worst nightmare and the answer to your problems. It's a real conundrum, isn't it?" I fire back.

Her eyes flash. "Where is the Connor who sits beside me at Callie's games and always has a smile for a little girl who idolizes him, even when the bitchy fucking moms are talking shit?"

The shit-talking is something I'm accustomed to. Frankly, I'd be more surprised if it stopped. "As if I'm going to disappoint a little girl who's already lost everything."

She arches a brow.

It dawns on me a second too late that she's the same, only in woman form.

"What about the Connor Grace I spent Christmas with? Where is the man who dressed up like an elf to make a little girl's second Christmas without her parents less of a nightmare?"

I'm angry that she's bringing that up, using that moment of weakness against me. Because that's what it was. I didn't want to be alone on Christmas. Not again. My parents had taken my sisters, their husbands, and Meems to Cabo, and I found out from Meems when she asked when I was arriving. They left it to me to tell her I wasn't, because I hadn't known they were going. Shortly after that, Roman had sucked me into his holiday plans, along with Mildred. It was the best Christmas I'd had in years. But admitting that is handing her my weakness on a platter.

"That guy isn't here," I tell her.

"That's bullshit, and you're a liar." She leans across the center console and shocks the hell out of me when she presses her lips to the edge of my jaw. "Tell that Connor I expect him to come out and play, whether he wants to or not. I'll walk from here." She hops out of the car, slamming the door before I can stop her.

CHAPTER 11
DRED

"What are you doing, Ms. Mildred? We have staff ready to help move you in!" Cedrick looks like his head is about to explode. He recoils slightly. "What is *that*?"

"Dewey isn't a that. He's a majestic and adorable hedgehog." I hold up the cage. "Dewey, meet Cedrick." Dewey is curled in a ball, hiding in the corner. He isn't a fan of car rides. "He's a little shy. He just needs some time to acclimate." Like me.

I lean in to kiss Cedrick's cheek, and Connor's frown deepens as heat rises in his cheeks. I wish I could see inside his head to understand his reaction. Over the past few days, his text messages have been gentler, less terse.

"Boxes of bricks incoming!" Flip appears, carrying a stack so high his eyes are barely visible.

"Those are my special edition hardbacks." I couldn't bear the idea of leaving them behind for an entire year. Or my comfort reads. I have a plethora of both. They're my literary security blankets.

"At least let me get the house dolly," Cedrick says.

"Probably a good idea since the closest bedroom is half a kilometer away," I agree.

"There's an elevator to the second floor," Connor replies.

"Of course there's an elevator," Flip says from behind his box wall.

"You can leave those there." Connor points across the foyer to the elevator tucked into an alcove. I somehow missed it the first two times I came here. "The staff will feel better if they can help." He turns to me. "I thought when you said you had it covered you meant you'd already lined up movers."

I motion to my friends, who are also his teammates. "Who needs movers when you have hockey players?"

"I would have come to help if I'd realized this was your plan."

I can't tell if he's hurt or embarrassed or some other emotion. I suppose I could have been more forthcoming, but considering our last conversation, this was the preferred option.

"Oh wow! This place is amazing!" Hammer rolls one of my suitcases into the foyer.

"So cool!" Rix follows with another.

"The architecture is unreal." Hemi adds a box to Flip's pile by the elevator.

"It's like a princess's castle." Essie sets a tote next to the boxes and bats her lashes at Nate.

He adds his own boxes to the growing pile and whispers something in her ear. I look away as Essie grabs the front of his shirt and pulls his mouth to hers. I never really believed myself capable of the kind of love my friends and their partners share, and now it seems even more out-of-reach.

"Connor, your family has a beautiful home." Lexi offers him a smile.

"My grandfather built it." Connor rubs the back of his neck, clearly uncomfortable as more people pile into the grand foyer, including Tristan, Dallas, Roman, and Hollis.

My friend invasion is intentional. I knew I'd have to move in eventually, but I figured we'd be married first. If I don't get time to find my equilibrium, neither does Connor. My friends and I are a package deal, and he needs to get used to them being around.

"You want to give us the grand tour?" Flip asks.

"It's more than twenty-thousand square feet. It would be a long tour," Connor mutters.

"Right." Flip gives me a look that says, *one of us is trying*. "I'll just grab some more boxes."

Before Flip can make good on that, several men appear out of nowhere, wearing polo shirts with name tags that bear the same logo that adorns the front gate. They're carrying more of my things.

"Do all of these people work for you?" Rix asks.

"This is the grounds and maintenance crew. The property spans several acres, so we have a full staff." Connor's eyes slide my way, maybe assessing my reaction to how extra his life is.

"That's wild," Rix muses.

"It's definitely next-level," I murmur.

"You'll adjust," he replies.

I make a noncommittal noise. That's an honest concern.

"I believe there may be perishables in here, Mr. Grace." Two men appear in the doorway, each holding one handle of a massive cooler.

"I brought lunch!" Rix exclaims. "I hope that's okay."

"That's amazing, thank you," I assure her before Connor can jump in with one of his blunt replies. "Maybe we should take the food to the kitchen. I'm sure Rix would love to see it."

"That would be great!" Rix is vibrating with excitement.

"I'll join you." Essie bounces over to Rix.

"We'll all join you." Connor seems resigned to being roped into the tour he didn't want to give. He leads the pack, the staff behind him with the coolers. I shouldn't be surprised that he doesn't wait for me, but the prick of disappointment is interesting.

Flip falls into step beside me. "It's a good thing we have the Find My Friends app, huh? You could get lost in this place."

"I hope there's a way to send a distress signal," I half-joke. "I wonder if there's a map."

"It would be helpful for sure." Flip drops his voice. "There's more than a million dollars just in vehicles parked out front."

"Betty will feel a little out of place when I bring her here."

Connor looks over his shoulder when Flip laughs, but he doesn't fall back to walk with us.

We enter the main kitchen, which is a beautiful combination of modern and classic design, but continue through another door to a state-of-the-art industrial chef's kitchen. This mansion was designed to hold a family, a big one, where entertaining happens frequently.

Rix is about to hyperventilate. She flits around, introducing herself to everyone while Tristan stands back and watches with a smile. The staff fall instantly in love as she helps them unpack the coolers, explaining each dish.

Once Rix is finished with the kitchen tour, we're ushered into the formal dining room, where I ate dinner with Connor and Meems the other day. Meems is escorted in a minute later by Cedrick.

Her face lights up. "Oh, this is wonderful! It's been ages since we've had a full table!"

I head toward her at the same time as Connor, and her smile widens as he gently skims my arm with his fingers. She takes one of our hands in each of hers and we both bend to kiss her cheek at the same time. Someone snaps a photo.

We guide her to the table, and Connor tries to put her at the head, but she refuses, making him take it. He looks uncomfortable, but also like he belongs there. Meems sits on his left, and I sit to his right.

There are a chorus of hellos and reintroductions.

Meems presses her hand to Connor's cheek, her smile wide. "Now you know why I wanted you and Dred to move in here."

"So you could throw dinner parties?"

"And so I can get to know all of your friends, dear."

He opens his mouth, probably to say something about them being *my* friends, but I cover his hand with mine and squeeze. "Thank you for opening your home to all of us."

"Thank you for loving my grandson."

My heart breaks a little at the tic in Connor's jaw, and the reminder that none of this is real for anyone but Meems. But she's happy, and that's what matters.

The staff brings in platters of food, and we pass them around family style. Flip is seated to my right, watching intently as I interact with Meems, like he's trying to piece together the reasons that brought me to this decision.

"Some of you went to the Hockey Academy with Connor, didn't you?" Meems asks.

"Us three." Dallas points to himself, Tristan, and Flip.

"It's lovely that you're all still so close after all these years, and playing on the same team." Meems looks to Connor. "For a punishment, it certainly turned out to be a good thing for you, didn't it, dear?"

"Hard to be a bad influence on my sisters when I wasn't in the country," he agrees.

Flip's eyebrows rise. "The Hockey Academy was a punishment for you?"

"There was another program in Europe that I'd been invited to attend that summer, but my parents felt I didn't deserve the opportunity, so they sent me to the Hockey Academy instead," Connor explains. "If they'd known they were giving me exactly what I wanted, they would have made a different choice, I'm sure."

I file that away with the other pieces of Connor I've collected.

"You didn't belong behind a desk." Meems pats his hand. "Now, how did all of you become friends with our Dred?"

Flip raises his hand. "I'll take credit for that."

Connor sits back, listening and watching while my friends—*our* friends—weave a story that pulls us all together, including him. He seems to soften over the course of the meal, especially when Lexi and Roman jump in with praise for him.

He's accustomed to being the media's scapegoat for his team when they've had a bad game. He's not used to having friends or being accepted exactly as he is.

Neither was I until Flip came along.

I tentatively cover Connor's hand with mine.

His eyes dart to me in question. I offer him a reassuring smile, and he returns an uncertain one of his own. He turns his hand over, curving his fingers around mine. Warmth works its way up my arm and moves in a slow wave through my body, pooling low in my belly. That same warmth settles in Connor's cheeks. I can feel our friends' eyes on me, trying to figure it all out.

They're not alone. It's the same for me. Maybe for Connor, too. Our goals might not be the same, but they align, and we feel like an unlikely team.

After lunch and a promise to Meems that our friends will be back soon, Connor and I walk them to the front door—I'm doubtful any of us would have found it without him as an escort. All the boxes have disappeared, probably waiting for me in my bedroom, wherever that is.

I collect hugs, tucking them into my heart to keep it full once they leave.

"I'll call you later," Lexi promises.

And then it's just me and Connor and a whole lot of awkward tension with my shields gone.

"Let me show you to your rooms." He opens the elevator door and ushers me inside.

"Okay."

Three walls are mirrored, providing an unparalleled view of Connor's regal face and cut body.

He pulls the wrought-iron gate closed and presses the button for the second floor. The temperature seems to rise several degrees in the confined space and his proximity. He's so tightly wound, his emotions locked down most of the time—unless he's on the ice. Then all that tension and aggression are unleashed. And in rare moments, like with Callie and Meems, I see the soft side of him.

I wonder what he's like in the dark, when no one else can see.

"What?" He rubs the edge of his jaw.

"Just thinking."

"About?"

"You."

We reach the second floor, and he opens the gate, motioning me ahead of him. He points down the hall. "Left off the elevator. We're in the west wing."

"Left off the elevator," I repeat. "Of course there are wings." I fall into step beside him, counting the doors.

"What about me?" he asks.

"What about you, what?" We pass door three.

"What were you thinking about me?"

I glance up at him. The muscles tense in his jaw, like he's waiting for the blow. He probably is. That's what he's used to from so many people in his life. Media comments about him always start with *He's an excellent player, but...*

He's too emotional, too aggressive, not a team player.

"Just trying to figure you out," I assure him.

"Good luck with that." He pushes the door open and steps aside to let me pass. "This is you."

"Holy shi...zzle. This is my bedroom?" It's like falling backwards through time, into an era where ballgowns filled closets and well-read women were rare and kept secret.

"Yes. It's yours." Connor looks wildly uncomfortable standing on the threshold.

I tilt my head. "Where do you sleep?"

"In my bedroom."

"Where are my things?" I glance around the room, but it's perfectly tidy, not a single box in sight.

Dewey's enclosure has been set up in the corner. But it's not the one from my apartment, it's new, much bigger, and somehow manages to fit the space.

"Everything has been put away for you." He swallows. "May I come in?"

"Are you a vampire? You need to ask permission?"

His brow furrows.

Fuck, he's stupidly hot when he looks disconcerted.

He tugs at his shirt cuffs. "You might not want me in your personal space."

"You were in my apartment."

"That's much different than your bedroom."

"You're fine."

He steps over the threshold, and I'm almost surprised he doesn't burst into flames as he passes through a beam of sunshine. He crosses to the first door and pushes it open. "This is your closet. All your clothes are in here."

I glance inside. My entire wardrobe takes up maybe ten percent of the space. If that. The closet is also bigger than my previous bedroom.

Connor brushes past me to open the next door. "And this is your private bathroom."

I follow him inside and shriek, clambering into the clawfoot tub. "This is my new favorite place to read." I stretch out on a sigh. It's huge and deep and perfect.

"It's probably more comfortable when it's full of warm water," he says wryly.

"And bubbles. You can't forget the bubbles."

"Of course not." He tucks his hands in his pockets.

I pull myself out and examine the rest of the space. The details are incredible, from the patterned tiles in the floor to the wallpaper that tells a story. It's the most beautiful bathroom I've ever seen. I open drawers and check the medicine cabinet, which is fully stocked with all the things I could possibly need, including feminine hygiene products. I immediately take inventory of everything and wonder how much I can reasonably take to the library and share with Everly. She's always complaining that the group home stocks her least favorite brand of tampon.

"There's more. Let me show you, and then you can get settled." He leaves the bathroom and I follow, mostly out of curiosity as to what *more* there could possibly be.

He stops in front of an ornate bookshelf and tips the figurine of a woman reading a book forward. I gasp, thinking he means to let it fall, but then I'm gasping for an entirely different reason as the shelf swings inward.

"Secret passageways? What the hell, Connor?"

"Thank my grandfather." He inclines his head. "Captive future brides first."

"I'm not your captive."

"Aren't you, though? You signed away your freedom for the next year," he reminds me.

I leave that alone and squeeze by him, far too curious to waste time arguing about my freedom and what exactly I've agreed to. "Oh my sweet heaven." I grab Connor's arm and nearly swoon into him. "I might spontaneously orgasm."

He looks down at me, eyes flashing with heat. His lip curls, and for a moment something primal and needy passes between us.

But before the embers have a chance to spark and flame, he steps out of reach. "I'm just across the hall. I'll leave you to explore." He disappears back through the bookshelf, but the heat in my belly doesn't leave with him.

I wasn't lying about the potential spontaneous orgasm. I'm standing in the middle of a library—a big, beautiful library. It's climate controlled, based on the temperature, the walls lined with ornately carved shelves, filled with endless tomes. A huge cherry desk sits in one corner of the room, a perfect place to work. In another corner is a grand fireplace with two high-backed chairs and plush footstools. But the most amazing part is the domed glass turret at the far end of the room. In the center is a plush velvet area rug with a stunning chaise lounge, bookended by coffee tables. It's like a private snow globe that overlooks the blooming gardens.

It is the most incredible space I've ever seen.

And for the next however-many months, it's mine.

I can hardly believe it.

I remind myself that it's temporary. Eventually I'll have to part with it.

But I'm used to having and losing.

CHAPTER 12
CONNOR

Despite the temptation to check on her, I leave Mildred alone for the rest of the afternoon. She agreed to move in without an actual fight, and she even brought all her friends over—though probably as a safety measure, and so they could see for themselves that she wasn't being treated like the captive I said she was. But it made Meems deliriously happy. And it felt nice to be part of something, even if it isn't real.

I knock on her door at dinnertime, but get no answer. I try the library, but it's empty, so I resort to texting.

> CONNOR
> Dinner is usually served at six.

> MILDRED
> Thanks. I'm with Meems in the living room.

Of course she's hanging out with my grandmother.

I find the two of them playing Connect Four.

"I haven't played this since you and your sisters were young. I'd forgotten how much I loved it," Meems says, motioning to the seat next to Mildred.

"I was maybe six when I played my first game of Connect

Four," Mildred replies, dropping another red circle in. "One of my foster families loved board games. We played them all the time. That was the home I stayed at the longest."

"How long were you there?" Meems asks.

"Almost nine months. Before them I only lasted a few months in any one place, if that. The foster parents in that home were great, Darryl and Mindy." She smiles fondly. "They were so patient with me and Hector. Especially Hector. He could be a real hellion."

That means for three years after her parents died, she was shuffled from home to home. And the longest she'd ever stayed in one place was less than a year? She'd just get settled, and then it would end. It must have been impossible to feel secure, to form attachments. "What happened that you had to leave that place?" I ask.

"Mindy got pregnant. They wanted to be able to focus on their baby." She drops in another red chip.

"I'm so sorry," Meems face falls.

"Don't be. It was an amazing nine months. They were great foster parents, and they deserved to have a baby of their own."

Ethel appears. "Dinner is served when you're ready."

"Perfect timing." Mildred drops another chip in. "Connect Four."

She stands and offers Meems a hand.

I spend dinner watching her with Meems, unable to take my eyes off her. She's the definition of a miracle. By all rights, she should have followed in her parents' footsteps, but here she is, a beautiful gift.

"You grew up in Toronto, right?" Mildred asks Meems as we eat.

"I did. My father was a contractor."

"Did he build this place?"

She shakes her head. "No. This was a wedding present from my husband."

"He built you this house?"

Meems nods. "He was very much about grand gestures. And he wanted to find a way to make me happy."

"How old were you when you got married?" Mildred asks.

"I was barely eighteen," Meems replies with a faraway smile.

"I can't even imagine being married at eighteen." Mildred laughs.

"Neither could I." Meems chuckles. "But it was a marriage meant to strengthen our families."

Like my parents' marriage.

Mildred's expression changes. "Did you love him?"

She laughs. "At first no, but I learned to."

I was young when my grandfather passed. I didn't know him well. He was sometimes cold and remote, like my father. But everything about him changed whenever Meems walked into a room. "He adored you," I blurt.

"He learned to." Her smile is impish and full of secrets. She turns her attention back to Mildred. "My husband was a businessman, and marrying me was an opportunity for our families to grow. I don't think he ever meant to fall in love with me, and I surely never meant to fall in love with him. But it happened anyway."

Mildred slips her hand into mine, just like she did at lunch.

I love it and hate it.

It's not real affection. It's a show for Meems. But her deep approval makes it worth it. So I don't pull away, even if eating with one hand is a challenge. It means cutting my chicken with a fork like a toddler with no table manners.

After dinner, Meems heads back to the guesthouse, leaving me and Mildred alone.

"Thank you for spending time with Meems," I tell her.

"Board games are my happy place." She shrugs. "And I've never had a grandmother—not one I had a chance to know, anyway. Lucy is an incredible woman. It's not a hardship to spend time with her."

I want to say something nice, like it's not a hardship to spend time with Mildred, either, but the words get stuck in my throat. As if a compliment from me will mean anything. "I hope she makes this easier for you."

"She's a joy to be around." We climb the stairs to the second floor, and Mildred says, "My step count is about to go through the roof."

"You'll get used to it after a while," I assure her.

"It's never been safe for me to get used to nice things," she admits. "The past few years, since Flip moved into the apartment across the hall from me, have been the most stable of my life."

"Because of how you grew up." This risks digging at her wounds, but I want to understand her.

"My whole life was transient. Before I went to university, I'd never stayed anywhere for more than a handful of months at a time. And the first few years of my life weren't good. I'm grateful that I have very few memories of the time before my parents died, because the ones I do have are…not worth remembering." She stops outside her bedroom door and looks up, her soft, dark eyes meeting mine. "I'm a different kind of broken, Connor."

I'm usually the one putting up walls, but tonight Mildred has beat me to it. I can't tell if it's a warning, her fear, or both. "What happened to you?"

The saddest smile tips the corner of her mouth. "I survived when I probably shouldn't have." She disappears into her room, the door closing with a quiet snick.

That's just what I was thinking earlier. I want to follow her inside and learn more about her life. I want to hold her. To hug her. To offer to keep her safe.

But I'm a contract she's fulfilling, not the love of her life.

I grew up in a home of affluence and excess, with a father who expected perfection and obedience and a mother who desperately wanted to fit into the role assigned to her. My sisters and I were Grace children, and our lives were not our own to live. I wanted for nothing materially, but things don't replace love or acceptance.

But to have neither? How bad were Mildred's first few formative years?

She's used to struggling. To instability. To suffering. Maybe that's why this arrangement works for her. Because she already knows what the end will look like, and it's better than the unknown.

I slip into the bedroom reserved for me since childhood. I stayed here on occasion when my parents went away without me and my sisters. Everything is dark wood finishes, draped in dark blue velvet. I'm accustomed to the beautiful excess, but I try to see it through Mildred's eyes.

I check my phone for the first time in hours.

> **MOTHER**
> I've arranged a venue walk-through for you and Mildred. A tux has been sent over in an appropriate color. I expect you to wear it and not embarrass me or enrage your father with another outlandish suit.

If it isn't black, white, or beige, it's considered outlandish. I fight the wave of guilt over what my mother must endure on my behalf. *"Why can't you just do what you're asked for once, Connor? Why do you always have to make your father angry? Why can't you just be good?"* But it's a choice to be the person my father pushes around, just like it's my choice to lean into the bad reputation I've earned and wallow in it.

> **MOTHER**
>
> Please ensure that your fiancée is dressed appropriately as well. Your father was not happy about the photos from the engagement party. He said Mildred looked like a harlot and none of those photos were acceptable for a media release, let alone an article in The Hotelier.

CONNOR

I also have new messages from my sisters. I brace myself, because they're often on the receiving end of my parents' disdain after an event where I've done something to embarrass or displease them, which is always.

> **ISABELLE**
>
> I have pictures from the engagement party, and I've been meaning to share them all week!
>
> How cute are you?

An image pops up. My finger is tucked under Mildred's chin, and her eyes are closed, while mine remain slightly open, my lips pressed gently to hers. My father is wrong about the dress. Mildred is stunning.

That one kiss has been all I can think about whenever I look at Mildred's pretty mouth. And now I have a picture to go with the memory.

> **PORTIA**
>
> That fucking suit. 😒 Mother nearly lost her mind.

I grin at the profanity. Portia only has a potty mouth in our siblings group chat.

> **CONNOR**
> She's very adamant that I wear black for the venue walk-through I've been informed is taking place.

> **ISABELLE**
> I might need to go out of town for the weekend if you decide not to.

> **PORTIA**
> I'll arrange a spa weekend. You know our brother can't help poking the bear whenever he gets a chance.

> **ISABELLE**
> If we could all be so brave.

> **CONNOR**
> I'll arrange your spa weekend. Niagara on the Lake is nice this time of year.

> **PORTIA**
> It's so quaint. 🖤

We message back and forth for a few more minutes, my sisters dropping in their requests for spa services while I make reservations. The weeks leading to the wedding will be a challenge for them, since they're the ones who deal with our parents and their expectations on a daily basis. My father uses our mother as his puppet, and she dutifully plays the role.

Once I have everything arranged, I sign off for the evening and get ready for bed. I lie there for a while, mind unwilling to settle with Mildred just across the hall. I can't get the picture my sister sent out of my head. Or the memory of how soft Mildred's lips were. How she tasted faintly of strawberries. For a moment, everyone ceased to exist but her and me.

— 🖤 D ♦ A ♦ R ♦ L ♦ I ♦ N ♦ G 🖤 —

I wake with a start, and the hairs on the back of my neck stand on end. Then I hear it again—a soft, muffled, feminine cry. I shake off the vestiges of sleep, roll out of bed, and step into the hall. Another soft wail comes from behind Mildred's door. I pause with my hand on the knob. I don't want to invade her privacy, but that forlorn sound repeats, the pitch high and panicked.

I turn the knob quietly, heart hammering as I push the door open. The bedside lamp is still on, casting a glow over Mildred. She's tiny in the massive king bed. Her dark hair is splayed across the pale sheets. The comforter is twisted around her legs, and she thrashes wildly.

I cross the room, throat tight as her mournful wails grow increasingly frantic.

"Mildred." I call her name twice more, but she stays locked in the nightmare.

I reach out and shake her shoulder. "Mildred, wake up."

She sucks in a gasping breath, eyes flipping open. She screams and scrambles away from me, hitting the headboard. "No! I don't want to!"

"Mildred, it's me. It's Connor." I raise both hands. "You're safe. It was a nightmare. No one will make you do anything you don't want to." That's not entirely true, though, because there are things she'll have to endure over the next year that she probably won't enjoy.

The nightmare fades, and her eyes clear. Between one blink and the next, her arms are wrapped around my neck, and her trembling, sweat-drenched body is pressed against mine. I stand there for a moment, frozen.

I'm shirtless. Wearing only boxer shorts. Mildred is dressed in a thin cotton sleep tank and shorts. Goose bumps rise along her arms, her damp skin cool to the touch.

"It's safe. I'm safe," she mumbles into my neck, the words on repeat.

"That's right. You're safe here." I carefully curve my arms

around her, and she squeezes tighter. I cup the back of her head and gently stroke her hair, breathing in her vanilla-and-strawberry shampoo. "It's okay, Mildred. You're okay. It was just a dream." But as I say it, I wonder if it's true, or if it was a memory haunting her sleep.

Holding her feels good, though, and for a selfish, horrible moment, I wonder if she'll have more nights like these, where she needs comfort from me.

Eventually her grip loosens, and her warm fingers slide over my shoulders. She sits back on her heels, eyes darting around, not meeting mine. "I'm sorry. I didn't—new places are..." She shakes her head. "I'm fine. I'm sorry I woke you."

I want to reach out and stroke her cheek, but I don't want to scare her. "Don't apologize for things out of your control."

She licks her lips, eyes on her clasped hands. "I'm fine now."

I stand there for a moment, letting the teeth in that lie sink in. I clear my throat. "I can stay with you, until you fall asleep again." I could hold her while she fell asleep, protect her from the ghosts that haunt her. Be something more than the man she made a deal with.

Her eyes lift, finally meeting mine. Yearning flickers in their chocolate depths. I feel it in the marrow of my bones. "Really, I'm okay. The first couple of nights are always the hardest. Then it gets better."

I want to press, but I don't. "Okay. I'm right across the hall."

She nods and slides back under the covers, sorting out the comforter.

I head for the door.

"Connor?"

I look over my shoulder.

"I'm sorry my demons woke you."

"I'm sorry you have them at all."

CHAPTER 13
CONNOR

When I arrive home from practice, there are three vehicles I don't recognize in the driveway. For a moment I wonder if Mildred has invited her friends over. And if she has, is it for protection against me, or because she's becoming comfortable here? I don't want to examine my feelings about either too closely.

Chatter comes from the living room, Mildred's laughter ringing out, warming the air. The room is full of cameras, lighting equipment, and people I don't know.

In the middle of it all is Mildred, wearing a stunning dark purple gown, her hair and makeup done, looking the picture of sophisticated elegance. I wish I could appreciate it more, but I thought I'd have a moment to myself before I had to deal with more than Mildred and Meems.

Practice wasn't the worst, but the whole team is off-kilter. It's Ryker's first season in net, and Romero is new on defense, and it's his first year in the pros. My engagement to Mildred is another layer of tension. We all need to find our sea legs.

"What's going on?" I demand.

"Oh, you're home!" Meems's wide smile makes it difficult to

remain irritated about the fucking invasion of what's supposed to be *my* living room.

"I'm home." I bend to kiss her cheek.

"I arranged an engagement photoshoot for you! Isn't Dred beautiful? Your suit is steamed and ready in your room. Go put it on, and we can get started."

"Mildred is always stunning." I cross my arms. "We took photos at the engagement party. Why do we need more?"

"Because I would like official pictures. Go get changed."

Arguing is pointless. Besides, clearly she's excited, and that's the entire point of this whole charade. Plus, Mildred is already cooperating.

Twenty minutes later, I'm dressed in a black suit with piping that matches Mildred's dress.

When I return, Meems is beaming like a fucking spotlight.

I approach my fiancée, and she gives me a slow once-over. I can't decide if it's for Meems and the photographer's benefit, or because she actually appreciates how I look. I do the same. Fake ogle, real ogle, she doesn't know the difference.

The dress, while modest, draws attention to her luscious curves. Makeup hides the circles from the nightmares. Every night so far, she's woken up screaming. I've been sleeping with my door open so I can get to her sooner. I've also been sleeping in a T-shirt. Each time she clings to me, and I hold her until she stops shaking. I don't want the bad dreams to continue, but I also want a reason to touch her, and now I have a nicer one.

"Let's start in front of the fireplace," the photographer instructs.

Mildred and I move into position.

"Sorry about this," I mutter, unsure where to put my hands. It's easier when she's the one hanging on to me.

"I don't mind. Lucy is over the moon," she whispers.

"A little closer, you two. Act like you like each other," the photographer jokes.

We close the space between us. All her softness and warmth press against me.

One of the assistants steps in to position us, adjusting my hand so it curves around the dip in her waist. Mildred's hand slides up my back and rests between my shoulder blades.

"Beautiful. Hold that pose." She snaps several photos.

Each position requires more contact than the last. This is apparently fine with me when Mildred is having a nightmare and needs me to calm her, but here, in front of these people...I don't know. It's different. I'm constantly told to relax my shoulders.

This is an excessive amount of closeness. I don't think I've touched anyone for this long in my entire life. At least not on purpose. I'm hyperaware of Mildred's curves and how good she feels tucked against me like this.

"Okay, let's move to the staircase."

I help Mildred to the stairs and hold her hand as she navigates them in heels.

"Oh, this is perfect. Dred, can you move up one step so you don't have to tip your head back quite as far?"

She moves up a step and still has to look up, but we're closer to eye level now.

"Excellent! Now look into each other's eyes," the photographer instructs.

Mildred turns toward me, and the entire front of her body presses against mine. She settles one palm on my chest. With the other, she moves my hand to her hip.

"Tap into your inner competitor and pretend it's a staring contest," Mildred whispers, maybe trying to alleviate some of the obvious tension.

Unfortunately, my body is starting to react to her closeness in highly inconvenient ways. If I don't get some space soon, she'll be made aware. "Looking at you is quite the challenge."

Her smile falters. "Dick of the Millennium award is coming your way."

"That's not what I meant."

"Then what—"

"Everything okay up there, you two?" the photographer calls.

"Everything's fantastic!" Mildred lies. "My fiancé isn't used to being photographed out of his hockey equipment."

The photographer laughs. "Why don't you kiss your husband-to-be?"

"I don't—" I start to object.

"You didn't have a problem kissing me in front of your family at our engagement party, but three people you don't know is a problem?" Mildred mutters through a fake smile.

"Meems is watching."

"Meems was at the engagement party," Mildred argues.

"Everyone is watching us." And we're arguing. About kissing.

"Well, give them something to watch, Connor," she challenges.

My gaze drops to her pretty, full lips.

She drags her pink tongue across them, arching a brow in challenge. "Better make it good."

My dick gets irritatingly excited about her sass and the prospect of tasting her mouth again. I tuck a finger under her chin and dip down, bracing for the onslaught of sensation.

The camera goes off in rapid-fire succession as I brush my lips over hers. She's sweet like strawberries. The tiniest whimper escapes her. I start to pull back, but her nails bite into my skin and she tilts her head, lips parting, stroking along the seam of my mouth with her tongue.

It's like tossing a lit match into a vat of gasoline. My need for more is all-consuming.

I open for her, which is an exceptionally awful idea. Because the moment our tongues brush, kissing her like this is all I ever want to do for the rest of my miserable fucking life. The world could turn to dust around us, and I wouldn't care. I snake an arm around her waist, pulling her tighter against me. My hand slides into her hair, angling her head so I can deepen the kiss.

Mildred makes a soft, surprised sound as I sweep her mouth again and again. I want to get lost in this feeling, in her softness, in feeling something good. In her. I run my other hand over her hip, curving around the generous swell of her ass.

"Connor, dear, remember where you are," Meems calls, her voice laced with humor.

"We definitely got the shot," the photographer says with a slightly uncomfortable chuckle.

Which is when I realize I've been trying to climb inside my fiancée's mouth. I wrench free and put some space between us. Mildred stumbles back, eyes wide and glassy. I catch her before she can tumble down the stairs. A flush works its way up her chest and into her cheeks.

"I need a minute." I spin around and rush up the stairs.

"Just, um...I'll be back, too." Mildred's voice is pitchy.

I stride down the hall, heading for my bedroom, my self-loathing on fire. Mildred is on my heels, making it impossible for me to close the door behind me without slamming it in her face.

She glances around at my bedroom. She's never been in here before.

I grip the back of my neck. I'm such a fucking asshole. "I shouldn't have done that."

She moves closer, deeper into my bedroom. I don't want the memory of her in here. I don't want her to leave.

Her eyes glitter with emotions. "Run away, you mean?"

"Kissed you like that." My jaw clenches. My cock aches. My disgust is at an all-time high. She's not here because she wants to be. She's not my fiancée because she enjoys my company. She's here to save herself from a lifetime of struggle and to give Meems hope that I won't end up sad and alone.

"I kissed you back, Connor." She's right in front of me, close enough to touch.

"You didn't really have a choice, did you?" I say through gritted teeth.

"There's always a choice." She settles a palm on my chest, but I can't handle the contact.

Everything is heightened, and all I want is to feel her lips on mine and her soft tongue. I want her moans and her sighs and the feel of her skin under my fingers. But that's a level of complication neither of us needs, so I step back out of reach.

"I'm overstimulated," I snap.

She raises both hands. "I'm sorry."

I turn away so I can adjust my erection, which is bent at an uncomfortable angle. "I need a moment, and you being in here is the opposite of helpful."

I'm met with silence.

I sigh. Why do I always have to be an asshole? Mildred doesn't deserve my bad mood. It's not her fault I'm painfully attracted to her and struggling to manage my fucking hormones. "I'm—"

I turn around so I can explain myself, but she's gone.

Her disappearance is an effective solution to my problem below the waist. But when I'm finally in control enough to return to the living room, the photographer is gone as well, and my fiancée is nowhere to be found.

CHAPTER 14
DRED

"I wish my gran read these kinds of books." Tally's eyes are wide, and her cheeks are red.

"I bet Dallas's granny would totally read steamy romance," Hemi muses.

"My grammy only reads autobiographies," Rix sighs.

"My grandma loves cozy mystery," Hammer says. "And my mom only reads self-help books."

"I have loved romance my entire life. I wanted to be Cinderella when I was a little girl," Essie confides. "But my hair wasn't the right color, plus her stepsister situation wasn't all that great."

"Isn't that the truth," I agree.

"No one would be surprised to hear that Callie's favorite is Merida." Lexi rubs her baby belly.

"Not even a little," I laugh.

"I always loved Pocahontas and Mulan," Meems says thoughtfully.

"That tracks." I grin.

She winks.

She's been all smiles since the girls arrived for "book club" an hour and a half ago. It's a new thing I sprang on them post-engagement photoshoot. I used the fact that we have an actual library as an excuse. But honestly, how could I not when I've been granted access to my very own personal library? It has nothing to do with needing insulation from Connor and the second kiss I can't stop thinking about.

All it took was an invitation, and a time and date, and here they are. I'm sure they thought they'd have a chance to dig into my reasons for this development in my relationship situation. However, Meems is the hostess with the most-est, so they haven't had an opportunity. But they're inadvertently getting to know the primary reason I'm here, in this gorgeous space, so there's that.

We've already made a list of books to read for the next several months, most of them selected by Meems, and now we've moved on to other topics, with the girls carefully sidestepping the wedding.

"I have the coolest idea for the library gala!" Hammer slaps her knee.

"I'm all ears," Hemi says.

"You're throwing a gala?" Meems perks up.

"We're raising money for programming. We do it every year, but Hemi and Hammer offered to help and they run one for the Terror that's wildly successful." Far more profitable than the ones we've previously run for the library. Any money we can raise to fund our community programming is great, but it can be a lot of hours of extra work without much payoff. I have high hopes this year. I want to build on the teen programs already in place for kids like Everly and Victor who could use more adult support in their lives.

"Hammer and I run an auction for the team in the spring. It's always a lot of fun," Hemi explains. "What's your great idea for the gala?"

"Some kind of bookish backdrop for photos. Maybe featuring all the banned books?" Hammer suggests.

"Oh! Oh my gosh!" Essie claps and her eyes go wide with excitement.

"Did you have a wedding idea?" Rix teases.

Essie bites her lips together. "No."

"That's a yes."

"More of an idea for a future Halloween party. We can put a pin in my idea and focus on the library gala. I kind of like the idea of *Alice in Wonderland*, you know? But featuring all the banned books, too."

"I really love this." I'm excited about leveling up this event.

We continue to discuss the gala for a while, tossing around ideas.

Eventually, Meems brings up the wedding. It's inevitable. We can't all get together without it becoming a topic of conversation.

"I'm so excited to see all of you in your bridesmaid dresses." Meems's eyes light up at the prospect. "And you in your wedding dress."

"Us too!" Lexi tosses in, eyes darting between us.

"I hope you don't mind, but I peeked at the dress book Courtney had sent over. You've flagged some beautiful options," Meems says.

This is news to me. I haven't flagged anything. In fact I'm barely over the engagement party. I haven't even thought about a dress.

"I wondered if I'd, oh—" Connor stops short in the doorway. He's dressed in black pants and a dark Henley. He looks polished and poised and completely out of his element. "I didn't realize. Sorry to interrupt."

"You're not interrupting. We were just talking about the wedding and some of the dresses Dred has marked," Meems says.

Connor's eyes dart to me, cheeks flushing as he rubs the back of his neck. "Right, yeah." He licks his lips.

"Connor will have to share which ones are his favorite," Lexi remarks.

"Oh yes! Where's the wedding book! We all want to see," Essie adds.

"Oh, uh..." Connor seems at a loss for words.

"Why don't you grab it for us," I suggest.

His expression makes me believe it's the very last thing he wants to do, but he gives us a curt nod and disappears down the hall. The lack of time it takes for him to return tells me a lot about the location of the book.

I shift over to make room for him on the couch and he sets the book on the coffee table. His ears are bright red as the girls move closer for a better view. They ooh and ahh, pointing out their favorites. And I note, as we flip through the pages that each page is marked with a post it and a number in the corner.

Connor's ears never calm down while we browse the wedding book, and his leg is pressed against mine, his warmth seeping into me. He cracks a small smile when Hemi brings up Tristan's near suit-fiasco at his and Rix's wedding this summer. None of us knew about it until after the fact.

Eventually the girls head out and I walk them to the front door. Lexi laces her arm with mine and whispers, "Is that the first time you've seen that book?"

I dip my chin.

"So he picked all those out."

"Or his mother did," I offer.

"Doubtful."

The girls hug me goodbye.

I don't have time to read into the wedding book because Connor meets me in the hall. He tucks a hand in his pocket. "My mother sent that book over a couple of days ago. I wanted to make it easier for you, so I went through it first."

"That was nice of you."

He frowns. "I wasn't being nice."

I tip my head. "What were you being then? Efficient? Controlling?"

"That's not—"

I pat his cheek. "Regardless of the reason, I like your top three." Then I skirt around him and head upstairs. The wedding magazine isn't in the library anymore, though, which means Connor has it tucked away somewhere. Probably in his bedroom.

Whatever his reason, I like that he's been looking at dresses for me.

And that seems both dangerous and enticing.

CHAPTER 15
DRED

"I'll try not to waste your entire day off," Connor informs me as he drives. It's not an apology, but it's not *not* an apology.

"I really don't mind." Today is our venue walk-through and meal selection for the wedding. "Plus, we get to eat, so that's a bonus, right?" I'm trying to keep things upbeat, but Connor looks stressed, which isn't helping my own.

"Hopefully that will balance out the fact that you'll have to deal with at least one of my parents at some point."

Connor has been different since the photoshoot—*since the second kiss*—and the girls' book club night. He's almost always remote and awkward, but since that photoshoot make-out session—which I have replayed incessantly over the past few days while soaking in the clawfoot tub—the pendulum swings between those states have shifted. He's something else now, too. And so am I.

I often find him staring at my mouth—maybe thinking about the kiss the same way I do. It was surprisingly gentle, but also full of the kind of pent-up longing and need that curls a girl's toes. *This girl's toes.* So it makes sense that I find myself wondering about the other things he could do with his talented tongue, and how I would not be opposed to finding out more about his off-ice skill sets, regardless of the parameters of the contract I signed.

But that's a dangerous game to play. Keeping sex and feelings separate would be possible if this only lasted a couple of months, but a year—however insignificant in the span of a lifetime—is still a lot of days spent with one person. Especially since the more time I spend with Connor, the more I like him. He's broody, closed off, emotional, and wildly, intensely devoted to his Meems. It's that last part that's hitting me in my soft places. And of course, the kisses.

"I can handle your parents," I tell him.

They're not difficult to read. His mother seems jealous of her son and his ability to give his family the middle finger so he can do what he loves. Her disdain isn't for me, but for what I represent, which is the flipside of her pampered, spoiled life. His father is an elitist dick, based on our limited interaction. I'm sure it angers Connor's parents to no end that their only son has chosen to marry someone way below their social standing. He should be marrying the daughter of one of their rich friends, not the local librarian.

"Why don't they support your career?" I know, in the vaguest sense, the answer to this, but I want to hear it from him.

Connor glances at me, then refocuses on the road. His jaw tics. "It's a waste of my Ivy League education, and I should be making them more money by taking my place in the family business, like I'm supposed to."

"But hockey careers don't last forever. Roman is the exception, not the rule, and even he retired at forty."

"That's correct."

"So why can't you do this now and shift gears later?" That they used his time at the Hockey Academy as punishment speaks to how out of touch they are with their son.

"It's about family loyalty, and ticking the appropriate social boxes. I wasn't supposed to play a sport where I could lose teeth and break bones in my face. To them, it's like a prince becoming a gladiator. It's beneath our social standing. They don't understand why I won't give it up. They don't understand me. It doesn't help that Meems supports me and hasn't cut me out of her will the way they cut me off when I signed my first contract."

"What do you mean they cut you off?"

"They froze my accounts. I expected it, so it wasn't the shock they'd hoped it would be."

"Did they do it thinking you'd change your mind and come work for them?"

"That was my father's hope."

"Wow. That couldn't have been easy." I imagine what it would be like, raised in a home where he never wanted for anything. Where staff took care of basic needs and every meal was prepared, served, and cleaned up for him. How jarring must it have been to go from a world where everyone took care of everything to suddenly having to do it all himself?

"I had a lot to prove, to them and myself. The first year was eye-opening."

"What about Meems? Did she help?"

"She tried, but I wanted to do it on my own."

"So they don't agree with your chosen profession, and they don't want you to marry me."

"They don't know you."

"No, but I'm like hockey, beneath your social standing," I point out. "Yet they're putting all this effort into a wedding they also don't agree with? Why? It doesn't make sense."

His hands tighten on the wheel. "This wedding is a way for my father to put me in my place."

That they're willing to spend all this money after they cut him off seems contradictory. "I still don't get it."

"It's a power move. My father wants a flashy wedding that will be featured by local news outlets, because he loves the attention. And he wants the world to know that his son, and the sole male heir to carry on the Grace name, continues to be a disappointment because I'm marrying someone outside of his world."

"Wow, that's..."

"Psychopathic?"

"Calculated. What about your mother? Where does she fit into this?"

"She married up when she took the Grace name. My father pulls her strings, so she'll do whatever he asks of her."

"She sounds like a prisoner."

"She chose to marry him, and she stands by that decision." He grips the steering wheel. "They're putting us on display with the hope that I'll do something to embarrass myself or ruin what's left of my career," he explains flatly. "They want me to be out of options, so I have no choice but to join the family business. They think they're doing what's best for me."

I want him to be joking, but it's clear he isn't. "That's awful."

"Everything is about money and business with my father, and my mother is his pawn, unfortunately."

"Well, screw them." I want to say we can skip the big wedding and just elope, but this isn't for us. It's for Lucy.

A hint of a smile appears. "I'm glad to see I chose wisely with you."

He pulls up to the valet of the Grace Hotel. It's the most expensive place to stay in the city.

"Please wait. I'll come around and get you," Connor instructs as the attendant opens his door.

He steps out of the car, rising to his full, imposing height, and transforms from Connor Grace the hockey player and my fiancé, to the son of Duncan Grace, billionaire. His thick biceps flex under his perfectly tailored black suit with wine piping, and I take a moment to admire this enigma of a man, villain not only to the hockey world, but his family as well.

He rounds the hood and gives the other attendant permission to open my door. I slip my fingers into his waiting palm, and warmth shoots up my arm.

He moves in close as I rise, the fingers of his free hand skimming the length of my arm. To anyone watching, it looks intimate—and feels it too. He dips until his lips are at my ear. "The media are waiting for us in the hotel lobby. I assume they're here for the photo op, courtesy of my mother. We'll pause for a few seconds so they can get their shots, but don't answer any questions, okay?"

"Right. Okay." I nervously smooth my hands over my hips and wish I had my hair tie rather than this bangle that rubs against my already irritated skin.

"Just smile and don't look directly into the cameras."

"Got it." I reflexively smooth his lapel, even though he looks perfect.

"You're engaged to a Grace. It doesn't matter that I'm considered the worst of them. The name is armor lined with cashmere. Remember that when the media start slinging their arrows."

"How do you deal with this all the time?"

"I grew thorns." He straightens, his expression shifting to arrogance. "Come on. Let's get the hard part over with."

Connor guides me to the entrance, his fingers pressed against the dip in my spine, keeping me grounded. The cameras flash as soon as the doors open. I shift my gaze away, looking up at him. He smiles down at me, probably as a reminder that I'm supposed to do the same. The way it softens his harsh, noble features makes my heart stutter and my own lips curve up.

He stops once we're inside the hotel lobby, hand curving around my waist, pulling me closer. The media closes in, the frantic clicking and flashes overwhelming. When I'm out with Flip and the Babes, we usually go to the Watering Hole, where they're treated like normal people. Even on club nights, we go straight from the car to the VIP entrance to avoid this nonsense. But there's nowhere to hide.

This much attention is disorienting and uncomfortable. I fight to keep my smile in place, to not let panic take hold, to keep the heat from rising in my cheeks.

"Mr. Grace, can you confirm the rumors that your fiancée is pregnant?"

"Mr. Grace, is it true that your contract with the Terror is in jeopardy now?"

"Mr. Grace, will you be joining the Grace empire now that you're about to be married?"

"Ms. Reformer, is it true that you're also involved with Flip Madden?"

Connor pins the last reporter with a glare and makes a circle motion with his finger. Two security guards step in and remove the offender.

"I should not have to remind you that there are *no questions* for the future Mrs. Grace," he calls out. Then his lips find my temple. "Just a few more seconds, darling."

The cameras click furiously at the tender affection. I tip my chin up, and our gazes meet. Connor's eyes search mine, soft and warm, full of secrets and a gentle apology. I wet my bottom lip and arch a brow. The media seem to like it when he's exerting his dominance, followed by sweetness. His smile darkens, and then he bends, pressing his lips lightly to mine.

For a moment the world stops turning, and all that exists is him and me, the softness of his lips and the heat of his fingers tightening on my waist.

But it's over just as quickly as it begins. I'm disoriented as he rushes me past the photographers and camera crews. He raises one hand as we pass, his other arm still wrapped protectively around me.

His mother stands on the other side of the mob, her expression remote as she waits for us to reach her. "Your fiancée needs media training."

"Mildred did fine. Some warning that you'd invited the media would have been nice."

"The media are always invited. You're featured in the gossip rags often enough to know this." His mother gives him an irritated look. "Quite the spectacle at the end."

He smiles placidly. "Isn't that what this was about, Mother?"

"Your father won't be happy."

"He never is."

She sighs, her shoulders melting for a moment. "Why can't you just make it easy for once? You're a Grace. People are interested in your choices, good and bad." She finally turns to me and adopts what I expect is supposed to be a smile, but mostly she looks tired. "I'm sure this is all overwhelming for you."

I echo Connor's smile. "I spend a lot of time in hockey arenas, which are notorious for being overwhelming, I can handle a few nosy photographers."

Her expression softens for a moment, but then her phone chimes and she rolls her shoulders back, her face a mask of arrogant indifference. "I have a meeting. Everything has been arranged for your walk-through and tasting. Please do make selections so we're not left guessing." She air-kisses my cheeks and does the same to Connor before striding off.

"I apologize for my mother," Connor mutters.

"She seems stressed more than anything."

"It's the effect I have on her. On all of them."

I skim the back of his hand with my fingers. "I'm sorry they don't understand you."

"Come on." He laces our fingers and guides me to the escalator that will take us to the second-floor event spaces.

Everything about this hotel screams luxury. We pass a conference center and head for the ballroom.

A man dressed in a hotel uniform approaches us, a smile plastered on his slightly panicked face. His name tag reads *Henrick*. "Mr. Grace, you're early. I would have met you in the lobby and escorted you up here."

"I know my way around my family's hotels." He inclines his head toward me. "This is my fiancée, Mildred Reformer."

"Ms. Reformer." He nods and half-bows.

"It's just Dred."

He looks to Connor, as though he's seeking clarification or permission.

I jump in with an explanation, hoping to break the tension. "It's a nickname. Mildred is pretty spot on, considering my profession, and Dred makes me feel like less of a nerdy librarian and more like I belong on some secret superhero squad."

Connor's face grows ten times more attractive as a half smile tips the right corner of his mouth. I wish the photographers had followed us up here, so he'd have another reason to put his lips on mine again. That is a problem, but I'll deal with it later.

"Okay, Dred." Henrick relaxes a little. "Would you like to see the ballroom where your reception will be held?"

"That would be great."

He leads us down the hall to a set of beautiful white-and-gold double doors. Opening them with a dramatic flourish I sincerely appreciate, he ushers us inside.

"Oh, this is amazing." It's fairy-tale beautiful. Chandeliers dripping crystals hang from the ceiling, and the room is a soft cream with gold accents. The floor is polished wood, the round tables are draped with cream tablecloths, and an array of napkins and chair covers in a variety of fabrics have been laid out for us.

But it's the sheer size of the room that has me leaning in to whisper, "This is huge. How many people are coming to this shindig?"

"All of your friends and everyone my parents know," Connor says.

"And your friends," I add.

"I don't have many of those, as I'm sure you've come to realize."

"What about the guys on the team?" I know from Lexi that he's closest to Kellan Ryker and Quinn Romero, and that he's stayed tight with some of his other Hockey Academy connections.

"They're teammates. That's different."

"What about Kodiak Bowman?" Kodiak and his wife attended Tristan and Rix's wedding this past summer.

Connor makes a noise but doesn't disagree.

I hug his arm and tip my chin up. He bends to give me his ear again. "I think you're so used to being the scapegoat that you've forgotten you can be something else."

His expression turns wry. "What are you, an inspirational calendar?"

I roll my eyes. "Oh, fuck you."

His grin turns lascivious. "As I've mentioned, I'm happy to write that into our agreement anytime."

Henrick clears his throat.

I drop Connor's arm and put a few inches of space between us.

Henrick's face has turned red. "Your private tasting session is through here." He motions to a set of doors.

We follow him into a small room where a table has been set for two. Low lighting and flickering candles give it a romantic air. Connor steps up before the waitstaff can and tucks my chair in, then takes his own.

Two servers put our napkins in our laps and pour us water, then offer us a selection of handcrafted cocktails. I opt for a lavender-rose gimlet, and Connor declines, noting that he's the driver. The servers bring out the first course, which is a decadent lobster bisque, drizzled with lemon butter and garnished with tarragon. Next is fresh pear and walnut salad on a bed of baby greens, sprinkled with gorgonzola cheese, including a vegan option for those who don't consume dairy. Every course looks like art and tastes divine.

Connor samples each item wearing the same intense expression. It's hot, but also, it defeats the purpose of this adventure.

When we have a moment to ourselves, I lean forward. "Isn't this supposed to be fun?"

He frowns. "I'm sorry?"

I motion to the crab-stuffed mushroom caps. "This is probably the best food I've ever tasted, and you're over there looking like you're being graded on your table manners."

His jaw tenses, and his gaze shifts to the side.

My smile fades, and I sit up straighter. "Oh my gosh, were you actually graded on your table manners?"

Last year when we spent Christmas Eve with Roman, eating Thai takeout, I was entirely too fascinated by his impeccable table manners. Especially when I was used to Flip and the way he protects his food like someone's going to steal it before he can finish. Connor is meticulous to the point of being rigid. But maybe it's not because he wants to be. Maybe that's how he *has* to be.

"My father kept a wooden spoon on the table," he admits.

I glance at his elegant hands, his knuckles scarred in places. I assumed hockey was the culprit, but maybe I'm wrong. "I'm so sorry."

"It's fine." He forces a smile. "Good table manners were an expectation in my house, and I always had to learn everything the hard way."

"It's not fine, Connor." I cover his hand with mine as a long-buried memory surfaces, and for some reason, I feel compelled to share it with him. Maybe so he doesn't feel alone? "One of the foster homes I stayed in briefly was very…strict. Especially with portion control. It was…tough." We were always hungry. It made us feral. Unruly. Punishable. "On my first day, one of the boys tried to sneak an extra roll, and the foster dad hit him so hard the wooden spoon *and* the boy's hand broke."

His name was Wyatt. He'd been eight at the time, and I'd been seven. By then the number of foster homes I'd been to was nearing double digits.

Connor's fingers close around mine, voice low and gritty. "How long were you there?"

"I made sure I was enough of a problem that they got rid of me almost right away." Bad behavior could be effective, but it often came with painful consequences. Sometimes they were worth it, but not always. By the time I was eight, I'd learned that saying the right thing in front of the right person could be just as good a way to escape the bad stuff.

"I did the same," he whispers. "But they never really got rid of me."

"Lucky for me, I guess." Our worlds are so different, but now I know it's true—underneath we're the same. Broken. Discarded by the people who were supposed to love us the most. But Connor has been turned into a villain, and I became a savior. Maybe even now I'm becoming his. Would it be so bad to have my own villain? To be a soft place for him to land?

"More for me, I think."

I shake my head. "Always so content to be the bad guy."

"I'm good at it."

"You're not the only one." I move my chair so I'm beside him, shove all my silverware into a pile, and prop my elbows on the table.

He laughs, and it's a beautiful sound.

The server brings the next course, and his eyes go wide at the mess the table has become. He steps in to fix the silverware.

Connor raises a hand. "Leave it, please. My fiancée is being a menace." He winks at me, and I grin back.

"Of course, Mr. Grace." He removes our plates and sets something artful and unidentifiable in front of us. I miss part of the explanation, too busy trying to comprehend what's in front of me.

I wait until the server disappears before I say anything. "This looks like pretty cat food."

Connor just about falls out of his chair, he's laughing so hard.

I vow immediately to try my hardest to put a smile on his usually serious face. I defend my position. "It really does seem like something a cat would happily consume."

He dabs at his eyes with his napkin, still grinning. "Please say that in front of my mother."

"Uh, never. But you can't tell me I'm wrong."

"You're not wrong about the appearance."

"Are you going to explain this, or do I have to look it up?"

"It's steak tartare."

I wrinkle my nose. "That's raw beef, isn't it?"

"Mostly raw, yes."

"Doesn't beef taste best with some grill marks and a little charcoal?" I bite my lips together for a moment. "I don't want to waste food, but I don't think this is my thing."

"You have to try it before you say no to it," he says.

"Can't you just try it and tell me what you think?"

"That's not how it works."

I blow out a breath and feign exasperation. "Fine, but you have to go first." This is better. No more falling into the sadness of the past. Both of us seem to have been through enough.

He pops a forkful into his mouth and chews while making intense eye contact.

"You would make an incredible poker player."

"I used to take everyone's money back at the Hockey Academy. Unsurprisingly, it did not help win me friends." He gathers a small bite on his fork and lifts it to my mouth. "Your turn."

"How does it taste?"

"Like you'd expect."

"Not helpful."

The side of his mouth quirks up. He continues to hold the fork in front of me. I stick my tongue out and poke at the bit near the end. Then retract to get a sense of the flavor.

"What are you doing?"

"Discerning the likelihood of activating my gag reflex."

"I don't know that it would be on menus if it was a horrible experience."

"Agreed, but texture is a thing for me."

His expression shifts. "You don't have to do anything you don't want to, Mildred. Apart from the one obvious thing."

"I wouldn't have agreed to any of it if I found you unpalatable." I wrap my fingers around his wrist and take the offered bite.

I chew quickly and swallow.

He arches a dark brow.

"It's not as unappealing as I expected, but I'm right about the texture. I also think some of my friends might have questions, and Flip will definitely think you're trying to feed him cat food."

"That guy used to swallow sandwiches whole at the Hockey Academy."

"I believe it. He still eats every meal like it's his last most of the time. He used to eat brown sugar sandwiches with margarine when things were particularly tight." Flip still has some serious food insecurities, as does his sister, Rix.

Connor frowns. "Why brown sugar and margarine?"

"They didn't have anything else."

He blinks at me as true understanding dawns.

"Kind of explains why he was so offended about the sandwich you defiled."

His cheeks flush, and he bows his head. "It was such a stupid thing to do."

"I'm sure at the time it felt like reasonable retaliation for your last clean shirt." I push my plate toward him. "Here, you can eat mine, too."

"I don't want to eat either of them. My father knows I hate steak tartare, which is likely why it's on the tasting menu."

"Ah, I see. Well then..." I pull the plate back toward me. "We'll eat them in homage to Flip, who hates wasted food."

"You'd do anything for him, wouldn't you?" Connor asks, envy in his tone.

"Almost anything. I wouldn't sleep with him, but we protect each other."

"Why didn't you ask him for help with your apartment?"

"I didn't want it to change our friendship. But his story is not mine to tell."

"Something happened, though." Connor's eyes stay locked on mine, probing.

I nod, but say nothing else.

"Between the two of you?"

I can't tell if it's curiosity, jealousy, or something else that's driving his questions.

"No, before he knew me."

His shoulders ease.

"On the count of three." I dig my fork into my steak tartare.

He does the same, and we both take a bite. I'm glad the portion is small, and I only have two more bites before I decide it's enough to feel like it's not a complete waste.

The courses that follow are all incredible, each sample better than the last. The seared scallops are to die for, and so are the potato puffs and braised carrots.

And then they bring out three types of gelato.

"I already know which one is the winner before I've even tasted them," I declare. "But I'm not telling you until we've tried them all."

Connor shifts sideways, one arm draped over the back of his chair.

I like this version of him, and I want more of it.

"Which one would you like to try first?"

I shake my head. "That's too easy. You pick the first one, and we taste it at the same time."

He digs into one that looks like chocolate, so I do the same. We pop the bites at the same time. It's smooth and creamy, but also fudgy and rich with notes of salt and caramel.

"Thoughts?" Connor asks.

"Delicious."

"Agreed."

We set our spoons in the glass and move to the next one.

It's yellow with purple ribbons through it. The tart flavor bursts on my tongue. "Lavender lemon?"

"Hemi would love this, wouldn't she?" Connor goes back for a second spoon. "Dallas always brings her lavender lattes."

"He does. They're her favorite. And peach anything."

He moves to the pink scoop of gelato between us. Instead of bringing his spoon to his own lips, he lifts it to mine. I open for him, and the sweet-tart taste of strawberry, threaded through with vanilla, melts over my tongue, sharp and creamy and luscious. My eyes fall closed, and I hum contentedly.

"This one's my favorite," Connor murmurs.

My eyes pop open to find him staring intently at me.

I swallow the bite. "You haven't even tried it."

He sets the spoon down and brushes his thumb along my bottom lip. "I don't need to." He licks the pad, eyes darkening. "You already told me it's your favorite."

"What about your favorite?"

"I already have it."

CHAPTER 16
CONNOR

We're running drills today as preseason shifts into full swing. Romero and I flank Madden as Ryker prepares for the shot on net. His confidence is growing steadily.

Stiles skates behind the net, Bright moving into position close to me. Madden passes to Stiles, but I'm ready when he tries to pass to Bright. I steal the puck, tap it to Romero, and he shoots it down the ice.

"Nice pass, Grace." I expect a barb to follow, but Madden takes off after the puck, Stiles and Bright on his heels.

Palaniappa is at the other end of the rink, defending McEwan, the new backup goalie. I watch the easy way Stiles, Madden, and Bright play together. They're cohesive, moving like extensions of each other.

"Man, those three are something, aren't they?" There's awe and envy in Romero's tone as Madden easily slides the puck past McEwan.

"They've had a lot of years on the ice together," I remind him.

"And they spend a lot of time together off the ice, too," Ryker adds.

I feel more like part of this team lately. I expected it to be the opposite this season with my engagement to Mildred, but instead of hating me for it, Madden's been accepting. They all have, actually. Not for me, I'm sure, but for Mildred. Regardless, it's been good for preseason.

After practice, where Ryker only let one goal in, we hit the locker room, shower, and change back into street clothes.

"Dred seems good. She told me about the venue walk-through. Said the food was fantastic."

I look up, surprised to find Flip making conversation with me.

Bright, Stiles, and Palaniappa glance our way, apparently just as surprised as me.

"She tell you about the steak tartare?" I ask.

"Oh yeah." He laughs. "Dred and texture are a real thing."

"I witnessed that firsthand. It wasn't her favorite, but she refused to waste it." She would have lost her mind if she knew what it would have cost per person.

"That's my fault." He grins, his smile fond. "I hope she didn't suffer too much on my behalf."

A spike of unfamiliar jealousy shoots heat down my spine. He's important to Mildred, and she's important to him in a way I've never experienced with anyone other than Meems.

"Dessert made up for it."

"She said as much. If you want to make her smile, just bring her something with strawberries in it."

"Yeah. I've noticed." Her little moan, the way her eyes fluttered closed... I want more of that.

"Good." He runs a hand through his hair. "I'm sure you have all the wedding stuff covered, but, uh, if you're still looking for someone to make the cake, Rix has a lot of friends who do that kind of thing, and she'd love to help."

"Okay. Yeah." I'm sure my mother has some kind of plan, but her wishes aren't mine, and anything I can do to make Mildred feel included in this process and not steamrolled by my controlling parents is a win for me.

"I'll shoot you her number."

"Yeah, absolutely. That would be great. Thanks, man."

"Anything for Dred."

I expected more animosity from Flip, but maybe we're on the same page with this. He's willing to let the past stay where it is for the sake of his best friend. Or maybe he's being nice because he doesn't want Mildred to feel responsible if we have a shit season on account of the dissension between us. His motives seem more selfless than mine, regardless.

On the way home from practice, I get stuck behind a beater. Sixty kilometers an hour seems to be its max speed, and it looks like it's one pothole away from falling apart.

When it turns onto Meems's street, I have more questions. Like, what asshole would let their grandmother/wife/employee/teenager drive this heap of shit when they live in this neighborhood?

And then it pulls into my driveway. I assume whoever is behind the wheel must be lost, but no, the hand that reaches out of the car is adorned with the ring *I* put on it. Which means it's my *fiancée*. My mother would lose her mind if she knew the woman I'm about to marry has been driving around in a car with more rust than the *Titanic*.

I follow my fiancée down the driveway, past the Rolls-Royce and the McLaren, to the back where the garden staff parks—this lot is closer to the grounds and means less of a walk to the greenhouse.

Mildred parks her car beside a blue Camry, purchased by Meems for Barney, our head gardener. The staff here are well taken care of. My future wife's car is in the worst condition by far.

I park behind her.

She doesn't get out right away, though. In fact, she takes so long I give up on waiting her out and walk up to her window. A muffled voice filters through, but it's too quiet for me to catch the content. At first I think maybe she's on a call, but a few choice words bleed through. She's listening to an audiobook, and based on what I catch, it's a romance novel.

She runs her hands up and down her thighs, her lips are parted, and her eyes are closed. Her tongue peeks out, and one hand leaves her thigh to pop the top two buttons on her cardigan. She's wearing a simple pink V-neck shirt underneath, with just the barest hint of cleavage. Her fingers trail back down, hands sliding between her thighs, chest rising and falling faster. Her mouth drops open, her hips roll. I might not be able to hear the words coming through the speakers, but I sure as hell hear the soft moan that tumbles from her lips. She shudders, and her hands go to the steering wheel, gripping tightly as her head falls forward. I have no idea what I just watched, but I sure as fuck want it to happen again.

I knock on the window. She shrieks and flails, head whipping my way. Her eyes flare, her cheeks flushed. She cuts the engine. I try the door, but it's locked.

She grabs her oversized bag, hugging it to her chest with one hand, and fumbles with the lock.

When I open the door, it groans loudly. "What are you doing?"

"What are you doing? You scared the shit out of me!" She pokes my thigh and brushes her hair away from her face.

I take a step back.

She pulls herself out of the car. Her skin is dewy.

"What just happened in there?" I narrow my eyes. "What were you listening to?"

"A book." Mildred adjusts her cardigan and shoulders her purse, eyes anywhere but me.

"Why are you flushed?"

"I got to the good part." She lifts her chin, defiant.

"What does that mean?"

"Exactly what I said."

We stare each other down.

I cross my arms. "You're not going to elaborate?"

She smiles serenely. "I don't think I need to."

Did I just watch my fiancée have a contactless orgasm? Is that a thing? And if it is, I would really love a front-row seat to the next event. I leave that alone, mostly because I don't want to leave it alone.

I must think about kissing her a hundred times a day. I constantly wonder how her hands would feel on my skin. If I'd like it. If it would feel as nice as her mouth. If I'd feel something other than apathy with her. And now I'll think about her sitting in her car, eyes closed, lips parted, possibly getting off without so much as a single caress.

I switch gears, because she still hasn't agreed to amend our contract—not that I've asked in a way that denotes my seriousness on the matter—and I won't push for things she doesn't want to give. "Did you drive this to work?" I motion to the car.

"No." She rolls her shoulders back. "I drove it to the subway station halfway to work because I had an appointment this morning."

"What kind of appointment?"

"The doctor kind."

Panic hits me. All doctor's appointments recently have been full of bad news. "Are you okay?"

She raises a hand, her voice gentle. "I'm fine. It was my yearly checkup."

"Oh." That's a relief. "This car is a heap of shit."

She places a protective hand over the side mirror, which is attached to the car with red duct tape. "Do not talk about Betty that way. You'll hurt her feelings." She rubs the mirror lovingly. "Or is this you telling me you don't want me to drive it because you're embarrassed that it's worth less than your shoes?"

"I'm not embarrassed. I don't give a shit if you want to drive a Barbie pink Batmobile. But this is not safe. It looks like it would barely make it to the corner store."

She crosses her arms. "Well, it's all I can afford."

We haven't reached the one-month mark on our relationship,

so no money has been deposited into her account. "What kind of car do you want?"

"You're not buying me a car when the one I have is perfectly fine."

"It's not perfectly fine. The side mirror is held on with tape." I give it a tug, and it comes off in my hand. "And not very securely."

"What the fuck, Connor?" She grabs it from me and cradles it to her chest. "Do I go around breaking your things?"

"It was already broken!"

Her defiant edge is back. "Well, so am I. Are you going to pull me apart too?"

"Mr. Grace, is everything okay?"

Barney is standing fifteen feet away, holding a bucket of fresh flowers.

Mildred shoves by me and heads for the house.

"Everything's fine, apart from my fiancée's car." I make a note to fix the problem as soon as possible. She needs a safer vehicle, and I can certainly afford to put her in one.

I leave Barney in the driveway and follow Mildred through the employee entrance, but she's disappeared.

"Dred! How was your day?" I hear Ethel call from the kitchen and head in that direction. "What do you have there?"

"One of Betty's ears." She shoots a glare over her shoulder at me.

"Who's Betty?"

"My car."

I can't help myself, I follow her into the kitchen.

"Oh! How did that—" Ethel's eyes go wide, and she jumps off her stool, standing at attention when she sees me. "Mr. Grace, I'm so sorry. I didn't see you there. What can I do for you?"

I frown and glance around the kitchen. Every single person is now standing in the same position—backs straight, hands clasped in front of them, wearing slightly panicked expressions.

And they're all staring like they're waiting for me to bite their heads off.

"I don't need anything," I assure them, attempting a friendly smile. *Except for my future wife to stop being angry about a side mirror.*

"He needs a time-out." Mildred points at me.

"He needed a lot of those as a child," Ethel says.

"Did he now?" Mildred pulls a stool up to the massive island.

"He needed less time studying and more time outside," Norm says defensively.

I like Norm the best, I decide.

"I didn't mean to break your car," I say.

"Are you sure about that?" Mildred pats the stool next to hers. "You can come sit with us if you promise not to break anything else."

I do, because I'm too curious not to, and I want to be part of whatever this is.

Ethel sets a plate of cookies in front of us, and the rest of the staff gives Mildred their undivided attention.

"Today's library adventures are brought to you by the two high school kids," she begins.

"Was it the one who always gets up to no good?" Norm asks, settling in the seat across from her.

"Maybe. Maybe not." Mildred's eyes light up. "So this patron has been dating this boy for a while—"

"The same one she got caught in the family bathroom with?" Ethel asks.

"She'll never tell," Norm nudges her arm.

"Right, what happened this time?"

"Well, apparently one of my young reader has discovered spicy romance, and the two of them were sitting on the floor in one of the aisles, reading together." Mildred pauses. "With their hands down each other's pants."

Norm laughs. "Cleaner than the bathroom!"

"Not by much!" Ethel gives his shoulder a playful shove.

Norm's expression shifts to alarm. "Please tell me Dorothea didn't find them."

"Is she the one who thought we were having an afternoon delight in your breakroom?" I ask, probably so Mildred's attention is on me for a moment, and so I can feel included.

Mildred gives me an amused look. "Is that how you interpreted her reaction to your being somewhere you weren't supposed to be?"

I shrug. "Yes?"

"Hmm..." She turns back to Norm and Ethel. "Dorothea didn't find them, thank goodness."

"It was you, wasn't it?" Ethel's eyes are knowing.

"It sure was."

"What did you do?" Myrna, one of the part-time kitchen staff, takes a seat at the island, and Ethel passes her the cookies.

Everyone is so relaxed and happy, waiting for Mildred to continue with story time.

"I'm sad to say neither of them got their happy ending." She presses her hand to her chest for dramatic effect. "However, after much embarrassment and some tears on the part of the boy who could not seem to get himself under control for quite some time—"

"Blue balls suck," I mutter.

Everyone's eyes are suddenly on me. The staff looks scandalized.

"Norm, back me up! They're super uncomfortable."

He nods. "Yes, Mr. Grace, you're right."

"Are you just saying that because you feel like you have to agree with me?"

"No, sir. It's been quite a long time since I've had the unfortunate experience, but I can attest to the discomfort."

"That's very helpful information." Mildred grins.

"Don't get any ideas, little menace," I mumble.

"Too late, villain," she quips, then turns her attention back to the staff. "I sent them off with their own copy of the book, and my young reader is now signed up for our romance book club."

"Hopefully the boy learns a thing or two!" Ethel giggles.

The room bursts into laughter and applause, quickly devolving into tales of teenage bad behavior.

Eventually we're shooed out so they can finish preparing dinner.

"How often do you do that?" I ask as Mildred turns toward the stairs to the second floor.

"Do what?"

"Hang out with the staff."

She pauses with her hand on the newel post. "Most days. I used to live across the hall from my best friend. I don't anymore, and I miss that. They help fill the void." She disappears up the stairs.

I don't follow.

Half an hour later, Mildred and I are sitting at the dinner table. I can't shake my fiancée's disappointment that Meems won't be joining us. Instead Meems is taking dinner with one of her friends in the guesthouse. When I asked them both to join us, Meems brushed me off, saying I needed time with Mildred without a chaperone. She spends time with the staff every day, she hangs out with Meems all the time, and she goes over to Madden's to play board games. But the only reason she's willing to sit here with me is because of a contract.

"I don't want you to feel trapped," I blurt.

"This place is enormous, Connor. I hardly feel trapped." She spears a roasted potato.

"That's not…" I push my chicken around on my plate. My stomach twists uncomfortably. "Besides playing board games, what do you and Madden do when you hang out?"

She tips her head, eyes fixed on me. "What do you do with your friends, Connor?"

I drop my gaze. Embarrassed. Frustrated. I don't socialize outside of hockey. I avoid hanging out with my teammates because I'm the bad apple. I don't spend time with my sisters because it causes tension with our parents.

Mildred sighs, and it's a soft, sad sound. "I beat him at board games. We watch stupid TV. We talk and laugh and complain about the weather, and we eat cheap food because Flip has a habit of buying things on sale in bulk. That's what we do. Normal friend stuff."

The uncomfortable jealousy I can't seem to escape when it comes to Madden takes hold. Even though I took one of the people who means the most to him and claimed her for myself, he's still nice to me—giving me pointers on how to make his best friend happy.

"You should hate me."

Mildred pushes her chair back.

Of course she's leaving now.

What did I expect her to do? Tell me I'm wrong? That I'm not making her miserable most of the time? That this isn't the worst decision she's ever made?

She rounds the table and stops beside my chair. She smells like strawberries and vanilla, and I want to ask her to stay, but I can't. I won't.

She takes my face in her hands and tips my head back, her soft chocolate eyes meeting mine, so full of sadness I could drown in the hurt I keep causing her.

"I don't need to hate you, Connor." She bends, and her hair tickles my skin as her warm, soft lips brush my cheek. "You do it enough for both of us."

CHAPTER 17
CONNOR

Mildred took her plate with her when she left, so I finish my dinner alone, but only because I don't want to waste food. I now have some odd sense of needing to right an ancient wrong regarding my fiancée's best friend. Besides, not eating well will affect my on-ice performance. It's been a solid start to preseason, and I don't want to fuck it up.

I shock the hell out of the staff when I show up in the kitchen with my empty plate. The laughter stops, and everyone stands when I enter.

"Mr. Grace, was your dinner insufficient?" Cedrick asks.

It really sucks that I put everyone on edge just by existing. "No, dinner was great. I just figured I'd save you the trouble of collecting my plate since I'm going out to see Meems."

He takes the plate and cutlery. "It's my job, sir."

"Sometimes it's nice when someone makes it easier, though." I rub the back of my neck. "And can you all stop calling me Mr. Grace, please? I know I look like him, but I'm not my father." And I never want to be. All the art I put on my body is a reminder of just how different we are. He would never defile himself the way I have, and he's been very vocal about his disdain for my choices, career and body art included.

"What would you prefer?"

"Just Connor, please."

Cedrick smiles. "Of course, Connor."

If Mildred was with me, they'd all be smiling. "Do we have strawberries?"

"Yes, Connor, would you like some?"

"Not now, but they're M—Dred's favorite, so maybe something with strawberries for breakfast."

Ethel beams. "I'll browse my recipes."

"Great. Thanks."

"You're welcome, Connor."

I leave the kitchen, feeling like I've at least made some progress with the staff. I pass through the breezeway, and the cool evening air is a reminder that long sleeves will be mandatory soon as I rap on Meems's door before I enter. The lights are on, but the living room is empty.

"Meems?" It's not even seven. I check the four seasons room with a view of the expansive backyard and her favorite gardens, but she's not there, either.

"Meems, you in there?" I knock on her bedroom door, but still no response. Panic hits, swift and cutting like a blade. The emotions sweep through me before I can corral them, nearly taking me to my knees.

I push the door open, heart hammering in my chest. Meems is in bed, still and tiny. She seemed okay earlier. What if... *Please don't let her be gone.*

I'm not ready to be without her. I'm not ready for a world in which she doesn't exist. She's the only person in my family who understands me, the only one who has always been on my side. But it's more than that. If I lose Meems, I have to let Mildred go, and I don't want to yet.

I cross the room, begging a God I've never put faith in not to take Meems away from me for wildly selfish reasons.

Meems's back expands and contracts, quelling the panic. For now.

There will come a day when my fears are reality. I know that, even if I don't want it to be true.

I kneel beside her bed and press my lips to her forehead. She's cool, no fever. *Thank God.*

She stirs, and I pull back, wishing her body was strong enough to withstand surgery. Maybe more time with Mildred will get her there. Maybe she can heal us both. *Give her more time, please.*

"Connor?" Her warm, soft palm presses against my cheek. "What time is it?"

"Seven." I take her frail hand and kiss the back of it. "You feeling okay?"

"I laid down after dinner because I was tired. I was only supposed to sleep for half an hour."

"It's okay. If you're tired, you're tired, Meems."

"I am." She nods groggily. "So tired these days."

We were warned this could happen. Her heart is working so hard. Too hard. "Maybe we should make a doctor's appointment."

"I'm tired of those, too."

"I know, but I need you to be healthy so you can see me get married." The sooner the better. I need to talk to Mildred about the timeline.

"Dred is so good for you." She smiles. "Where is she?"

"In the house. We finished dinner a while ago." *She was sweet, and I was my asshole self.* "You want me to read to you tonight?"

"Maybe just a page or two. Don't skip any of the good parts."

At least her sense of humor is still intact. "I won't, Meems." I grab the book from the nightstand and sit on the edge of her bed. She settles back against her pillows with a sigh.

I only manage to read one page before she's asleep again. I replace the bookmark and rub my cheek, the one Mildred's lips were pressed against briefly when she called me out on my own self-loathing. "I don't know how to talk to Mildred when you're not around," I admit. "I need you to stay so I can get better at it."

I kiss her cheek and turn off the light. On the way back, I stop in the staff quarters and ask Cedrick to check on Meems before he goes home for the night. I walk down to my office to tackle a few emails, including a request for an update on Mildred's apartment.

The back rent has been handled, so she's no longer at risk of being evicted. But I want to solve the problem indefinitely, and the best way to do that is to make her the owner rather than the renter of the apartment. However, the new owner is resistant to selling the unit. From a financial standpoint, I understand. It's a high-end building, and the rentals generate more income over time. But everyone has a price. It's just a matter of figuring out what it is.

It's closing in on ten by the time I leave the office. I pause outside Mildred's bedroom door. Her light is still on. I should apologize for making dinner uncomfortable.

I knock, but don't get a response. Seems to be a trend tonight.

I try again, but still nothing, so I resort to texting. No buzz comes from the other side of the door, though. She's probably in the library.

I walk down the hall, take the first right, and step inside the library through the other entrance. The lights are dim, so it takes several seconds for my eyes to adjust. She's curled up on the couch in the glass dome, a blanket covering her legs, pillow behind her head, and a book lying open on her chest. Her glasses are askew. I carefully remove the book, tucking the bookmark in before I close it and set it on the side table, then I remove her glasses, wiping away the fingerprints before I gently fold the arms. Those I slip into the breast pocket of my polo.

I don't wake her. Not yet. I want this moment, where I'm not the person tying her to a life she doesn't want but is willing to accept so she can keep the things and people she values most. What would it feel like to be loved like that by her?

That will never happen.

"Mildred?" I stroke her cheek.

She doesn't shy away from the touch. Instead she turns toward my fingers, as if the contact is welcome. Maybe we're similar in that respect. Most of the time I feel starved for contact. I fear it and crave it. That kiss during our engagement photos plays on an endless loop. The warmth of her lips, the softness of her body against mine.

"*I kissed you back.*"

"Dred." I understand the nickname to be ironic now, because the only thing I dread these days is her deciding to leave. It doesn't sound right coming out of my mouth.

Her eyes flutter open. She feels for her glasses.

"I have them right here."

She stretches like a cat and hums. "I fell asleep."

"You did. In the library."

"I do almost every night," she murmurs and rolls on her side, toward me, pressing her cheek into her pillow. "I like being surrounded by stories."

"Your bed is probably more comfortable."

"It is."

I brush a tendril of hair away from her face. I shouldn't, but she's unguarded, not quite awake enough to tell me to fuck off and keep my hands to myself.

She raises a hand, curving it around mine. Holding on to it. Her eyes are closed again, but the hint of a smile plays on her lips.

"Then why not read in your bed?"

"It's too easy to get used to nice things," she says.

Why does everything she says make me wish I was a different person? "You can take the bed with you when you go back to your own life."

"It won't fit in my apartment." She relaxes again, sleep trying to reclaim her.

She'll stay here all night, if I let her.

I tuck one arm under her knees and slide the other behind her back, carefully lifting her into my arms.

"What are you doing?" She nuzzles into my neck, nose pressing against my collarbone.

"Putting you to bed."

"I was fine on the couch." Her hand settles on my chest.

"A couch is not a bed." She feels good in my arms. Like she belongs there. Like she should be mine.

I carry her through the library, using the secret entrance to her bedroom, and tuck her in, setting her glasses on the nightstand.

She blinks up at me in the hazy darkness. "Isn't it so much nicer when you're not hating yourself?"

"Who said I stopped hating myself?"

Mildred presses her hand to my cheek. "You came to find me."

I let my eyes slide closed, absorbing the warmth of her touch. How would it feel to curl my body around hers and hold her all night? I could keep her safe from the nightmares. I could feel something other than longing.

"Now's when you kiss me on the forehead and say good night, Connor."

"Did you read that in a book?"

"Maybe." She tips her chin up.

I bend and press my lips to her forehead, her temple, and her cheek. The itch under my skin ceases. The yearning quells, just for a moment. "'Night, Mildred."

CHAPTER 18
DRED

DRED
Rix, how in the world did you manage to go to school full time, work part time for an accounting firm, make meals for half the Terror, and still plan a wedding without having a nervous breakdown?

RIX
I had Essie.

ESSIE
And dick. She also had lots of dick.

DRED
Ah, that's clearly what's missing from my equation.

HEMI
I guess this means you haven't jumped on that yet.

DRED
It would certainly complicate this already complicated relationship.

IF YOU CLAIM ME

HAMMER

But it could also be a perk!

ESSIE

I bet he's a demon in the sheets. The quiet, reserved ones always are.

HAMMER

Same with the grumpy ones.

DRED

I may or may not have already wondered these things.

RIX

I vote you find out, for research purposes.

ESSIE

You just want one of us to be as freaky as you.

HEMI

I'm pretty sure Dallas and I could give you a run for your money.

LEXI

😊

DRED

Rub salt in the wound, why don't you? I'm very grateful for my ability to orgasm without even touching myself.

TALLY

That's a thing?

How is that a thing?

That can't be a thing!!!

SHILPA

It's a thing.

DRED

It's my turn in the fire, I guess.

TALLY

I'm twenty, not a teenager. No one has to worry about corrupting my poor innocent mind. I've been to parties where people were boning on the living room couch (which is gross, by the way) while the people who sat beside them played video games (and an onlooker cheered them on).

DRED

Please tell me you didn't stay at that party long.

TALLY

Obviously not. I was worried about getting an STI just from breathing the sex air.

How did I not know contactless orgasms were a thing?

RIX

To be fair, it's not super common.

SHILPA

This is true.

TALLY

How not common is it?

DRED

It's rare. I probably should have led with that.

I probably shouldn't have said anything at all. Although I'm highly appreciative of how easily my friends have accepted my decision and are supporting me without pressing me for details I'm not ready to give. New messages pop up in my private chat with Lexi.

LEXI

Once again, proving your magical unicorn status.

Why have you never shared this special talent?

IF YOU CLAIM ME

DRED
Most people are shocked and then jealous.

LEXI
That's fair. I would be jealous if I didn't have my very own personal and dedicated orgasm provider.

DRED
Daddy Roman 🐻

LEXI
Can I tell you how excited I am for him to dress up as Santa again this year? 😊

I need to stop talking about this.

My pregnancy hormones are out of control.

Me and the girls will be there to pick you up in about twenty minutes. How are you doing?

DRED
Today is the kind of day I wished I partook in the herbal variety of stress relief. I'm nervous. Even the full-contact self-administered orgasms aren't taking the edge off.

LEXI
You could ask Connor to help you out.

DRED
It's an idea.

But probably not a good one.

LEXI
Seeing more than just his pretty face these days?

DRED
The way he loves his Meems is hard to ignore.

So many things about him are now—like the furrow in his brow every time he looks at me, as though he's trying to figure out what to say.

Or how the past four nights, after I've fallen asleep on the couch in the library, like I do every night, he's come in and carried me to bed. And every night his kiss migrates, moving closer to my mouth.

He's fine when Meems has dinner with us, but on those evenings when she's too tired—which is becoming increasingly, alarmingly frequent—and it's just the two of us, he struggles not to say something that could be hurtful, if interpreted incorrectly. Most of the time I can decode the message under the words, but today I'm stressed.

My wedding is in two weeks—when Connor said it would be a short engagement, I thought maybe a few months, not a handful of weeks. But he's worried about Meems's health, and frankly, so am I.

The wedding I can handle, but the bridal shower being thrown by his mother at his sister Isabelle's house today terrifies the shit out of me.

Meems and all my friends will be there as a buffer, but I won't have Connor as my bodyguard.

DRED

I have to put my dress on, and it'll take another ten minutes to get from my bedroom to the front door, so I'm signing off until you get here.

LEXI

You've got this. And we've got you.

I toss my phone on the bed and head for the closet. Another dress appeared yesterday. This one is exceedingly modest, but also beautiful. I could probably have bought a brand-new car twice over with the amount of money spent on dresses for me recently. Or fund a soup kitchen for a year. Which is gross to think about. But it also gives me pause when I consider the library gala and how different it could look this year, and how easy it would be to fund all the programs if I changed the scope of my thinking.

I shove those thoughts aside. They're not helpful. When I get my first check I'll donate to ease my guilty conscience.

I change into the dress and transfer the necessary items from my purse to my matching clutch. I grab a handful of bracelets from my dresser and thread them onto my left wrist to cover the raw skin and faint bruising left behind from the hair tie. I've switched to a scrunchie recently, which helps, but the skin isn't quite healed yet. I hate that I've resorted to this old behavior, and that it's mostly subconscious.

I make sure I have everything before I leave my room, carrying my high heels since it's half a kilometer from my room to the front door. I was only slightly exaggerating about how long it takes to get from one end of the house to the other.

Connor is sitting in the living room with Meems when I arrive. I smile at her outfit. Meems loves statement pieces just as much as Connor seems to, and together she and I make quite the pair. Our dresses are mirrors of each other. Hers is teal with wine piping and mine is wine with teal piping. This is intentional. And not just because it's cute, I've come to realize. It screams solidarity, and it's a giant fuck you to Connor's parents and their apparent love of sad beige dresses.

Connor stands, eyes moving over me in a way that's become familiar and flattering. He approaches, lighting up with the same anticipation I feel. He only touches me when Meems or someone else equally important is there to witness it—and when he carries me to bed every night.

"You look stunning." He runs his fingers gently down my arm, clasping my hand in his.

Is it just for Meems's benefit, or does he feel the same electric tension swirling between us? Either way, my stomach flutters as he brings my fingers to his lips. His lips quirk as he pulls me closer.

Normally I would enjoy this part—being close to him,

breathing in the sandalwood and citrus of his cologne, reveling in the feel of his strong arms wrapped around me, marveling at the way everything about him softens when he holds me like this. Okay, I still enjoy this, but... "Easy to smile when you're not the one walking into the lion's den," I whisper.

That wipes the grin off his face. Guilt is swift on its heels.

"You've already sent the message that we three are a team, Connor. No need to keep firing arrows by dressing us like twins."

"I'm sorry." There's real apology in his tone.

"Mmm... Best to find a way to make it up to me that doesn't have dollar bills attached to it." Despite myself and the tension flaring between us, or maybe because of it, I tilt my chin up.

The remorse swimming in his eyes makes me regret saying anything. He'll spend the next few hours swirling in self-loathing, and by the time I get back with Meems, he'll have returned to his shell. So instead of waiting for him to kiss me, I slide my hand up his chest and curve my fingers around the back of his neck. I tug gently, and he drops his head.

"I love the dress," I say against his warm lips. "And Meems looks adorable." I flick his top lip with my tongue and step quickly out of his arms so I don't end up sucking face with him in front of his grandmother. Ignoring the chemistry these days is a challenge, mostly because I haven't. Instead I've been doing things to purposely wind up in his arms.

Making it through an entire year without falling into bed with this man will prove difficult. My previous intrigue has shifted, and most of the time I find that I like him, even when he's being a problem.

Connor rubs the back of his neck. "I have something for you."

"Besides all of this?" I motion to my attire.

"It's little." He slips his hand into his breast pocket and retrieves a a small box. Freeing the lid, he reveals a stunning gold charm bracelet interspersed with teal and wine gemstones. And of course Meems has one to match.

"This is beautiful," I murmur, running my fingers over the delicate chain. "Will you help me put it on?"

His smile is radiant and something I want to see more of. "Of course." He carefully frees the clasp and adds to the string of bracelets already decorating my wrist.

Meems is all smiles. "You two are perfect."

"Mildred is perfect. I'm just better with her at my side," Connor says.

I stifle a laugh. Surprisingly, he looks serious.

"Let me get a picture of the two of you before you go." He pulls his phone from his pocket, and I stand beside Meems, posing for a few photos.

Briefly, I wonder what this memory will be like for him. What will it be like for me? All these celebrations of love, and the only part of it that's genuine is the way we feel about the woman connecting us to each other.

My phone buzzes. "That's Lexi."

"Did she bring the girls?" Connor's face lights up.

"She did not. Callie has hockey practice, and Fee is coming with Tally since they're both at Tilton."

"Ah, right." His face falls.

My heart melts a little at his disappointment. "We can go to her game next week." It's been a challenge to make them with all the wedding preparations, which has been unfortunate.

He offers us both an arm and nods. "I don't want to keep missing them."

"Me either."

Connor walks us down the steps and helps us into the car. He stands there with his hands shoved into his pockets, looking stupidly delicious and equally worried as we drive off.

Meems and I sit in the back seat, while Hemi is in front with Lexi.

"When will we have book club again?" Meems asks on the short drive.

"Soon, hopefully. It's been busy with all the wedding prep and season startup for Connor."

"We'll have to plan a date once the wedding has passed," Lexi suggests.

The drive over is the fun part of this event, and it basically goes downhill from there.

Courtney's smile slides right off her face when Meems and I enter her daughter's home, but she quickly recovers and ushers us in with a forced smile. I assume it's the matching dresses. Or at least what they represent. Connor's family seems like a ball of wool unraveling, and I'm trying not to get tangled in the mess.

Portia waits until her mother is out of earshot before she whispers, "You and Meems look cute. This was Connor?"

"It was Connor," I affirm.

She gives me an empathetic smile. "He should know better."

I come to his defense. "I think he's just trying to find a place to fit."

She laughs. "He's never tried to fit into this family."

"Maybe he did, but it didn't work, so he stopped trying," I suggest.

"Connor has always done his own thing," she assures me.

"It can't be easy."

Her expression shifts to confusion. "Connor has never liked to make things easy for himself or anyone else."

"I imagine it must have been lonely for him, always feeling like he was on the outside, never feeling understood."

Isabelle comes down the stairs and squeals when she sees me, effectively ending that tense conversation. I'm grateful for Isabelle and her sweetness, and even more thankful when the rest of my friends show up. They're a huge ball of happy energy, insulating me from the haughty stuffiness of Connor's mother's friends. Everyone is so proper and stiff.

I'm not huge on being the center of attention, but I'm thrust into the middle of the room so I can open the endless gifts. Three-thousand thread count sheets imported from Egypt, a collection of wildly expensive wines, designer embossed sweaters with Mr. and Mrs. Grace on the front. Every gift is grander than the last, like it's a competition to see who can give the best one.

So when the Babe Brigade—bless their wonderful, sweet hearts—present me with a spa day that they'll all be joining me for, I almost burst into tears of gratitude. I could really use a girls' day.

"You're included as well, obviously," Lexi says to Connor's mom and sisters.

"I have someone who comes to the house monthly," Courtney replies.

"I'd love to go," Isabelle says at the same time.

Portia looks like she might explode from the sudden tension in the room.

Lexi just ignores it. "Great! It'll be a fun day! Roman sends me there all the time, and they're wonderful." She turns to Courtney. "Maybe you could just join us for lunch. Your aesthetician is sort of like your stylist, right? Going to someone else feels a lot like cheating."

Portia laughs shrilly, then sinks into her chair. I have so many questions about her.

I diffuse some of the discomfort by offering an embarrassing, pointless story. "Once I trimmed my own bangs. I was between stylists because I'd moved." And I couldn't really afford regular trips to the salon, but everyone is listening, and Portia is no longer receiving looks from her mother for her outburst of laughter, so I continue. "But my ability to cut a straight line was not the best, so I had to keep trimming."

"Oh no..." Isabelle covers my hand with hers.

"You see where this is going, right?"

"How short were they?"

"*So* short. It was around Halloween, so I really leaned into it. I dyed my hair black and went as the girl from *Kill Bill*."

"What's *Kill Bill*?" Courtney asks.

"A movie from the early two thousands," I explain.

"That's a real commitment to a bang cut gone awry," Lexi says.

"I like to own my mistakes." And apparently tell stupid stories because I didn't put up a fight when my future in-laws said they were throwing a bridal shower. I am so lucky to have the friends I do.

"My mom used to cut mine and Flip's hair, because of money," Rix chimes in, obviously not wanting me to be alone in the land of embarrassing stories.

At Isabelle and Portia's confused expressions, Rix offers more of an explanation. "We were poor."

"Oh. I'm sorry." Isabelle looks genuinely sad that this was the case.

Rix shrugs. "It's all I knew, and we have great parents and a house full of love."

I love how she unintentionally humbles these women, and how easily she talks about what her life was like growing up. "Except once Flip asked me to cut his hair, and it did not go well."

"This is one of my favorite stories!" Essie claps and hugs Rix's arm.

"Same! So, my older brother Flip, who is Connor's teammate and Dred's bestie, decided he wanted a special haircut for grade nine picture day, and despite my lack of hair-cutting experience—"

"—other than with our Barbies," Essie chimes in.

"We thought we were so good," Rix says.

"Bless our idiot selves." Essie puts her hand over her heart. "We were awful."

"So awful." Rix smiles. "But Flip had misplaced faith that I could handle the task."

"How old were you?" Hammer asks.

"Like, ten, right?" Rix looks to Essie for confirmation.

"About that, yeah."

"I can't believe Flip has never told me this story before," I muse.

"Then you'd want to see his grade nine pictures." Rix grins.

"Please tell me you have them."

"Absolutely. I'm saving them for the photo slideshow at his wedding, if he ever gets married."

"He'll get married," Tally pipes up.

Fee hides a smile behind her glass of soda.

Seems like that torch Tally has been carrying since high school is still burning brightly.

"How bad was the haircut?" Portia asks.

"So bad," Rix replies.

"So, so bad. He looked like he'd gone a round with a weed eater and lost," Essie adds.

"And then my mom came home."

"You must have been in so much trouble," Isabelle whispers.

Rix snorts a laugh. "My mom thought it was hilarious. It was Flip's fault for encouraging me. After that, she taught me how to use the electric trimmer. He looked like a tennis ball for his photos. Ironically, or probably unsurprisingly, he rocked that buzz cut."

Essie nods her agreement. "That was the year Flip got cute."

"The girls were relentless after that." Rix rolls her eyes, but she's smiling. "He kept the buzz cut until winter, and then grew his hair back because Canadian winters aren't kind."

"Amen to that," Hammer agrees.

Connor's sister jumps in with a story of her own. "Portia and I tried to cut each other's bangs once, too. Except our hair was dry."

"Oooh, that's a rookie mistake," I say with empathy.

"It was so bad." Isabelle turns to Portia. "Yours were better than mine."

She grips her sister's hand. "True, and I'm still sorry."

"Remember when we begged Connor to help us fix it?" Isabelle smiles.

"He laughed so hard at us."

"We deserved it." Portia's smile is wide. "But he brought us a whole pile of scarves and made us promise not to tell you he'd aided and abetted," Portia explains to Courtney.

"Is that why he needed all of those scarves?" Meems slaps her thigh and laughs.

"Oh my goodness, Connor got them from you?" Portia's jaw drops.

"That makes so much sense now," Isabelle adds.

"How old were you girls? Junior high maybe?" Meems asks.

"I was grade seven. You were going into eight." Isabelle looks to her sister for confirmation.

"That's right. I was so worried I wouldn't have bangs for picture day in the fall." Portia nods.

"Don't you remember the trunk full of old clothes you girls used to play with when you were young?" Meems smiles.

"It was the only thing you girls wanted to do when we went to see Meems," Courtney says. Even she seems caught up in the memories.

"You'd dress Connor up," Meems adds.

Isabelle and Portia laugh. "The things he tolerated."

"You made dresses out of the scarves, and then he'd have to untie all the knots for you," Meems says. "That day of the bangs disaster, he drove over, picked them up, and said he'd be back later to explain."

"That's right! He didn't have his G2 license yet, but he took the car anyway," Isabelle says.

Courtney blanches. "That's why he took the car?"

The humor in Portia's voice disappears. "He got in so much trouble for that."

"He never told on us, though." Isabelle shares a look with her sister. "He just accepted the punishment."

"Which was what?" I ask.

"He'd been offered a placement at a hockey program in Sweden, but that was the summer he went to the Hockey Academy instead," Portia replies.

"Ah. Well, he's still close with those guys, and look where he is now. Seems like it worked out in the end," I say, trying to lighten the suddenly somber mood. I've just opened their eyes, and hopefully they'll start to see Connor differently, just like I have since I became his fiancée. He's damaged, but he's loyal, even when he's the one who gets hurt.

Meems, bless her amazing, but overworked heart, asks to go home shortly after that because she's tired. Courtney tells me to leave the gifts, and she'll have them delivered to the house for us.

The girls all hug me, whispering words of encouragement, and Lexi, Hemi, Meems, and I climb back into Lexi's car. I'm sure my Babe chat will be blowing up later, but we spend the car ride back to Grace Manor talking wedding stuff.

"That was a good thing you did," Meems says a little while later as I get her settled in her favorite chair in the guesthouse.

"I just want to open their eyes, so they see the same Connor we do," I explain.

"You're doing a wonderful job of that." She squeezes my hand.

"Thank you. It means a lot to hear that from you."

I leave Meems to rest and cross through the breezeway into the mansion, planning to stop in my room so I can check on Dewey and change before I go in search of Connor.

As soon as I enter my room, Dewey makes excited snuffling noises. He's popular with the staff, and they're more than happy to spend time with him while I'm at work. I open the cage and pick him up, cuddling him.

"How's my cute baby?" I kiss his little face while he squirms and smile when I catch a hint of Connor's cologne. "Has someone else been giving you snuggles?"

I arch a brow, and he wiggles around, a permanent smile on his adorable face.

"I think you have a new fan."

I transfer him to one hand and pluck his water dish from his enclosure. There are woodchips in it, which happens on a regular basis. I cross over to the bathroom and stop short when I reach the threshold. The clawfoot tub is full of pink bubbles.

"What is all this?"

Dewey snuffles.

There's a tray across the center with a stack of my favorite, well-worn books, a steaming mug of tea, and a plate of chocolate-dipped strawberries. A notecard sits on top. I set Dewey's water dish aside so I can pick it up.

Flipping it open, I run my fingers over the pretty cursive.

Mildred,

My sisters and Meems had the most amazing time. They haven't stopped messaging about how much they adore you.

Thank you,

Connor

Dewey nuzzles my neck, and I turn to kiss his head. "Maybe you're not the only one with a fan."

CHAPTER 19
CONNOR

We get our asses handed to us when we play against New York on an away game. It sucks, but they have Kodiak Bowman. Just when we think the guy is at the top of his game, he gets better.

Flip points at me. "We're taking you out tonight."

I glance to my right, where Quinn is shrugging into his dress shirt. The guy is a literal freckle factory.

Quinn arches a ginger brow, a sage smile curving his mouth. "He's talking to you, not me."

Flip does seem to be looking at me when I turn back toward him. I shake my head. "I'm good, man."

He snorts a laugh. "You're marrying my best friend in a week and a half. You're not getting out of a bachelor party. We're in New York City!" He motions to everyone. "Besides, Bowman's already set everything up. You can't disappoint him."

"That's dirty." Of all the guys I played with at the Hockey Academy, Quinn and Kodiak were the two I stayed tight with.

His eyes light up. "Not as dirty as fucking my sandwich."

"You fucked my shirt first," I remind him.

"His last *clean* shirt," Dallas chimes in.

Flip shrugs and claps me on the shoulder. "I promise it'll be a fun time, and no one will be fucking anyone's anything."

Typically I avoid nights out with the team. I'm not particularly social at the best of times, and I'm used to being a problem—for my family, for my team, and now for Mildred. I don't want my reputation to rub off on Kellan and Quinn, or any of the newer players on the team. It'll upset my fiancée if I say no, which I can't have, because an unhappy Mildred could lead to an unhappy Meems. In truth, I don't mind when Mildred is annoyed with me. In fact I love it when she tips her chin up and regards me with defiant eyes. I'm thrilled anytime her attention is on me. But I'm realizing it's even better when I earn her smile of approval.

"Where are we going?" I ask.

"Bowman picked the place, so it'll be low-key," Quinn assures me.

Flip orders cars for the team, and we end up at a rooftop bar. It's been rented out, so the entire space is ours for the night, which means no fans asking for pictures and no grainy photos taken out of context.

Kodiak greets me, pulling me in for a hearty back slap. "I miss having you on my team." His smile is wry and questioning. "I must have been pretty wrapped up in my own shit not to notice you and Dred were a thing when we were in Aruba this summer."

"I think we were all wrapped up in our own shit." It's not a complete lie. There was more going on in Aruba than many people realized. Especially when Tristan's estranged mother showed up uninvited. Thankfully I was able to handle the problem without Tristan finding out she'd been there until after the wedding.

"Well, I'm happy for you, man. It looks like Toronto has been a good move."

"Yeah, it's working out." Better than I could have imagined, at least for now.

Quinn steps in to give Kodiak a brotherly hug, followed by my teammates. The ass kicking we took tonight has stayed on the ice, where it belongs.

Some of my former NY teammates come over to congratulate me. I wonder if this is how Flip feels all the time. Accepted. Included.

Dallas hands me a shot, and then another and another. I down them, but make a trip to the bar to grab a water. Tristan is leaning against the rail, his phone in his hand. He finishes his message and slides the device into his pocket.

"Everything good?" I ask.

"Yeah, just checking on the wife. She's in cooking mode with Essie."

I nod. "Mildred's bachelorette party is tomorrow." It's in her calendar, marked with celebration emojis. All the events in her calendar have an emoji beside them.

He rolls his empty beer bottle between his hands. "Those ladies always show up for each other when it matters—kind of like this team will, if you let them."

"Flip organized this for Mildred, not me," I argue.

"I mean, yes and no. Dred is special."

"I know." I thought it would be easy enough to bring her into my world, get her to spend time with Meems and make my grandmother happy. I meant to give her space and just be on the periphery. But I haven't, and I don't want to. It's selfish, but I can't seem to stop myself. "She means a lot to a lot of people."

The bartender hands him a beer.

I ask for a water, and a scotch on the rocks.

"She does, and she brings the good out in people." He glances over his shoulder. "Flip, uh, he made some choices that weren't great for him for a while."

Everyone's heard the rumors about Flip Madden. But since I've been on the team, the guy has pretty much taken on monk status. Before that, he was constantly on the hockey sites. Not that it's anyone's business what he gets up to behind closed doors, but he didn't try to hide it, and the media ate it up.

"It's easy to get accustomed to being used in this career. We can be leveraged by our own coaches for better trades, the media likes to shine a spotlight on us to get more clicks, and fans want a piece." Tristan shakes his head. "It can be a vicious cycle, and for a while, Flip fed the beast. But then Dred came into his life and taught him what it means to be a friend who doesn't want to fuck him—literally or figuratively. She became his nonjudgmental sounding board. He's a loyal guy, and he's especially loyal to her. So he'll support her exactly the same way she's supported him these past few years, no questions asked. Flip made some big mistakes when Bea and I started dating. He doesn't want to repeat them with Dred."

"They love each other." I wish I could say that without sounding jealous.

"They do. In a completely platonic way. They're like siblings."

"Is that hard for Rix?" My sisters are close to each other, but they're not particularly close with me. Rix and Flip are tight, though.

"She has the same kind of friendship with Essie, so she gets it. But there's no chemistry between Dred and Flip." He side-eyes me. "Unlike the two of you."

I glance at him. "She's smart and kind and perceptive and beautiful." And a million other things that make her alluring. Every time I look at Mildred, I want to feel the softness of her lips against mine.

"All good reasons to marry her," he says pointedly, then takes a long swig of his beer. "A big part of Flip helping Bowman put this together is to show Dred he's on your side." He rubs his bottom lip. "You and I know how hard family can be, but Dred, she made her own. And if you want, it can be yours, too."

Everything I'm being given—feeling like I'm part of something—will disappear when this thing with Mildred ends.

Getting in tight with her people will only make it harder for her in the end. But I don't say any of that. I just nod. "Thanks, man. It means a lot."

"Finish your water, Grace. It's time for more shots!" Flip slides between us and slings an arm around our shoulders.

"Aren't you always telling the girls shots are a bad idea?"

"Yup, but bachelor parties are the exception."

We take our shots, and I order another water—because exception or not, I don't want to yak on the flight tomorrow.

The party rolls on, and I manage to eat some food along the way to help soak up the alcohol. It's closing in on one in the morning when Kodiak's wife, Lavender, shows up with another blonde. Kodiak rushes his wife, folding his huge arms around her and picking her up. He shoves his face into her neck like an excited puppy.

Quinn's eyes light up as he and the blonde move toward each other. He scoops her into a hug, and his eyes fall closed as he turns his head into her hair. Whoever she is, there's history between them.

Thankfully, the arrival of these women winds the party down.

Quinn claps me on the shoulder. "I'm crashing at Lavender and Kodiak's tonight. I'll meet you at the airport in the morning."

"Sure thing."

The blonde hugs his arm and rests her head against his shoulder as they leave the bar.

"What's the deal there?" I ask Tristan.

He shrugs. "That's one of the Butterson girls. She and Quinn grew up together."

"Huh." So did Kodiak and Lavender.

Flip orders cabs for the rest of us, and we return to our hotel, where all of us disappear into our rooms.

I strip out of my suit and stumble to the bathroom to brush my teeth. I'm good and hammered, despite my water consumption. I climb into bed, phone in hand, and set three alarms—morning will be rough. In the process, I see I have new messages from Mildred, who I've saved in my phone with a tongue-in-cheek spin on her nickname.

> **DREDFUL MENACE**
> Nice game tonight.
>
> **DREDFUL MENACE**
> Lexi tells me Flip and Bowman organized a bachelor party for you. Don't let Flip buy you too many shots.
>
> **CONNOR**
> Wish I would have seen this earlier.

I close my eyes for a second. She'll be asleep. It's one thirty in the morning. But my phone buzzes on my chest, startling me awake.

> **DREDFUL MENACE**
> Flip has a horrible penchant for shots. You should take a painkiller now. I'm sorry about tomorrow's suckage, but I hope you had fun.
>
> **CONNOR**
> Why are you awake?
>
> **DREDFUL MENACE**
> 😊
>
> **CONNOR**
> Did you fall asleep on the couch?
>
> **DREDFUL MENACE**
> Maybe.
>
> **CONNOR**
> I'm sorry I'm not there to put you to bed.
>
> **DREDFUL MENACE**
> Me too.

The inching dots appear and disappear a few times. So I add a bit to encourage her.

CONNOR
It's my favorite part of the day.

DREDFUL MENACE
Tell me why.

I'm drunk, and my thumbs feel like sausages, so I switch to voice-to-text, but I have to stop and start again a few times because my words are slurring.

CONNOR
Because I get to hold you, and you let me.

DREDFUL MENACE
Why do you think I do that?

I hit the call icon.

She answers on the second ring. "Hi, Connor."

I try on the nickname she's so fond of. "Hi, Dred."

She hums into the phone. "Say my full name, please."

"Mildred." I like the way it sounds better. And it makes me feel like I'm not everyone else. "Are you still on the couch?"

"I am." She sighs, and the sound washes over me in a wave of heat. "Because you're not here to carry me to bed."

"You like it when I do that?"

"Mm-hmm." Her voice is soft and breathy.

"Why?"

"Because we're the same, both afraid to ask for what we want."

Another soft sigh, the rustle of her blanket. I can picture her, curled up on the couch, blanket half-covering her, cheeks pink, skin warm, hair fanned over her pillow.

"What do you want, Mildred?"

"What do you want, Connor?"

I smile, because this is her way, always throwing the question back at me, proving she's right. For once, I let my guard down and give her honesty. "I want the softness of your lips on mine. I want to know what my name sounds like when you moan it." There's a beat of silence. "What do you want, Mildred?"

"Ask me again when you're home."

I chuckle. "Good night, little menace." Now I guess I know how she feels most of the time when I give her half answers or none at all.

"Good night, sweet villain."

CHAPTER 20
DRED

"Where are the Babes taking you tonight?" Connor stands in the open doorway of my "dressing room." It's between my private bathroom and the walk-in closet. The three-way, full-length mirror to the right of my vanity gives me an incredible view of my fiancé. He's wearing a black T-shirt that hugs his biceps and shows off the stunning artwork that ends halfway down his forearms. He's also petting Dewey, and it's so sweet my teeth ache.

Obviously this makes it a challenge to focus on getting ready.

I manage to pass my mascara wand over my lashes without poking myself in the eye. "Dinner and girl time is what I've been told to prepare for."

He lets Dewey climb onto his shoulder. "They didn't give you any specifics?"

"Nope." Lexi took the reins and she's pregnant, so I can safely assume there will be no club. "I've been told Lexi and the girls will pick me up at six."

Connor rubs the edge of his jaw. "You're coming home tonight, though."

My stomach flips at the worry in his tone, and how much I like that he calls this place my home. It's starting to feel like one, which is as dangerous as it is alluring. I slide my mascara wand back into the tube and meet his gaze in the mirror. "Yes, I'm coming home tonight, Connor."

"Okay." The single word drips with relief.

I was at work when he arrived home from New York this morning, and the moment I walked through the door I had to rush to get ready for tonight. We haven't had time to talk—not about the flowers that showed up at my work this morning or the lunch that was delivered for the entire staff. Or how his bachelor party went. He appeared in my bedroom a few minutes ago and has spent the time since watching me put on makeup, while absently petting Dewey.

I push my chair back and stand, smoothing my hands over my hips. Connor's gaze tracks the movement, his eyes darkening. I don't know how much of last night's conversation he remembers after we switched from texting to a call. He was drunk, so probably not much.

My phone pings. "Lexi's here." Looks like any questions will have to wait. I adjust my bracelets, then grab my bag, a cardigan in case I get cold, and my shoes. "Walk me out?"

"Of course." He puts Dewey back in his luxury hedgehog condo.

Connor is silent as we walk down the hall, though he glances at me every few seconds, like he wants to say something, ask something, admit something. But he doesn't.

The elevator ride to the first-floor foyer is electric with tension, but I don't break, and neither does he. After we step out, I pause to put my heels on, using Connor's shoulder for balance. And an excuse to touch him.

Connor opens the front door. A stretch limo has pulled up in front of the stairs.

Flip's head pops out of the sunroof. "It's bestie party time, bride-to-be!"

"I didn't know Flip was coming." Connor looks both relieved and apprehensive.

"Bestie privileges mean he gets to partake in the estrogen fest." I wave and note that much like Connor, Flip looks a little rough.

The door opens, and Callie comes bouncing toward us. The rest of my friends' smiling faces appear at the windows as Connor holds his arms open and catches her. Lifting her off the ground, he gives her a big squeeze. "How's my favorite goalie?"

"I get to go for dinner!"

"That's great! Are we still meeting at the rink after to shoot the puck?" Connor asks as he sets her down.

"Yup! Roman bought me a new stick!"

"I can't wait to see it."

Callie takes my hand, pulling me toward the limo. She clambers back inside and pats the spot beside her.

"Please don't feed Dred too many shots," Connor says, leaning down to look inside.

I pat his chest. "I know my limit."

"Doesn't mean everyone else will." His eyes fall to my lips.

I curve my hand around the side of his neck and feel his pulse hammering there. "Don't worry, Connor. I'll be a good little menace."

"That's what I'm worried about."

"I won't do anything to make your life more difficult than it already is," I assure him.

"I appreciate that, but it's not what I'm worried about."

My heart stutters. I push up on my toes, kiss the corner of his mouth, and climb inside the limo. The entire Babe Brigade greets me with shrieks and hugs and laughter.

We leave Connor standing at the bottom of the steps. One hand is tucked in his pocket, the fingers of the other rubbing the place my lips were.

Lexi gives me a knowing look.

"How are *you* feeling?" I ask Flip.

"Probably just as bad as Tristan," Rix pipes up.

"Dallas was in rough shape when he got home," Hemi agrees.

"Ash wasn't too bad," Shilpa says.

"What happened last night?" Callie asks.

"The team took Connor out after the game," I explain.

"Oh." She nods knowingly. "He stayed up too late."

"Exactly," Lexi says.

"I get grumpy when I do that."

"Me, too."

The rest of the girls and Flip chime in with their hearty agreement.

Fee and Tally are already at the restaurant when we arrive, as are Connor's sisters. My friends greet them with enthusiastic hugs.

"We invited a couple extra guests to join us for dinner," Lexi says. "They should be here soon."

"Who else is coming?" I can't see Lexi having extended the invitation to my work colleagues, especially not Dorothea.

I find out a second after I ask the question when a pair of arms wrap around me from behind. "Dred!"

"Everly?"

I spin around, my smile widening as I take her in. She's wearing a slightly too big dress, and Cordelia, the woman who runs the group home, is standing behind her. "Cordelia!"

"I'm just dropping Everly off for dinner."

"What? No! You have to join us!" I turn to Lexi. "There's room, isn't there?"

"Of course."

"It's settled, you'll stay for dinner, unless you're needed elsewhere," I amend.

"We have to pick Victor up from his piano lesson in two hours. He says hi, by the way," Everly explains.

"Excellent. You can bring him takeout." I introduce Everly and Cordelia to everyone and we get settled at the table, with Everly ending up beside Fee and Tally, since they're the closest in age. She fits right in, and it makes my heart so happy that Lexi managed to invite her.

Isabelle is quick to warm up and Portia eventually relaxes, too, laughing and smiling as we talk about the wedding preparations and my first experience with steak tartare.

"Why would someone want to eat raw steak?" Everly asks.

"That is a great question," Flip commiserates.

"I don't think I'll ever be able to look at it the same way again," Portia says.

"I used to feed it to Duchess, our family dog," Isabelle admits. "But we had to get rid of her because Dad said he was allergic."

"That's sad. I've always wanted a dog. Once Victor and I went to a foster home with a dog. He was always chewing through his leashes," Everly says. "What did you do with the raw steak after you gave your dog away?"

"I had to be vegetarian," Isabelle explains.

"Until you went to university," Portia says, connecting all the dots.

"What happened when you went to university?" Everly asks.

"I lived on campus, away from home, so I didn't have to eat raw steak. I could eat whatever I wanted." Isabelle smiles impishly.

"You could have cake for breakfast?" Everly's eyes are wide.

"I could and sometimes I did," Isabelle confides.

"I want to go to university," Everly declares.

Everyone laughs and Cordelia tells her she needs to work hard and get good grades.

Isabelle grabs her sister's arm. "Please, do not tell Mother any of this."

"Of course not." Portia makes the lips-zipped gesture and tosses the imaginary key aside.

Whenever I spend time with them, it's like they discover a new piece of their family puzzle right along with me. It seems everyone has been hiding stuff from each other, and Connor isn't the only one who's struggled.

Dinner is full of laughter, and Portia and Isabelle tell us stories about Connor growing up.

"Remember when Mother made him take piano lessons?" Isabelle says.

Portia rolls her eyes. "He hated them so much."

"So much, but she wouldn't let him play hockey unless he spent two hours on the piano first," Isabelle adds.

"Why make him play piano before he was allowed to play hockey?" Flip asks, clearly confused.

"They didn't want him to play," I explain.

"Why not?" Flip's eyes are wide. "He's a natural. He's one of the best defensive players in the league."

"It's physical, it's violent, you can lose teeth, break bones, and it doesn't require a university education," Isabelle explains uncomfortably.

"But almost all of us played for our university team," Flip replies.

I jump in. "They wanted him to work for Grace Hotels."

Understanding dawns. "Right. Gotcha." Flip sits back, expression pensive.

"So he had to learn how to play piano?" I ask, turning back to the sisters.

"At first he just banged away for two hours, but he gave himself a headache, as well as everyone else," Portia replies.

Isabelle grins. "And then he moved on to learning the most annoying songs and practicing them until all our ears bled."

I prop my chin on my fist, always interested to hear more about young Connor. "Did he get better?"

"Not at first." Portia sips her cocktail.

"But he wanted the time for hockey." Isabelle runs her finger around the rim of her glass, expression far away. "Every two hours on the piano meant an hour of hockey, and he was desperate for time on the ice."

"I'm sure." I nod. "Imagine being forced to do your least favorite thing to be able to do your most favorite."

"I don't think I've ever loved anything as much as Connor loves hockey," Isabelle says thoughtfully.

"Do you remember his recital piece?" Portia asks.

I'm wildly fascinated by them—perfect hair, perfect skin, perfect everything. Poised, proper, and almost extensions of each other. It's clear that they rely heavily on each other for everything. And why wouldn't they, when it's them against everyone else?

"Unforgettable." Isabelle nods.

"What did he play?" Callie asks.

"'Nothing Else Matters'," Portia says.

"By Metallica?" I grin. Of course he would pick something like that.

"It's so pretty at first—" Isabelle starts.

"Father was so angry after his performance—" Portia continues.

"But he was so good." Isabelle shakes her head.

"I bet he still is—" Portia agrees.

"—but he won't play anymore. Though maybe for you he would," Isabelle muses.

"Maybe." But I don't know that I'll ask him to. He's been punished enough in his lifetime.

We shift our conversation away from Connor to talk about the lessons *we* took as kids. Rix enrolled in every free cooking class under the sun, Hemi was a master debater and took scrapbooking, Lexi (no surprise) lived and breathed hockey—just like Callie and Flip, and Hammer loved working on graphics and graphic design. Tally and Fee both loved dance, but Fee's passion lies in art. Portia and Isabelle have a laundry list of things they've dabbled in, from golf to dance to piano. I joined clubs in school, but I didn't have many foster homes willing to part with the money to put me in lessons. Everly echoes this, but jumps in to say that she joined the drama club at school this semester and likes to work on the sets. Some of the parents also provide snacks, like pizza and subs, which she clearly enjoys.

Everly and Cordelia have to leave to retrieve Victor and we send them off with takeout for him and dessert. Roman picks up Callie at the end of dinner, and any disappointment at being left out of what's next disappears when he reminds her Connor is meeting them at the local rink to shoot the puck around for an hour.

As soon as she's gone, Lexi's eyes light up. She looks to Hemi. "Is it time?"

Hemi nods. "Oh, it's time."

Hammer shimmies in her seat, and Tally claps excitedly.

"No shots," I declare.

"How about fun shots, with fifty percent juice?" Essie suggests.

"No shots," I repeat.

"You say that now," Flip says.

"The bachelorette scavenger hunt begins!" Lexi pulls a set of typed cards out of her bag and passes them around the table.

I scan the list. Almost every clue is a literary reference.

"The only person who isn't allowed to look up these quotes is the bride-to-be." Lexi winks at me.

Shortly thereafter, we leave the restaurant and head for what we've determined is our first stop.

"This was you, wasn't it?" I prop my fist on my hip and give Rix a knowing look when we arrive. We're standing outside an adult store that was designed with vaginas in mind.

"What makes you think that?" she asks, eyes wide.

"The clue says, *Rix has a full crisper, so she doesn't need to visit this spot on Wooley Street.*"

Hammer elbows Tally in the side, while Hemi covers her mouth with her hand.

Thankfully, Flip is too busy trying to decode the scavenger hunt list to catch this.

Lexi leans in and whispers, "A crisper full of what?"

I pat her shoulder. "Stay in the dark, my friend. It's safer there."

We file inside the store. Isabelle and Portia, who I expect to be totally out of their element, shriek excitedly and head for the vibrator wall. They're like kids in a candy store.

Flip finally looks up from his phone. "Whoa. I'm just going to sit right here." He points to the chairs outside the change rooms.

"Head down, my friend."

"Yeah, seems like the safest option."

Lexi links her arm with mine. "You having fun?"

"I really am. Thank you for doing this." I never thought I'd get married, let alone have a group of amazing friends willing to go to all this trouble to throw me a bachelorette party.

Tally and Fee have stopped in front of a wall of pleasure devices. Tally's head is tipped to the side, lips pushed out. "What is that?"

"Ask Lexi. She has one," Fee says loudly.

I snort a laugh.

Lexi shakes her head. "Fuck my life."

"Lexi!" Tally grabs the device, which is attached to the wall with one of those cords so people can look at it, but not pocket it. I don't know why anyone would want a sex toy that's been handled by hundreds of people, but apparently some people prioritize pleasure over being sanitary.

"I got this." I pat Lexi's arm. "It simulates oral sex. You put it on your clit, and it does all the work. That way you don't have to rub it like you're trying to make a genie appear."

Tally nods. "Oh, that's handy."

"Very," Lexi agrees. "Although mine doesn't get much use these days."

"I'm going to wait outside." The door tinkles as Flip disappears through it.

Tally smirks.

Lexi and I exchange a look.

We spend more time than is reasonable in the store, and

Portia and Isabelle come out with bags full of goodies. Flip frowns when he notices Tally also has a bag, but if he has thoughts, he keeps them to himself. She's a full-fledged adult. She's in her third year of university and has been living in an apartment on her own since her first year.

From there, a passage from one of my favourite romance books, takes us to a cupcake shop. We indulge in dessert and drinks, filling in our scavenger-hunt cards, and then a quote from Shakespeare leads us to a bookstore that serves spiked coffees and teas. Finally, with a flourish, Lexi hands me the last envelope, and we make it to the final stop, a local pub for trivia night.

And because we haven't imbibed enough, of course trivia turns into a drinking game. Every time I get a question right, I have to drink. This would be fine if I didn't know the answer to almost all the questions and feel compelled to give the correct one. But things being what they are, I keep draining glasses.

After a while Lexi accompanies me to the bathroom, because I'm no longer steady on my feet. I'm a lightweight, and three margaritas —plus whatever else I had earlier that I can no longer remember clearly—are kicking my ass. "This has been so fun." I try to move my bachelorette sash out of the way, but it's impossible. I hang it over the door. "Are you having fun even though you can't drink?"

"I'm having a great time," she assures me. "Connor's sisters are really gelling with the Babes."

"Right? I'm happy about that. Sometimes we just need to step outside our comfort zone." I do my business and straighten my dress, then retrieve my sash. I can't figure out how to get it back on. "I think I might be a little drunk." I open the door and stumble out.

Lexi catches my arm. "You're usually a one margarita girl."

"Yeah. Three is a lot for me." Reality is starting to hit, but it's softened by the booze. "I can't believe I'm getting married in a little more than a week."

She pushes my hair over my shoulders. "You don't have to go through with it if you don't want to. Everyone will understand."

I shake my head. "I don't want an out. And that's not just the margaritas talking," I whisper. "I think...I like him? We're so similar. We both have damage from people who were supposed to love us." My words are stumbling over each other. Sometimes I feel like I'm made of Swiss cheese. I take her hands. "I don't know if I'll ever really find the kind of love you have, Lexi. This might be my only chance, and selfishly, I want it. I want the fairy tale, even if it isn't real, even if it comes with a wicked mother-in-law, and even if it means I marry the hockey world's misunderstood villain."

"We're all someone's villain," she replies. "Maybe you get to be his angel."

"I would like that."

When we return to the table, Tally is talking about going to a nightclub, but that's never been my scene. I can only handle so much before I'm on sensory overload. There's too much contact with people I don't know, too many unknowns. So when we head out, I thank my friends for a fantastic night and take a car to Grace Manor.

Connor meets me at the front door. He's dressed in black joggers and a black T-shirt, the art on his arms on display.

I blink at him. "Did you wait up for me?"

"My sisters texted. So did Lexi and Flip."

"Flip texted you?" I press a hand to his chest and kick my heels off, groaning at the relief.

"To tell me you were coming home, and that there were no shots, but you're a lightweight."

I nod vigorously. "I am such a lightweight."

"Let me carry you to bed, darling." He dips down and tucks an arm behind my knees and another behind my back, sweeping me off my feet.

I loop my arms around his neck as he steps into the elevator, and press my face into his warm skin and inhale.

"Are you sniffing me?"

"Maybe." He smells like sandalwood and citrus, with a hint of mint.

A few moments later, he steps off the elevator, but as he approaches my door I murmur, "Your room."

He halts.

I lift my head and meet his wary gaze. "I want to stay with you tonight."

His jaw clenches and releases. "I won't touch you when you're drunk, Mildred."

"You're touching me now."

"You know what I mean." His fingers flex.

"I'm not asking for sex. I just want closeness."

"Why?"

I sigh, suddenly feeling the weight of everything. "Let me pretend this is real. Just for tonight. Please."

He regards me with impassive eyes before he presses his lips to my temple. "Okay."

A single lamp illuminates his bed. But it smells like him, feels like him—dark and broody, a mystery I want to solve. He carries me to his bed and carefully sets me on the satin comforter.

His gaze roves over me, nostrils flaring. "Let me get your pajamas."

"I'll take the shirt you're wearing."

"Mildred." His eyes darken.

I grin. "Connor." I pull my dress over my head.

"You're a Dredful menace." But he looks up at the ceiling and removes his shirt, tossing it on the bed. "Tell me when you're decent."

I unclasp my bra, letting it fall. Then thread my arms through the sleeves and pull the shirt over my head. It's soft and smells like him. "I'm decent."

His eyes drop, and he sucks in his bottom lip, exhaling

harshly. He reaches behind me and pulls the covers back. "Under you go."

I slide up the bed, settling against the pillows as he pulls the covers over me, then moves around to the other side and climbs in. It's a massive king. There are two feet of satin sheets separating us.

But just like I'd hoped, he stretches out his arm, inviting me in. I slide over to nestle into his side. The light clicks off. I throw my leg over his and settle my palm on his stomach.

"Mildred."

"You're warm." It feels safer in the dark with him, where he can't see all the things I want in my eyes. "Don't worry. I won't be more of a menace than you can handle."

He sighs and moves my hand to his chest, thumb brushing over the bracelets. "Can I take these off for you, darling?"

"Okay." He can't see what's hiding underneath.

He carefully removes them, one by one, setting them on the nightstand.

"Tell me what you want again," I whisper.

He presses his lips to my forehead, and I sigh.

"That sweet sound."

I kiss the edge of his jaw. "What else?"

"You here, like you are right now."

I nuzzle closer, lips on his cheek. "What else?"

"To play board games with you every night when I don't have an away series."

"We can do that." I cup his cheek and turn his head toward me. "Anything else?"

"You're not going to remember any of this in the morning."

"I might."

His eyes search mine in the darkness, glittering and warm, full of emotions I can't pin down. "What do you want, Mildred?"

I brush my thumb along the contour of his bottom lip. Love is scary, especially the kind where you give your heart and soul to someone. But I can almost believe we're something more, something special, and I want to hold on to it, even if it's fleeting. "For you to kiss me good night."

His breath breaks against my lips.

"Please," I whisper.

He lightly skims my cheek, thumb resting under my chin. There's a soft brush of lips, a gentle press that lingers. Then parting lips and sweeping tongues, his quiet moan mixing with mine, and his fingers in my hair. I want to climb into this moment and stay here. Live inside this kiss—in his gentleness, in the sweet oblivion of darkness where all that exists is desire, and our damage can't get in the way.

But then it ends. Like everything does.

"Good night, darling."

"It is now."

CHAPTER 21
CONNOR

I knock on Mildred's bedroom door. It's rehearsal dinner day and she's been preparing for what seems like hours.

"Come in!" she calls.

I peek my head into the room. She's standing by the vanity, homemade bracelets scattered across the marble top. Her eyes move over me in a way that's become pleasantly familiar.

"You look great," she says, running her hands nervously over her hips.

"So do you." She's dressed in a floor-length, dark purple dress. The lines are simple and crisp, which flatter her curvy figure. "I have something for you."

She arches a brow. "Because the dress, shoes, and bag weren't enough?"

"Well, you can't go to the rehearsal dinner naked, darling."

"It would be a statement, and so would an off-the-rack dress from JCPenney."

I cross the room. "My parents would be furious. Post-wedding, you can shop wherever you like."

"You make it sound like I was asking permission." Mildred looks up at me, eyes flashing with defiance.

"You don't like the dress?" I agonized over the right one; the softness of the fabric, her comfort, how beautiful she would look.

"That's not what I said."

I can't get a read on her emotions, other than nervousness. "If you'd prefer to change into something else, you're more than welcome." I give in to the urge to skim the length of her arm. "But I picked it out for you thinking you might like it, and it didn't cost anyone's arm or leg." Lexi mentioned that Mildred isn't used to extravagant gifts, and that I might need to adjust accordingly, so I did. "I just want tonight to be as pain-free as possible for you."

Her expression softens. "I love the dress. There's just a new one for every event. I hate having a closet full of clothes I'm not supposed to wear again."

"You can wear them as often as you like. And if there are too many for you, they don't have to stay in your closet. We can donate them."

Her eyes light up, and relief washes through me. "I'd like that. There's a prom dress program at the group home not far from my work."

"Then that's where we'll take them." I pull the jewelry box from my pocket and flip it open. It's a necklace of diamonds, the one in the center a soft pink. It's definitely extravagant, but it complements her dress. "This belonged to Meems. My grandfather gave it to her the night of their rehearsal dinner, and she gave it to me a few years ago, probably hoping I'd get here faster." I smile, and she laughs.

"It's beautiful," Mildred whispers.

I swallow my anxiety. "I'd love for you to wear it tonight, but only if you want to."

"It would be an honor." Her fingers go to her lips, and she nods.

I free the necklace from the box, and she turns to face the vanity, moving her hair aside. Behind her ear is a tiny shooting star tattoo, yellow and white with a purple and blue tail. I refocus my attention and carefully clasp the necklace at her nape.

My fingers brush her shoulder, and she covers my hand with hers, our eyes locking in the reflection.

"We can pretend it's real again tonight," she whispers, eyes full of the longing that's become impossible to ignore lately.

I hold her gaze and bend to press a gentle kiss to the top of her spine. "It's perfect on you."

The tension between us has been growing like ivy since she spent the night in my bed after her bachelorette party. I woke alone, and it hasn't happened since, but she also hasn't returned the borrowed shirt. Every night when I carry her from the library to her bedroom, she's wearing it.

My phone chimes in my pocket. A message from Cedrick informs me the car is ready. "It's time to go." I bend and scoop up her shoes.

Mildred finds her clutch, then grabs a handful of the bracelets scattered across the vanity.

"Let me help you with those," I offer.

"It's okay. I've got it." Half the bracelets scatter across the floor. She frantically shoves the remaining ones on her wrist, then crouches to retrieve the rest.

I drop to one knee beside her and gather the closest bracelets. They're old and worn, with names on some and designs on others. They remind me of friendship bracelets from high school days.

I gently take her hand, but she snatches it away. Her head is bowed, wrist turned into her body.

The fallen bracelets dangle between my thumb and forefinger. "What about these?"

"Just let me have them." Her voice shakes, along with her hand.

"What are you hiding?"

"We need to go."

"In a minute. They can't start without us." I gently flip her hand over, palm up, and slide the remaining bracelets onto her wrist. The inside, by her pulse point, has a few small scabs, but there are also scars, old and not so old. I run my thumb over the raised skin, the ache in my chest impossible to ignore. "Mildred?"

Her eyes slide closed, and her shoulders sag.

"Hey." I cup her cheek in my palm as fear slithers down my spine. "It's okay. Talk to me. Tell me what this is."

"It's embarrassing," she whispers.

"I fucked a sandwich, darling. I'm pretty sure I've cornered the market on embarrassing."

She huffs an unsteady laugh.

I lift her wrist and press my lips to the tender skin. "Please talk to me. I'm worried right now, and I just want to keep you safe."

Her eyes lift, and I see the ghosts she's so good at hiding lurking in their uneasy depths. "I usually wear a hair tie or scrunchie on my wrist. I snap it to cope with stress. It's an old habit."

Understanding twists my stomach. "And you've been under a lot of stress lately, because of me."

"You are not the source of my stress," she clarifies. "There's been a lot of change."

"I've tried to make it easier."

"I know. And I appreciate that."

But dealing with me and my family hasn't exactly been a walk in the park. It doesn't matter who caused the stress, it's that there's too much of it for her to handle. "You wear the bracelets to hide the marks."

She nods. "Some of them are from the group-home kids I grew up with and some are from my foster siblings. The good ones, anyway."

"You are such a beautiful miracle." I don't deserve her, but I pull her into my arms anyway, hugging her tightly.

She returns the embrace, and it feels like she's comforting me instead of the other way around. "I'm okay. I promise you don't have to worry," she whispers against my throat.

How can I not worry? I cup her face in my palms. "We're almost through the hard part. Just tonight and the wedding, and then we have a break from all the shit with my family. We're in this together, okay?"

Her eyes search my face, her bottom lip sliding through her teeth. She nods, and her palm settles against the side of my neck. "We're in this together." Mildred leans over and kisses the corner of my mouth.

My phone buzzes a second time.

We rise, and Mildred steps back, but I catch her hand in mine. And she doesn't let go.

CHAPTER 22
CONNOR

"The presentation is art." Rix takes a photo of her plate before she picks up her fork. She's done this with every course. "And everything is so delicious!"

"Aside from your cooking, this is the best meal I've ever had," Flip agrees.

There's a murmur of agreement from my teammates, who start discussing their favorite foods from Rix.

"Thank God there's no steak tartare tonight," I whisper in Mildred's ear.

She chuckles. "Or ham and cheese sandwiches."

I laugh loudly, earning a disapproving look from my father.

The rehearsal was not seamless. Mildred kept pulling at her bracelets when my mother expressed her displeasure with something, which was often. Each time, I'd lace our fingers and kiss the inside of her wrist, and I only left her side when it was unavoidable. Thankfully, now that the formal part is over, she's much more relaxed, laughing and smiling with her friends.

Just before dessert is served, Portia and Isabelle push their chairs back and tap their water glasses to get everyone's attention.

The table quiets.

"We wanted to thank everyone for coming tonight to celebrate our brother and Mildred, who we are so incredibly grateful for."

My teammates hoot and holler. The Babes clap. My parents look scandalized by the noise. I tip Mildred's chin up and press my lips to hers for several seconds longer than is appropriate.

"Dred, we're so excited to welcome you into our family as our sister!" Isabelle clears her throat, already emotional.

"But we promise to leave the bang trims to our stylists," Portia adds.

The girls laugh. The guys look confused. At least I'm not alone.

Mildred pats my leg under the table. "I'll explain later."

"Thank you so much for inviting us to be part of your wedding party, Dred. You have such welcoming, wonderful friends, and it's so easy to see how our brother could fall for you."

Mildred mouths *thank you* to my sisters.

Their connection is genuine, and I'm struck with a wave of sadness, knowing that all of this is a lie, and when it ends, hearts will be broken over more than just the loss of Meems.

"Connor..." Portia smiles softly.

"Our big brother." Isabelle hugs her arm.

They've always been like this, finishing each other's sentences, even though they aren't twins. They were close out of necessity. They needed each other to survive in our house. Because I made it so difficult.

"It took us a long time to really understand how much of a protector you were growing up." Portia links pinkies with Isabelle.

"You were great at keeping the boys away," Isabelle adds, maybe trying to lighten the mood.

"At least until you went to the Hockey Academy—" Portia adds.

"—and then to boarding school."

"We missed you so much when you were gone." Portia's voice cracks, and she reaches for her water.

Mildred squeezes my hand under the table and dabs at her eyes with a tissue. So does Meems.

Without me around there was less dissension, but I also couldn't be a distraction for my parents. So all their attention went into making my sisters the perfect daughters. And they are, but I question how happy this life makes them.

"We're so glad the Hockey Academy brought you all these amazing people," Portia continues, motioning to the team and their significant others. "And we're ecstatic that you've found your person." Portia turns to Mildred. "Thank you for letting our brother into your heart."

"To finding your forever." Isabelle raises her glass.

Everyone toasts, and Mildred and I stand to accept hugs from my sisters.

"You two don't have to get yourself in shit over me," I whisper to Isabelle.

"We wanted to say those things. You've been taking the heat off us your whole life." She squeezes me tightly.

I want to ask more questions, but not with my parents as an audience, so I leave it for now. They take their seats, and Flip stands.

He smooths his hands over his thighs and exhales an unsteady breath. "I'll never forget the day I met you—either of you, really."

Our teammates from the Hockey Academy chuckle.

Flip rubs the back of his neck sheepishly. "But, Dred, you showed up in my life exactly when I needed you."

"You needed board games," she quips.

"I did. So fucking badly. Sorry about the language." He clears his throat and pulls a set of cue cards from his pocket. Tugs on his tie. Takes a sip of his water. "Since the day I became your neighbor, you've become one of the most important people in my life, Dred. You're my family. My other sister, and I'm so lucky to have you. Every single person at this table is better for having you as a friend, as a future daughter-in-law, as a fiancée."

He makes eye contact with me, and it's not full of warning, but something else, something more like awareness, maybe. And a plea to treat her with the kindness and love she deserves.

"You listen without judgment, you stand by your friends no matter what, you are viciously loyal, aggressively loveable, and unbelievably compassionate. We see it every time you set up another program at the library, and when you show up for the people you care about."

"You all do the same for me." Mildred wipes under her eyes.

I stretch my arm across the back of her chair, and she leans into me.

"The way you give to everyone around you and expect nothing in return is awe-inspiring." Flip turns his emotion-filled eyes on me. "Connor, you are so lucky to have the honor of loving Dred. Take care of her the way she always takes care of everyone else, especially her beautiful heart." The *or else you'll have to answer to me* remains unspoken.

I nod. "I promise I will." And I mean it. Because as I sit here, surrounded by the people who love Mildred the most, I see exactly what Flip is saying. I don't want to lose her.

Her reasons for doing this are motivated entirely by love—for her friends, for Meems, for the people she helps with the programs she builds at the library, for every kid she spends time with who doesn't have a mother. And I want that for myself. I want a right to her warmth and love. I have found something special, *someone* special, and by chance and circumstance she's agreed to be my wife.

She's mentioned wanting to pretend it's real, so maybe if I do things right, she'll want more than just pretend. Then she could be mine forever.

CHAPTER 23
DRED

"You look stunning." Lexi adjusts my dress, fussing over me in a way that feels maternal.

"I cannot believe I'm getting married." I turn to face her.

"As in, you want to do a runner, or you're excited, or somewhere in between?" She holds up a finger. "And let me preface this by saying that any of those, or a combination, or an alternate version, is completely acceptable. And whatever you need from me, I'm right here with you—getaway car, hug, emotional support." She opens her arms, and I step into them.

"I don't want to run." I squeeze her and step back. "Thank you for being such an incredible friend."

"You've done the same for me. How are you feeling? Honestly."

"Nervous. I care about him, Lexi." These past weeks have shown me a different side of hockey's most-hated player. He's someone else when no one is watching.

"He cares about you, too." She takes my hands in hers. "Even villains have a heart."

The knock on my dressing room door startles us both. "Your bridal party is here!" Rix calls.

It's really happening.

Lexi opens the door, and the girls flood in. Everyone has their own style of dress, but they're all wine red.

"Oh wow! You look like a princess, Dred!" Callie's eyes are wide with wonder.

Lexi steps in front of her before she can throw herself into my arms. "Are your hands clean?"

She gives her sister a look.

"Roman made her wash them before she came in here," Fee assures us with a wink.

I bend to hug Callie. "Are you having fun this morning?"

"So much fun! I love weddings! Essie did my makeup, and they have the best snacks, and I love my dress, and we all look like we're straight out of a fairy tale!" She barely takes a breath before she continues. "Will Connor be my uncle Connor now, like you're my aunt Dred, even though we're not really related?"

"I think Connor would love to be your honorary uncle." I'm on the verge of tears.

Lexi must realize it, because she asks Callie to get something from her purse, and then I'm enveloped in more hugs and my hand is wrapped around a glass of something bubbly.

"Take a deep breath," Hemi says.

I suck in some much-needed air.

"Your mascara is waterproof, so you're all good," Essie assures me. That she managed to do all our makeup *and* be part of the wedding party makes her a superhero.

"Take a sip." Hammer taps the edge of my glass with a manicured fingernail.

I do as I'm told. It's a mimosa, and mostly orange juice by the taste of it, with a hint of champagne.

"You look stunning, Dred." Rix squeezes my free hand.

"You all look beautiful," I tell her. "Where's Flip?"

She smiles. "Waiting outside the door for you."

I look around the room, grateful for their friendship. "We should do this, then, shouldn't we?"

"Just let me touch you up." Essie steps in to dust my face with translucent setting powder.

I give myself a quick mental pep talk. I'm securing my future, saving Meems and Connor from heartache, keeping my family close, and for a year, this beautifully broken, misunderstood man will be mine. And I'll be his—maybe even kind of for real. I've at least glimpsed that possibility. No matter what happens, I don't think I'll make it out unscathed. But I'll take the risk.

We make sure I have everything I need, and then Tally throws the door open. The girls file out, moving aside to reveal Flip. He's dressed in a black tux, hair styled. He looks like he stepped out of the pages of a magazine. His expression warms when he sees me. "You are a vision."

"You clean up pretty good yourself."

Lexi touches my elbow. "We'll just give you a minute."

"Thanks."

My friends move down the hall to a beverage and snack station—they seem to be everywhere.

"Seriously, Dred, you are beautiful beyond words." Flip takes my hands in his. "You want this, right?"

I nod. "I want this." More than I realized maybe. I get the fairy-tale wedding I never dared to dream of, and my family stays close.

His eyes search my face. "I believe you."

"I know this hasn't been easy, but I appreciate you so much, Flip." There's so much more I want to say, but the words get caught in my throat.

"I'm always going to have your back." He kisses me on the cheek. "You're my family. Nothing will ever change that, okay?"

"Okay." Tears well, all my emotions bubbling to the surface. "I really needed to hear that."

He wraps his arms around me. "I will always be your brother, Dred, and I will always stand up for you, no matter what."

"I love you," I whisper.

"I love you, too," he murmurs then pulls back. "You ready to walk down the aisle?"

"I am."

Flip places my hand in the crook of his elbow, and we join our friends, who surround me as we walk to the hotel's wedding chapel.

My palms start to sweat as we reach the doors. My bridal party is huge. Lexi is my matron of honor, Shilpa, Hammer, Hemi, Rix, Essie, Tally, Portia, and Isabelle are my bridesmaids, and Fee and Callie are my junior bridesmaids. Connor's groomsmen are Kodiak, Quinn, Kellan, Dallas, Roman, and Tristan. Connor refused to pull his brothers-in-law into the mix.

It feels like it takes eleven years for the bridal party to make it down the aisle.

"How you feeling?" Flip pats my hand.

"Nervous."

"We can dip if you need to. No questions asked."

I look up at him and repeat the same thing I said to Lexi. "I don't want to run." That's the part that makes me the most nervous.

"I know. I was kidding." He squeezes my arm. "The way he was looking at you last night... He sees what the rest of us do."

I'm afraid to hope he's right, just as much as I'm afraid of the flutter in my stomach upon hearing that from my best friend.

The "Wedding March" begins—of course there's a harpist, because why wouldn't there be? It's the most beautiful wedding I've ever seen, and it's mine.

Flip takes a deep breath. "All right, Dred, let's get you married to the sandwich fucker."

I bark out a laugh, then choke the sound as we step around the corner. "Oh my God, there are so many people." Every seat is filled. Panic takes hold, and my mouth goes dry as cameras flash.

"It's okay. I got you. He's waiting for you. Eyes on Connor and nowhere else," Flip murmurs.

"Eyes on Connor," I repeat, and I can't stop the wide, genuine grin that breaks across my face when I find him. The groomsmen are all dressed in black, but Connor is wearing a deep maroon tux, and he is glorious. He looks every part the defiant billionaire's son. Regal, arrogant, unflappable.

His eyes spark when they meet mine, and he echoes my smile.

We're in this together.

I stay focused on the only thing that matters, keeping my promise to the man waiting for me at the altar. Flip grounds me, and Connor's promise carries me down the aisle.

When we reach Connor, I turn to Flip. "Thank you for being my best friend. I love you."

"I love you right back." He kisses me on the cheek and transfers my hand to Connor's.

They exchange a look, and Connor nods in deference. "I promise I'll take care of her."

Flip sits in the front row with the rest of the Terror crew. I smile and wink at Everly and Victor, who are sitting in the middle of them with a couple of my colleagues and Cordelia from the group home. They seem completely awestruck. Meems sits on the other side with Connor's parents and brothers-in-law. She's beaming, and my heart swells and breaks at the same time, because I've fallen completely in love with her in the short weeks since Connor and I made this pact.

Connor's wide, warm hand curves around mine, pulling my gaze back to him as I move into position.

"You take my breath away," he murmurs.

"You're trying to upstage me with this tux."

He winks. "I could never."

"But you tried."

We both smile, and it feels...right somehow that this serious, broody man is making jokes with me at the altar.

Lexi steps in to take my bouquet of night lilies, and we give our attention to the officiant, who looks slightly amused as he begins the ceremony. Connor's hands around mine and the warmth in his eyes ground me. *This is really it.* I'm binding my life to his—at least for now.

Connor holds my gaze, expression earnest as he says his vows. "Mildred Reformer, I vow, from this day forward, to put you first in all things, to cherish every moment with you, to give you comfort, to show you with words and actions that you are the most important person in my world. Your happiness is my happiness, your needs are my needs. I promise to take care of you, to honor you, and to give your heart the home it deserves with me, until death parts us."

The weight of his words settles in my heart, and I recite my own vows. "Connor Grace, you are the most incredible, loyal man. You love deeply, without reservation, and with inspiring conviction. I promise to cherish that love, to stand beside you and support you. It is an honor to give my heart to you and be claimed by you, until death parts us."

His eyes glimmer with satisfaction.

Connor is a steady counterpart to my shaking hands as we exchange rings. And then we're pronounced man and wife.

"You may now kiss the bride," the officiant proclaims.

"I've been waiting all day for this, Mrs. Grace."

My heart slams around in my chest as he cups my cheek in his trembling hand.

"My beautiful wife." He dips down for a tender brush of lips, soft and sweet. Gentle and chaste. At least until I part mine.

Connor makes a deep sound in the back of his throat and tilts my head, stroking inside. He deepens the kiss for a few knee-weakening moments while cameras flash incessantly, and then he pulls back, his grin wry as he takes my hand and faces the sea of people.

Our friends are smiling and clapping, boisterous, and a stark contradiction to the restrained golf claps from the rest of the attendees. Connor's mother looks furious, and his father's expression is a dark storm cloud. I'm sure slipping me the tongue in church is high on the list of no-nos.

Connor takes my arm and covers my hand with his when I settle it on his forearm. He bends, lips brushing my ear. "You're better than every single person in this room, and the important people already know it."

Even though my legs are unsteady, I let his words wash over me and infuse steel into my spine. I'm a Grace now. And even if it's only temporary, that name carries power. Cashmere-lined armor, like he said before. I feel the power in taking his name, in being his. I roll my shoulders back, and I feel his lips curve against my temple.

Everyone rises as we move down the aisle. I smile at my friends in the first few rows, then focus on putting one foot in front of the other. Connor leads me to the wedding party suite, which is different from the separate suites where we got ready.

We only have a minute before our friends will be here. I look up to take in the full glory of my...husband. "Holy shit."

"You okay?" He runs his hands down my arms.

"We're married."

"We are." He nods, his smile tentative. "I have something for you."

For a moment I expect him to pull a wad of cash out of his pocket, but instead he retrieves a tiny organza bag.

I tip my head, curious as he carefully loosens it, then moves my hand so it's palm up between us and shakes a small friendship bracelet into my hand.

I finger the beads that read *Mrs. Grace.*

He clears his throat. "I made it for you."

My gaze lifts to his. "You made this?"

"Yeah." He pushes his cuff up. "I have one, too." His reads *Mr Grace.*

My eyes prick. My heart stutters. I don't know if Connor realizes the significance of this, of how much those bracelets I've gathered all the road of my life mean to me; they're fragments of all the good parts.

It suddenly feels like someone injected novocaine into the top of my head, and it's running down my body like a waterfall. I grab the lapels of his tux. "You should kiss me again."

His eyebrows rise.

"Please. Now. I need a distraction, or I'll end up crying," I explain.

His brow furrows, and his expression darkens. "Regretting your choices already?"

"No, my feelings are big and your sweetness is hitting me in all my soft places. Please distract me, Mr. Grace."

"Whatever you need, Mrs. Grace." He cups my face in his hands and slants his mouth over mine.

The soft stroke of his tongue, the rough pads of his gentle fingers on my face, the comforting smell of sandalwood and citrus, and the warmth of his body pull me back from the edge of panic.

"Whoa, hey now!" Kodiak's deep voice breaks the spell.

I stroke my tongue against Connor's one last time before I break the kiss.

"We can give you a few minutes," Lexi offers with a smirk.

"It's fine," I assure them. Consummating our marriage isn't supposed to be on the table, let alone something that happens before we've even had photos.

I walk over and push open the door, waving everyone in. "We were just saying hi. Everyone, please join us!"

Our friends pile into the room, and bottles of champagne are popped and poured. After a minute, Connor's parents and brothers-in-law join us.

"You look lovely, Mildred," Courtney says through a practiced smile.

"Thank you so much. This is such a dream come true." I mean it.

"I'm sure it is," she counters.

Meems appears, bless her sweet heart, and takes one of our hands in each of hers. "I'm so thrilled to welcome you into the Grace family, Dred. You're going to make each other so happy."

I wrap my arms around her. "It's such an honor to be part of your family, Meems."

Her eyes are watery with unshed tears. "Thank you for bringing out the very best in my grandson."

My heart clenches, but I don't have time to respond, because Courtney commands our attention.

"The photographers are set up in the gardens. The wedding party should meet us out there in ten minutes." Her gaze shifts to me, and I wish I could read her expression. "Welcome to the family, Mildred."

I nod. "Thank you."

Julian holds out a hand to Isabelle.

"Izzy will meet you out there. She's part of the wedding party," Connor tells him.

Julian smiles tightly. "Of course. I'll see you shortly." He kisses Isabelle on the cheek and follows Courtney and Duncan out of the room.

"I hope he gets wasted and passes out early," she mutters into her glass.

I snort a laugh.

Her eyes go wide. "I'm just joking, obviously."

"Feed them shots. They won't know their ass from their armpit by the time dinner is over," Connor suggests flatly.

Photographs with the wedding party are full of laughter, and even my usually broody husband is all smiles as his teammates gather around him. I hope he feels like he's part of them today. I want what's happening between us, temporary or not, to show him that this team can give him the support and friendship he needs, just like they have for me.

The wedding party is then excused while Courtney directs the family photos. They're stiff and a little unpleasant, and then things get awkward when she decides they should have some mother-and-daughter photos.

"Are they serious with this?" I ask Connor.

"Oh yeah." He grabs two glasses of champagne and passes me one.

"But this is our wedding."

"They're paying for the photographer, though."

Courtney calls Julian and Bryson over so they can pose with Isabelle and Portia.

It astounds me that they can leave him out so easily. "Would you like Connor and me to join the sibling photos?" I call out.

Courtney startles.

Connor snorts a laugh into his champagne glass.

"Oh! Yes! Of course."

I down my champagne and spend the rest of the photo session inserting Connor and myself into every single one of them, because fuck his parents for leaving him out at his own damn wedding.

CHAPTER 24
DRED

Connor links his arm with mine as we walk back toward the hotel. "This reception is as much a business meeting as it is a flex," he explains, his voice low.

"Of course it is."

"All of my parents' contacts are attending, and some of them will be exceptionally interested in you."

"In an unfriendly way?" I ask.

"Mm, exactly." He rubs the center of my palm with his thumb. "So I might be annoyingly attentive this evening. I apologize in advance."

"You're my husband. You're supposed to be annoyingly attentive," I remind him.

His nostrils flare, and his gaze darkens. He brings my hand to his lips and kisses the back of it. "I'm glad you feel that way, wife."

The moment we step into the reception hall, the introductions begin.

Connor keeps a protective, possessive hand on my lower back as his father and mother introduce us to influential person after influential person.

Anytime someone asks when he's giving up hockey to join

the hotel empire—which is often—he deflects and asks them pointed questions about their own children and their career goals. The answer is often the same: They've joined the family business, of course.

Connor has spent his entire adult life defending his choice to play professional hockey. Yet they can't fathom why he would choose this path when the one laid out for him makes so much more sense. Every introduction paints a more vivid picture: He's a beautiful villain. And he's mine.

"Now that you're married, are you planning to quit hockey?" a bigwig in finance named Martin asks.

"Not until the league stops offering me contracts," Connor replies coolly.

"It's a rather violent sport," Martin muses.

"So is the world of finance," he retorts with an arrogant smile.

Martin chuckles. "Well, you won't end up with gaps in your smile from running a hotel business."

"My son might, since he tends to enjoy pushing buttons," Duncan says with a hint of warning.

"Especially yours, Father," Connor quips.

"Oh my gosh! Dred, your wedding is amazing! This is so cool! Thank you so much for inviting us!" Everly drapes herself over me like a blanket. Victor stands behind her with his hands in his pockets, wearing an apologetic smile.

"I'm so glad you could make it. Where's Cordelia?" I glance around for the group home's primary contact and guardian.

"She had to use the bathroom. They have an attendant in there who hands you a paper towel and cleans the sink after each person uses it. Like whoa." She makes a mind-blown gesture. "I didn't even know that was a thing. You look like a princess. Do you like my dress?"

"I love your dress." It's very nineties prom and completely suits her personality.

"I got to buy a brand-new one! We didn't even go to a

consignment shop. And Victor got a suit and people pinned it while he was wearing it!" She sucks in a breath.

"Did you have fun picking it out?" I'm halfway to tears at her excitement. I sent money to Cordelia at the group home so they could get something to wear.

"So much fun! And there are people here walking around with appetizers. They keep offering them to us, and we can just take them. They're so good." She drops her voice to a whisper. "I kind of wish I'd brought a container and a bigger purse so I could take some home."

"We can have a box packed up for you, if you'd like," Connor offers.

His father has moved on to a conversation with a group of businessmen and his sons-in-law.

"Hey! Hi! Oh my God. Wow." Everly is about ninety percent of the way to a full-on freak-out, and I could not love it more. "You're Connor Grace. Full disclosure, I'm not really into hockey, or like, sporty guys, but"—she gives him a double thumbs-up—"I like the suit." She turns back to me and mouths, *he's hot.*

I motion for Victor to join us. "Connor, I'd like you to meet Everly and Victor. They volunteer at the library with me."

"I'm only helping out because I need forty hours of community service to graduate, and also I got caught doing naughty things with a cute boy in the stacks." Everly wrinkles her nose and shrugs, like *oops.*

"Everly!" Victor chastises.

Connor smirks. "Was it my wife who caught you?"

I should not love the way *my wife* sounds coming out of his mouth.

"Uh-huh." Everly nods. "Better her than Dorothea, that's for sure. A library ban would suck." She flips her hair over her shoulder. "Then where would I get my cookies and juice boxes after school?"

"I do love a good juice box and cookie." Connor's amusement is written all over his face.

"But you love a good ham and cheese sandwich more," I fire back.

"Same!" Everly exclaims, apparently thrilled to have this in common. "But don't ruin it with lettuce, am I right?"

"Definitely no lettuce," Connor agrees.

The emcee makes an announcement that dinner will be served soon.

"We should find Cordelia." Victor takes his sister by the elbow. "It was very nice to meet you, Mr. Grace. Thanks for inviting us, Dred. It's been amazing."

"We'll dance later, okay?"

"I love dancing!" Everly exclaims.

Victor smiles and nods, then guides her across the room, stopping to grab an hors d'oeuvre from a passing server on the way.

"They're siblings?" Connor asks.

"Twins."

"She's the one you were talking about to the kitchen staff." His palm settles on my low back as he guides me to the head table.

"She is." I smile fondly.

"And they live in a group home?"

"They do."

"She's a little wild, but Victor seems easy," he observes.

"She is, and he is, but he won't be separated from her, and she has a hard time staying out of trouble." Last year I started the paperwork to become a foster parent, but as a single woman under thirty, with a modest income, and living in a small two-bedroom apartment, the odds were against me.

"So they're stuck in the system," Connor says.

"Until they age out, unfortunately."

Connor helps me into my seat, adjusting my dress so it doesn't get caught under the chair's legs.

He presses a gentle kiss to my shoulder, whether for my benefit, or that of the guests we're on display for, I'm unsure.

Cameras flash and click as I tip my chin up and touch my husband's cheek.

"There are an awful lot of photographers here," I murmur.

His eyes search mine, fingers skimming under my chin. "My father allowed media access just until dinner. They'll be gone soon."

I'm sure it looks like we're having a moment. And maybe we are. Because part of me wants this fairy tale to be real—to step into the roles we've agreed to and forget who we are outside them.

"You should kiss me," I whisper.

He narrows his eyes, expression pensive. "For them or for you?"

I go with honesty. "For me."

He presses his lips tenderly to mine. Neither of us tries to deepen it, to turn it into a spectacle. So it's over far too soon. But Connor takes his place beside me. At least we're not alone up here, sitting on thrones like royalty. We're insulated by our friends with Lexi on my right, and Kodiak on Connor's left.

Dinner is extravagant and exceptional. The servers keep topping up my champagne, and for once I indulge. Connor's parents are seated with Meems and Connor's brothers-in-law. My work friends and Everly and Victor are tucked into a corner, the rest of the Terror surrounding them.

I'm nervous when we get to the speeches, but Connor's parents keep it short and sweet, welcoming me to the Grace family and openly intimating their expectation that their only son will join the Grace empire in the near future.

Meems is next, and Connor meets her at the stairs, helping her to the podium. My heart stutters as he adjusts the mic for her before he returns to his spot beside me.

"She looks tired," I murmur.

"She is, but she's happy, so thank you for that." He kisses my temple.

I squeeze his hand as Meems talks about Connor growing up,

how he did things his own way and when he discovered his passion for hockey. "You've been in love with the sport since you picked up a stick, and for a long time nothing mattered more. You lived and breathed it. You took your dream, and against all odds, you made it yours. And then Mildred, Dred"—she smiles —"came into your life, into our lives, and I saw the change in you. I see it now." She motions to us, Connor sitting with his arm slung casually over the back of my chair, legs crossed. "Dred brings out that soft side of you that I've had the privilege of seeing my entire life. She brings so much joy and light and love into our lives and our home." Meems blinks back tears. "Dred, thank you for coming to us when we needed you the most. Thank you for seeing what I see, for loving my grandson the way he deserves to be loved. I'm so proud to call you my granddaughter."

I blink tears from my eyes, feeling horrible and wonderful at the same time. I adore her, and the whole point of this is to make her happy, which she is, but what if this act Connor and I have been putting on isn't one anymore—at least not for me? *What if I'm really in love with him?*

I don't have time to dive into a panic spiral, though, because Connor is helping me to my feet. We meet Meems at the podium.

"I love you so much." I hug her.

"I love you, too, sweetheart." She kisses my cheek.

Isabelle helps Meems back to her chair while Connor pulls out his pocket square and dabs at my eyes. "We're in this together, okay?"

I nod.

"You want me to do the talking?"

"Please."

He keeps his arm around me, tucking me into his side while he adjusts the microphone so it's at his height. "Mildred and I want to thank all of you for being here to celebrate this special day with us."

A round of polite applause follows, accompanied by raucous cheers from his teammates.

"Mom and Dad, thank you for so generously hosting this event. It's fairy-tale worthy, which is what my beautiful wife deserves." He gazes down at me. "Thank you, Mildred, for making my life so much fuller and for agreeing to be mine. I owe you the world."

My chin wobbles. I don't know what's true and what's not anymore. But he looks so earnest and handsome, and regardless, he's given me so much more than I ever expected. He tucks a finger under my chin and presses his lips softly to mine. Maybe for appearances. Maybe because he wants to.

The hall erupts in applause.

The bar opens back up, and the emcee announces the first dance.

Connor leads me to the dance floor and takes my hand in his.

"There are so many eyes on us," I whisper.

"Just follow my lead." His palm splays against my back, the heat soaking into my skin, grounding me. "Keep your eyes on mine, okay, darling? It's you and me against the world."

I finally understand what it must be like for Flip and the rest of the team—people always watching, always commenting, always having an opinion. And it's so much worse for Connor, because it's not just the hockey-watching nation that picks him apart. It's everyone else, too.

Connor pulls me close as the music begins, and I rest my palm on his thick shoulder. He's poised and elegant, just like his last name implies. I don't look anywhere but at him as he spins me around the dance floor, focusing on his gorgeous face.

When the song is over, our friends surround us in a bubble of protection. I loop my arms over Connor's shoulders, while he links his at my low back, improper and casually affectionate.

"This reminds me of high school dances," I muse.

"Did you go to many?" Connor sweeps a lock of hair off my cheek.

"Enough to know they were fun, but awkward. How about you?"

He shakes his head. "I usually had my privileges revoked for those kinds of things."

I can picture him as a sullen teen, angry at the world, lashing out and putting up a fight every step of the way, his arrogance a shield for the acceptance he couldn't find.

"For creating trouble so other people could stay out of it?" I arch a brow.

"You make me sound altruistic."

"Aren't you, though? The hero disguised as the villain," I muse.

"I'm not sure that's true, but I like that you think so."

The song changes, ending the moment, and Flip steps in to dance with me. Connor grabs Callie and spins her around the dance floor.

"That was some speech Connor gave," Flip says, eyes on mine, assessing, questioning.

"It was," I agree.

"His Meems loves you, eh?"

"Yeah, and I love her."

"Kodiak might have mentioned that her health isn't the best."

"She's doing okay."

"Connor's close to her though, yeah?"

"Stop fishing and just enjoy my wedding, Flip."

He laughs. "Okay. I'll leave it alone. At least until you get back from your honeymoon."

"Thanks. I appreciate it."

Tally and Fee twirl past us, giggling and smiling.

Flip's gaze follows them for a moment before he returns his attention to me. "Tally wants me to save her a dance."

I smile. "I'm sure she does."

His brow furrows. "You don't seem surprised."

I pat his chest. "I'm not. I don't think anyone in our friend group would be, to be honest."

"What do you mean?" His gaze darts over my shoulder for a moment, before returning to me.

I arch a brow.

"It's just a crush."

"A few years ago it was a crush, Flip. She's not a teenager anymore. She's an adult. She's in university, and before long, she'll be graduating and living life."

He shakes his head, unnerved. "That can't... I can't... I'm not a good choice for her."

"Maybe in the past—"

"The shit I've done." He squeezes the bridge of his nose. "I can't erase it, and she's too good for me."

"That's not true."

"Vander Zee would bury me."

I glance over at the Terror's head coach, sitting at a table, watching his daughter having a good time while wearing a serious expression. He's an intense guy at the best of times.

"Promise you won't let me make that mistake, Dred."

I sigh. *What am I supposed to say?* "I won't let you make a mistake."

CHAPTER 25
CONNOR

"That conversation looked serious," I murmur once Mildred is back at my side.

"His eyes are finally opening," she replies.

"You told him why you married me?"

Dred side-eyes me. "No."

"Then wh—" I glance over at Tally and Fee, whose heads are together. "The coach's daughter has a crush."

She hums. "Speaking of crushes, and getting over them, Callie seems to be smitten."

The music has changed to something more upbeat, and Tally, Fee, and Callie have started dancing with Everly and Victor. Callie looks up at Victor with stars in her eyes. And every so often, Tally's gaze moves across the room to where Flip is standing with Tristan and a few of our teammates, talking.

Meems approaches, arm laced with Isabelle's.

"Everything okay?" I ask.

"Everything is wonderful." Meems takes one of our hands in each of hers. "You two are beautiful together. I'm so thrilled I could be here to celebrate this day."

"Us too, Meems." I fold her into a gentle hug, and Mildred does the same.

She whispers something to Meems that makes her laugh.

"I'm going to walk Meems out to the car," Isabelle says.

"I can do that," I reply.

"I can come, too," Mildred offers.

"No, you join your friends on the dance floor." I tip my chin toward the Terror women. "You too, Izzy."

"Feel free to join us when you get back." Mildred kisses the edge of my jaw, links arms with Izzy, and shimmies over to her friends.

I walk Meems out of the reception, and we take the elevator to the lobby.

"Those twins from the library absolutely adore Dred," she notes.

"They do," I agree.

"She loves them, too," she adds.

"She has a big heart."

"She's good for you." Meems pats my hand.

"I think so, too."

When I return, my eyes are on the dance floor, but I'm cornered by my father and a few of his business associates and am sucked into a dry conversation I couldn't care less about. Eventually I'm able to excuse myself and join Kodiak and some of the guys from my team, who are hanging out by the bar, watching the women dancing.

I give Mildred her space to enjoy the evening, since we'll be spending the next few days together, just the two of us, for our honeymoon. The flush in her cheeks and her glassy eyes toward the end of the night tell me she's enjoyed the champagne. I can't blame her. I've had a few glasses myself. It's been quite the gauntlet since we started down this road a mere handful of weeks ago.

A little after midnight, I whisk my bride off her feet and carry her out of the ballroom while she waves to her friends and everyone throws confetti. Once the doors close behind us and the cameras stop flashing, we head up to the wedding suite. Mildred is quiet in the elevator, and I don't force conversation.

We exit on our floor and walk together until she stands in front of the double doors. "Are we sharing a room?"

"Yes, darling." I pass her the keycard.

"And a bed?"

"That's entirely up to you." I bend and slide my arm under her legs, lifting her off the floor.

She gasps and wraps her arms around my neck, exactly like she does every night when I carry her from the library to her bedroom. "What are you doing?"

"What does it look like?" I smile down at her. "Allow me the honor, Mrs. Grace."

She taps the card against the sensor, and I open the door and carry her inside.

"Oh wow." The suite is massive—and romantic, meant for people in love. The huge four-poster bed is littered with pink rose petals. Champagne chills in a bucket alongside a plate of chocolate-covered strawberries.

"Meems booked this for us," I explain as I set her on her feet.

"Of course she did." She turns to me, eyes full of emotion. "We made her so happy today."

"We did," I agree.

Her eyes move over me. "We're really married."

I tuck a hand in my pocket. "We are."

She nods once. "We should do shots."

My stomach sinks. I don't know what I expected. "Reality finally setting in?"

"Pretty much." She crosses over to the wet bar and lines up four shot glasses.

I shrug out of my suit jacket while she pours vodka into each glass, adding a dash of simple syrup and lemon. She passes me a glass and takes one for herself.

"To making the people we love happy and keeping them close." She clinks her glass against mine and downs the shot.

I do the same.

She passes me the second one, and we shoot again.

"Feel better?" I don't know what to do or say. She's stuck with me for the foreseeable future. I'm definitely the winner in this arrangement.

"A little." She leans against the bar, eyes glassy.

"I have something for you." I slide my hand into the breast pocket of my tux. I've been carrying it with me all day, waiting for the right time to give it to her. I pull the small, wrapped box out and pass it to her.

"You already got me a wedding gift." She holds up her arm and jingles the bracelet. "Now there's another?"

"Sort of."

She rolls her bottom lip between her teeth. "I didn't get you anything."

"You are the gift, Mildred."

She makes a sound and carefully unwraps the box. Inside is a piece of paper folded into the shape of a house. "What is this?"

"Unfold it and find out."

She sets the box aside and unfolds the piece of paper. She pushes her glasses up her nose, brow furrowing as she reads it, then lifts her eyes to mine. "These are ownership papers."

"I was able to finalize everything yesterday. The apartment is yours. You can rent it out, if you want. You can keep it as it is. If you need space, you have a place to go that belongs to you." I rub the back of my neck. "I want you to feel like you have agency and choices. You're my wife, and I'm your husband, but I don't ever want you to feel trapped in this with me."

She throws her arms around my neck. "Thank you."

I gently embrace her. "You don't have to thank me. I told you I would take care of it. The timing just happened to work out in my favor."

She cups my face in her palms. "Just say you're welcome, Connor."

"You're welcome."

She smiles.

"Is there anything else you need from me?" I ask.

She turns her back and bows her head. "I need you to help me out of this dress."

"Hmm... So you do." I steady my hands and begin unfastening the many, many buttons one at a time. Her skin is soft and warm, and she smells like strawberries and vanilla. All I want is to kiss a path up to her neck, but we're not here because we're in love.

"I've been thinking," she says.

"You make that sound dangerous, darling."

She glances over her shoulder, smile coy. "It's our wedding night."

"Yes, it is." I continue unfastening buttons, her white lace bra appearing.

"And you've mentioned on more than one occasion that we could make an amendment to our contract."

"I have done that, haven't I?"

"Very cheekily, I might add."

"I do have a tendency to be cheeky, don't I?"

"Mmm... Exceedingly cheeky," she agrees.

"Last button," I say.

She turns, holding the bodice of her dress in place. "What if we made a verbal amendment to our contract?"

"What kind of verbal amendment?"

She releases the bodice, and her dress slides down. She tugs it over her hips and lets it fall to the floor. Stepping out of the puddle of satin, she moves closer, dressed in nothing but her bra and panties. She's perfectly curvy and soft in all the right places.

"You look hungry, husband." She reaches behind her, eyes on mine as she unclasps her bra and lets it fall to the floor.

"And you look like everything I want, but don't deserve."

"What about what I deserve?" She hooks her thumbs into her lace and satin panties.

My mouth goes dry and my body heats as she pushes them

over her hips and steps out of them, bringing her close enough to touch.

"You deserve better than me."

"What if I don't want better? What if I like what I have?" Her eyes are slightly unfocused, but hot with desire.

"I'd say you're drunk, little menace."

"Maybe a bit." She runs her hands up my chest. "But it's our wedding night, Connor. We spent hours on display for all those people, now I'm on display for only you. What will you do with me?"

I clench my hands at my sides. I don't want her to regret her decision tomorrow. "I should put you to bed."

"I think you should touch me." At the tug of her fingers, my bow tie unfurls. "But first I want you out of this shirt." She drapes the black fabric across the back of her neck and starts unbuttoning it. I watch her, waiting for her to change her mind, to realize this is a mistake she doesn't want to make with me. But she pushes my shirt over my shoulders and sighs, nails running over my abs and up my chest. She traces the letters there, drinking in the art covering my skin. "God, you're beautiful."

"Only on the outside."

"Untrue." Her eyes lift. "You can convince everyone else that you're the bad guy, Connor, but I see you."

She's too gorgeous, too much to resist. And I don't want to anymore. I want this. I want her. Not the lie we're telling everyone else—I want this woman who protects the things she loves the most, who's offering me a piece of her that I have no right to, but still want to claim. I lift her onto the wet bar.

Mildred's eyes light up with triumph. She grabs the champagne from the bucket—it's already been opened—and sips directly from the bottle. "What are you going to do with me, now that I'm yours, Connor?"

I slip my fingers into the hair at the nape of her neck and tip her head back. "What would you like me to do, Mrs. Grace?" I brush my lips over hers.

She exhales on a needy whimper, parts her legs wide, and pulls me closer. "Make me come, Mr. Grace."

I trail my fingers down her side. "Demanding little menace." I angle her head, slanting my mouth over hers. She parts her lips on a low moan, letting me in as she guides my hand between her thighs.

My fingers glide over soft, wet skin, pink and pretty and all mine. She sighs, and her entire body softens as I ease one finger inside her hot cunt. She breaks the kiss and her gaze drops, eyes on my fingers as I slide out and add a second one, curling forward to massage the spot inside as I circle her clit with my thumb. A small tattoo decorates her hip, a single ladybug sitting on a strawberry blossom, pretty and delicate. I wonder if I'll find more secrets on her body when I have time to explore her. My mind nearly melts at the possibility.

Everything about her opens, the walls crumbling as she gives me a part of her I desperately want.

"Such a good husband." Her hand slides down her soft stomach, index finger swirling around her clit along with my thumb. She eases lower, skimming the fingers buried inside her, and on the next pump, she pushes inside with them.

"All you have to do is ask for more, if that's what you want." I withdraw my fingers, sucking her juices off them on a low groan. She drags my mouth to hers, licking inside as I push three fingers into her, stretching, filling. Mildred moans into my mouth, and I swallow it down with the taste of her.

She clutches my shoulder as she spreads her legs wider, still wearing my bow tie and her glasses. The champagne bottle nearly tips over when she sets it clumsily on the bar top. She grips my wrist while she fucks my hand, rolling her hips in time with the pump and curl of my fingers.

I memorize the moment, capture it and tuck it away so it's mine forever. And then she's coming apart. Clenching on my fingers, shuddering, whimpering my name.

Her hands frame my face as she sucks in my bottom lip, teeth dragging over the skin. "You should take me to bed and fuck me."

I pull back. "You will be entirely sober when you invite me into your body again."

Her bottom lip juts out. "Such a villain."

"The worst kind." I pick her up, and she wraps her legs around my waist as I carry her across the room. "It's time for bed."

Her lips are on my neck. "Shouldn't I take care of you?"

"I'm the villain," I remind her. "I think you should make me wait."

CHAPTER 26
CONNOR

The next morning I wake to the sound of my phone buzzing from somewhere in the room. I'm surprised to find Mildred tucked against me, little spoon to my big, warm skin touching mine. Our left hands are laced together, wedding bands next to each other.

She's my wife.

My wife.

I pulled her into this life with me, made her mine out of a selfish desire to keep Meems with me for as long as I can, and now, this morning...everything is different. It's not just about Meems and her happiness anymore.

Mildred has made a place for herself in my heart, and I don't want to let her go, even after Meems is gone. I want her to keep taking up space in my bed and my house and my life.

I would do anything for her—except walk away, unless that was truly what she wanted. Waking up with her in my arms... it's more than I expected it to be.

My phone buzzes again. And then both our phones buzz in tandem.

I expect awareness to hit and her to shove out of my arms,

regretting what happened last night. But she doesn't, and it gives me hope.

"Why won't it stop?" she grumbles. "What time is it? My head is not happy."

I lift mine so I can see the clock. "It's ten."

"What time is checkout?"

"Whenever we feel like. But we should be on the road by one."

"Where are we going at one?"

"It's a surprise." I planned a weekend away to give her a break from the whirlwind of the past few weeks. "Fuck."

She scoffs. "I offered myself last night, and you denied me. My head says *no thanks* right now, but you can try again later." She feels around for my arm and tries to pull it back over her.

I smile and press my lips to her bare shoulder. "We have to get up."

"You said we don't have to leave until one. That means I can sleep for at least another two hours."

"We have a brunch to attend."

She wriggles until she's on her back, all that warmth between us dissipating. Mildred throws her arm over her face. "If it's with your parents, you can go alone."

I arch a brow. "Do you really think I'd spring something like that on you with no warning?"

"No. You're everyone else's villain, not mine." She reveals one bleary eye. "If not your parents, then who?"

"Your friends."

"You have to stop calling them *my* friends since they're also *your* friends now, too."

Temporarily. Unless I can change the way Mildred feels about me. I throw the covers off. Otherwise I'll fold and we'll end up in bed for the next two hours instead of spending time with her—*our*—friends. "I'll get you a painkiller and let them know we're on our way down." I roll out of bed, grab a bottle of water from the fridge and painkillers from the care package in the bathroom—so smart—and return to stand over my wife.

Her eyes are still covered by her arm.

"Darling."

She groans but pushes up on her arms. The sheets slip down to her waist, revealing her lush breasts. Her hair is a wild mess, her cheeks flushed pink. She's stunning, unguarded, and *mine*.

Mildred makes disgruntled eye contact and sticks out her tongue. I set the painkillers on it and hand her the bottle of water. She drains half of it and flops back down. "I can't believe you let me talk you into doing shots last night."

"I suggested it was a bad idea. You seemed to disagree."

"I was already drunk."

She's different this morning. Maybe because the stress of the wedding is gone? Maybe because we finally gave in to the chemistry that's been eddying around us these past weeks, growing stronger by the day. "That's what you get for being a menace." I bend and press my lips to her forehead.

"I'm a cute menace, though."

"The cutest." I straighten.

Her eyes drop to my crotch, and her brows rise. "Looks like someone else is awake and excited."

She reaches for me, and I capture her hand in mine. "What do you think you're doing?"

"I haven't even seen it."

I fight a smile. "And you think right now, when we're already fifteen minutes late for brunch and you're wickedly hungover, is a good time to play show-and-tell?"

"You saw mine last night." Her lips push out in a pout.

"You can be as adorable as you want, but you're not in any condition to play with me." I cross over to the closet, needing to walk away before I break for her. And I need a moment to convince myself this is real, that I haven't somehow conjured it with my mind. I grab a pair of jeans and pull them up my thighs. "I hate being late, which we already are." I rearrange myself and tug the zipper up, fastening the button. I pull a shirt over my head and manage to get my arms through the sleeves before Mildred's arms wrap around my waist from behind.

I like this affectionate version of her. I want more of it. But we have all weekend to explore this new side of us. I hope.

I capture her hands and turn to face her. She's gloriously naked.

"I texted and said we'd be down in fifteen minutes." Her eyes are lit up with hope.

"I texted five minutes ago and said we'd be down in ten." I drop my head and drag my nose along the edge of her jaw. "Pretty little menace." I keep my hold on her wrists, pulling her naked body against me. "You're going to let me dress you, take you to see your friends, feed you, and hydrate you."

Her cute pout returns. "Why so sensible and sweet?"

"I can't be the worst all the time." I kiss her chin and forehead.

"What happens after brunch with friends?"

"We'll go for a drive. And later, when I have you all to myself again, you can play with me however you want." I gaze down at her, letting the rush of desire wash over me. "Do we have a deal?"

She sighs. "I suppose."

I grin and kiss her tempting lips. I release one hand and reach behind me to pluck a pair of panties from the drawer before I drop to my knee in front of her. Mildred lets me dress her in jeans and a sweater with a strawberry print with only minimal pouting.

She disappears into the bathroom for a moment to brush her teeth and hair, and then we take the elevator to the private dining room.

She frowns at me on the ride. "I take it back."

"You take what back, darling?"

"What I said about you being sweet and sensible. Postponing show-and-tell was an exceptionally villainous thing to do."

I kiss the back of her hand. "You're right. Taking care of you, making sure you're properly fed and hydrated is criminal."

"Utterly felonious really," she agrees with narrowed eyes. "And you wore that shirt to torment me."

"Another heinous crime. How dare I wear clothing in public and rob you of the opportunity to shamelessly ogle me? My offenses are really piling up this morning, aren't they, Mrs. Grace?"

"We were already late," she points out. "Ten more minutes wouldn't have been a big deal."

I throw my head back and laugh. Then I box Mildred into a corner. "My beautiful, feisty, gorgeous wife. In no world would ten minutes with you ever be enough."

"But it would have taken the edge off." Her cute pout is back.

I grin. "I think I like edging you."

She pushes on my chest, but hooks a single finger into my belt loop to keep me close. "Horrible villain."

I brush my lips over her cheek. "Perfect menace."

The elevator doors open.

I step back, and her hot gaze darkens. She brushes by me with a huff and starts speed walking down the hall.

"Darling!" I call after her.

She keeps walking.

"You're going the wrong way!" I shout, loving the way it feels to push her buttons like this.

She spins to face me, nostrils flared, expression reflecting her displeasure as she stalks back. I step in front of her before she can pass. We've gained the attention of several nosy staff and a few guests.

"You have every right to be annoyed with me. I'm being a problem. Your problem." *And I fucking love it.* "But people are watching, and while there's nothing my father would love more than to see us arguing in public the day after our wedding—because it will prove that I'm completely incapable of making anyone happy, especially not my own wife—I don't want to feed the media beast when there is a possibility of backlash for you." I hold her face in my palms.

Her expression softens, and she exhales a slightly annoyed breath. "You want to make me happy?"

"I do, yes."

"Then you better kiss me," she demands.

I press my lips gently to hers. "Is that better?"

Her eyes flash. "Make a scene, Mr. Grace."

I grin. "Of course, Mrs. Grace." I wrap my arm around her waist, pulling her tightly against me, and delve in.

Soft lips, warm tongue. Her vanilla-and-strawberry shampoo surrounds me. Mint and wet and want. Cameras click. Her nails dig into my biceps.

I pull back. "Can I feed you now, darling?"

She sighs dramatically. "I suppose."

I lace our fingers and smile in satisfaction as she rolls her shoulders back, wearing the Grace name with the kind of arrogance I'd hoped for.

The dining room is full of easy laughter and chatter when we finally arrive.

"Look who made it!" Tristan stands, his smile wide as he claps, and everyone joins in.

"I'm so sorry we're late. It's my fault. I didn't want to wake my wife this morning." I kiss Mildred's temple. "She's adorable when she's sleeping."

Mildred snorts.

Flip barks out a laugh. "Not how I would describe a sleeping Dred."

She fires the double bird at him.

"Mimosa?" Rix asks.

"No thank you. Just water and coffee. Lots of both." Mildred slides into one of the two remaining chairs, and I push it in for her.

Before I can take the seat next to her, Quinn approaches with his date, Lovey Butterson. Her dad is a former pro player, and a coach at the Hockey Academy.

"Kodiak and Lavender send their love. They had to fly out early this morning." Quinn gives me a back-pat hug.

"New York has a game tomorrow." I nod. "You two heading out, too?"

"Yeah. Lovey and I are stopping at the Hockey Academy, and then continue to Guelph to visit her grandparents."

"Do you play hockey?" I ask.

She shakes her head and laughs. "No, but I haven't had a chance to visit the new Hockey Academy location." Lovey hugs Quinn's arm. "Thank you so much for the invitation. We had the most amazing time." She smiles up at Quinn, whose ears have gone red.

"I'm glad you could make it on such short notice." I nod to Quinn. "I'll see you in a few days, yeah?"

"You bet." He claps me on the shoulder and leaves with Lovey.

I slide into the seat beside Mildred and stretch my arm across the back of her chair.

Lexi smiles as Mildred sips her coffee with a sigh. "Too much champagne last night?"

"My wife thought it would be fun to do shots when we got back to our suite," I explain.

Mildred shoots me a glare over the rim of her cup. "Seriously, Connor?"

"It was your idea, darling."

"You're not supposed to throw me under the bus."

"You never think shots are a good idea," Flip says.

Mildred shrugs. "Well, last night I did. I'm blaming it on the champagne I had before the shots."

"They were fun." I kiss her temple.

She side-eyes me. "For you, maybe."

"And you, but maybe you don't remember that part."

"Time-out, you two. There are minors at the table," Tristan reminds us. "You'll be alone again soon enough."

Dallas nearly falls out of his chair because he's laughing so hard. "Like you're one to talk! When you and Rix are in a room together, the temperature goes up five freaking degrees."

"Hemi might as well put you on a leash," Tristan fires back.

Dallas puts his arm around Hemi. "Who says she doesn't?"

Hemi smirks.

"Minors at the table!" Roman snaps.

Fee leans forward. "My bestie writes why-choose romance."

"What's why-choose romance?" Callie asks.

Mildred jumps in. "She means the choose-your-own-adventure books!"

"Oh, I love those!" Callie says.

"Me, too," Lexi agrees, exchanging a look with my wife.

"What's why-choose?" I mutter.

Mildred pats my leg and gives her menacing little smile. "I'll tell you later."

CHAPTER 27
DRED

Brunch was an excellent idea, even if it meant I didn't get to ogle a mostly naked Connor for more than a handful of seconds. I feel much more human after coffee, water, carbs, and time with just friends. By the time Connor and I finish eating, the car is already waiting, and all our things have been packed up and loaded. I hug everyone and climb into the passenger seat.

Connor and I leave the city and head north, leaving the highway after about half an hour, for less-traveled roads. We pass a town I lived in briefly. The location was cute, but the family wasn't a good fit. The farther we get from civilization, the more anxious I become until I finally crack. "Where are we going?"

"It's a surprise," Connor says airily.

I run my hands up and down my thighs. I would love a hair tie. But mine is packed in my bag in the trunk, so the only way to assuage my anxiety is to be truthful. "So...I, uh, I don't really like surprises."

"I promise you'll love it," he assures me.

Irrational panic takes hold. Normally I'd find a quiet place to disappear and give myself the time I need to feel all the feelings, but I have nowhere to go. "I'm sure I will, but my anxiety is at about a four thousand out of ten right now."

"You don't trust me to keep you safe?" Connor frowns, glancing at me. "You realize it's always in my best interest to keep you happy."

There's so much to that statement to unpack, but I'm not capable of digging into it in my current state. "It's not a you thing, Connor." I swallow past the massive rock clogging my throat. If I'm honest, maybe he'll understand. But he'll also have another broken piece of me to play with. Exposing my weaknesses to him is tricky. I've spent my entire life hiding the parts that bleed.

We're married, though. We're living together for an undetermined amount of time. Him using my vulnerabilities against me isn't in his best interests. He can't avoid my triggers if he doesn't know what they are.

"Every time there was a surprise growing up, it usually resulted in something bad."

"Bad how?"

I lower the window a little, needing fresh air. But then we drive past an orchard, and memories I've long kept buried explode in my head. Scents can do that—open a box I've forgotten existed and submerge me. My words die on a plaintive sound. All the stress of the past few weeks has weakened my defenses, and this onslaught shatters them like glass. I close my eyes and fight the wave of memories, but they're already on me.

"Mildred?" Connor's fingers brush mine.

Did I really think I could go an entire year without him learning these things about me? Something was bound to happen eventually. Some accidental trigger to set me off. Who knew the smell of apple blossoms would light the match and set my brain on fire? I fight to keep my voice steady.

"I was left a lot. In places I shouldn't have been." My thoughts are a flood, saturating my mind, sliding down my throat, choking me, making it impossible to continue.

The pretty flowers. The petals floating to the ground. The promise that my foster brother wouldn't be long. Stay in the car. We'll get ice cream later.

But he lied.

Waiting and waiting and waiting.

Stuffy. Too hot. Sunburn. Need the bathroom. Can't hold it.

Stay in the car.

Wet pants. Wet pants. Wet pants.

The sun heading toward the horizon.

The car door opening. Finally.

Apple blossoms and laughter turning to screams.

Yanked out of the car so hard my shoulder pops out of the socket. A stinging slap across the face.

Bad girl. Bad girl. Bad girl.

Back to the group home.

Another foster family.

Having and losing, having and losing.

Being three in my first home.

Before the foster families.

I cry and cry and cry until my voice gives out.

And then silence.

So much silence.

Blue-tinged mannequins.

Open eyes. Watching TV forever.

Three sunrises and sunsets.

Mommy and Daddy smell bad.

Silence stretches on.

Empty cupboards. Empty stomach.

Knocking on the door.

Knocking. Knocking. Knocking.

I'm not supposed to open the door.

A loud crack. Frantic voices. Uniforms.

A woman with haunted, sad eyes holds me and tells me I will be okay.

But I'm not.

And I never will be.

"Hey, hey..." Warm hands on my face pull me out of the past. "Mildred, baby, look at me, where are you?"

Connor's panicked eyes finally register as I fight my way out of the deluge and suck in a lungful of air—like I've been stuck underwater, like the memories have been pinning me to the floor of my mind. "I'm sorry." I gasp and shudder.

"You don't need to be sorry." He takes my shaking hands in his. "Is this okay? Can I touch you? Is it okay for me to touch you?"

"Yeah." I nod. "Yes, it's okay." We're parked haphazardly on the side of the road. I'm shaking. Shivering uncontrollably. Like I'm cold, but I'm not.

"Okay. You're okay. We're okay." He presses my hand against his cheek. "No surprises, darling."

"I'm sorry I don't like them," I whisper, hating that the past has come here with me.

"I'm the one who's sorry." He kisses the back of my hand, apology on his face and in his eyes, his voice cracking. "We're driving to Blue Mountain. We have a private cabin booked on a lake. It's pretty up there this time of year, and a short drive. I wanted to take you somewhere peaceful, because I know this whole thing has been a lot."

"I like the lake." I exhale another steadying breath.

"Me too. It's a nice escape." He kisses my knuckles, lips lingering on my skin.

"I'm okay now." I lock it all away. Put the pain in a box and keep it there. "It just hits sometimes...little things trigger memories. Like scents. Most of the time I can find somewhere quiet to go and just..." *Lose it in private.* "Cope."

He turns my hand over and kisses the inside of my wrist. It's healed now, the skin pinker than it should be, but no more scabs. "I'm here however you need me to be, okay? If you want to talk, or even if you don't, I'm here."

I believe he means it. I just don't know *how* he means it. He has to be here for me. It's his role, and I'm learning that Connor takes those seriously.

He believes he's the team scapegoat, and so he stays in that space, maybe because it's comfortable, maybe because it's the expectation and he doesn't know how to break it. For Meems, he's the boy who refused to bend to his parents' whims. To them he's the problem child who continues to be a problem because they don't understand him. So what does he think he is to me? The man I have to marry to keep the things I love? The man I chose to say yes to because I love his Meems as much as he does?

Or is it deeper than that now? Have all the lines blurred for both of us? It feels like they have, but I don't have a lot of relationship experience—by design. I'm guarded. I have baggage and some pretty intense attachment issues.

But I like him.

I'm attracted to him.

And he's attracted to me.

Yet this contract binds us with thorns that make it difficult to maneuver. It's the piece that forces us to be one thing when maybe we want to be something else.

"I'm okay," I tell him again. "And we can talk about it later, when I've had some separation from it, if that's okay with you." It's too deep a look down my well right now.

"Whatever you're comfortable with."

I don't know how to read him now, and I'm too stuck in my own feelings to be able to mine through his.

"We can keep driving." It's better than sitting here, feeling awkward for having a meltdown on what's supposed to be the start of our doesn't-feel-as-fake-as-it-should honeymoon.

"Okay." He leans over and kisses my temple.

I don't know if I want to melt into the seat from his casual affection, cry, or jump out of the car and run all the way back to Toronto. All three seem reasonable.

"Talk to me about the Hockey Academy," I say as we pull back onto the road.

Connor side-eyes me, and his grip on the steering wheel tightens. "I'm not talking about the fucking sandwich."

"I think you mean you're not talking about fucking the sandwich." This is better. I can handle verbal sparring, just not all the feelings that come from talking about my own past.

He huffs.

"Seriously, though. I'm not asking about the sandwich. And fucking a piece of bread has nothing on the shit Tristan does to Rix," I mutter the last part.

"I'm sorry, what was that?"

"Nothing."

"That was *not* nothing. What does Tristan do to Rix?"

"Like I'm going to give you dirt you could use to piss off Flip." Although they have been surprisingly cordial with each other lately. "I shouldn't have said anything."

"But you did say something. And pissing Flip off isn't in my best interest these days."

"Because it would piss me off also?"

"Because it would upset you, and I don't enjoy making you unhappy."

He doesn't elaborate on his reason for this, so I'm left to surmise on my own.

"I want to hear about your experience at the Hockey Academy," I press.

"Only if you tell me what Tristan does to Rix."

"I can't. It breaks girl code."

"I can't tell you about the Hockey Academy because it breaks bro code," he fires back.

I roll my eyes. "I'm not asking about your feud with Flip. I'm asking about the experience. You must have enjoyed it since you're still tight with Kodiak and Quinn, and it was more than a decade ago."

"Kodiak and Quinn are good guys," Connor agrees. "So are Tristan and Dallas, but they mostly sided with Flip because he's Flip." He sighs. "He's always loved. Even when he does shitty things. And I get it, because he's a good guy. He came from a tough beginning. He fought to be here harder than most. And being the son of a billionaire put me at a disadvantage at the Hockey Academy."

"Because the program is highly subsidized," I say.

"That's right. My parents could have sent me to the other hockey program I'd been accepted to overseas, but they chose the Hockey Academy instead. They wanted me to understand my place in the world. People believed I'd bought my spot in the program, so I worked hard to prove I hadn't. But I had a huge chip on my shoulder, and let's be real, I'm entitled as fuck."

"It's hard not to be when you have a literal staff of people taking care of everything for you," I reply.

"What my parents failed to consider is that I'm used to being on the outside. The Hockey Academy wasn't any different for me. I wasn't afraid of losing status, because the only status I had was the result of a family I didn't fit into anyway."

He pauses a moment and then shrugs. "When I made the pros I wanted to know what it was like to be normal. I lived in an apartment and figured out how to cook food and do my own laundry. The ultimatum had been set for me. If I didn't join the family business, my dad would cut me out of the will, and then where would I be? So I went to the Hockey Academy, and I let myself be put in another box. But I played my ass off, and I played the role I thought I deserved. And I hated that I hated Flip because I was jealous."

"Because he came from nothing, and everyone loved him." Of course they hated each other.

"He didn't know what it was like on the other side," Connor explains. "He didn't have a clue what it felt like to want for nothing, because he wanted for everything. But he had the one thing

I wanted—everyone's acceptance. People gravitated to him. He saw the good in everyone. And I wanted to be him."

He shakes his head. "I thought for sure he'd lose his shit over you and me, and he just...proved he's a stand-up guy." Connor's jaw flexes, and he gives me a sidelong glance. "And here I am, acting the hero by offering you financial security so my grandmother doesn't have to worry about me ending up bitter, angry, and alone. Which is exactly what will happen eventually, just thankfully not while she's alive to see it."

"But you're not alone, Connor," I argue. "You have a whole team who will be the family you choose instead of the one you were born into, if you let them. And what about Quinn? He's a real friend outside of hockey. He stood up for you at your wedding."

"He gets me in a way most of the other guys don't," Connor agrees.

"Why? What's different about him?" There's something about Quinn. He has an edge to him.

"He feels...cursed."

"Cursed how?"

"He's named after his uncle."

"And that's a bad thing?"

"His dad watched him die when they were kids."

"Oh my gosh. What happened?"

"They were jumped by a bunch of kids on the way home from school. Quinn's dad, Lance, survived, but his uncle didn't. His entire family fell apart, and Lance moved to the States to live with his aunt. He found hockey, and the rest is history."

"That would have been devastating."

"I'm sure it was. But Quinn's name is a weight he carries, and his dad's career was a strong one. Quinn finally gets his chance in the pros, but now he has the legacy to live up to."

It seems everyone has a history, dark secrets they carry with them. "It's the same for Kodiak, too, though, right?"

"Yes and no. Kodiak is a better player than his dad. He's in a league of his own. Quinn is just starting. He's fighting to keep his spot. He feels like he has to prove that it isn't his father's legacy that brought him here. He's terrified that he isn't good enough."

"And you?" I ask. "What are you terrified of?"

"Becoming like my parents."

"Seems pretty unlikely."

"I don't know about that. They're not married to each other because they like each other."

"They're together because they wanted to make their Meems happy?" I say cheekily.

He snorts.

"Then I stand by my original assertion that it seems unlikely you'll end up like your parents. Probably as unlikely as it is for me to end up like mine."

"You're a miracle," Connor says softly.

"Based on what I've seen of your parents, so are you and your sisters."

I switch gears and ask Connor to tell me stories about his sisters growing up. I'm always a little obsessed with other people's holiday celebrations. I don't have family traditions, so I'm interested to learn about them.

Eventually we pull off the highway. The trees are beginning to change colors up here, with vibrant reds, yellows, and oranges dotting the landscape.

"We're about a ten-minute drive off the highway, and Flip and Lexi know where we're staying. There's reception out here, and we're only a short trip to the closest town," Connor tells me. "And there are a bunch of permanent residents on the lake."

"I'm not afraid to be alone with you, Connor," I assure him.

"I just want you to feel safe."

The paved road turns into gravel, which pings aggressively off the side of his very expensive car, but Connor doesn't seem to care. We pull into the driveway and he parks, asking me to wait so he can open my door. I step out into the crisp afternoon, breathing in the scent of pine and fall leaves.

Connor grabs our bags, and I shoulder my purse and the small cooler bag of leftovers from our room and brunch. The trees form a canopy, the sun peeking through. I follow Connor down the path to a rustic but gorgeous wood cabin perched on the edge of a steep hill. He punches in the code and ushers me inside.

"Oh my gosh." I toe off my shoes and pad into the warm, homey space. I drop the cooler bag on the kitchen counter. The far wall is all windows, boasting a stunning view of the lake, the trees a bright wash of color, but it's the living room that has tears springing to my eyes. Two walls consist of floor-to-ceiling built-in shelves, filled with books, and there's even a recessed reading nook with enough space for two. In the center of the room is a couch and a coffee table, piled high with board games. A fire crackles invitingly in the hearth.

I turn to Connor, who stands a few feet away, wearing a hopeful expression.

"This is perfect, Connor."

A proud smile lights up his face at my approval. "Good. That's good. I hoped you would love it."

I cross over and wrap my arms around his waist. His strong arms encircle me, and I rest my cheek on his chest, comforted by the steady beat of his heart. "Such a sweet, thoughtful villain."

"Don't tell anyone. It'll ruin my reputation."

I look up, taking in his beautiful, harsh face. "Why did you do this for me?"

We could have gone anywhere. His family has a private jet. It would have been nothing to fly us to an island. But here we are, a short drive from the city, surrounded by books and board games.

"The past few weeks have been a lot, and yesterday wasn't easy for you, I'm sure. I thought you could use the quiet." His fingers trace gently up and down my spine, his voice dropping to a whisper. "And I want to make you happy."

"Why?"

His brow furrows. "Why do I want to make you happy?"

"Yes."

"It makes me feel good."

"Why?"

"Are you just going to keep asking why?"

"Yes, I'm drilling down."

"Why?"

"Because I think you have an ooey-gooey center, and I want to know what it tastes like."

The right side of his mouth quirks up. "I'm not a pastry, darling."

"You have all these layers. I want to see what's underneath them." And I want to know if we're on the same page. If this isn't just about making Meems happy and my financial stability. "Why is my happiness so important to you?"

"It just is."

"There has to be a reason."

His eyes dart to the side, and he sighs, like he's preparing to share something that makes him uncomfortable. "I like how I feel when I'm with you and you're happy. I like watching your face light up when I do something nice for you. I like this." He motions to our surroundings and hugs me closer. "Surrounded by your softness and warmth because I did something that pleases you."

He craves acceptance and connection as much as I do, longs for it in a way I understand. "You like me," I whisper.

His expression softens. "I've always liked you, Mildred."

"I like you, too." It's enough for now.

I tug on the back of his neck and push up on my toes. His mouth meets mine. Lips part and tongues sweep. I'm grounded by the hot press of his body. His fingers flex against my hip. My pulse thrums and an ache flares, heavy in my belly.

Sex has always been an act driven by desire for me, compartmentalized into a tidy box of pleasure. But the weight of who Connor and I are to each other and how we arrived here is shifting my world. Everything he does, every soft side he shows me, chips away at the armor I've built. I want to find out what it's like to be part of him more than I want to protect my own heart.

"I'd like to see the bedroom."

CHAPTER 28
DRED

Connor laces our fingers and leads me across the rough-hewn hardwood floor into the bedroom. Like the living room, the wall facing the lake is all windows. Pines and maples frame the cabin, but don't obscure the view. Vases of fragrant night lilies dot every surface in the room. To the right, in front of the windows, is a barrel chair piled with pillows and throw blankets, a table stacked with books beside it. From the spines I can see they're my favorites.

Connor doesn't have to tell me he likes me with his words, because he keeps showing me with his actions that he pays attention to the things that bring me joy.

"This is incredible," I whisper.

Connor exhales a relieved breath. "Good. I'm glad I got it right."

I turn to face him. "It's perfect. All my favorite things are right here." I settle a hand on his chest. "You promised I could play with you when we were alone again."

He hums his agreement. "I did say that."

"And we're definitely alone."

His eyes darken as my fingers drift down his broad chest. "Then it looks like I'm yours to do with as you please."

I slide a hand under the hem of his shirt, the fabric bunching as I smooth my fingers over his warm, tattooed skin. Connor bows to make it easier for me to pull the shirt over his head. He straightens and runs a hand through his hair, smoothing out the strands. They settle obediently back into place.

I trace the cursive letters on his chest that spell *Catch Me* above a falling angel. His entire chest, stomach, arms, and back are covered in pieces that tell his story. Some are vibrant in full color, like the landscape that frames his chest on either side of the black-and-white angel. Flowers trail over his right shoulder, leading to a wolf on his bicep. Trees wrap around his forearm, and a gorgeous, full-color loon floats on the surface of a calm lake. His left arm is covered in mythology, gods and angels from history tumbling across his skin. "Your art is magnificent." I skim the wings of the falling angel, his muscles jumping under my touch.

"I'll tell my artist you said so the next time I see her."

A spike of heat shoots down my spine. "You must see her fairly regularly."

"Most of the pieces require multiple sessions."

"I'm sure that's a real hardship for her." I don't mean for it to come out with bite, but it does.

He grins. "You sound jealous, wife." He cups my cheek in his palm.

"Maybe I should come with you next time," I suggest. "So I can see if there's anything to be jealous of." How deep into his life will he let me go? How close do I want to get?

"If you'd like." He tucks my hair behind the ear with the falling star tattoo. "Maybe you want to add to your own art."

"I just might." I pop the button on his pants and pull the zipper down.

Connor's lids are low, his eyes sparking as I tug his pants down his thick, muscular thighs, leaving him in nothing but boxer briefs and socks. He's all taut muscles—broad shoulders, a defined chest, and rippling abs all painted in stunning designs. His deep V disappears under the black waistband of his boxer briefs. His erection presses against the fabric.

He watches me intently as I follow the line bisecting his abs and gently cup him through his boxers. His eyes slide closed, and goose bumps rise along his skin as I curve my hand around him through the cotton and stroke from base to tip. Connor's head falls forward on a deep groan.

When was the last time I touched someone like this? It's been ages since I've come for anyone but myself—apart from last night.

My hand leaves his body, and his eyes flip open, flashing with disappointment. Until I pull my sweater over my head and let it fall to the floor—then they ignite with lust.

"Would it be fair for me to undress you if you're undressing me, darling?" His voice is low and guttural.

"Was it fair of you to deny me the chance to touch you last night?"

"You were in quite the state," he reminds me. "I wanted you to have a clear head before you started doing things you might have reconsidered come morning."

"But you denied me again this morning," I remind him as I trace the letters on his chest.

"In the name of hydration and time with your friends," he counters as he kisses the back of my hand. "Evil, I know, but I was thinking of your personal well-being and happiness."

I sigh. I was hungover this morning. I doubt I would have appreciated him the way I can now. "I suppose, in the spirit of giving, we could undress each other."

"Mm..." He kisses my shoulder and reaches behind me, flicking the clasp of my bra. "Such a sweet, generous wife." The fabric slides down my arms, and I let it fall to the floor as Connor drops to one knee. He rids me of my pants, then my socks and panties. But he doesn't make a move to touch any aching part of me. Instead he presses his lips to my strawberry blossom and ladybug tattoo. "So pretty and delicate."

He looks up at me. "What should we do now that all our secrets are on display, darling?"

I pull myself up onto the bed and slide back, patting the space to my right. "Come join me."

He climbs up and stretches out. I'm five six, so slightly above average, but Connor is huge, well over six feet of broad, thickly muscled, tattooed man. Yet I feel safe with him, comfortable and protected. When his head rests on the pillow I straddle his thighs and settle my bare pussy over his still-covered erection.

Connor exhales on a groan. "Little menace."

Palms splayed on his chest, I roll my hips, rubbing my clit against him as I dip down and brush my lips over his. Between one breath and the next, he flips us over.

"What are you doing?" I run my fingers through his hair. "I thought it was my turn to play with you."

"I've been thinking about that." He kisses my chin. "And how unbalanced things have been."

"Unbalanced how?" I'm already breathless and aching for his touch.

Sure, I can get off without contact, but it takes so much mental effort. Everything has to be perfect, my mind clear with no distractions and the right voice in my head, whispering all the things I want to hear.

He peppers kisses along my jaw. "You've been playing with me for a while now, being sneaky about it, like the pretty devil you are."

"I don't know what you're talking about." My eyes fall closed as his lips skim my neck. His tongue presses against my clavicle, followed by a gentle grip of teeth that sparks heat between my thighs.

"Of course you don't." He takes my earlobe in his mouth.

"What sneaky things have I done?"

"Falling asleep in the library every night."

I bite back a grin. "I'm not being sneaky. I like it there, and it feels safe."

"You like it when I carry you back to bed."

I love it when he carries me back to bed. "I'd be fine on the couch," I assure him in a bored voice. "I've told you as much."

He makes a noise in the back of his throat, lips skimming my collarbone. "You never have enough blankets."

"I don't need more blankets when you insist on relocating me every night," I argue.

"You're proving my point, darling, not your own." His cheek brushes my nipple, and he lifts his gaze. "Close your eyes for me."

"Why?"

"I want to play a game with you."

My apprehension must be written all over my face.

"If you don't like it, we'll stop. But I think you might not be opposed." Another soft kiss. "Have I taken good care of you so far?"

I swallow down the anxiety. "Yes."

"Do you trust that I always want to make you happy?"

I soften at the hope and fear swimming behind his eyes. "Yes, Connor, I trust you." I close my eyes.

The weight of his body leaves me.

I crack a lid. "What are you doing?"

"Eyes closed." When I comply, he leans over me and presses his velvet lips to each lid. "I'm going to worship every inch of you, like a good, devoted husband."

His hair tickles my neck as he kisses the hollow of my throat.

The sound of our breathing fills the room, and the bed dips just before his hair brushes my collarbones. Anticipation makes my heart race as he leaves several open-mouthed kisses on the swell of my breasts, the deep rumble from his chest heating me from the inside.

His breath tickles my skin. "Would you like to keep playing?"

"Yes, please."

His fingers find mine, and he brings them to his cheek. "Can I trust you to keep your eyes closed?"

"Yes, you can trust me."

"Such a sweet menace." He kisses my fingertips and the warmth soaks into my skin, rushing through my veins.

Something tickles my stomach—not his fingers, or his hair or his mouth. I gasp and shiver. "What is that?"

"Tell me how it feels." Another soft sweep across my belly, followed by the scrape of his teeth on the edge of my jaw.

I moan and sigh, already in love with the discordant sensations. "It's a...feather?"

"That's right, darling." His lips close around a nipple, sucking softly as that feather brushes between my thighs. He follows with a nip of teeth, a gentle swipe of tongue, and a rough suck.

Every time I think he plans to kiss or touch me where I want it most, he moves away. His mouth dips lower, past my navel. Warm, wet kisses anoint my overheated skin, my soft sighs and his groans filling the space around us.

All I am is want. I'm drenched in desire as sensation spirals. I grip the sheets, toes curling as he circles and circles, closing in.

"Connor, please..." I whimper.

"Do you want the game to end?" His lips brush the juncture of my thigh with every word.

"You're pure evil." I groan, hips rolling against nothing.

"The devil himself," he agrees.

He pushes my legs wide, and then his hot mouth is on me, tongue sliding over sensitive skin, the sharp bite of teeth against my inner thigh. The featherlight brush of his hair across my stomach nearly undoes me.

I'm shaking with need. Desperate for release.

And then his tongue glides through my slit, and the nip of teeth sends a shockwave through me. Connor's deep groan vibrates against me, followed by deliciously rough suction. I bow up off the bed, toes curled, sheets fisted in my hands.

His mouth leaves me for one painful, interminable moment. "Open your eyes and look at me when I'm feasting on your perfect cunt, darling," he demands.

I blink against the sudden brightness, taking in the sight of my husband, his broad shoulders forcing my legs wide, tattooed arms looped around my thighs, dark eyes heavy with lust.

He licks up the length of me and latches onto my clit. I come in violent waves, moaning his name, pussy contracting around nothing as he laves me. It's intense—overwhelming and not enough at the same time. I grip his hair and yank viciously when I can't take any more. He presses a kiss to my clit and prowls back up my body, lethal and gorgeous and mine—*for now*, I can't help reminding myself. I vow to enjoy every last minute while I have him.

"I need you inside me." I push his boxer briefs over his hips —somewhere along the way his socks have disappeared, maybe while he making me come with his mouth? Freeing his erection, I hook my leg over his hip, pulling him on top of me.

Connor gazes down at me, gentle fingers sliding into my hair. "Let me get a condom."

There's a heart-shaped box on the nightstand. He flips it open, grabs a foil square, and quickly rolls it down his length. And then he settles between my thighs, erection sliding over slick skin. Time slows. His face is a mask of desire as our bodies align.

He tenderly cups my face in his hands, the tremble nearly imperceptible. "If we go forward, we can't go back," he whispers.

"I know." I touch his cheek. "Please, Connor."

He pushes inside in one smooth stroke, a full-body shudder rolling through him.

This is so much more than sex. It's more than sensation and

need. I feel my heart opening as his lips brush mine and he whispers my name like a prayer.

In this perfect place, hidden away from the rest of the world, I can forget about the contract I signed. About the time limit we've set. About the reasons I said yes.

Here in this moment, I am claimed and claiming. I'm his, and he's mine. And I never want us to end.

CHAPTER 29
CONNOR

I wake up wrapped around my wife for the second time in as many days.

My *wife*.

Mildred's breathing is slow and even. We stayed up late last night, giving in to the chemistry that's been steadily building over the past several weeks. I'm afraid to move, to break this peace. What if last night was a culmination of all the stress of our engagement? What if she changes her mind and decides sleeping together is a bad idea?

Unfortunately, my bladder is screaming at me, so I carefully slide my arm out from under her and ease out of bed.

When I return a minute later, Mildred has rolled into my spot and stolen my pillow.

She cracks a lid when the floor creaks. I freeze, waiting to see what will happen. She blinks at me, eyes still heavy with sleep, but her gaze warms as it moves over my mostly naked form.

She shifts over and pats my pillow. "Come back and cuddle me."

Relief is warm in my veins. I climb back into bed and stretch out next to her, slipping my arm under her.

She moves into the crook and wiggles around, grumbling,

"Still not close enough." She pulls herself on top of me, tucking her head under my chin.

"Are you feeling exceptionally affectionate?" I run my hand up and down her back, skimming the tiny doves tattooed below her shoulder blade that I discovered last night. "Or are you horny?"

"Probably more the former than the latter, but you're poking me in the stomach, and other parts of my body are getting ideas, even if they're a little sore. Should I move? Is this too much for you?"

"It's not too much." I like that she wants to be close to me, whatever the reason.

"Do you want to be this close to me?" She traces the angel wings on my chest.

"Yes." I run my fingers down her spine. "I'll take any excuse to be in your orbit, no matter how villainous."

"Did your parents hug you when you were a kid?" She kisses my chest, right over my heart, as if she already knows the answer.

"Not really. We had nannies. Sometimes they were affectionate, but those ones never lasted long."

She lifts her head, chin resting on my chest. "Why not?"

"Jealousy, probably? Once I called one of the nannies Mom by accident. She was gone the next day." I was five. My mother had been in the other room and overheard. She slapped the nanny. I'll never forget my mother's rage, the nanny's shock, or how angry I was at myself for ruining something good.

"I'm so sorry." Mildred slides her arms under my back and squeezes me.

I wrap my arms around her and squeeze back. "I'm guessing you didn't get many hugs, either."

"No." She rests her cheek on my chest so I can't see her eyes, but I hear the sadness. "My parents were too high to pay attention to me most of the time. And when they did… Usually it was better if they just ignored me or forgot I was there."

Rage, violent and consuming, hits me in a rush. If they weren't already gone, I would hunt them down and find a way to make them pay.

She kisses the bottom of my chin, probably sensing my sudden tension. "I survived all the bad things, Connor."

"You shouldn't have had to endure them in the first place."

"Neither should you, but here we are. Bad parents are bad parents. It doesn't matter if they're poor drug addicts or rich assholes. They do damage, and we either survive and thrive to spite them, or we repeat history." She shifts, pulling herself higher. "I'm going to kiss you now, and we're going to stop talking about things that hurt us and instead we'll focus on the things that make us feel good, okay?"

"Yes, darling."

―◆・D・A・R・L・I・N・G・◆―

"You're terrible at this game." Mildred is all smiles as she kicks my ass for the tenth time at Mastermind.

"Or maybe I'm letting you win so I can see your face light up with evil glee," I offer.

"Or maybe you're just really bad at it," she quips.

"It is a possibility," I agree. "I haven't had nearly the same opportunities as Flip to hone my board game skills."

"Practice makes perfect."

"As evidenced by your winning streak."

Mildred uncrosses her legs with a groan.

I frown. "Are you okay?"

"Oh, I'm great. Just not used to sex with a hockey player." She stretches her legs and wiggles her toes on another groan.

"Why don't I run you a bath, and you can have a soak?" I suggest.

"What will you do?"

"I'll sit with you." As if there's anything else I'd rather do.

She perks up. "In the bath?"

"I barely fit in there on my own, and we both know if I get in with you, there would be no relaxing, and we'd only add to your soreness."

She gives me sweet-menace eyes. "What if I want to add to the soreness?"

I kiss her forehead. "Bath first. Then we'll see if you're ready to play with me again."

"This is my honeymoon! Shouldn't I get to decide if I'm ready to play with you or not?" she calls after me.

I poke my head back into the living room. "It's my honeymoon, too."

I leave her pouting and start the bath, adding strawberry-vanilla bubbles. I grab her book from the nightstand and move one of the occasional chairs next to the tub before I return to the living room.

"I can walk." Her voice is laced with amusement as I scoop her up.

"You should save your energy." I nuzzle into her neck. "In case I decide you're in good enough condition to play later."

"The important parts are in perfectly good condition. It's my thighs that are sore." She kisses my neck. "And my abs. And basically everywhere else."

"It's interesting what you deem unimportant." I set her on the bathmat.

The tub is positioned so it, too, has an amazing view of the lake. Candles cover the surface of the vanity and the small table next to the bath. I even poured her a glass of sparkling grape juice, since she usually reserves alcohol consumption for nights out with friends.

"It's so pretty in here."

"It matches you, then." I peel her out of her clothes. Every time it feels like unwrapping the most precious gift. Once she's beautifully naked, I help her into the tub.

She sinks into the hot water with a groan, the bubbles covering all her soft, tempting parts. She reclines, letting her hair spill over the edge as her eyes fall closed. "Oh, this is nice."

My chest warms with satisfaction.

I nab one of her many scrunchies from the vanity and move behind her. Running my fingers through her hair, I gather the thick strands and pull them into a messy bun, securing it.

"Thank you."

"My pleasure." I move the book from the chair and take a seat. "I thought I could read to you."

"My very own narrator." She sinks down until her chin brushes the bubbles. "Go on, then."

I flip to a bookmarked passage and skim the contents.

"And don't skip the spicy parts," she warns, still smiling.

"I wouldn't dare." I start reading, the scene playing out, tension shifting on the pages and in the room as the hero and heroine push each other's buttons. "These two should just fuck and get it over with," I muse as I flip the page.

"Soon. It's all about the buildup." She sighs.

"Have you read this one before?" I flip to the next page, skimming ahead.

"It's a comfort read."

"There's a lot of tension for a comfort read."

"That's the point."

I continue where I left off, the conflict between the two rising right along with the heated tension. And then they break. The water sloshes as Mildred shifts, her hands disappearing beneath the surface as the hero's fingers skim the heroine's curves and slide into her panties.

Mildred's eyes meet mine. "Don't stop reading."

"Are you playing without me?" I shift to sit on the edge of the tub.

"If you got in, you could play with me, too." The water laps against the swell of her breasts.

"I think I like the view from here." I drag my fingers through the bubbles, displacing them, giving me a brief glimpse of her hands dragging down her thighs, and then her delicate fingers dipping between.

I keep reading for a few more paragraphs, the hero and heroine giving in to the chemistry raging between them, eyes flicking up to Mildred between sentences, taking in her parted lips, pink cheeks, and lust-filled eyes as the couple embraces their basest, darkest desires and he fucks her in the stairwell of their apartment, where anyone could find them. Mildred shudders and sighs, eyes falling closed as she reaches her peak. *That's my wife.*

When the scene ends, I set the book on the chair and grip the edges of the tub, leaning down to brush my lips over hers as I whisper, "What's your darkest fantasy, darling?"

Her bottom lip slides through her teeth, gaze shifting to the side, hands still between her thighs. "Why?"

"Because I want to know what gets you hot, aside from me reading to you." I drag my hand through the slowly dissipating bubbles.

"I don't want you to judge me," she whispers.

"My sweet wife." I thrill at the way she softens whenever I say those words. I brush my lips over hers again. "I did unholy things to a sandwich out of spite. I won't judge you for the things that turn you on."

She bites back a smile, and her eyes search mine. I see the moment she decides she can trust me with this part of herself. "Being watched, watching, the thrill of being somewhere we could get caught."

"Like when I caught you in your car, listening to one of your books?" I ask.

Her eyes spark. "Yes, exactly like that."

I let my fingers dip under the surface, skimming her thigh. "I like watching you." I brush her hand out of the way. "The way you soften." I ease a finger inside her, pumping slowly. "The pretty sounds you make."

She whimpers.

"How quiet you'd have to be if I fucked you somewhere I shouldn't." I rub her clit. "Like the dining room table at home while the staff are in the kitchen."

She moans.

"Or your favorite couch in the library while Ethel is cleaning your rooms."

"Oh, God..." She arches and groans.

"In the powder room during a family gathering at my parents' house."

Her hips swivel, and she grips her breast.

"Or maybe you'd prefer my childhood bedroom?"

She grips the tub, water trickling over the edge.

"I'd love to eat your pretty cunt while you're sitting on my desk—with my family downstairs, talking about things that don't matter, completely unaware that I'm having dessert before dinner."

She comes apart for me, shaking and moaning.

When she's capable of moving, I help her out of the tub. It's warm today, and boats are sprinkled over the lake. Canoes and kayaks drift by. I move her to stand in front of the window, dry her off with a fluffy towel, and pluck her lotion from the vanity.

"Do you think they can see us?" she murmurs.

"I hope so." Goose bumps rise on her skin as I press my lips to the nape of her neck. I take my time, rubbing lotion into her, starting with her arms, moving down her back and thighs before I stand in front of her, smoothing lotion over her breasts, stomach, and legs.

When my wife is moisturized, I sit her in the chair facing the window, spread her wide, drop to my knees and bury my face in her sweetness. She slides her hands into my hair, legs draped over the arms of the chair, eyes fixed on me as I lap at her, suck and nibble and fuck her with my tongue until she comes all over it.

I strip off my shirt, pull her to her feet, and help her into it before I open the sliding door.

"What are you doing?"

"Fulfilling a fantasy for both of us." I take her hand and lead her outside, onto the deck. There are people on the water, and we can hear our neighbors laughing and talking next door, likely also enjoying the warm weather and the beautiful view.

I move her to stand in front of the railing, my chest to her back, and place her hands on it, my fingers laced through hers. I kiss a path up her neck, lips at her ear. "Would you like me to fuck you right here, with our next-door neighbors close enough to hear your pretty whimpers?"

She pushes her ass out, rubbing against my already hard cock. "Oh my God, yes."

"You're always safe to change your mind, Mildred, if you decide it's not what you want." I kiss her cheek.

"I know." She tips her head back, seeking my lips.

I cover her mouth with mine, sliding my other hand down to cup her through the fabric of my shirt. She rubs herself against me, and I push my joggers down, freeing my cock.

The neighbors laugh and the smell of something cooking on the barbecue filters over. I release Mildred long enough to pluck the condom from my pocket, tear it open, and roll it down my length.

Mildred grabs the railing and pushes her ass out. Flipping her shirt up, I run my hand over her soft skin, dipping between her thighs to stroke her clit before I grip my cock and rub the head between her pretty pink lips. She hums quietly, glancing over her shoulder, her bottom lip between her teeth.

I curve one hand around her hip and push inside. She moans, not quite as quietly as I'm sure she intends. I grin when her eyes flare and the conversation next door ceases for a moment. I lean into her, cock sliding deeper, lips at her ear.

"Shh, darling, unless you want our neighbors to know how lovely you sound when you're being fucked."

She shudders, pulsing around me.

"Little menace, are you coming for me already?" I whisper.

She nods, lip sliding through her teeth.

"Maybe you do want them to know how well I take care of my precious bride." I pull my hips back, sliding out to the ridge, then slam back in.

She sucks in a breath, legs trembling.

"See that couple in the kayaks on the lake?" I nod to the water, and her gaze follows mine. "I'm sure we look like a sweet couple, just enjoying the view." I gather up her shirt, twisting it, exposing her from the waist down. "But they can't see your gorgeous cunt dripping pretty cum down the inside of your thighs the way I can, and they can't hear the sweet sounds you make when I fill you up, can they, darling?"

"N-n-no."

"But you wish they could, don't you?" I kiss her cheek.

"Oh my God," she groans on a whisper.

"It's okay to admit it, darling." I pull out and slide back in. "I wish they could see how stunning you are when you're stretched around my cock, but then I'd have to end them because you're mine, aren't you?"

"I'm y-y-yours," she stammers.

Birds flutter in the trees above us, squirrels skitter away, and the easy laughter from next door has disappeared. Quiet, scandalized whispers follow. "They know, darling."

She makes the most beautiful mewling sound.

"We should give them something to talk about, shouldn't we? Maybe we can help spice up their sex life."

She moans, wantonly, perfectly. I kiss her cheek.

"Hold on, darling, we're going to make a scene."

She scrambles to grab the railing as I grip her hips and pound into her. Our skin makes wet slapping sounds, and Mildred's moan makes the birds take flight, expressing their displeasure at the disturbance.

She comes, my name the most glorious, desperate whimper,

and I fuck into her one last time, holding her tightly as the orgasm rushes through me. We're both panting and sweaty, neither of us giving a shit about being quiet.

Our neighbors' sliding door closes with a bang.

"I hope they took notes."

Mildred giggles, and it's the most beautiful sound. "Who's the menace now?"

"Me." I carry her back inside and keep her in bed for the rest of the day.

CHAPTER 30
DRED

It's everything I can do not to groan as I drop into a crouch and slide the book back onto the very bottom shelf in the fiction section of Toronto Central Library. I shut down the memories that accompany every ache and pain. It's a real shock to step into reality after the weekend away with Connor. *My husband.* And my thighs don't lie—it was one hell of a weekend.

Annulling this marriage isn't an option anymore since we consummated the hell out of it on every surface available.

I grip the edge of the trolley with one hand and the shelf with the other and grit my teeth as I stand, my quads screaming. I might need to join Essie for yoga classes if I plan to survive the next year.

On the upside—or the downside, depending on what part of my body is commenting—Connor is on an away series for the next four days, so my poor thighs will have a chance to recover. I finish shelving the rest of the books, then return to the front desk.

My stomach lurches when I see a familiar figure standing there, talking to Dorothea. I leave the cart next to the return bin and rush over, palms already sweaty. "Mr. Grace, this is unexpected. Is Connor okay? Is Meems?" She was fine when I left this morning. Tired, which is common these days with the strain on her heart, but she was happy. Every doctor's appointment is status quo right now. She still doesn't qualify for surgery, but her heart is holding on.

He regards me with cool indifference. "Shouldn't you know these things since you live in my mother's house, and you're married to my son?"

Dorothea gives me a disparaging look, like she agrees—fuck you very much, Dorothea—and disappears into the office, leaving me alone with Connor's father. I ignore his question. Obviously Meems is fine and so is my husband. One of my friends would be standing here if the latter was an issue. The way my chest tightens at the thought is telling.

I clasp my hands then drop them to my sides. "How can I help you?"

His eyes move over me. "I doubt you have skills I would deem helpful, although my son seems to believe otherwise."

The way that one sentence picks at deep, old wounds is startling. No wonder Connor can't stand himself most of the time. To have one of the people who's supposed to love you unconditionally constantly shred your self-esteem would be devastating.

Anna, one of the local unhoused women who often spends time here, lopes by with a coffee. Her family has been around to clean her up and take her to the thrift store recently, based on her attire.

Duncan's lip curls as she waves hello, and he tucks his hand in his pants pocket, turning back to me. "How much of your programming here relies on outside funding, would you say?"

"I... A lot, I guess." We have monthly meetings to discuss our funding, apply for new grants, write proposals to acquire donor money for the accessible programming. We rent out spaces to local community organizations to bring in extra money and allocate it for resources.

He nods and hums. "Through the foundation, our family

donates an exceptional amount of money to worthwhile organizations."

"I can imagine you do."

His smile turns cold. "I suppose until recently that's all you could do, wasn't it? Just imagine."

I swallow past the horrible lump forming in my throat.

"Do you think you're worthwhile?"

My stomach twists. "I don't understand what you're asking."

His icy gaze holds mine. "Don't you, though? You're nothing but an opportunistic whore. Having the Grace name will never make you one of us. You're nothing but a distraction for my son. He'll get tired of you, *Dred*."

Duncan smooths a hand over his tie, lip twitching with satisfaction. "Don't get comfortable, sweetheart. Everything you have can disappear." He snaps his fingers. "Just like that." His smile is full of malice as he spins around and walks away.

I reach for the hair tie around my wrist, but there isn't one.

Everything he's accused me of is a fresh slice on an unhealed cut. This morning money appeared in my bank account and a big part of me ached over it, because the weekend I'd just spent with my husband had felt so real. I'd shared pieces of myself with him, invited him inside me. But the fragile fairy tale broke the moment that money hit my account. I can care about Connor, but it doesn't change the fact that I signed a contract to be his wife.

My body is numb, my blood turned to ice in my veins. A young woman comes up to check out a book, and I woodenly go through the process, attempting polite and friendly when all I feel is devastation. Once she's taken care of, I slip into the breakroom, hoping to have a minute to calm the hell down. But Dorothea is in there with several other staff, and the tone is somber.

"What's going on?" A sinking feeling amplifies as I absorb the faces of my colleagues. They look as destroyed as I feel.

"We just lost our biggest donor." Kenny runs a rough hand through his hair.

And in that moment, I'm certain it's the work of the man who just walked out the door. That he'd spite Meems like this, just to hurt me, takes my breath away.

"We'll have to cut so many programs if we can't find a new one," Odette says.

"Do we have anywhere else to pull from?" I already know we don't. All that money for services rendered is likely accounted for. The fundraising gala will be more important than ever if we've just lost our primary funder.

"We'll have to audit everything that isn't necessary," Dorothea informs us.

Anxiety grips my heart. "Will we have to cut programs that are already in session?"

"I'm not sure yet," she admits. "We'll have to run all the numbers, but anything that isn't tied to schools or doesn't have city funding will likely have to go."

That's basically everything under my umbrella. "I can start writing proposals. Maybe we'll be able to bridge the programming." The moms-and-tots programs, all the things I've set in place, are at risk—all because Connor's father wants to cause me pain for wearing a name he doesn't think I deserve.

But maybe he's right. I didn't earn the Grace name. I just happened to be the damsel in distress, looking for a way out of the hole that had been dug for me. I'm using Connor, and Connor is using me. It comes with a price, and this is it.

But it felt like something real this past weekend. It's felt like something real for a while.

"We'll figure it out," Kenny says. He looks to me. "You could talk to your husband. I'm sure he'd be happy to help."

I look at him blankly. Telling Connor will only cause more problems. And I certainly cannot tell Meems and risk the strain on her already struggling heart. But I can run the numbers for my own programs and pull from my enhanced savings. "I'll see what I can do."

I spend the rest of the day researching grant opportunities and emergency funding sources between my regular duties, feeling exhausted and overwhelmed by the time I leave work. My phone pings with new messages as I trek up the steps of the subway to my car, which is currently one of Connor's cars. Driving around in a Rolls-Royce is highly conspicuous, so I park on the subway line and take the train to work. Connor took Betty to the mechanic, and she's undergoing extensive surgery because I refuse to give her up, and Connor refuses to let me drive her until she's been serviced properly. This is the least-expensive car option available in Connor's garage, unless I let him buy me something new, which I will not.

> **MEEMS**
> Cedrick will not bring Taco Bell home for me.

> **DRED**
> It is a questionable life choice.

> **MEEMS**
> It's what I feel like eating today. Nothing else will do.

> **DRED**
> 😊 You have to eat, Meems.

> **MEEMS**
> I know. And I will eat Taco Bell.

> **DRED**
> 😊 What do you want?

> **MEEMS**
> Doritos Locos Taco Supreme combo and birthday churros.
>
> Please.

> **DRED**
> Not the healthiest options, but okay.

MEEMS
Can you also stop at McDonald's and get me a nugget Happy Meal with a vanilla shake?

> **DRED**
> 🙁 What about some vegetables?

MEEMS
There are potatoes.

> **DRED**
> They don't really count, especially when they're deep-fried.
>
> Also, these don't seem like the best choices for someone who is hoping to have heart surgery.

MEEMS
I ate oatmeal for breakfast and grilled chicken and vegetables for lunch. I deserve a treat once in a while.

> **DRED**
> Okay. I'll get you all the bad things, but only if you'll also eat a side salad.

MEEMS
Deal.

CHAPTER 31
CONNOR

There are two minutes left in the third period. Ryker has managed a shutout, and we are up one goal against New York. I get into position as Bowman barrels down the ice with the puck. Madden is on his tail, trying to steal, but this is Bowman, and his stick-handling skills are second to none.

But I have the benefit of years with him on the ice. I've learned every move he has, and I understand his subtle shifts in posture, anticipating what's next.

"Watch his wrist shot," Ryker warns.

I see what he's saying half a second before Bowman makes his move. It's all the time I need. I manage to deflect it, passing the puck to Romero, who shoots it to Madden.

He takes off down the ice, Stiles and Bright flanking him. New York's defense is still trying to get into position. Madden sees the opportunity, lines it up, and shoots the puck. It goes wide, but Stiles snags it, passing to me. I assess the odds. I can pass to Madden, but everyone is on him, and Bowman is in position, so I send a prayer to the hockey gods and take the shot. Another player tries to intercept it, but instead he taps it with his blade, changing the angle and sending it through the goalie's five-hole.

Romero and Bright slam into me, whooping and giving me back pats. The last minute of the game is a scramble, but we maintain the shutout and win the game.

It's a whirlwind after that, and we're all riding the high of the win when we reach the locker room.

Madden gives me a chin tip. "Nice work out there tonight, Grace. That was a beautiful goal."

I brush off the compliment. "We would have won regardless."

"Doesn't make it any less impressive."

"He's right. That was beautiful, and every goal counts," Romero agrees. "Especially against New York."

"Thanks." I nod to Madden.

He grins and pats me on the back. "Maybe it's the Dred effect."

"Maybe." I drop my head to hide my grin and focus on unlacing my skates.

I didn't want our honeymoon weekend to be over. I wanted endless days of board games and reading her spicy romance aloud, breakfast in bed, exploring every inch of her body on repeat, making her come, hearing my name tumble from her lips on a whisper, a moan, a plea. But reality called, and I had to answer.

Two more days and I can get my fill of her again—if she wants me. If she wasn't just caught up in the honeymoon vibe. Or maybe she was stuck with me for those uninterrupted days and fucking was a way to pass the time.

We shower and change into suits. A couple of the guys suggest grabbing drinks in the lobby bar, but pictures of me at a bar with my teammates a few days after my wedding will bring the vultures out.

Saying no to the team without an explanation, even though no one expects one from me, isn't helpful. Mildred is right. If I let them, these guys could be like family. If I shift my role with my team—and the people Mildred cares about the most—maybe I'll be so ingrained in her life, she won't want to give me up.

"I'd love to hang out, but the media are looking for a reason to put me in the headlines." Whether it's related to my career is irrelevant. "I'd like to stay out of their viewfinders when potential fans are around."

Madden nods. If anyone understands the gravity of this, it's him. "Why don't we hang in my room then?"

"That sounds good." I appreciate the pivot.

On the way up to Flip's room, I check my messages. I have new ones from Mildred. I've changed her contact in my phone to reflect our relationship status.

MY DARLING WIFE
Beautiful goal.

CONNOR
Thanks. How was your day?

MY DARLING WIFE
It was fine. You going out to celebrate the win?

CONNOR
Heading up to Flip's room for a bit. But I can stop in mine first if you want a call.

That's what I should have done in the first place.

MY DARLING WIFE
Don't do that. Go hang out with the boys. We can talk tomorrow.

Something feels off, and I want to dig around in that message and read into it, but I'm afraid to.

CONNOR
Everything okay?

> **MY DARLING WIFE**
> Just a busy day at work and I'm fading. I'm going to snuggle with your pillow. Have a good night.
>
> **CONNOR**
> 'Night, darling.

---D·A·R·L·I·N·G---

The following afternoon, after we've landed in Boston and settled into our rooms, we hit the ice for practice, and I decide to pump my coach for information. Aside from Flip—which I still don't love thinking about—Lexi is Mildred's best friend. If there's something going on, she might know about it before I do.

I'd like that to change. I'd like to be the person Mildred comes to first with every worry, secret, and piece of good news, but that will take time. And I'm not above digging to ease my own worries.

"Callie has a game tonight, right?" I ask conversationally as Coach Forrest-Hammer and I pass the puck back and forth.

Coach nods. "She does. I'm so grateful that Roman and Hollis can trade off during away games, especially with Fee in university this year. And Dred is a great backup when we need it," she adds.

"Mildred loves going to her games," I confirm. "We both do."

"She does," Coach Forrest-Hammer agrees. "But it's a lot to ask, and her circumstances have changed significantly recently."

"Have you talked to her today?" I ask.

"I talk to her every day." She arches a brow. "Have you?"

"She's my wife." As if that's an answer. I roll the puck down my stick and pass it to her. "She seem okay to you?"

Coach Forrest-Hammer shrugs. "A little distracted and tired.

She mentioned having a bunch of proposals to work on. The wedding stuff has kept her busy, so it might just be catch-up."

"Right. The last few weeks have been intense." We've been sprinting since she agreed to marry me. Maybe I'm right and now that we're back to real life, she has regrets—about marrying me, about letting me into her body, about sharing her secrets.

"You could send her something to let her know you're thinking about her," Coach suggests.

"That's a good idea." And one I should have thought of.

"It doesn't have to be elaborate." She flips the puck on her stick before sending it back to me. "Sometimes small and thoughtful can mean more than something extravagant."

"Noted."

"You care about her," Coach says softly.

"Does that surprise you?"

"Just because this started as something else doesn't mean it can't change, Connor. Roman and I are proof of that. So are Hemi and Dallas, and Hollis and Hammer, and Rix and Tristan. Where we end up doesn't have to be defined by where we began."

I open my mouth, but then Coach Vander Zee skates over, ending that conversation. Still, it hits where it's meant to. After practice, I check my phone and see that I have new messages.

> **MEEMS**
> You need to take your wife shopping.

> **CONNOR**
> Sure.

> **MEEMS**
> Her pants have holes in them.
> On purpose.

> **CONNOR**
> That's fashionable these days, Meems.

But I do love the idea of spending time with her, watching her try on clothes, dressing her in beautiful things.

CONNOR
I'll take her when I get back.

CHAPTER 32

DRED

HEMI
Watering Hole in an hour?

RIX
I can make it!

HAMMER
Obviously you know I can make it.

A picture of the two of them standing in the office together follows.

SHILPA
Please enjoy each other while I enjoy my sleeping nugget.

A photo of a tired but happy Shilpa snuggling her passed out baby follows.

TALLY
I have dance practice. Miss you. Sending my love!

LEXI

I'm in.

DRED

I wish I could, but proposals are calling my name. Eat some potato skins in my honor!

A new message pops up from Lexi in our private chat.

LEXI

You've been working on proposals for days. No pressure either way, but are you sure you can't take a little break?

DRED

I'm almost finished. Maybe later this week, though?

LEXI

Okay. Let me know if there's anything I can do to help.

DRED

Thank you. I appreciate you.

I toss my phone on the desk in the library at Grace Manor and flop back in the chair, removing my glasses so I can rub my tired eyes. Even if I hand over everything in my bank account, almost every program I have will have to be cut after this loss of funding. I've been scrambling since we got the news, and it's been a full-time job creating proposals for all of them. There's no guarantee the committee will see the value in them.

I haven't said anything to Connor. If he pushes, I'll tell him everything, and then his already tumultuous relationship with his family will be even more strained. I worry about the ripple effect on Meems, and his sisters.

Last night when he came home, we spent time with Meems, and then I dragged him straight to bed. I needed the escape and the connection. It seemed like he needed it just as much. And sex is a great way to keep our mouths and bodies busy and away from difficult topics.

My head is a mess, and my heart is already way too involved.

Two hours and another finished proposal later, Connor appears in the library. "I thought I'd find you in here." He's fresh from practice, dark hair styled and wearing a pair of jeans and a long-sleeved Henley, sleeves pushed up his forearms revealing a sliver of the story on his skin. He looks like he stepped out of an advertisement. He's also carrying takeout.

I close my laptop. "Just taking care of some work things."

"Still playing catch-up?"

"Yeah." I smile, but it feels stiff.

"You seem stressed." He sets the takeout on the desk, eyes moving over me.

"Work can be that way this time of year."

"Can I do anything to help?"

I reach for him, and he comes to me.

His palms curve around the armrests, and he leans down until our lips touch. "Besides distract you with kisses." He backs up, brows pulling together. "Or maybe it's you distracting me."

The problem with letting him in is that eventually he'll be able to read me in ways that will make it hard to hide things from him. I run my nails along his scalp, something I know he loves. "Did you bring me my favorites?"

"I did. Although they're my favorites, too."

"What about Meems?"

"She went to a friend's to play bridge, which means I get time with my wife." He kisses me again. "Are you hungry?"

"For food or you?"

"Food first. You can have me later."

"Such a meanie."

"So awful that I want to make sure you're nourished before I take you to bed and make you come until you're delirious."

I nod solemnly. "The absolute worst."

He smiles and I laugh, relieved that the time apart hasn't

changed things and glad for the break from the incessant worry. We unpack the takeout containers and settle in to eat. My appetite has been off since the day his father stopped by the library, but Connor went to the trouble to get all my favorites, and he's right—I won't be able to focus on anything if I don't eat.

"How was practice?" I pour dressing on my mango salad.

"It was good. This season feels different." Connor spoons tamarind curry over his rice.

"Different how?" I ask.

He taps his chopsticks on the edge of his plate. "Like I'm part of the team."

My heart squeezes. "And you haven't felt that way with the Terror before?"

"I haven't felt that way anywhere before," he admits.

"Not even when you were playing for New York?"

He shakes his head. "Having Kodiak on my side made it easier, especially since he was the team's golden boy, but I was still a problem. And then I was traded to Toronto and became even more of a problem."

"Because of Flip."

"Partly. But I have a reputation for pushing people's buttons, on and off the ice. I'm a good distraction."

"What's changed?" I ask, keeping my voice casual. He's opening up, letting me in.

He drops his head, eyes on his plate. "I want to be more than that." Connor clears his throat. "My entire life I've played this part. I've always been the outsider. It's all I've ever known, on and off the ice."

"But not anymore?" My stomach flips and twists. These feelings I have for Connor keep growing.

"My parents believe I chose this career to spite them, and I've fed into the belief that all I can be is the bad guy. But I want to leave more than a legacy of problematic behavior. I want to deserve my place on my team, and it's not just me who's affected anymore."

"You mean Meems?"

"I mean you. If you have to be married to me, at least you can be married to a player whose team doesn't hate him."

I set my plate aside and take his from him, moving it to my desk. I shift from my chair and settle in his lap, linking my fingers behind his neck. "My sweet villain."

"Not sweet at all. I want these things for entirely selfish reasons."

"And what reasons are those?"

"It makes you soft for me." He threads his fingers through my hair and kisses the edge of my jaw.

"Putty in your evil, plotting hands," I agree.

He pulls my mouth to his and licks inside.

I'm suddenly ravenous for him. Needy and desperate. Also, I'm terrified that if this conversation continues, I'll tell him my own truth, and that could change everything.

I slip out of his lap to kneel between his parted legs. His eyes darken as I run my hands up his thick thighs and reach for his belt.

"What are you doing, little menace?"

"What does it look like?" I unbuckle his belt, pop the button, and pull the zipper down.

"Like you have plans for me."

I slip my hand into his boxer briefs, my fingers closing around his length. He's already hard. I free him from the fabric and stroke him. His eyes heat, and he watches me with rapt fascination as I leave open-mouthed kisses on the shaft, working my way up to the head. I meet his hot gaze as I take him between my lips, licking him, sucking him.

"You're so beautiful." He skims my bottom lip with his thumb as I fuck him with my mouth, reveling in the way it feels when he looks at me like this—like I'm his world, like I'm the only thing he wants.

He frames my face with his hands, eyes flaring as he holds me immobile, his cock halfway down my throat.

"Connor, I didn't realize you were home. I was coming to see if Dred needed anything before I retired for the night," Ethel says from what sounds like the other side of the room.

I freeze, but I'm hidden behind the massive desk. Ethel has no idea I'm on my knees sucking off my husband.

He strokes my cheek with his thumb, the other hand leaving my face.

"We're fine," he grinds out. "Thank you, though. She just stepped out for a minute."

"Ah. I see. Well, tell her I said good night."

I apply suction.

His fingers press firmly against the hinge of my jaw. "I'll do that. Have a good night, Ethel," he says through gritted teeth.

"You too, sir."

Several seconds pass before his hands are on my face again, and he slides out of my mouth, tipping my chin up to kiss me roughly. "Did you want Ethel to know you were trying to swallow my cock, darling?" He rises, pulling me with him, and strips me out of my shirt. His lips ghost mine, fingers curved around my jaw. "Should I bend you over your desk and fuck you right here, with the door wide open, where anyone can walk by?"

I moan against his mouth.

He grins darkly. "I'll take that as a yes."

He spins me around, pulls my leggings and panties down, and moves me into position. A thrill shoots through me as he gently runs his hand down my spine. My chest and stomach meet the polished wood surface, and I turn my head, cheek pressing against discarded papers. Our half-finished dinner plates are a few inches away, takeout containers next to them.

He slips his fingers between my already trembling thighs. "Such a pretty, wet cunt." He pushes two fingers into me and folds over me to kiss my cheek. "I think I'll eat you later, when we're in bed and I can take my time. How does that sound, wife?"

"Yes, please."

"Such a sweet little menace." His fingers withdraw, and he quickly rolls a condom down his length and sheaths himself inside me in one smooth stroke. His body covers mine, his mouth at my ear. "You feel so fucking good, Mildred. So wet and hot and perfect." He slips a hand between my legs to rub my clit.

I come, spasming around him, groaning his name.

"Louder, darling, they can't hear you in the kitchen."

The heat of his chest leaves my back, and his fingers dig into my hips as he fucks into me, hard and fast. My pussy makes wet sucking sounds with every thrust, and it's all I can do to hold on and enjoy the ride as I careen into bliss, moaning his name through another orgasm.

And then he's close again, lips at my ear, whispering dirty praise as he comes. We don't make it to the bedroom before the next round. Instead, I end up on my back on the desk with Connor on his knees, my legs thrown over his shoulders as he buries his face between my thighs and makes good on his promise.

CHAPTER 33
DRED

I've just changed into something that isn't covered in my cum and Connor's saliva when my phone pings with new messages. I find it on the floor under the desk. My stomach lurches as Victor's name appears several times. I gave him and Everly my cell number when they started volunteering, so they could let me know if they would be late. Obviously I gave them the green light to contact me if they ever needed anything, be that school- or life-related. Their last message before today was me thanking them for their gift. Cordelia told me they paid for all on their own, which makes it even more special.

> **VICTOR**
> Are you at the library?
>
> I think maybe your shift is already finished.
>
> Everly is locked in the bathroom in the café down the street. She said she can't come out, and I don't know what to do.

> **DRED**
> I'm taking it Cordelia isn't an option?

VICTOR

Not really. Everly already got in trouble once today, and she'll be in even more trouble if I tell Cordelia. And I know she'll be in trouble no matter what, but she's really upset, and I just don't know what else to do.

DRED

Got it. I'm texting Everly now.

VICTOR

Thank you. 🖤

DRED

We'll get it worked out.

I switch to the private messages with Everly to start damage control.

DRED

Hey! Can you tell me what's going on? Victor seems concerned.

The inchworm dots appear, and it takes a minute before a message finally comes through.

EVERLY

I got my period on the way home, and I had to stop at the café. But it was a flood and my favorite jeans are ruined, and I can't leave the bathroom because I don't have anything to cover it up. I did my laundry yesterday, but then I forgot to put it in the dryer and everything stinks and I can't get another turn until tomorrow and I have no options and I will die of embarrassment if I have to leave the bathroom looking like a shark attacked my vagina.

> **DRED**
> I can be there in less than half an hour with a pair of pants. They won't be a perfect fit, but they'll be better than your current situation. Is there anything else you need?

> **EVERLY**
> Maybe tampons. The kind from the machine here suck. And they're a dollar each.

> **DRED**
> On it. I'll be there as quickly as I can.

I rush to my bedroom—most of my things have been moved to Connor's room, but a few items remain. I grab a pair of jogging pants and a variety of feminine products and stuff them all in a bag.

Connor's on the way up the stairs holding two plates of dessert as I'm on my way down.

His gorgeous brow furrows. "Where are you going?"

"I have a work emergency." Not a complete lie.

"Why are they calling you now? You're already bringing your work home with you and now this? It's after eight. Tell them you can't do it."

"There's no one else to handle it. I'll be back in a couple of hours."

He blocks me from descending. "I don't want a wife who lies to me."

"Well, that wasn't in the contract, was it, Connor?" We had such a nice night—if one considers being bent over a desk and fucked until my legs gave out nice, which I do—and now here I am, running out on him.

"A lot of things weren't in the contract, Mildred," he reminds me. Unfairly.

"You don't get to be picky about the kind of wife I am." Especially since I'm also the kind who tried to swallow his entire cock less than an hour ago.

I try to move around him, but he's fast, and bigger than me, so he blocks my every move.

"You're going to end up wearing that dessert in a moment, husband," I warn.

He arches one dark, delicious eyebrow. "Don't threaten me with a good time, wife."

I go with brutal honesty in the hope that it will ick him out. "Everly got her period. She's locked in a bathroom at a café and doesn't have a spare pair of pants. I'm bringing her some."

"Why is she asking you for help and not the group home?"

"Because she's somewhere she's not supposed to be already, and she's trying to avoid more trouble."

"Why didn't you just tell me that in the first place?"

"Because it's not your problem to solve."

He raises his chin and looks down at me with assessing, arrogant eyes. "I'm your husband. You're my wife. If you have a problem, I have a problem."

I wish he wasn't so hot when he's being like this. "Well, right now you're getting in the way of me solving a problem."

"I will drive you."

Arguing won't get me anywhere. "Fine."

"Good."

"Really leaning into the villainy, aren't you?" I snap and motion for him to lead the way.

"Oh, yes. It's positively evil of me to pick up all your favorite things for dinner, make you come so many times your legs give out and you almost lose your voice, then surprise you with a special dessert in your private library, but change plans and offer to drive you to help teens in need solely because I want to spend time with you." He sets the cake on the side table and picks up my jacket. "And it's an unbelievable level of horridness that I want to make sure you're warm since it's getting cooler at night."

"Or maybe you're just being a controlling psycho." I slide my arms into the sleeves, and he frees my hair from under the collar.

"Oh, darling, let's not kid ourselves. If anyone has control here, it's you." He kisses the edge of my jaw. "I would follow you anywhere, even into a burning building."

I unsuccessfully try to ignore the way my heart flutters. "We should take the cake for Everly and Victor," I suggest.

"I agree."

"I can carry it." I pick up both pieces and follow Connor out to his Rolls-Royce. He opens the door for me, takes the pieces of cake, and waits until I'm buckled in before he passes them back.

We're out on the street, heading for the café before he asks, "Why didn't you want to tell me where you were going?"

"Can we talk about this after we deal with the situation?" I get the sense if I tell him before, he'll blow a gasket, and having him angry while dealing with two parentless teens—one who hates rules and the other who hates broken ones—will be a recipe for disaster.

"You're keeping something from me." It's not a question.

"And you aren't?" I throw back at him.

We're both keeping plenty from each other. Whatever this was supposed to be has shifted in an irreversible way. I have feelings that don't align with the contract, and owning those while I'm already on edge seems like a bad plan.

He's silent for the rest of the drive, either stewing or brooding.

"I'll be out with the twins in a few minutes," I tell him when he stops at the curb in front of the café.

"I'll come with you."

"Everly is a fifteen-year-old girl who bled through her jeans and locked herself in a bathroom. You're a high-profile pro hockey player and very interesting, especially since you've married a commoner. She's crampy and bitchy and emotional and doesn't need the extra attention."

His nostrils flare.

I lean in and kiss his cheek. "Please tone your broody down a few notches. These two have been through a lot, and they need gentleness. You're welcome to reengage the furrow once we're home."

"I don't like that you're keeping me in the dark."

"I don't think you'll like being in the light any better, but I'll explain once this situation is dealt with and we're on the way home." I leave him in the car and enter the coffee shop.

Victor is standing by the bathroom, talking to a store manager. His expression shifts to relief the moment he sees me. "Dred, thank you so much for coming."

"Of course."

"Are you their guardian?" The manager gives me a doubtful look.

"Is that relevant?"

"That young woman has been in there for forty-five minutes!" He points to the bathroom door. "She's not even supposed to be here! She routinely comes in and orders a black coffee and a day-old scone and refills her coffee cup three times." He says it like it's a criminal offense.

"Refills on coffee are free," Victor says quietly. "It says so right on the sign above the drip coffee. And she didn't come in here for coffee, she just came in to use the bathroom."

"The bathroom is for paying customers! And she takes advantage of the policy."

"Then maybe you should change your policy," I say coldly. "And do you really think a teenage girl would lock herself in a gross public bathroom for forty-five minutes if she didn't have a good reason?"

The bell above the door tinkles. I glance over my shoulder. Every single head turns as my husband enters. I try to see him as others do, and not as the man I've started sharing a bed and a life with.

He's the picture of elegance, even in jeans. Dark peacoat, polished shoes, perfectly styled hair, and an air of arrogance that makes people take notice. He moves toward me, Victor, and the unhappy manager.

"I asked you to stay in the car," I remind him.

"I never agreed to your order, Mrs. Grace." He kisses my temple.

The manager's eyes bug out. "Oh my God, you're Connor Grace."

"It seems that way." He gives the manager a patient smile. "I believe we have a teenager in need locked in a bathroom. My wife is here to assist, and I'm happy to hand out some Terror swag for the minor inconvenience having me here might pose."

Connor pulls a stack of hockey cards out of his breast pocket and a felt-tipped pen, leaving me open to deal with Everly. Three minutes later, she's dressed in a pair of ridiculously oversized joggers, I'm holding a bag of ruined jeans—she was not being overdramatic—and Connor signs his last trading card.

We troop out to his car, and Everly and Victor pile in the back.

"Where to now?" Connor asks jovially, his dark attitude tucked safely away for now.

I twist in the passenger seat. "Can either of you explain why we're here and not Cordelia?" She's the group home's main point of contact for me.

Everly slouches in the seat and crosses her arms. "The manager banned me from the coffee shop, but it was the only place open with a bathroom, and obviously I needed one so I took my chances."

Victor and I exchange a look.

"Is that the only reason?" I press.

"I said I was going to the library, but I got the days mixed up and you weren't working, and that guy I was seeing for a bit was there. It got awkward, so I left." She sighs. "I wasn't causing problems. And then I got my period and ruined my favorite jeans!"

"We can get you new jeans," Connor says.

"I don't have money to buy new clothes," Everly replies.

"I have money. We'll go to the mall." Connor waits for me to pass the cake that's sitting on the dash to Everly and Victor before he starts driving.

I glance in the rearview mirror.

Victor and Everly are mouthing things to each other while holding their slices of cake.

"We can just go to Value Village. It's closer than the mall," Everly pipes up.

"What's Value Village?" Connor asks.

"A clothing store," I offer.

Five minutes later, we pull into the parking lot of a strip mall that contains a few big-box stores and a Value Village.

Everly and Victor hop out of the car.

Connor frowns, but exits the vehicle, and we follow them in.

I hand them both a shopping basket. "Go wild, kids."

"I don't need anything new," Victor replies.

"You might find something you like, though. And you can pick a few things for the other kids at the home."

His eyes light up. "Okay. I can do that." He heads for the men's section.

"This is a used clothing store," Connor murmurs.

I slip my arm around his waist. "They can't show up with designer clothes, Connor. The other kids at the group home will be jealous, and they could get rolled for their outfits. Or they'll just sell them, because the money is more important than brand names."

He gazes down at me, expression intense. "Do you know this from personal experience?"

I shrug. I've seen plenty of kids fight over shiny things. "Everly's too feisty not to get into it with people, and I'd like to save her from the potential fallout."

"You really care about these two," he muses.

"I understand their life."

We spend the next hour shopping for clothes. They pick something for each of the kids in the group home, and Everly comes out with two new pairs of jeans, a few shirts, and a sweater. Victor picks a button-down and a pair of dress pants for job interviews. We stop for food on the way back, which they eat in the car.

I accompany Victor and Everly into the group home so I can explain the situation, leaving out any details that might add to their trouble. Connor stays in the car this time.

Fifteen minutes later, I slide back into the passenger seat with a sigh.

"Everything okay?" he asks.

"They'll be fine." As far as group homes go, it's a good one.

We're halfway home when Connor finally asks the question I've been avoiding. "What secret are you keeping from me, darling?"

"Maybe we should wait until we're home," I suggest. I'm tired and sad. Everly and Victor have a group home with amazing staff, but it's not a replacement for a loving family and a stable environment. They have each other, but they deserve so much more.

"It's that bad?" Connor's voice sounds strained.

What scenarios must he be spinning? What secrets have people kept from him that make him so closed off and distrustful?

"We rely on donations to help fund most of the programs I run at the library, and that funding was pulled earlier this week." I start off with the truth that has less bite. "So I've been writing grant proposals."

"Why didn't you tell me? I can help with this. How much does the library need? Who was the donor, and why did they pull their funding?" Connor volleys questions at me.

I run my hands down my thighs and press my nails against my knees. "I don't have all the details, but I believe it was probably a division of Grace Hotels. A foundation, perhaps?"

"Meems wouldn't pull a donation from the library."

"No, she wouldn't," I agree.

He turns onto his street, brow furrowed.

Now to tell him the hard part. "Your father paid me a visit at the library while you were away." I don't need to say more. The dots are already connected.

"What did he say to you?"

"Nothing he doesn't believe is true."

He punches in the code, and the gates open. "Tell me what he said, Mildred."

"I don't really want to," I say softly.

Connor parks and we exit the vehicle. He follows me up the front steps.

Cedrick opens the door.

I force a smile.

"Is everything all right?" Cedrick asks.

"We're fine," I lie.

"Mildred and I would like privacy for the remainder of the evening," Connor clips out and heads for the elevator.

"Yes, sir." Cedrick rushes off, leaving me alone with my angry husband.

Thanks for the save, Ceddy.

Connor waits until we're in the elevator. "Tell me."

I'm too tired and sad to fight with him. "He said I would never be a Grace."

"You're my wife. You are a Grace."

"He also said I was a whore."

Connor's eyes flash, and for a moment I see the hockey player who doesn't mind being the villain on the ice. "That fucker."

"He's not wrong, though, is he, Connor? You're paying me to play this role." I hold up my hand with the massive diamond ring on it. "And we're fucking, so doesn't that make me exactly what he says I am?"

My stomach twists as his expression darkens.

"Nowhere in our contract does it say you're obligated to sleep with me."

"But we still have a contract." And isn't that the piece that I keep circling back to?

These feelings I have don't sit inside the written agreement. And his outrage at his father's behavior could be tied to so many things. Is he angry because he truly cares, or is it because my unhappiness directly affects all the things that are important to him?

I don't know for sure, and I'm too exhausted to handle whatever the truth might be.

"You are not a whore, Mildred. You are my wife, and you are a Grace whether my father likes it or not."

I wait for him to say more. To give me a piece of himself. To tell me the contract doesn't matter. But this is Connor. He's no more likely to hand me his heart than I am to hand him mine.

And where does that leave us but a standstill?

CHAPTER 34
CONNOR

I reinstate the funding for my wife's library programs by cashing in a few investments. I don't say anything to Meems, because I don't want to cause her stress, or my wife for the same reason. But I stew over the situation, marinate in my anger and frustration. Self-flagellate over the fact that I should have anticipated something like this, and I failed to put safeguards in place to protect Mildred from harm. Now she's overworked, and her colleagues are just as stressed as she is.

Of course Meems set up donations to the library through the company. Of course my father performed a financial audit and saw the opportunity to shit all over my wife, because he's an entitled, power-hungry asshole.

But more than that, it's the things he said to her, the way he cut her down, made her feel like less. Made me question her intentions when she got on her knees for me. Was she proving him right? Was she stepping into the role like I do with my family? It's hard to separate myself from my choices and not impose them on her.

And that's why I expect Mildred to stop sleeping in my bedroom, even though it's now *ours*. I expect her to stop sleeping with *me*. But she doesn't do either. Every night she climbs into bed. And each night I stretch out an arm, inviting her in. But I never stop being relieved when she snuggles into me and lets me soak up her warmth. She lets me kiss her in the dark, touch her, get inside her.

Still, the contract hangs over my head, its implications compounding. Does Mildred stay because it exists? Is financial security still her motive? She and Meems grow closer all the time. When I'm away, they play board games together, eat dinner together, and act like family should. They smile and laugh and love. I want all of it to be mine too, but I'm unsure what's real and what's linked to the money in Mildred's account. She never says anything about it.

Then today I get home from hockey practice to find a balloon arch and a huge banner that reads *Happy 75th Lucy* being fixed to the wall by Cedrick and Norm. My beautiful wife is standing in the middle of the room with her hands on her hips, directing them.

"Up a couple of inches, Cedrick." She tilts her head. "That's it! Right there!"

I stop several feet away, not wanting to startle her. "What's going on?"

She stiffens slightly, but doesn't turn. "We're throwing Meems a birthday party."

"I would have helped you organize this." More likely I would have paid people to organize it.

"It's just a small get-together." She still won't make eye contact.

"Who's coming?" Meems loves Mildred's friends. They get together every other week for book club, which seems mostly like an excuse to hang out and eat junk food.

Her jaw tics. "Your family."

"What?"

She turns to face me, finally, guard up, eyes flashing with defiance. "I invited your family over to celebrate Meems's birthday."

"Cedrick and Norm, can you leave us for a moment?"

"Of course, sir." They hastily finish tacking the banner in place and hustle out of the room.

"Why would you invite my family *here*?" I have yet to confront my father. In part because I don't want him to retaliate further, but also because I'm concerned I'll cause him bodily harm and end up in a cell. Apparently my time has run out.

"I thought it would be better to host here so Meems can excuse herself when she's tired." Mildred bridges the gap between us and smooths her palms up my chest. "I also thought it would be preferable to spending an afternoon at your parents' house, and I didn't feel as though Meems or your sisters should be punished because your father has feelings about me that aren't positive."

God, I fucking love you.

The thought is a shock, and those words stay locked inside me. "Are you sure you're not punishing yourself, darling?"

"I've been punished more than enough by other people," she informs me. "I don't need to do it to myself, too."

"You married me."

"Marrying you wasn't a punishment, Connor, even if you'd like it to be."

The doorbell chimes.

"They're here. Don't start a fight before we even get to cocktails." She kisses me on the cheek and threads her arm through mine.

"That's a very tall order."

"But isn't there real satisfaction in having your father come to the house you live in?"

"Mm..." I bring her hand to my lips. "You have a point, Dredful menace."

I can only imagine the feelings he must have about the fact that my wife, who he bullied, called a whore to her face, and whose job he put on the line, has invited him to the house he believes he deserves.

"Ahhh! Dred, we've missed you!" My sisters envelop her in a hug while my parents hang back, my brothers-in-law behind them, looking awkward.

"I've missed you, too!" Mildred says with genuine affection.

Mildred turns her bright smile on my parents, and instead of waiting for the customary air kisses from my mother, she pulls her in for a hug. I wish I could bottle Mother's shock.

Mildred links arms with my sisters and ushers them into the living room where Meems is waiting. I want to sit next to my wife, but my sisters flank her before I can get there.

Drinks are served and appetizers set out. My mother sips her martini, looking awkward and out of place in the Victorian-era chair she's claimed as hers.

"You've already started traveling, haven't you?" Isabelle asks.

"Yeah, the official season is underway," I say. None of my family watches hockey.

"Will you travel with Connor?" my mother asks Mildred.

She shakes her head. "No. I have work."

"Of course you do." Mother turns to me. "How is...work for you?"

I clear my throat. I'm shocked that she's asking about hockey. "It's been a solid start to the season."

"That's good." Mother turns to Portia. "Oh! You should show Meems your concept drawings for the living room makeover!"

So I guess we're done with that...

Julian and Bryson excuse themselves to the billiard room. Then Mother takes a call that she's been "waiting for all day." Portia and Isabelle want to see what Meems has done to the guesthouse, and that leaves me alone with my father.

"Your wife has certainly made herself comfortable here," he says flatly.

"Well, it is her home, so I suppose that makes sense." I swirl my scotch in my glass. "Mildred told me about your visit to the library."

A hint of a smile curves his mouth. "It's been weeks. I'm surprised it's taken you this long to bring it up."

"It wasn't a conversation I wanted to have on the phone, where you could hang up."

"You could have come to me sooner, asked me to reinstate the funding in person. Although you do tend to meet problems with violence."

"The only fights I get into are on the ice."

"Yes, I'm aware." He inspects his nails. "Such a waste of education. I should have sent Portia to Harvard instead of you."

"You owe my wife an apology."

"Why, when everything I said was true?" He stares down his nose at me, sighing with frustration. "Your problem, Connor, is that you never fall in line. You constantly make things harder than they need to be. I thought your career would finally be the end of it, but I misjudged your commitment to making this family look bad."

"Watch yourself, Father. You're in *my house*, and Mildred is *my wife*."

He throws his head back and laughs. "She's a user, Connor. She doesn't want you. She wants this life." He motions to our surroundings. "She comes from nothing. She *is* nothing. And it's only a matter of time before you come to your senses and see the truth. She's a distraction. A project, even. She makes you feel important, but she's still just a whore."

"She is not—"

He sneers. "You can dress her up in expensive clothes and put pretty jewelry on her, but she's still a filthy little slut who opens her legs for you in exchange for a comfortable life. Use her all you want. Get your money's worth, Connor, but then get rid of her so you can find someone who will help you fit into this family instead of turning yourself into a complete outcast."

I push out of my chair, shaking with rage as I grab the lapels of his suit jacket. "Keep pushing, and you'll need to visit Mother's plastic surgeon."

He grins. "The truth stings, doesn't it, son?"

"You want to fuck with me, go right ahead, but you don't fuck with my wife, ever."

"Connor."

At the sound of Mildred's unsteady voice, I release my father and step back. I spin around as my sisters and Meems round the corner, followed by my mother.

"Dinner is being served in the dining room," she says softly.

Based on the way she can't meet my gaze, I worry how much she overheard.

Dinner is wildly uncomfortable. Conversation is stilted. Mildred barely touches her plate. Mother talks about how desperately Grace Manor needs a makeover. Julian and Bryson complain about public funding. My father and I trade thinly veiled insults.

"I've had enough." Meems sets her knife and fork down.

Everyone turns their attention to her.

"This..." She motions between me and my father. "...is unbelievable." She tosses her napkin on the table and pushes her chair back.

I get up to help her. "Meems."

She raises a hand and uses the other one to grip the edge of the table. Her eyes are on fire. "I don't know what is going on between you two, but this...pissing contest is juvenile and uncalled for."

"Your grandson—"

"He's your son!" she snaps.

Mildred looks utterly stricken. She pushes back her chair and rounds the table. I watch her transform, become the woman who saves teenage girls from embarrassing bathroom situations. "Okay, Meems, put your firecrackers away. They're grown men. They can work their own shit out." She offers her hand, and Meems takes it. Mildred whispers something to her, and she nods.

They link arms, and Mildred turns back to my family, who

wear varying expressions of shock. "Thank you for coming for dinner. You're welcome to stay for cake, as long as it doesn't end up on the walls. But Meems is done with company."

And with that, she steers Meems out of the dining room, leaving my family staring after them. Three seconds later, my parents get into it. But my mother's fire won't last long. She's too afraid to lose what she has.

I leave them, going in search of my wife and Meems so I can apologize.

I find them in the kitchen with Ethel, Norm, and Cedrick.

Mildred slides over and pats the empty stool between her and Meems. "Come on, Connor. You're a sweet enough villain to deserve cake and ice cream."

CHAPTER 35
DRED

"These boys are on fire tonight." Rix pops a chocolate-covered peanut in her mouth.

"They're playing so clean these days," Hemi notes.

"It's good to see in such a transitional year." Hammer snaps a picture and sends a message to either Hollis or her dad, or both. They might be retired from the league, but they're still invested in the team. They're both coaching tonight at the Hockey Academy; otherwise they'd be here, too.

Roman worked closely with Kellan and Connor last season to get them ready, and it feels like all that hard work is paying off.

"Connor has really stepped it up this season." Shilpa cradles her little nugget in her arms. He's wearing an adorable pair of earmuffs, and he's totally zonked after two periods of being snuggled and passed.

"It's been a good season for him," I agree.

"Seems like maybe you're responsible for that shift." Essie nudges me.

"I don't know that it's a me thing..."

"Seems like a you thing." Hemi arches a brow.

"He's getting along with everyone on the team, even Flip," Hammer notes.

Tally looks up from her phone with a disgusted expression.

"Everything okay?" I ask.

"Yeah, sorry. Cammie's at Chase's game tonight, and my ex is hitting on one of our other friends. She didn't want to tell me, but she felt like it would be better coming from her instead of someone else." She tucks her phone in her pocket. "I don't care who he dates, but he's kind of flying his douchebag flag by flirting in front of one of my closest friends, you know?"

"I'm sorry, Talls." Fee hugs her arm.

"It's fine. He's a dick. He just needs to stop being so creepy and find new people to hang out with."

"Maybe *we* need to attend one of Chase's games," Rix suggests.

"And bring our boys," Hemi adds.

Tally's eyes light up with glee, and a side of vindication. "It would be such a shitshow," she breathes. "But also probably worth it."

Tally's boyfriend from last year wasn't a fan favorite. They broke up at the end of summer, when pictures surfaced of him making out with a girl from his hometown. Apparently, he'd been dating her *and* Tally the whole time. Mostly Tally was annoyed by all the online chatter and irritated with herself for not seeing him for what he was sooner, but she bounced back quickly.

"Oh! You know what we need to do?" Hemi taps her lip.

"Go over things for the library fundraising gala?" I ask hopefully. It's taken a back seat with the wedding and writing all the proposals.

Hemi nods. "We have loads of time, but I'd love to get most of it ironed out in the next few weeks."

"Agreed." I try not to sound overly eager, but I would love for this gala to give the library a soft cushion after what happened with Connor's dad and pulling the funding. It's been reinstated, and I'm sure it has everything to do with my husband, although he hasn't mentioned it. "Now that I'm settled, I'll be able to give it more of my attention."

The girls jump in, throwing out ideas, and Hammer pulls out her phone to take notes.

The Terror win the game. It's a Friday night, and they have a three-day break, so we decide to go out and celebrate. Under normal circumstances, I would bail early because the club scene is not my jam, but not this time. I've been living in a mansion on the edge of the city, missing the easy access I used to have to all my friends. Before I could walk across the hall or down the street; now it's a drive with some planning.

And if I'm stepping out of my comfort zone to spend time with them, so can my husband.

The rest of them all live within a few blocks of each other, so Connor and I join the crew and stop at Rix and Tristan's for a quick wardrobe change.

"You can borrow something from my closet," Rix tells me. "And we wear the same size shoe."

"That won't be necessary," Connor assures us. "Cedrick will be here in a minute with options." He holds up his phone to show me the car moving on the map. "He's bringing several dresses and shoes, so you can pick whatever you'd like."

"It's after ten! Cedrick probably wants to go to bed."

"And he will, after he drops off dresses and shoes, darling. Don't worry, he has tomorrow off."

"You're unbelievable."

"The most heinous, obviously. How dare I want you to be comfortable in your own clothes when we make spontaneous plans to go out with friends?"

"You two are so cute." Rix hugs Tristan's arm. "Aren't they?"

"Adorable," Tristan agrees.

"Don't encourage him." I scowl as Connor beams.

Half an hour later I'm wearing a dress that shows off every curve I have and a pair of shoes that probably cost as much as a month's rent. I won't even think about the price of the dress.

Connor's hand is placed protectively—and possessively—on my back as we enter the club. His brow is deliciously furrowed, and his jaw is tight.

"You're rather tense," I observe.

"I wonder why," he grumbles.

"If you didn't want me to wear the dress, you should have said something." I'm poking the bear. Intentionally.

"I thought when I said I liked it the best you would choose something else."

"So you *don't* like this dress?"

"No, I love this dress. You look fucking edible. I hoped the reverse psychology and honesty would work in my favor and push your defiant little buttons."

"Guess that backfired, eh?"

"Immensely, yes."

"Does that mean you plan to spend the night broody and glowering?"

"It's quite possible."

The air around us is now vibrating with bass.

"Oh! This is my favorite song! Let's dance!" Tally grabs my hand, and I wave over my shoulder, my smile widening as Connor's expression darkens.

Quinn claps him on the shoulder and hands him a drink.

"Connor looks like he wants to eat you alive," Tally shouts.

"He's pretty annoyed that I'm wearing the dress he said he loved," I reply.

She frowns. "I don't get it."

"I think he'd rather she just wear it for him, and not for everyone else," Rix explains, motioning to all the bodies surrounding us.

"Oh! That makes sense. I can't wait until I have someone who gets all territorial over me." Tally flips her hair over her shoulder and glances toward the guys. "And not the way my ex was."

"Gotta say, I'm glad you've moved on from him." Hemi side-hugs her.

"Me too. I know he wasn't everyone's favorite. Especially not my dad's." She rolls her eyes. "At least I never had sex with him."

"Small mercies." I exchange a look with Rix.

"Not that he didn't try…" Tally rolls her eyes. "They always try. Half the reason he wanted to date me was because he knew I was a virgin. He did the whole candles-and-sex-soundtrack thing once. He wanted to be able to tell his friends he popped my cherry. And then he lied and told them he did anyway—and also that I'm a shitty lay."

My eyebrows rise. "This guy sounds like a high-level douche." Flip better never find out about this or he'll bury him.

"I got him back by telling the girlfriend of one of his friends that he was a premature ejaculator."

Rix wrinkles her nose. "Was he?"

"Oh yeah. He always came in, like, under two minutes. And I never got to come." Tally crosses her arms and pouts—but only for a moment before the beat is too much to resist and she's dancing again.

"Sounds like a selfish asshole." Hemi takes Tally's mostly empty drink and sets it on the bar rail behind her.

"So selfish," Tally agrees.

I'm unsurprised when Tristan joins us a few minutes later. Dallas and Hollis are next, and then a familiar tattooed arm snakes around my waist. I tip my chin up and Connor gazes down at me, eyes hooded.

"You better not be here to drag me off the dance floor," I warn.

He pulls me tighter against him. "You know the old saying, darling. If you can't beat them, join them."

"So you're here to dance with me?"

"I'm here for the foreplay." He drops his head, and his lips skim my cheek and stop at my ear. "All these eyes on us. My hands on you."

Heat works its way down my spine, settling between my thighs. "Evil to the core."

"You're the menace who wore this dress," he reminds me.

"You're the one who said you loved it."

He runs his hand down my side. "You're the one who didn't play by the rules."

I reach up and skim the shell of his ear. "Hard to play by the rules when I don't even know what they are."

"I suppose I should have finished the thought in my head, and then you would have known that while I love this dress, you wearing it in a club full of people makes me lightly homicidal."

"And possibly horny." I spin and press my ass against him, feeling his hardness.

"Possibly." He turns my head, tilting my chin so he can cover my mouth with his.

It's a soft kiss. Sweet. Until he sucks in my bottom lip and lets it slide through his teeth. "Do you know what I can't stop thinking about?"

"Fucking me in the front foyer when we get home?"

"You'll be lucky if we make it out of the car." His hand moves lower, pressing firmly against my low belly as he rolls his hips.

"Tell me more about that," I suggest.

"I'd like you to tell me more about the time I caught you listening to your audiobook in the driveway."

A thrill shoots down my spine. "What do you want to know?"

"I know you better than I did then." His fingers splay across my stomach, pressing illicitly close to the crest of my pubic bone.

"You do," I agree on a soft moan.

"I know how you sound when you're about to come." He kisses the edge of my jaw. "And I know you get off on the idea of being watched."

My nipples tighten, and my panties dampen.

"And here we are, in the middle of a nightclub." He bites my earlobe. "Surrounded by our friends, and based on the way you're biting that lip of yours, you're dangerously close to coming, aren't you, Dredful menace?"

"Y-yes." Everyone is lost in their own world, bodies moving, engaged in their own foreplay. But there are eyes everywhere. Someone is watching. Noticing.

"Do you know how much I want to feel your pretty, wet cunt squeezing my cock?"

My moan gets lost in the bass as heat spirals through me and my knees buckle. Connor spins me around and works his knee between my thighs. His hand curves around my ass, pulling me tight against him. His lips drop to my ear. "I can feel you coming, little menace." And then his mouth is on mine, swallowing my plaintive sounds.

I melt into his arms. We don't say goodbye to our friends. As soon as my legs will hold my weight, he whisks me out of the club and into his car.

"Take your panties off," he demands once we're on the road.

I shimmy them down my thighs. Connor holds his hand out, and I drop them into his palm. He groans as he brings them to his nose and inhales deeply.

"Oh my fucking God." I shudder and dig my nails into my thighs.

"Are you coming again?"

"Maybe," I say through gritted teeth. The roll of my hips gives me away.

Connor almost misses the turn. He makes a hard right, then straightens out the wheel, easing off the gas. His hot hand lands on my thigh, squeezing. I part my legs for him, and he skims my clit. My body is on fire, and I'm on the verge of combusting.

We turn onto our street, and he punches in the code for the gate. As soon as we're through, he shifts into park and wraps his hand around the back of my neck, yanking me over and into a kiss. With that, we're frantic, insatiable. He throws open his door and steps out into the cool fall night. I clamber over the center console, and he pulls me out of the car with one arm while he frees his cock with the other.

He hurriedly rolls on a condom, and then I wrap myself around him and he presses me against the side of the car. Our gazes lock, my heart skips a beat, and then he fills me in one rough, glorious thrust. Our mouths clash, tongues lashing. Connor fucks me into oblivion at the mouth of the driveway. I can't get close enough, will never be full enough. I want him in ways I've never wanted anyone.

And then he softens. His hold gentle, his lips tender on mine as he fucks me still. I think I could love him, if he would let me.

CHAPTER 36
CONNOR

"Where's Dred tonight?" Meems asks as Norm and Ethel fuss over her, making sure she's comfortable before they leave us to eat.

"She's visiting a friend."

Meems brightens. "Her Babes?"

I smile. "Uh, no, she's playing board games with Flip," I explain.

"Ah." She nods knowingly. "And how do you feel about that?"

"He's her best friend."

"That's who he is, not how you feel," she presses.

I cut my parmesan green bean in half and spear it with my fork. "He's her family. They've been a support system for each other for a long time."

She widens her eyes and waits.

"I mean, obviously I'm jealous. But I know there's nothing going on between them." Mildred sleeps beside me every night. I'm the only man who gets to touch her, kiss her, love her. *But I've never said those words.* "Their friendship is easy. They're very close."

"She's an easy person to love," Meems says.

"She is," I agree. I want to claim her forever. To make her love me back. "But I'm not."

"That's not true," she argues.

"My father hates me."

She sighs, her expression softening as she sets her fork on the edge of her plate. "He doesn't understand you. Your father is very much like your grandfather. His entire existence is a business transaction."

"But Pops loved you," I point out. *How am I any different when my own marriage is based on a contract?*

"He did, but that took time. And unfortunately for your father, I was the *only* person your grandfather was soft for. You can't escape genetics, but you also have pieces of me and your mother. You have kindness and compassion."

I don't see these things about myself. I'm not selfless. "Mother lets my father walk all over her. My sisters do the same with their husbands."

Meems sighs. "I hoped that Courtney would soften your father the way I did your grandfather. But instead of softening him, he hardened her. Your mother is too conditioned to be what everyone else wants. You played your part, but you never stepped in line for either of them." She reaches out to squeeze my hand. "It isn't hate they feel. It's frustration, confusion, fear. The ultimate failure as a parent is being unable to see your children for who they are. It isn't your fault they don't understand you."

Growing up, they always wanted me to be more like so-and-so's son. After my sisters married, they wanted me to be more like Julian and Bryson.

And now here I am, still defiant, still a disappointment, still seeking acceptance where there is none. "What if I don't know how to love any better than my father?" I feel like I'm running toward a cliff, and what lies at the bottom is an unknown that could ruin me.

Because I'm falling. I've fallen already. And I'm afraid of the landing.

Meems reaches across the table and takes my hand. "You love me."

"It's a different kind of love."

Meems is the only person who has accepted me for who I am and doesn't put her own aspirations on me. Well, Mildred doesn't push me to be something else, but I don't know if that's because our relationship is transactional. Just like my mother is bound to my father for the good of her family, Mildred is bound to me for the good of hers.

But when we're alone at night, it doesn't feel transactional. And it didn't feel that way when we were out with our friends last week. She seemed genuinely happy—not just with them, but with me, too. For the first time in my life, I feel like I fit somewhere, and it's all because of her. She's shown me how to make that happen. But if I lose her, then what?

"Different yes, but still valid. All love is important," Meems says. "You also love Mildred."

I nod. "I do."

"And she feels the same way."

I focus on my plate. Chemistry is not the same as love. "What if I can't be a better man than my father?" *Does Mildred soften me? Am I hardening her?*

"You already are a better man. You didn't marry Dred because she was going to further your career ambitions."

But I didn't marry her because I loved her at the time either. I do now, but at the beginning she was the answer to my problem. I used her softness and need against her. I could have just given her the money. She could have posed as my girlfriend for the next year, and wouldn't that have made Meems happy, too?

Sitting beside her at Callie's hockey games, watching her love that little girl like she was family made it easy to propose that contract. She came from nothing, had no one, and has managed to weave herself into the hearts of all these people without effort. Mildred is wholly loved by the people in her life. I wanted that same love for myself. Wanted to know what it felt like to be surrounded by friends who care deeply. And now I have it. I have her. "I worry that I don't deserve the kind of family Mildred has created for herself."

"My dear sweet boy." Meems squeezes my hand. "Mildred isn't the type of woman who would give her heart to someone who doesn't deserve it."

"I know." The problem is, I took it under false pretenses, and I don't know how to ask to hold it on my own.

—— D · A · R · L · I · N · G ——

It's closing in on nine thirty by the time my wife gets home.

She smiles when she sees me lounging on the couch in the library. "Why am I not surprised to find you in here?"

"It's your favorite place to be." *And if I can't have you beside me, I spend time in the place you like the most.*

She drops onto the couch next to me, and I stretch my arm along the back, hoping she'll slide into the gap. I'm not disappointed. She tucks herself into my side and checks out the cover of the book I'm reading. "Did you just pick up the first book on the pile?"

"I did. I was flipping through the tabbed chapters."

"Those are all my favorite parts."

"So you like the steamy stuff and the heartbreak."

"It's the dark moment before they figure out their way back to each other. But I only like it because I know they work it out in the end."

I want to ask her if she thinks we could work out, but it feels like too much of a risk. I set the book down and press my lips to her temple. "How was game night with Flip?" The tightness in my chest is ever present when we talk about him. I fear I'll never be as important to her as he is.

"I kicked his ass, which is not usual." She follows the seam on my pants with a fingernail.

"Sounds like there's a but in there."

She looks up at me, eyes a little sad. "He's struggling."

"Personally or professionally?"

Flip is at the top of his game. He's having an amazing season. He has the best scoring record on the team, and he's pushing his way into the top ten in the league. But just because he's doing well doesn't mean he feels great about it.

"They don't always function independently of each other."

People outside of this career don't realize how easy it can be to go from the top to the bottom. And with all the positive press he's been getting comes a resurgence of the negative coverage from the past.

"So both then?" I ask.

She nods and tries to get closer, so I pull her into my lap. I want this with her, these moments when she lets her guard down and shares with me, even if it's about the person I'm most jealous of. Maybe especially then.

"Are you worried about him?"

"Yeah." She shifts and kisses my neck, inhaling deeply. I can't see her face to understand what's going on in her head. "He started to see what we all see about Tally at Rix and Tristan's wedding, and now that he's aware, he can't make himself unaware."

"Ah. That's tricky."

"And now he's realizing how his past choices could affect his present and his future. He doesn't feel like he deserves to have a person," she says.

I nod. He and I have that in common. The difference is, I'm selfish enough to try anyway. "Time can change a lot of things."

She skims the edge of my jaw with a finger.

"What else is going on in that busy head of yours?" I ask.

"The holidays will be different this year."

"What do they usually look like for you?" I run my fingers through her hair.

She lifts her head, kissing my chin. "Typically on Christmas Eve I put food baskets together for the unhoused people who frequent the library, drop off gifts at the group home, and eat Thai takeout."

"Seemed like fate threw us together last year."

"Mm-hmm... It did," she agrees.

Last year we ran into Roman at a local Thai restaurant and ended up at his place for Christmas Eve. It inspired a plan to make Lexi and her sisters' Christmas less difficult since it was their second holiday without their parents.

"What about Christmas Day?" I ask.

"I usually go to the soup kitchen in the morning and help prepare dinner."

I stroke her cheek. "Do you ever do anything for yourself?"

"All of that is for me. I get to brighten other people's days, and I'm not alone during the holidays."

I want to tell her she doesn't have to be alone ever again. I'll spend every Christmas with her for the rest of my life.

She traces the shell of my ear with a fingertip.

I can't promise her this Christmas will be easy, but I can take her mind off the things that weigh her down—and my own as well.

I press my lips gently to hers. Her warm, soft hand curves around the back of my neck and she angles her head, allowing the kiss to deepen. Weeks have turned into months and time is slipping through my fingers. I don't want to lose her, but I don't know how to deserve to keep her.

Mildred shifts to straddle my lap as we explore each other's mouths. I run my hands down her sides, settling on her hips, needing her closer.

We break long enough to rid each other of our shirts, and her bra. Before she can reclaim my lips, I dip down and capture a nipple, laving the tight peak, then sucking softly.

I need her under me, her hands in my hair, my name a moan on her pretty lips. Laying her on the couch, I stretch out over her and carefully remove her glasses, setting them on the table behind her head. I brush my lips over hers. "Let me take care of you, darling."

Her fingers slide into my hair as I kiss a path down her throat. I tease her nipples, relishing every gasp and moan, alternating gentle suction with sharp bites.

When I reach her navel, I rid her of her jeans and panties and sink to the floor, hooking one of her legs over my shoulder and pressing her other thigh open, her knee against the back of the couch. I turn my head and bite the inside of her thigh, making her gasp and roll her hips.

Her toes curl against my side, her voice breathy as she lifts her shoulders from the couch. "I left the door open."

"Everyone is asleep." I kiss my way along the inside of her thigh.

"They might not be." She bites her bottom lip when I suck her skin.

"Then they'll know I take care of my wife's needs." I continue my path to the apex of her thighs. "And you look so lovely spread out like a feast for me."

"Such a good villain."

"Every moment of every day."

Mildred sinks back into the couch, eyes darting between me and the door as I drop open-mouthed kisses on her skin. I suck and tease until she's pleading in desperate whimpers.

"So sweet when you're begging for my mouth." I lap at her, and she writhes under me, hands in my hair, nails biting into my scalp. "So beautiful when you're coming on my tongue, wife."

Mildred bucks and moans, body shaking as she comes in waves. And I can't get enough. I nab a condom from my wallet and roll it down my length, then fit myself between her damp thighs.

Our gazes lock and her eyes flare as I sink into her, filling her, claiming her.

"You feel so good." Her fingers skim my cheek.

"Like heaven," I agree.

She wraps herself around me, pulling me closer, my body pressing her into the couch. Her soft skin under my fingers, her warm breath breaking against my lips, the scent of strawberry and vanilla, and the taste of her on my tongue.

We kiss and fuck and cling and pant.

She comes again, gorgeous, unguarded, and mine.

I want her to stay. For this to last.

I want to love her for the rest of my life.

CHAPTER 37
CONNOR

Mildred and I spend Christmas Eve morning handing out care packages to those in the local unhoused community. She knows every person we greet by name. She introduces me as her husband, and every time, they tell me how lucky I am to have her. Of course I agree.

After the library closes at noon, we stop at the group home to drop off presents for the kids. It's clear Mildred is particularly excited to see Victor and Everly, and so am I.

Mildred hands me a box. I glance inside. "Where did you get all this?"

"Ceddy gave it to me. He found it in the storage shed with the holiday stuff, and I said we could put it to use."

"I doubt everyone in here is a Terror fan."

"Toques and hoodies are always welcome. So are baseball caps and T-shirts. They won't care what team it is, just that it's new and the logo is cool." She grabs one of the elf hats from last year. "Come here."

I bend and pucker my lips. She kisses me and ruins my hair with the elf hat, and I don't even care.

When we enter, Mildred barely has time to set the boxes down before Everly attaches herself to her like a koala clip. "I wasn't sure if you were coming today, 'cause now you're married and have family events to go to and stuff."

Mildred hugs her tightly. "As if I would miss Christmas Eve."

Victor appears, wearing a smirk. "Hey, Connor. Nice elf hat."

I dip my chin. "I think it suits me."

"Definitely." He hangs back, waiting for Everly to release Mildred before he moves in for his own hug.

Everything about him softens as he folds his arms around her.

She has this effect on everyone. People fall in love with her kindness and warmth.

More teens come down the stairs, almost all of them seeking hugs. They look at me with wide-eyed curiosity.

One boy's mouth pulls to the side. "You're Connor Grace."

I tuck a hand in my pocket. "I am."

"You married Dred."

"I did."

"You must be really nice," he says decisively.

"She makes me nicer, if I'm honest."

A minute later, a lanky teen wearing a sour expression drags himself down the stairs. When his eyes find me they flare. "Holy shit." He looks to a younger, equally lanky kid. "I thought you were lying."

He shrugs. "Sometimes I tell the truth."

The lanky kid stands off to the side, eyes darting to me.

Mildred hugs my arm. "Connor brought some special gifts for all of you."

I'm suddenly surrounded by chatty, eager teens. I pass out hats and shirts and jerseys. Some of them hug me, others ask me to sign their swag. It's humbling and gratifying, especially with the way it lights up Mildred's face.

After we finish handing out loot, we're invited to stay for coffee and afternoon snacks. The coffee is godawful, but the cookies are good. Mildred talks to Cordelia, the house guardian, about her funding proposal in hopes to create additional opportunities for kids to earn their community service hours at the library since it's been so successful for Everly.

Unfortunately, we're expected at my parents' so we are forced to excuse ourselves. I'd rather stay with the kids and drink shitty coffee and eat cookies, but I can't disappoint my sisters, who are excited to see Mildred.

The twins stand at the window waving, Everly hugging her brother's arm, both of them looking sad and happy at the same time as I help Mildred into the passenger seat of my car.

"What's Christmas like at the group home?" I ask.

"They have a Secret Santa gift exchange," she replies. "Some of the kids might have supervised visits with family members, and the kids who can't have a family visit or don't have family make dinner together."

"Do Victor and Everly see their parents?"

Mildred shakes her head. "No, their parents aren't allowed visits."

"Why not?"

"Mom is a sex worker with addiction issues, and Dad is incarcerated."

"That's sad."

"It is, so the group home is better." She shifts, angling her body toward me. "What is Christmas like with your family?"

I shrug. "Usually my parents take my sisters and Meems somewhere warm."

"Can Meems travel this year?"

"No, but the rest of my family is flying out after dinner tonight."

"Have you ever gone?"

"When I was younger. My schedule doesn't allow it now." And they stopped asking years ago.

"Of course not." Her voice softens with sadness. "But we'll have just as much fun together this year as we did last year."

"It'll be even better," I agree.

Once we arrive home, we change into formal dinner attire, as is the dress code for the evening. Then Mildred comes down the stairs carrying a huge box that's decorated like a wrapped present.

"What is that?"

She tips it forward, showing me the contents. "Gifts."

"For who?"

"Your family." She says this like it's the most logical thing in the universe, like my parents aren't stuck-up assholes every time we see them.

"But I already took care of the gifts." I get my family the same thing every year: spa gift certificates for my mom and sisters, and bottles of expensive imported booze for my father and brothers-in-law. Meems—I go all out for, though. Every year I get her something different. Last year I picked out a new winter coat with a matching hat and gloves for her ladies' nights. This year I bought her a special reading chair for the guesthouse because she falls asleep in it so often.

"You took care of the gifts from you. These are from me." She kisses my cheek and passes me the box as Meems appears.

Mildred's gaze slides to me, brow quirked. "Matchy-matchy, aren't we?"

Mildred is wearing a black-and-wine plaid dress, and Meems is in green and black. Both have gold accents. My jacket is the same wine color as Mildred's dress, and my tie picks up Meems's green.

Meems's smile is wry. "Connor has always had a thing about color coordination."

I shrug. "We're a team."

"We absolutely are." Mildred smiles warmly as she holds out her arms, linking the three of us. I walk my girls out to the car, help them in, and make the short drive to my parents' house. Just a few hours and then my unpleasant family obligations are fulfilled for the holidays.

When we arrive, my sisters greet us with hugs and enthusiasm instead of air kisses, and we're ushered into the living room.

"Wow." Mildred smiles wryly. "That's quite the tree."

I hum my agreement. It fits my parents' white-on-white décor.

Mother comes over to give us air kisses, eyeing my suit with disapproval.

"What's all this?" She peers at the loudly wrapped box full of smaller, less-loudly wrapped gifts, like whatever is inside might jump out and bite her.

"Presents," Mildred says brightly.

"Did you wrap them yourself?" Mom asks.

"That's my favorite part of the season." Mildred carries the box, which she refused to relinquish to me for reasons I don't understand, into the living room and sets it next to the monochromatic, professionally wrapped gifts already under the tree.

Julian arches an eyebrow, first at the gifts, then at me. "That's quite the suit."

Bryson coughs into his glass.

"Isn't it fun?" Mildred kisses my cheek, ignoring their rudeness. "We definitely need pictures with Meems before the night is over."

I want to keep Mildred at my side so she can be my personal shield of sunshine and warmth, but my sisters pull her and Meems to the couch so they can fawn over them and talk.

Julian's phone goes off. "I'll be back in a minute. I need to take this."

Bryson follows him. Can't say I'm sad that I don't have to field work calls on Christmas Eve.

My father moves in, expression reflecting his disdain. "I see you're planning to ruin family photos again this year."

"I didn't want to disappoint you by showing up in something you couldn't criticize." Looks like we're starting the night slinging arrows.

"You definitely excel at disappointing this family," he agrees.

I expect the barb, but it still hits sharper than I'd like. "I guess it's good that I've stopped trying to win your favor, then, isn't it?"

"You could make family events less stressful for everyone if you stopped being such a brat."

"Why do you think I act this way?" I ask, hoping I sound casually indifferent.

"To get attention."

"That's exactly right," I agree. "Because if you couldn't be disappointed in me all the time, you'd have to find someone else to be disappointed in. At least the heat is off my sisters and mother when I'm around."

My gaze shifts to my wife on the couch, flanked by Isabelle and Portia, who are smiling and laughing. Usually Christmas is tense. Unpleasant. Everyone waiting for Dad and me to draw swords and start fighting. Because I can't help myself. Or maybe because it feels too risky to try anything else.

"Why don't we open some gifts?" Mildred says, eyes on me. She hastily tacks on, "Unless you have a specific order you do things in? I don't want to mess with tradition."

"We usually have dinner first," Mom says.

"We can change it up this year for Mildred, though." Isabelle squeezes my wife's hand. "Do you always open presents first?"

Her cheeks flush. "Oh, uh, I don't really have family traditions, so we can do whatever works for everyone else."

Portia and Isabelle are quiet a moment. They glance at each other as they put the pieces together.

Mom surprises me—and I think everyone else—when she says, "We could open one gift before dinner." She turns nervously to my dad. "Couldn't we, Duncan?"

"Of course we can," Meems cuts in, beaming at Mildred. "New family members call for new traditions."

"You can just open the gifts I brought." Mildred hops up, her smile bright.

She hands a gift to everyone, and when she offers one to me,

I pull her into the oversized chair with me and nuzzle her neck. "I'd rather unwrap you."

She elbows me in the ribs. "Behave."

"What if I don't want to?" I'm doing exactly what my father said, being a brat. The family problem. Mildred didn't ask for this. *Shit.*

She turns toward me, searching my face as the sound of tearing paper fills the room. "This is not for me. This is you reacting to something, and later you'll tell me what it is."

Isabelle and Portia squeal with excitement, dragging my attention away from Mildred's unimpressed gaze.

My sisters pull on their toques, helping each other adjust them.

Mother frowns. Meems is grinning widely, and my brothers-in-law and father appear confused.

"I like to knit," Mildred explains. "I make hats and mittens for people who frequent the library, and everyone needs a winter hat, so..." She shrugs, and I wrap an arm around her, kissing her temple. She doesn't elbow me this time.

"We should take a picture," I suggest.

"Oh, I—" Mother starts.

"Oh yes! Let's set up the tripod so we can all be in it!" Isabelle says. "Last year Connor missed the family photo!"

Because I also missed Christmas in Cabo.

Portia adjusts her hot pink hat with BBB knitted into the brim and hops to her feet. My sisters could not be happier. My brothers-in-law look annoyed. But miraculously, my family gathers in front of the fireplace and don their knitted toques. The guys' all have the Terror logo knitted into them.

"These are impressive," I say as Mildred adjusts my hat. I wrap my arm around her and pull her close as Isabelle rushes back into place.

"Everyone say *cheese*!"

We must take fifteen pictures before Portia decides one is

good enough to share. I Airdrop it to the family and immediately post it on my socials, much to my father's irritation.

The kitchen staff informs us that dinner will be ready shortly.

My sisters are busy fixing their hair, Mom is trying to talk to Meems, and my brothers-in-law are refilling their scotches.

Mildred squeezes my hand. "I'm just going to use the restroom before we sit down."

"I can show you," I offer.

I follow her down the hall, and she glances over her shoulder, making sure we're alone before she pulls me in with her and closes the door. "Are you okay?"

"Shouldn't I be the one asking this question?"

"What happened with your father?"

"What always happens. He fires arrows, and I fire them back and hate myself for it, so no one wins."

She cups my face in her hands. "You don't have to protect everyone else by always falling on the sword. Just a couple more hours. That's all we have to make it through, and then it's just you and me and my pretty, festive underwear that you're welcome to take off with your teeth."

A spark springs to life inside me. "Can I see them now?"

"No, because if you do, you'll want to spoil your dinner." She pushes on my chest when I try to pull her closer. "Be a good villain now, and you can be a bad one later."

I sigh, drop my head, and breathe her in. "Okay. But only for you."

"And Meems."

"Mostly for you."

Something in her eyes shifts at my words, and I don't know what it means. I panic a little and force a saucy grin. Being the problem is always my default. "And also because I want access to these festive panties of yours."

She pushes up on her toes and presses her lips to the edge of my jaw. "We stick together."

Two hours and twenty minutes later—most of which has

been spent biting my tongue and imagining punching my dad in the face—we arrive home, put Meems to bed—she fell asleep during gift opening, which gave us an excuse to finally leave—and head to the elevator.

"You did great tonight." Mildred runs her nails down the back of my neck as we close the gate and head to the second floor.

"I had a reason to behave." And I kept reminding myself that tomorrow will be better, as it's just us and the special surprise I've set up for her.

My intention is to take Mildred up to bed and thank her with my mouth and fingers and cock, but before we get there, I find my patience and good behavior have run out. I can't get her naked fast enough. I just want to erase all the things that make me hate myself, to blanket over all my fears, to get inside her like she's gotten inside me.

I back her into the corner of the elevator car, drop to my knees, tug her panties down—they are festive, as promised, with little sprigs of holly all over—throw her leg over my shoulder, and bury my face in her.

She shoves her hands into my hair and rides my tongue, her moans and whimpers echoing off the walls. I'm still fully dressed when I roll a condom down my length, pin her against the wall, and drive into her. The relief is overwhelming. Hot and tight and soft.

"Mine." I bite the edge of her jaw. "You're mine." I kiss her and fuck her and fall deeper. "Tell me you're mine."

"I'm yours," she whispers.

And I wish it could be true forever.

CHAPTER 38
DRED

I wake on Christmas morning wrapped around a pillow. Some of my past holiday experiences have been wildly unpleasant, but last night was the most joyous Christmas Eve I've ever had. Post sex in the elevator, Connor carried me to bed and spent the hour that followed being an absolutely villainous demon by making me come until I was delirious. Then he spooned me to sleep, lips on my shoulder, nose against my neck.

I roll over, seeking his warmth, but I'm met with cool sheets and an empty space where his body should be. I crack a lid and glance around. He's not where I usually find him on off-practice or game mornings—reading the paper in the chair by the fireplace. I roll back the other way and find my glasses.

A mug of coffee sits on a warmer, along with a bowl of yogurt topped with strawberry compote and a note with my name propped next to it. Anxiety sweeps through me. *What if something happened to Meems*? Connor would wake me if something bad happened. Still, my hands shake as I unfold the note.

Merry Christmas, darling.

I had to take care of a couple of things and didn't want to wake you since I kept you up so late. I'll see you soon.

XO

Connor

I read it over twice more, getting stuck on the XO. Waking up alone on Christmas morning isn't unusual, but I thought this year I would have a pretty new memory to tuck into my heart.

I throw off the covers and use the bathroom. By the time I'm done putting on clothes, my Babe Brigade chat is blowing up.

> **RIX**
> Merry Christmas, Babes!
>
> **SHILPA**
> The three of us wish you the happiest holidays! We've been up since five, and Ash was hoping Pavin would be able to unwrap his gifts, but so far he's more interested in his feet than anything else.

A picture of their adorable baby boy follows, lying on the floor with his toes in his mouth.

> **HAMMER**
> My view this morning.

Hollis's back in a pair of plaid pajama pants and a Santa hat follows.

> **LEXI**
> My view isn't quite as nice. A Christmas baby would be welcome about now.

Lexi's swollen belly and the phrase LOADING pops up.

> **HEMI**
> Wishing you the most amazing Christmas!

A selfie of Hemi and Dallas with their families in the background comes next. They're up in Muskoka where both their parents live.

> **ESSIE**
> Happy holidays, my loves!

A photo of Essie and Nate appears. Nate's attention is on Essie, not the camera.

I cross over to Dewey and carefully lift him out of his cage, giving him a little love before I put his Santa hat on and take my own selfie. I send it, along with a *Merry Christmas*.

A moment later, a message pops up in my private messages.

> **LEXI**
> Everything okay?

> **DRED**
> I don't know. I woke up alone.

> **LEXI**
> ☹

> **DRED**
> He left a note saying he had to take care of something. I leave for the soup kitchen in half an hour.

> **LEXI**
> Maybe he had to pick something up?

> **DRED**
> I'm sure that's it. I'm excited to see you and the girls later today.

> **LEXI**
> I can't wait, and neither can they. You're welcome to come earlier.

> **DRED**
> Thanks. I'll message when I'm finished at the soup kitchen.

I eat half the strawberries and yogurt and sip my coffee, but my stomach is twisty. Where would he have to go on Christmas morning when everything is closed? I set the spinning thoughts aside, put Dewey back in his cage and feed him, then grab my purse and head downstairs.

The front door swings open as I'm putting on my running shoes.

"This looks like something out of a movie!" a familiar voice makes my heart skip a beat.

A moment later Everly appears, followed by Victor and my husband.

"Dred!" Everly drapes herself over my back and hangs off me like a human cape. "Merry Christmas!"

"Hey, hi." I cover her arms with mine.

Connor stands behind Victor, hand tucked into his pocket, a small smile on his lips.

I open my arms for Victor, and he steps into them. "Merry Christmas, Dred."

"Merry Christmas, Victor."

"We're coming with you to the soup kitchen!" Everly exclaims.

"And then back here for Christmas stockings and brunch," Connor explains.

"And then we can explore this place, right?" Everly asks.

"You can explore this place," Connor agrees.

"That sounds amazing." I'm lucky my voice doesn't crack with the emotions clogging my throat. There are probably zero chances I will make it through today without shedding a couple of very happy tears, but I'm holding those for later.

I grab my purse, and we leave the mansion. Victor and

Everly climb into the back seat, and Connor follows me to the passenger side.

"I'm sorry you woke alone. I tried to get back before that happened, but I hope the surprise makes up for it," he says.

"More than you know." I hug him. "This is a chart-topper Christmas surprise."

His lips touch mine. "I'm also sorry about my lack of control last night."

"I'm not. It's nice to be needed," I admit.

"I could have needed you in a more civilized manner."

"I didn't mind."

He appears to get lost in my eyes for a moment.

Everly presses her face against the window.

I laugh and pat his chest. "We should set a good example when the children are watching."

He kisses me on the lips. "Hm, good point."

Connor helps me into the car, and we drive across town to the soup kitchen. The four of us spend the next few hours preparing Christmas dinner for people who can't afford to make it themselves. It's sweaty, intense work, but everyone there does it with a smile, because afterward we'll return to a house full of love with a warm meal of our own.

Soup kitchen prep tackled, we pile into the car with Everly and Victor and drive back to the mansion.

Meems is in the living room in her favorite chair when we traipse in. She's wearing a green dress, her hair done, looking like she's ready for a night on the town.

"Isn't this a picture!" Her smile is wide as she takes in the four of us. "Merry Christmas! How was your morning?" She pushes out of her chair, and I hug her gently.

"So amazing. We made two hundred pounds of mashed potatoes." My forearms will probably be sore for the next couple of days, but it's so, so worth it.

"I helped make cranberry sauce," Everly adds. "This place is amazing! That tree is huge! I'm Everly. We met at the wedding, but it was huge and there were hundreds of people, and this is my brother, Victor. Thank you for letting us crash your Christmas."

"I remember. It's so wonderful to see you again." Meems hugs them. "Connor said he had a surprise, and I can't think of a better one than this." She'd already fallen in love with them at the wedding.

"I feel the same way." My heart is overflowing with happiness and gratitude.

Connor crosses to the massive tree, which is piled with gifts that weren't there yesterday. He holds up stockings with Everly and Victor's names. "Who wants to open presents?"

"You have stockings for us?" Victor's eyes are wide.

"Of course. We all have one." Connor passes them out, and Everly and Victor sit on the floor cross-legged in front of the tree.

I tuck myself into Connor's side. "Thank you so much. These two are the best gift."

He kisses my temple. "I'm glad it makes you happy."

Everly and Victor dig into their stockings, oohing and ahhing over every little thing. There are standard stocking items, like chocolate and teenage necessities, but there are also gift cards for Everly for a local bookstore, and ones for her new favorite café where they don't give her trouble for drinking the unlimited coffee. Victor gets a STEM subscription box.

My stocking is strawberry-themed, and all my favorites are tucked inside—from my preferred body lotion to the bubble bath I splurge on occasionally. At the bottom is a tiny festive jewelry box with another bracelet, this one holiday themed and clearly made by Connor's hands. My heart swells when I realize he's made one for all of us, and he's wearing one of his own to match.

Connor kisses my temple after he opens each item in his stocking. I filled it with his favorite treats, including imported chocolates and maple fudge, as well as a pair of hand-knitted gloves and socks to match the toque I made. Meems added a few of his favorite childhood candies, and there are small gifts from the twins, too. He's so much more relaxed today, no longer in fight mode. And I feel like I'm part of a real family.

I want to hold on to this, nurture it and never let it go. The lines between reality and fiction have blurred. I wish I knew what Connor's intentions were. He's always focused on making me happy, and last night he said it was for me—not Meems. Is that possible?

Once the gifts are opened—Connor assures me he tried not to go overboard for the twins, but he was unsuccessful—we move to the dining room for brunch.

"You could have twenty people in here!" Everly exclaims.

"We used to host Christmas dinners every year," Meems explains.

"Not anymore?"

"My parents usually go away for the holidays," Connor explains. "Sometimes Meems goes with them, but she stayed home this year."

"You can't go because of hockey, right?" Everly drenches her pancakes in maple syrup.

"That's right." Connor nods.

Everly's mouth pulls to the side. "That's too bad."

"It's okay." He reaches out and covers my hand with his. "I have everything I need right here."

Everly's expression turns dreamy, and Meems's smile is radiant. I lean in to kiss his cheek, wishing I could see inside his head to confirm that this is the truth.

Everly and Victor stuff themselves silly on pancakes and eggs and a mountain of fruit salad, and after brunch, Connor takes Meems to the guesthouse for a nap. I don't want to get my hopes up, but the doctors have been cautiously optimistic. She still tires easily because her heart is working hard, but her naps have been shorter over the last several weeks.

Everly and Victor take the elevator to the second floor to explore—Everly can't get over the fact that there is a "for real" elevator—and she and Victor freak out over the library. Eventually they appear at the top of the stairs again.

"This place is amazing!" she shouts.

"It is," I agree.

"And huge!" She grips the banister, eyes alight with devilish glee. "I want to slide down!"

Victor grabs her by the waist and hauls her away. "This is not the movies, and we don't need a trip to the hospital on Christmas Day."

"I almost broke my arm doing that when I was a kid!" Connor calls out as he returns.

I turn toward him with a laugh. "This is not shocking in the least."

"Better me than my sisters."

I thread my arm through his, and rest my cheek against his bicep. "How's Meems?"

"Happy but tired." He kisses the top of my head.

Everly and Victor run down the hall to the east wing, shrieking and laughing.

"Thank you for bringing them here today."

"It was the least I could do after you endured yesterday. And you love them," he says.

"I do." I look up at him. *And I love you, too.* I want to say the words, but fear keeps them inside.

CHAPTER 39
CONNOR

"Thanks for inviting us to join you." I accept a back pat from Roman as we arrive at his place on Christmas afternoon.

"The more the merrier."

Mildred folds Lexi into a hug. More than once I've caught my wife on the edge of what I hope are happy tears today.

"I just want Mildred to be surrounded by the people she loves the most."

"I get it." Roman claps me on the shoulder and then turns to Meems, offering her his arm. "It is so wonderful to see you again, Lucy."

She smiles up at him, and he bends so he can hear whatever she's saying as he guides her into the living room.

Callie stands off to the side, looking a little unsure of herself.

I open my arms, and after a moment of hesitation that hits me right in the chest, she rushes over so I can scoop her up. "How's my favorite goalie?"

"Awesome! Roman and I went down to the gym and shot a stress puck around this morning before everyone else woke up. And Fee is back for a few weeks, and we're going to watch all our favorite movies together while she's home from university."

"That sounds like an amazing Christmas so far."

"Yeah. And Roman dressed up as Santa again this morning, but don't tell him I know it's him."

I make a lips-zipped motion and toss the imaginary key aside. "Did he bring any elves with him this time?" I ask quietly.

"He said they had the day off." She narrows her eyes. "And now you and Dred are a family, which is good because Dred deserves to have one."

"I think so, too."

I put her down, and she pulls me over to the tree to show me her gifts. Roman's gift-giving prowess is stamped all over the place. There's a huge stuffed axolotl that's nearly the same size as Callie, new hockey equipment, books, and clothes.

"Wow, you must have been really good this year, huh?"

"Mostly, yeah." She nods and fiddles with the end of her ponytail. "I sort of hoped Lexi would have the baby for Christmas, so I'd get to be an aunt, but she said the baby is still growing." Her lips push out. "I don't know though, 'cause Lexi's belly is really big. She looks like a balloon that's ready to pop."

I laugh.

"Can you imagine that? Just boom!" She makes explosion hand motions. "And instead of confetti, out comes a baby." She thinks for a moment. "Are you and Dred going to have a baby?"

"Callie!" Fee appears and covers her sister's mouth with her hand. "Sorry! She's fully focused on being an aunt these days."

Callie pulls at her sister's hand. "They're married. Married people have babies," she says defensively, wrinkling her nose.

Everly nods. "You and Dred would have really cute babies."

"Lexi and Roman's baby will be the cutest," Callie declares. "I'm going to go say hi to Victor." She stomps off.

Everly snorts an indelicate laugh. "Someone has some feelings."

"She had her and Connor's whole wedding planned out last year," Fee explains. "They were going to get married on the ice when she turned eighteen."

"I'm sorry, what?" I glance over to where Callie is now hugging Victor, still looking over her shoulder at us.

"She even asked me to draw their fictional ceremony," Fee confides.

"Did you?" Everly asks.

"Oh yeah. It was proudly displayed on her wall until he married Dred, and then it moved to the closet." Fee gives me a look. "But the picture of you riding the unicorn is still on her wall."

"You're not hard to look at," Everly blurts, then covers her eyes for a moment. She grabs Fee's arm. "Why don't you show me your art stuff?" She steers Fee away.

Mildred sidles up next to me. "What was that all about?"

"Apparently Callie had plans to marry me."

She laughs, then nods to the couch where Callie is sitting cross-legged, showing Victor one of her sketchbooks. "Looks like maybe that crush is shifting."

"He could be her babysitter," I mutter.

"Give it ten years."

There's suddenly a flurry of activity at the door, followed by loud feminine excitement. "Hollis and I are engaged!" Hammer shouts.

Mildred and Lexi rush over to check out the ring, followed by Fee, Everly, and Callie. Hammer's mother and Roman's ex, Zara, and her life partner, North, are there, too. Suddenly, Christmas turns into a whole different celebration.

After the whirlwind subsides, I end up standing with Roman, Hollis, and North, while Victor gets pulled in with the girls. He doesn't seem to mind the attention.

"Congratulations, man." I clink my drink against Hollis's.

"Thanks. I've been waiting for the right moment and figured I better get a move on before someone else jumped in to steal my thunder again."

I nod. "Sorry about my role in that."

He shrugs. "I had to stop worrying about making it perfect."

He sips his eggnog. "Dred said you surprised her with the twins today."

"I did. She's rather attached to them," I explain. "They make her happy."

"You make her happy," Roman replies.

"She's good for you." Hollis claps me on the shoulder. "You're having a great season, the best of your career."

I'm gelling with my team in a way I haven't before, and my stats are up. "She settles me." If not for Mildred, I'd have entertained Meems for a while today, gotten day drunk, watched bad movies, and felt sorry for myself. Instead I'm surrounded by people—everyone who loves her. My heart feels like it's expanding and contracting simultaneously. Would she choose me the way I would choose her, without the contract? I'm afraid to burst this bubble to find out. But I may burst if I don't.

Once everyone has arrived, we gather in the living room. Mildred settles in my lap since couch and chair space is at a premium. The kids lounge on beanbags.

"It's time for the Secret Santa gift exchange!" Roman calls.

"Yes!" Callie bounces to her feet. "Can I hand out all the presents?"

"Of course you can, kiddo." Roman ruffles her hair.

"I didn't bring anything for a gift exchange," Mildred whispers, suddenly panicked.

"I took care of everything, darling. No need to worry."

She looks at me. "Did you plan all of this?"

I skim her cheek with my fingers. "I wanted Christmas to be special for you."

"Such a lovely villain."

The warmth in her eyes makes me want to believe. "I don't even mind if people find out and it ruins my reputation."

She brushes her lips over mine.

"Hey! No making out in public! It's a house rule!" Callie gripes.

I laugh, and Mildred presses her face against my neck while our friends chuckle.

Callie hands out gifts. Mildred's Secret Santa gets her a new holiday outfit for Dewey. Everly receives a special hardcover copy of her favorite book, and Victor gets a new book with all his favorite hits arranged for piano. I shake my box. It's suspiciously light. I peel the wrapping paper free and carefully peek inside.

"What is it?" Mildred asks.

"It's...nothing."

She skims the shell of my ear. "The color of these tells me you're lying."

"What's your gift?" Callie asks.

"Yeah, Connor, what are you hiding?" Roman asks.

"This was you." I point an accusing finger at Roman.

He shrugs. "It's Secret Santa."

Everyone heckles as my wife tries to pry the box out of my hands.

"You don't want to do that, darling."

"Oh, I think I do."

"You might regret it when we're alone later," I warn.

"I'll take my chances." She digs her fingers into my ribs, finding the ticklish spot—she discovered it once when she kissed her way across my tattoos. It's enough of a distraction for her to wrestle the box free. She hops out of my lap and plucks the object from the box, tossing it to Hammer.

Hammer bursts into laughter. "It's perfect."

"What is it?" Callie asks.

Hammer holds up the annoyingly adorable, grinning, stuffed sandwich.

More people laugh than I would like.

"Why is the smiling sandwich so funny?" Callie asks, adorably oblivious.

"Connor really loves sandwiches," Lexi explains.

"Oh." She nods like it makes complete sense.

"I don't think the other sandwich was quite so joyous about its situation," Mildred muses.

"You do one stupid thing as a teenager, and you never live it down," I grumble.

Thankfully the sandwich discussion ends when Roman announces that it's time to set the table for dinner.

My phone buzzes in my pocket. My sisters promised to let me know when they landed, but it's not Isabelle and Portia. It's a message from my father, bitching about my social media posts. I leave it for now. He doesn't get to ruin a perfectly good day. I tuck my phone in my jacket pocket and leave it in the front hall. I have Meems, Mildred, the twins, and my team, and that's all that matters.

Callie ends up sitting between Victor and Roman at dinner, with Everly beside Fee. There seems to be an instant connection among those kids. They all know what it's like to be without parents. I stretch my arm across the back of Mildred's chair.

She kisses my cheek. "Thank you for making today so special, not just for me, but for the twins, too."

I smile down at her. "Are you happy?"

Her eyes sparkle, and she nods.

"Good. That's all I wanted."

Again, her expression shifts at my words, but this time, I refuse to panic. I want her to see what's in my heart.

We eat and laugh and talk. It feels good. I've spent so much of my life avoiding connections, afraid to have them and lose them. Now I just want to figure out how to make them permanent.

Meems is tired after dinner, so we thank our friends, gather our gifts, and hug everyone goodbye, congratulating Hammer and Hollis again on their engagement before we leave. The twins help Meems settle in the back seat while Mildred and I load the trunk.

"Do we have to take the twins back tonight?" Mildred asks quietly.

I shake my head. "Not until tomorrow, but they don't know yet."

Her eyes light up.

"If they want to stay the night, they can."

She throws her arms around me. "Thank you. This is the most incredible gift."

As I press my face against her neck, I want to tell her we can keep them forever, that we can be our own misfit family. But then she'd have to spend the rest of her life dealing with my family on the holidays—and a lot of other days too. And she's still bound to me by a contract. So I leave that thought inside my head and help her into the car instead.

Everly can't say enough nice things about Fee on the ride back home. We take Meems to the guesthouse, and when we return, the twins are sitting in the living room, their gifts neatly stacked.

"I guess we should probably get back, huh?" Victor says, working hard to hide the sadness in his voice.

Everly runs her hands up and down her thighs, looking just as unhappy.

"Do you want to go back tonight?" Mildred's voice wavers slightly.

They look at each other.

"Don't we have to?" Victor asks.

"I checked, and you're allowed to stay the night, if you want," I offer.

"Here?" Everly's eyes go wide. "With you?"

"Only if you want. We understand if you'd feel more comfortable in your own bed," Mildred says.

"No. Nope. No way. Those beds kinda suck, and the ones here look super nice." Everly looks to Victor. "You want to stay, right?"

"Yeah." He nods and swallows, voice cracking. "Yes, please."

"Okay, great." Relief eases the tightness in my chest. "Why

don't we pick your rooms for the night, and then we can watch a movie."

It only takes a minute for them to decide. We all change into comfy clothes, then make popcorn and hang out in the theater room to watch their favorite holiday movie.

It's late by the time we climb the stairs for bed. The twins seem caught somewhere between relentless excitement and overwhelming exhaustion.

They disappear into their rooms, which are down the hall from Mildred and me, but right next to each other.

Mildred loops her arms around my neck once the door to our room is closed. "Thank you for making this the most amazing Christmas."

"It was my pleasure." I press my lips to hers.

I would give her the world if she asked for it. I would give her anything if she'd just stay for me—not because she has to, but because she wants to.

"It was almost perfect," she whispers, fingers moving to the collar of my shirt. "Just one thing was missing."

I trail my hand down her side. "What was that?"

"You." She tugs my shirt from my pants. "Inside me."

"Let me fix that for you, darling." I allow myself to believe that what we are is more. That she doesn't owe me; she wants me.

We undress each other, and she guides me to the bed and pulls me on top of her. I can't get close enough, can't get enough of her hands on my skin or her soft whimpers and sighs. I want every part of her, not just her body, but her heart, too.

When I reach for a condom, she shakes her head. "Not tonight, please."

And with that, my heart leaps again. "You're sure?"

Mildred runs her fingers through my hair. "I'm on the pill. I trust you, and I want to feel all of you."

I shift my hips, the head nudging at her entrance. All it takes is a tilt of her hips, and I fill her in one smooth stroke. It's an avalanche of sensation, and I tumble into bliss. Into the warmth of her surrounding me.

I frame her face in my hands, eyes on hers as we move together. I'm in so deep. I'm too far gone for her. I'll never break free. I don't want to. Eventually she comes in glorious waves, and I follow, drowning in heady bliss.

Afterward, I clean her up and turn off all the lights. But I check my phone before I climb into bed and find a new email from Meems's doctor.

It doesn't seem right for it to have come today, but I fight the wave of anxiety, open it, and scan the contents.

I can just make out Mildred's silhouette in the darkened room as she sits up, the sheets rustling in the quiet. "Connor, what's wrong?"

"It's Meems."

"Is she okay?"

I look up and meet her eyes in the darkness. "She qualified for surgery."

CHAPTER 40
DRED

The week leading up to Meems's surgery is an unexpected roller coaster. Connor vacillates between doting, overbearing, and combative. His stress comes out in sharp comments and soft apologies.

Christmas feels like a million years and a whole relationship ago. My feelings for him have shifted. I feel like I've finally been given a family, rather than piecing one together myself. I care for him and Meems deeply. This marvelous place has started to feel like my home. And I'm terrified of what all this means.

I find myself desperate to feel connected to him. In the light of day, he shuts down, closes himself off. So every night, when the lights are out, I reach for him. It's safe in the dark, where our feelings can stay hidden behind desire.

But I'm out of time today.

And even though my husband is sitting next to me, he's far, far away. Every offer of comfort is met with terse denial. His family sits across from us, tanned from their week in the sun. His father is typing away on his laptop. Julian and Bryson are at work, because someone has to keep things running smoothly.

Courtney flips through a magazine, Isabelle works on an intricate design in an adult coloring book, and Portia holds a novel open, but she hasn't turned a page in ten minutes. Connor's knee bounces, and he taps on the armrest.

I tug at the scrunchie around my wrist. Neither of us has slept particularly well since Christmas Eve, and I'm exhausted, emotionally and physically. Plus, right now, I'm drowning in the tension of it all. "I need a coffee. Does anyone want anything?" I ask.

"The coffee here tastes like bathwater," Courtney grumbles.

Isabelle closes her coloring book and stands, setting it on the chair. "I'll come with you."

I look to Connor. "Can I get you anything?"

"I'm fine." His jaw tics.

My heart aches. I stand and move in front of him, blocking everyone's view with my body. His gaze stays locked on his bouncing knee.

I lean down and press my lips to the top of his head. "I won't be long."

I'm afraid to leave him alone with his parents, but I can't protect him if he's shutting me out. I still haven't had the guts to bring up the conversation we desperately need to have. If Meems doesn't survive, my happiness is no longer important, and if she does...well, that wasn't part of the contract.

Isabelle slips her hand into mine and squeezes. "It'll be okay."

"It should be me reassuring you, not the other way around."

"You're close to Meems. Closer than I am. She always loved Connor best," Isabelle says.

"She understands him," I murmur. I thought I did, too. I thought we were becoming something real, but now I don't know.

"I know Connor can be closed off," Isabelle whispers as we start down the hallway. "But he's scared right now."

"We all are." And he's slipping away from me. I don't know how I'll survive if I lose them both.

"But Connor more than the rest of us," she says softly. "Apart from you, Meems is the only person he loves like this."

My stomach twists, because Connor doesn't love me. *Does he?* a voice inside me demands. It's what my presence in his life brings him that connects us. *Isn't it?* That's what I always tell myself. *But why?*

"You've changed him, Dred. So much. Once Meems makes it through the surgery, he'll be okay. He just needs to get through this part."

"We all do," I agree.

She hugs me tightly. "Thank you for being here. I know it isn't easy."

His family is messy, but I know his sisters care. And he cares for them, too. *So maybe he can love me*, my mind chips in before I can shut it down.

Isabelle releases me, and we continue down the hall until we reach a Tim Hortons. I get coffees and Timbits for everyone.

Portia accepts a coffee and so does Connor, and I leave the others sitting on the table, in case anyone changes their mind. Then it's back to waiting, the knot in my stomach constantly growing, my fears compounding. Two hours into the surgery, a nurse comes in with an update. Her posture and expression make my already roiling stomach sink.

"The doctors are working hard to replace the valve, but it's been touch and go," she says. "We lost Lucy briefly, but she's stabilized now."

Everything inside me goes cold.

"Can they still replace the valve?" Portia asks.

"They're doing their best," the nurse replies.

Connor runs a rough hand through his hair. "This is supposed to make her better, not fucking kill her!"

"Connor, get ahold of yourself," his father snaps.

I settle a gentle hand on his forearm. His sleeves are pushed up to his elbows, some of his tattoos on display. "Let's go for a walk."

"I don't want to go for a walk! I want the doctors to do their job!" he barks.

I pull back, hands raised. "Yelling at them, or me, won't make the outcome any different."

His anger quickly morphs to guilt, and he looks away.

Isabelle and Portia are wide-eyed. His mother looks embarrassed, and his father smug. Like the outburst is expected.

"You'll have to excuse our son. He has a temper," Duncan says to the nurse.

"He's hurting and afraid," I counter. "Look at yourselves." I motion to the four of them, sitting in a row, with no space for their son. "What did you expect when you turned him into an island?" I turn back to Connor and extend my hand. "Let's go for a walk."

He complies, but he still doesn't meet my eyes. And I don't know the impetus behind his actions.

In the hallway, his gaze remains on his feet, jaw tight. "I'm sorry I yelled at you. You didn't deserve that."

"Me too, and no, I didn't." I turn to him. "But this is a really difficult situation. What can I do, Connor? What do you need? I'm trying, but you're shutting me out."

"I just need her to live." He pulls me against his chest. "I need her to stay. I need this not to be the end."

I nod, my cheek rubbing over his shirt. Selfishly, I want the same things—not just for him, but for me, too. Because without her, where will we be? I can't get him to talk to me. He'll hold me now, but he won't give me more of himself.

We loop around the hospital a couple of times, and then return to the waiting area. The next two hours feel endless.

When the doctor finally comes in, Connor grips my hand, squeezing so tightly my bones grind together.

"She made it through," she tells us.

The room exhales a collective breath.

"Thank God." Connor deflates.

"She's not out of the woods yet, though," she cautions. "The next few days are crucial, and we'll be keeping a close eye on her."

"When can I see her?" Connor asks.

"She's still coming out of anesthesia, but you can go in and say hi. Two at a time, though. And only for a minute."

"Go with Isabelle," Connor's father says flatly.

Connor doesn't argue, and he doesn't look at me as he leaves the room, following his sister.

I'm thrilled Meems made it through, but I'm afraid of what's coming next—and what version of Connor will be on the other side of this.

CHAPTER 41
CONNOR

I'm failing at protecting the goalie tonight. We're down by two, and Ryker, Romero, and Palaniappa are working double time to make up for my shitty performance.

I'm frustrated, and I can't focus. Meems is still in the hospital after five days, and I'm here, on the ice, a two-hour flight from home. She turned a corner after the first forty-eight hours and is doing much better. So I made the decision to be with my team instead of her and my wife. I needed to get away. To find some perspective. To put some distance between me and Mildred.

But I'm not performing. So when Ottawa tries to score again in the second half of the third period, I lose what's left of my frayed cool and trip their lead scorer. I'm looking for a fight, so when I have the chance, I hit him in the place it hurts most. And he reacts, giving me a reason to drop my gloves. That results in a five-minute penalty, which is the last thing my team needs this late in the game.

Vander Zee looks like he's ready to murder me. I can't see Coach Forrest-Hammer because she's in the box, but I can imagine how unimpressed she'll be. Ottawa scores again at the end of my penalty, widening the gap. We can't recover, and it's our second loss in as many games—a trend that can't continue if we want to secure a spot in the playoffs.

The mood is somber as we enter the locker room. Romero claps me on the shoulder. "Don't get too up in your head. You have a lot going on."

"It's not an excuse." I shouldn't be here, but I can't be at home. I'm drowning in worry and in wishing I could talk to my wife. Yet I'm too afraid to be honest.

Vander Zee comes in with the rest of the coaches. "This team has been working hard to prove we can succeed without Hammerstein and Hendrix on the roster. But this shit—where you let the other team get under your skin and play like testosterone-fueled rookies—won't fly. We might as well hand over our spot in the playoffs if we keep this up. Get changed, get rested, and get your heads back in the game so we can beat Montreal in two days."

He leaves us to shower and change. No one is in the mood to go out because there's nothing to celebrate. I can already predict the news around tonight's game. People will question whether I'm back to my old ways. They'll wonder if the past few months were a blip, speculate that there's trouble in paradise.

They won't be wrong, either.

Meems's time here might be extended another decade, and while I'm relieved and elated, I didn't plan for this outcome, and I don't know what to do. Because I believe keeping Meems means losing Mildred.

When I leave the locker room, Lexi is in the hall with the other coaches. Her gaze shifts my way, and the disappointment on her face is more than I can deal with. She's always been on my side, but right now she looks pissed.

She pulls me aside. "I know you have a lot going on, but you're a better player than this."

"Maybe I'm not." I voice the thoughts in my head. "Maybe the last few months were a fluke."

She crosses her arms atop her swollen belly. "I know what

you did out there to set him off, and the only reason you would stoop that low is because you're looking for someone to take out their frustration on your face. Don't forget that I'm aware your grandmother's surgery is a stressor, and that there is far more to this than just her recovery."

"I don't know what you're talking about."

"For fuck's sake." She huffs. "Does Mildred know how you feel?"

"It doesn't matter how I feel. It wasn't part of the deal, and she deserves better."

Coach shakes her head. "If this is the version of you she's getting, then yeah, I'd agree. Get your head on straight, Connor. Figure your shit out and stop bringing your personal life onto the ice."

I blink at her. "Are you done?"

"No, actually." Her expression hardens. "You're about to blow up your life and your career because you're too afraid to face your own feelings. You're not the only person who stands to lose something here." And with that, she turns and walks away.

I go back to the hotel and run into Romero in the hall on the way to my room.

"Hey, man, I know today's game was rough, but don't be too hard on yourself," he says. "I know the situation with your grams has been weighing on you."

"I don't deserve a pass for fucking up the game for my team."

"You didn't fuck it up by yourself," he counters. "We were all out there, too."

"I made it worse." I pass the card over the sensor.

He's quiet for a moment. "I'm going to Ryker's room to hang out for a bit. You should come. We can talk strategy for the next game."

"Better if I don't spread my bad mood around." I shoulder my door open.

"If you change your mind, we're in room six twenty-six."

"I won't, but thanks."

He leaves me to stew in my own self-loathing.

My phone buzzes with a message. I pull it out of my pocket, almost hoping for one from my father, so I can get into it with him, too. But he doesn't watch my games.

> **MY DARLING WIFE**
> Hey, how are you?

I stare at the message for long minutes. *I'm fucking awful. I let my team down, I'm away for three more days before I can see Meems again, and I'm certain that when Meems is in good form again, I'll have to let you go.*

> **MY DARLING WIFE**
> Meems had a good day. They have her up and walking around. We played Connect Four and she kicked my ass. The doctors said if she keeps improving they could release her as soon as next week.
>
> Please respond.

> **CONNOR**
> That's good news.

> **MY DARLING WIFE**
> Can I call you?

> **CONNOR**
> Not right now.

> **MY DARLING WIFE**
> Are you out with the team?

> **CONNOR**
> I just can't talk.

> **MY DARLING WIFE**
> Are you okay?

The answer is no. I'm not remotely okay. I'm scared. I'm

fucking everything up. But I can't tell her the truth when there are hours and too many miles separating us. And I'm terrified her feelings won't match mine.

CONNOR

I'm fine. I just don't have the energy to talk.

The dots appear and disappear three times.
She doesn't respond.
Which is what I asked for. *Dammit.*
The next morning when we're boarding the plane, I overhear Flip talking to my wife on the phone. Of course she went to him. He would never shut her out. He's her best friend, the person she confides in the most.
When I lose her, he'll be there to help her move forward. And I'll be exactly as Meems feared I would be: alone.

CHAPTER 42
DRED

"I vote this is where we watch all the playoff games." Tally stretches out in the leather recliner in the theater room at Meems's, her bowl of popcorn on the tray in front of her and a margarita in her hand.

"I agree," says Rix.

"Same!" Hammer drops into the seat next to Rix.

"We should have movie nights here in the offseason," Essie suggests.

"I love that idea!" Hemi hits the button to adjust her leg rest.

"It's a great room," I agree. But I don't make any promises. I have no idea what things will look like next week, let alone during playoffs.

It took more than twenty-four hours for Connor to finally call me after the shitty game against Ottawa, and all he asked about was Meems. He didn't want to talk about the game, nor did he ask how I'm handling all of this. I don't know where the Connor I married has gone, and it's eating me alive.

"I can't wait until the boys are home tomorrow." Rix passes around the box of cookies Tristan sent her.

"I'm sure the produce in your fridge is also excited for his return," Tally mutters, not quite under her breath.

Rix throws her arms in the air. "It was one time!"

"One unforgettable time," Tally adds.

"Gotta admit, I'm not the biggest fan of these long on-the-road stretches, and neither are my lady parts," Hemi says.

"Same. Batdick is nice and all, but he leaves a lot to be desired in the post-orgasm-cuddles department." Hammer sighs.

Essie's eyes light up. "Hollis is totally a cuddlebug, isn't he?"

"The biggest," Hammer confirms.

Essie gets a dreamy look on her face. "So is Nate. We could probably get away with a double bed because he's always wrapped around me all night long."

"Dallas will lie on top of me on the couch and tell me he's still not close enough." Hemi laughs.

"Tris and I always start out cuddling, but he's like a furnace, so I have to worm my way out of his hold. But he requires a point of contact throughout the night, and I always wake up in his arms again," Rix admits.

"That's really sweet." Tally presses her hand to her heart. "I have a full-body pillow that I cuddle with every night, and I look forward to the day I replace it with a real-life boyfriend."

"It'll happen," Essie assures her.

"What about Connor? Is he a cuddler?" Hemi asks.

"Um... I'm probably more the cuddler of the two of us, but he entertains it." I'm questioning all of it now, though. Every night he stretched out his arm and invited me over—was it because he wanted to, or because I wanted him to?

The night before he left for the away series, he fucked me in the dark and let me fall asleep in his arms, but I woke in the middle of the night to find him turned on his side, away from me. And he left the next morning without saying goodbye.

I grown accustomed to the closeness and started taking it for granted—the little notes he'd leave inside my books during away games, and lunch showing up out of the blue at work has stopped with this series. Now there's just silence or short, tense conversations, mostly over text. No banter. No back-and-forth. No *I can't wait to spend time with you in the dark.*

I keep trying to convince myself it's just the stress of Meems's surgery. But I'm far too aware of my own history of shutting down for self-preservation to believe I'm wrong. By shutting me out, is he trying to protect his heart the same way I've always protected mine? I wish the contract wasn't this wall of uncertainty between us, making it impossible for me to trust my intuition.

The Babes and I settle in to watch the game, and I cross my fingers that tonight goes well. I don't know what to expect when Connor gets home tomorrow, and I'm hopeful a win will ease some of the tension, at least for him and the team. The first period goes well, with the Terror shutting out Montreal and scoring a goal. That trend continues in the second period, and Connor seems to be keeping himself in check. He has some chippy moments, but he avoids a penalty.

Everything goes sideways seven minutes into the third period, though, when Flip gets tripped and ends up slammed into the boards by another player.

There's a chorus of gasps that echo through the arena—and the women in this room.

Tally knocks what's left of her popcorn to the floor. Her eyes are glued to the screen, hand covering her mouth, eyes wide with fear.

Essie gives me a look as she reaches out to console her. "He's getting up. He's okay."

"What if he has a concussion? What if he's out again like he was last season? He had such a hard time when he hurt his ankle..." Her voice trails off as she glances around.

"Did you visit him when that happened?" Hemi asks.

"I brought him homemade mac and cheese and Good n' Plenty because they're his favorites." Tally wrings her hands. "I just wanted to see for myself that he was okay."

"It's okay, Tally. We know you have feelings for him," Rix says.

"What?" Her eyes dart around. "I—I don't... What are you—?"

Essie squeezes her hand. "It's okay. We're your friends."

The color drains from her face as we nod. "You all know?"

"We've been friends for a long time, Tally," Hammer explains.

Her bottom lip trembles. "How long have you known?"

Hammer shrugs. Rix and Essie exchange a look.

Hemi is apparently the only one of us with the balls to admit the truth. "For a long time."

"Oh my gosh, do you think he knows?" She slaps her palm over her mouth and tears stream down her face. "I'll never be able to face him again. I'm so embarrassed."

We spend the next half hour consoling Tally, trying to talk her off the emotional ledge. My heart aches for her—especially after she finds out through Rix that Flip is probably out for a few games with a concussion.

Toronto loses the game by one goal in the last two minutes, making them 0 for 3 on this away series.

At the end of the night, the girls take a teary Tally home, and I head upstairs. I stand inside the bedroom I've been sleeping in for months and wonder how much longer I'll be here.

I change into pajamas and call Connor. I hate that I'm surprised when he picks up.

"Hey." It's just one word, but his tone speaks volumes. It's short, clipped, guarded.

I feel like we've rewound back to September, when he showed up at my door with a contract and a way to solve my financial problems. "How are you?"

"Fine. How's Meems?"

"She's gaining strength every day." It's the truth. She's bouncing back in the most beautiful way.

He sighs. "That's what the doctors are saying, so it's good to hear it from you, too."

"I'm sorry about the game tonight."

"It is what it is."

I hug his pillow to my chest, wishing I could confront him, force him to be honest. "Why won't you talk to me?"

"What do you want me to say, Dred? We had a shit series, and I'm at fault for a lot of it, and now our lead scorer is out with an injury." His frustration bleeds through in his tone. "Look, I don't have the bandwidth to do this with you. It's been a crap week. I'm tired, and we have an early flight."

I'm still stuck on the fact that he called me Dred. He only ever uses my full name or darling, or little menace.

He clears his throat. "I'll see you tomorrow."

"Safe travels," I reply woodenly.

"'Night." He ends the call.

I curl myself around his pillow and promise myself that this is the last night I'll spend in this bedroom. I'll wait until Meems is managing on her own, but then I have to go. I won't allow myself to be what Connor's father accused me of.

I hate everything about this plan, but I've survived worse.

CHAPTER 43
CONNOR

The house is eerily quiet when I arrive.

The first thing I should do is go see Meems, since she's home now, but my headspace is rotten, and I can't handle her disappointment over my game play and attitude during the away series. So I take the elevator upstairs to unpack, shower and get my emotions under control.

The last three games have been some of the worst of my career. It's as though the universe gave me one good thing, and then decided everything else had to be taken away to balance it out.

I step into my bedroom, breathing in the comforting scent of my wife's strawberry lotion. I drop my bag, my doomsday mood darkening as I take in the space, registering that something isn't right.

Dewey's enclosure is missing.

I cross to the bathroom, stomach already in knots. Mildred's things have vanished from the vanity. I throw open the doors to the walk-in closet. Everything I've ever bought for her hangs in neat rows, but her favorites that came with her, as well as her work clothes, are gone. The same with the contents of the dresser.

I stalk across the hall, anxiety and anger warring as I burst through her bedroom door. Dewey grunts his surprise. Relief hits hard and fast, followed by more anger. She left, but she stayed.

Because she's bound by a contract that doesn't have a clause in it for the current situation. *If she leaves, she doesn't get the money.* And wouldn't it serve me right? I locked her into this. I saw an opportunity and claimed her, with strings and a promise of compensation for her time.

My father was right, again. Of course she's tired of my shit. I'm tired of it. Being the scapegoat for my family and my team is exhausting. But I've convinced myself it's better—or safer, at least—to be the villain everyone expects than to try and fail to be the hero. Or even just be myself.

Mildred is my wife, and this is my family's home, yet I don't feel like I have a right to be in here when she's not here. So I go back to our bedroom—my bedroom—unpack my bag, and cross to the bar. Scotch won't make things better, but it might help me forget the mess I've made of my life.

I pour three fingers into Mildred's favorite crystal glass and drop into the chair she likes. That's over now. I made sure of it. My phone buzzes with a message, and then another and another. I slip it out of my pocket, ready to put it on do-not-disturb, because I'm in no mood to deal with anyone, but the messages are from my sister.

> **ISABELLE**
> Are you home?
>
> Have you seen the news?
>
> It has to be a lie.

I dial her number, already bracing for the shitstorm. It must be bad if she's messaging me.

"What's going on?" I ask as soon as she picks up.

"Have you seen?"

"I just walked through the door, and before that I was on a plane, and then in my car, so I haven't seen anything. What happened, Izzy?" I wouldn't be surprised if I've made it onto my dad's radar with my poor performance this past series, always dragging the Grace name through the mud.

"It can't be real. It has to be fake." She hiccups through a sob.

I rub my temple and work to keep my tone even. It's not Isabelle's fault I've turned my life into a shitshow. "What has to be fake?"

"There are pictures of Dad and, and—and, oh my gosh, I think I'm going to be sick, Connor." The phone clatters, and it's followed by heaving.

"Izzy? What pictures of Dad?" I put her on speaker and perform a quick search on the Grace name. There are a few hits about my recent performance on the ice, but they are hugely overshadowed by my father. "Oh fuck."

"It's not real," she says, her voice a little steadier now. "It's a deep fake. Someone used AI to make those. Father wouldn't do this."

I don't know if I envy my sister's faith in my father or pity her willingness to keep her head buried in the sand. I can't even imagine how horrified my mother must be.

The images, while grainy, are damning. It's very clear that it's my father, and that the fair-haired, much younger woman in the pictures is *not* my mother. The compromising positions can't be explained away either.

I squint. "Is that his secretary?"

"It's not real," Isabelle practically pleads. "This will ruin us."

"It'll ruin our father," I correct. And possibly stain the Grace name.

Our family is about to be raked over the coals.

"Just tell me everything will be okay, Connor," my sister begs.

"It'll be okay. Think about all the times I've been in the media. It just bounces right off. You're a Grace. It's armor."

"It doesn't feel like armor right now. It feels like a curse."

"I know. But we'll get through it, Izzy."

"Oh God, Julian just got home. I'm a wreck. I need to get myself under control before he sees me. I'll talk to you soon. I love you."

She hangs up before I can say it back.

My world feels like it's crumbling around me. So I do what I do best. I send my father a single text, firing an arrow.

CONNOR
Who's the embarrassment now?

CHAPTER 44
DRED

I put my car in park and snap the scrunchie on my wrist a few times. No more walking on eggshells, or living in this state of limbo. Which means confronting my husband. I can't keep spinning in questions with no answers.

"Give me strength," I murmur as I leave the warmth of my car and step out onto the heated garage floor.

It's been too easy to get used to this level of comfort. I take my time walking through the mansion, climbing the stairs to the second floor slowly, memorizing the feel of the banister under my fingers. My stomach churns as I approach the bedroom I've slept in every night for months.

I never meant to let Connor into my heart this way, but I'm here, in this place of uncertainty, and there's only one way out. The bedroom door is ajar. I take a steadying breath and push it open.

My husband sits in my favorite chair, holding a half-empty glass of scotch, looking every bit the angry, regal billionaire son. I will him to stand, to open his arms and tell me he's sorry for shutting me out this week, that he's been overwhelmed, that he's just as scared as me. But he remains seated, jaw set, eyes empty.

I've already lost him.

Or maybe I never had him.

But I ask the question, because I need to know my next move. "Who are we to each other?"

He taps his index finger on the arm of his chair, expression impassive. "You're my wife, and I'm your husband."

"That's not what I mean."

Before Meems's surgery, it felt like we were moving toward something deep and real, and now the rug is being pulled out from under me.

Again. Still. It's the story of my life.

"What do you mean then, Dred?"

My nickname is a knife through my heart. I'm being reduced, minimized with a single word. He's hurting me on purpose, pushing me away. But he doesn't get to be the villain with me. I won't give him the satisfaction of walking away without pulling the truth out of him, no matter how much it hurts. "How do you feel about me, Connor?"

His jaw tics, and his fingers press into the arms of the chair, but he remains silent, unyielding. I see his father in him now, and it terrifies me.

But I move closer anyway, even though it feels very much like I'm cornering a scared animal.

"What do you feel for me, Connor?" I ask again.

"Gratitude." He crosses and uncrosses his legs. "You gave me back the person who means the most to me."

That hurts, the way it's intended to. My next question scorches its way up my throat. "How much of my happiness these last few months has been tied directly to Meems and how much of it was actually about me, if anything, Connor?"

"Making you happy made Meems happy," he states simply, as if it should be obvious.

As if there's nothing more to it. As if we haven't shared a bed for months. As if he hasn't held me every night like I'm precious.

"And what about you? Did it make you happy?"

"My happiness is irrelevant, Dred."

"Stop calling me that!"

"Why? It's what everyone else calls you."

"You are not everyone else!"

He shrugs. "But what if I am?"

"Why are you shutting me out like this?"

"I'm not," he says flatly.

"You are," I argue. "Everything you're doing right now makes me feel like I'm all the things your father accused me of." And I refuse to allow myself to be used so Connor can escape whatever is happening inside his heart and his head. I know there's something.

His throat bobs, and he rolls his head on his shoulders. "You signed a contract. You agreed to marry me for financial security. And I don't blame you. If I was in your position, I would have done the same thing." He motions between us, voice void of emotion as he continues to eviscerate my heart. "This was never real. I saw an opportunity, and I took it. So did you."

Every word feels like salt rubbed into an open wound, one that's festered since childhood. The little girl who was too broken to fix. The one people took home and hoped would be the daughter they'd always dreamed of. But I never was. The part of me that could trust an adult to take care of me, to put me first, had been shattered.

I'm a charity case.

Broken.

Dispensable.

I always have been. Like everyone else, Connor felt bad for me. He saw me as a chance to make the one person who has his heart happy. And he took full advantage of every single weakness I have. He used my soft, flawed heart against me.

He drops his head, shielding his eyes from me. Cutting off my link to his emotions. But now I'm angry. All those years spent broken taught me how to recognize it in others. And I hate being lied to.

This started as a contract, but somewhere along the way,

things shifted. Connor might not want to admit the truth, but I was more than an obligation to fulfill, and he was more than just a ticket to a better life.

I fell for *him*. Not the angry son of a billionaire. Not the hockey player who became a villain on the ice and welcomed all the negative attention because it affirmed what he already believed about himself. I didn't fall for this closed-off version of the man who handed me a marriage contract.

I fell for the man who took care of me when I slid into a pit of memories I couldn't escape on my own.

He gifted me the twins for Christmas.

He gave me a room in this house he knew I would love.

He played board games with me.

Read books to me.

Cuddled me.

Fucked me.

Brought my fantasies to life. He made me believe in the possibility that I could have a family. That I could be loved.

And I'm angry that he's so cavalier. Just taking it all away—from me and from himself.

He's twisting our time together into something with too many sharp edges, erasing all the good parts of him like they never existed.

His jaw clenches, and he grips the arms of his chair.

I wait for him to own some part of his truth.

But instead he slices my heart in two.

"I don't want you here."

CHAPTER 45
CONNOR

I can't handle the hurt in her voice or the sting of my own feelings. Mildred has no idea about the shitstorm that's about to hit my family, or her, because she carries the Grace name. I wish I could give her a piece of the truth, but what good would that do either of us? This isn't a life she wants. I'm not the person she should be tied to.

The silence that stretches between us is agonizing, but her next words tear my soul apart.

"I thought you were better than your father." Her voice cracks with emotion. "You're not a better liar, but you're just as cruel."

I lift my head at the last part.

Any of the softness I've come to love has disappeared. I ruin beautiful things, as evidenced by what I'm doing to her, to me, to what she means to me.

Her cold gaze meets mine. "I pity you."

"You shouldn't." I don't deserve anything but her wrath.

She turns around and walks out.

It takes every ounce of restraint not to run across to her bedroom and tell her she has to stay. That she can't leave. She has an obligation to fulfill.

But hasn't she already done that?

She mended Meems's heart, gave her something to keep fighting for. And for that I'm eternally grateful, so forcing her to stay to incur more of my vitriol seems like a torment she doesn't need. And I already hate myself enough right now.

Half an hour later, there's movement in the hall. I do us both a favor and stay where I am.

Eventually Cedrick appears in the doorway, his expression stricken. "Mrs. Grace has taken her personal effects and is preparing to leave the manor."

My stomach feels as though it's trying to turn itself inside out. I nod.

"If I may be so bold, maybe you would try to talk to her and request that she stay?"

"She should be able to leave if she wants to."

He stands there for a long moment before he clears his throat. "Madame Grace is speaking with her now. She's asked that you come down."

I thought I would have time to prepare for this. Might as well rip every Band-Aid off and let all the wounds bleed at the same time. "I'll be down shortly."

He leaves me alone.

I stall another twenty minutes, but I don't want Meems to have to come to me.

She's waiting for me in the living room when I descend the stairs. She doesn't look sad, or frail, or like she had heart surgery less than two weeks ago. She looks like a wrathful angel.

She points to the chair across from her. "Sit."

I follow her orders. My throat is tight, my mouth dry, my eyes burning. I've ruined my life, and I have no one to blame but myself. I deserve her disappointment and her anger.

"When will you stop sabotaging yourself?"

"She left me," I point out, stupidly.

"Why are you pushing her away?"

"The family's about to be dragged through the mud, thanks

to Father. Mildred doesn't need to be put through that, too." It's a weak excuse that holds no merit.

"Your father's idiot choices are his own, and yes, there will be shit flinging, but it's not as though she hasn't already endured it. Now try again, with the truth this time."

"Mildred ran into financial issues back in September."

"What does this have to do with anything?"

"I'm explaining." I run a hand down my face. "I saw how much she cared about you, and how much you cared about her, so I told her I would take care of the situation...if she agreed to marry me. I didn't want you to think I was going to end up alone, so I made her sign a contract."

Meems throws the closest object at me, which thankfully is a box of tissues and not something she'll regret breaking. She also has terrible aim, so it hits me in the arm and drops to the floor. "You made her sign a contract?"

"I did it for you! I wanted you to be happy!"

"I would have been more than happy for Dred to be your girlfriend. You didn't need to make her your wife."

"She never would have stayed with me otherwise! My own family can't even stand me."

"You silly, ridiculous man. You will fight anything, won't you?" She sighs and shakes her head. "You always manage to do things the hard way, even when you have alternatives."

"What other option did I have?"

"You could have done what I suggested in the first place and asked her out on a date," she points out.

"She never would have said yes. Her best friend hated me." It'll be present tense again once he finds out she's left me, and why.

"She said yes to marrying you," Meems argues.

"Only because she didn't have another option."

"Didn't she?" She shakes her head. "Always and forever the hard way. Even when you were a little boy."

"Nothing has changed, obviously."

"Shut up and listen," Meems snaps.

I shut my stupid mouth.

"There was an event." She rolls her eyes to the ceiling, trying to remember the details.

"There was always an event," I supply, unhelpfully.

She shoots me a look. "Your father always needed to throw a party so everyone could celebrate the amazing things he did, and you and your sisters were always on display. Your sisters loved the dresses, at least for the first couple of hours, because they could pretend they were princesses."

"The fairy tale worked for them," I mumble.

"For a time, yes. But it never worked for you. You hated the suits. You despised being made to look like a miniature adult when all you wanted to do was play hockey." She shakes her head sadly.

I would endure just about anything to get on the ice, but I always hated the parties. Hated all the people, the socializing, being something I wasn't.

"This one night you refused to get dressed. Your mother was furious. Your father was too busy to help, because God forbid he be a parent outside of the title. The staff couldn't persuade you. And the moment you saw a chance, you bolted and hid. They had to search for you for over an hour."

I remember that night now. I was supposed to have a hockey game, but my parents had deemed the party more important. I knew what it would look like. Hours of sitting in chairs like dolls —not being able to move, run, play, or have fun. No time on the ice. "I hid in Dad's office."

"And you broke your father's favorite statue," she adds.

My father had been enraged, red faced and livid. He'd yelled and railed and spanked me so hard it hurt to sit for days.

"You still had to sit through the party, and you lost your hockey privileges for a week."

I remember that part, too. The boredom had nearly killed me.

"You were always mischievous, Connor. It's one of my favorite things about you—that and the fact that you refuse to fall in line when it doesn't suit you. But when you find yourself in trouble, you don't look for a way out of it, you find a way to make an even bigger mess. All you had to do was tell Mildred the truth. You could have owned the way you feel about her, but instead, you've done everything in your power to cut her down and shut her out."

She's right. That's exactly what I did.

Meems's expression grows sad again. "Anyone who sees the way you look at her knows you're in love. All you had to do was tell her, and she would have been yours. Now you'll have to work ten times as hard to fix the things you've broken."

"I don't deserve her."

"Not with the way you're acting right now, no. This is you self-sabotaging, Connor. You do it in your career, with your family, with your teammates. The only person you hadn't done it with was *me*. Except now here we are. You married the woman of your dreams under the guise of making *me* happy. You should have owned your feelings for Mildred from the start, because if you're honest with yourself, they existed long before you locked her into a contract."

"I knew she was a good person."

"And you liked her!"

"I liked her," I reluctantly agree.

"And you fell in love with her!"

I look at my hands.

She sighs. "All you had to do was rip that contract up. That was it."

"But then she would have left," I whisper.

"No. That's what you were afraid she would do. So instead of putting yourself on the line, you made sure that's what happened." Meems pauses for a moment, waiting for me to acknowledge this truth. Finally I nod. "You want to fix the mess you've made? Do something that makes you proud of *yourself*, so other people can be proud of you, too."

She pushes out of the chair and crosses over to me. Her soft, weathered hand rests against my shoulder, and she bends to press her lips to the top of my head. "Stop breaking your own heart."

CHAPTER 46
DRED

Heartbreak gets two thumbs down from me. Moving back into my apartment feels simultaneously right and wrong. And it is mine now; I own it. It's a wedding gift I won't part with.

I nearly had a heart attack when the cleaning woman let herself in while I was in the shower crying my heart out an hour ago. Apparently Connor has had someone come in every other week to dust and vacuum, like he was ready for this. Like he expected me to leave eventually. Because he believed I wouldn't want to stay. And now here I am, heart in tatters, frustrated and angry that he pushed me to make this decision because of his own fears.

There's a knock at my door, and then it swings open because I've left the security latch off for Flip. He's laden with grocery bags and a huge tub of ice cream.

I burst into tears.

He sets the groceries and ice cream on the closest surface and opens his arms. I fall into them and sob all over his shirt.

"I'm sorry." He heaves a sigh. "I'll kick his ass, if you want."

"Maybe…" I hiccup.

He lifts me so my feet are dangling and carries me over to the couch. Once I'm arranged in a not-awkward position, I continue sobbing into his shirt. For the briefest moment, I wish my feelings for him weren't solely platonic. Flip is broken too, but at least I *know* that he loves me, even if it isn't the kind that dreams are made of.

When I can finally take a full breath, and I'm not hiccupping my way through every attempt at speaking, Flip grabs us both a drink, piles two bowls with half-melted ice cream, and settles in next to me, letting me hug his arm.

Before I can explain everything, there's another knock on the door. "Hello?" Rix's questioning lilt filters down the hall.

"Maybe Flip's checking on the place," Tristan says.

"We're in here!" I call out.

Tristan and Rix appear in the living room a few seconds later, Tristan carrying several containers, likely filled with Flip's weekly food-plan items.

Rix's eyes go wide. "Dred? What happened? Are you okay?"

"Connor and I are over."

"What? Why? But he's so in love with you." She wraps me in her arms.

Flip gets two more bowls of ice cream, and they join us in the living room for sad story time.

"I fell in love with him, and he fell in love with me, but he refuses to own his feelings," I explain.

Flip nods slowly. "Do you want to start from the beginning? Because usually people marry each other *after* they fall in love, not before."

That he's made it this long not knowing the whole story speaks to how amazing he is as a best friend. And the rest of my friends showed up for me too, the whole time.

So I start from the beginning—with Callie's hockey games and Connor coming to the library looking for Meems's books, me putting together who she was and how connected I already felt to her before Connor proposed the arrangement to alleviate the possibility of me losing my apartment, and then signing the contract."

Tristan arches a brow. "You signed a contract to marry him?"

I explain the parameters.

Flip's expression darkens. "You know I would have helped you with the apartment, and I wouldn't have made you sign anything."

Tristan and Rix share a look.

"What's that about?" Flip motions between them. "You can't tell me you think what he did was okay."

"We both stood to gain something," I reason.

"Connor did a lot more at our wedding than just fix the accommodations," Rix says.

"What do you mean?" Flip asks.

"My mother showed up," Tristan explains.

My eyes widen. "What? When?" Tristan hasn't seen his mother since she abandoned their family when he was twelve.

"The day before the wedding. I didn't see her, but Nate did. I wasn't there, but Essie and Nate explained what happened after the wedding. Connor paid her off. He gave her three million dollars to stay out of our lives. He made her sign a contract, too, saying she'll have to pay it back if she ever tries to contact one of us again. And he refuses to accept any form of repayment."

"He said it was our wedding gift," Rix adds.

"Wow." Flip runs a hand through his hair. "That's...wow."

This absolutely sounds like something Connor would do, especially considering the circumstances. I let my head flop back against the couch cushions. More tears fall. "This just makes what's happened so much worse." I pinch the bridge of my nose.

"Maybe he's scared, like I was?" Tristan offers.

I nod, and Flip hands me a tissue.

Tristan and Rix stay for a few more minutes, but then leave me and Flip to talk with a promise to call later.

"I wish you'd come to me with this, Dred." Flip's sadness is written all over his face.

I set my ice cream soup aside, taking his warm hand in my cold one. "But you understand why I couldn't ask that. Even if we didn't want it to, it would've changed our relationship. I couldn't take that risk. Our friendship is too important. Connor felt...like a safe person to make that arrangement with. He loves his Meems so much, and I love her too. I thought I could play the role and keep my heart out of it."

"But that changed for both of you."

"At first I thought... I thought he was just doing these things to make me happy because it made his Meems happy. It made sense. The more content he kept me, the more real it would look to everyone else, right?"

He nods. "It definitely looked real by the time you got to the wedding."

"I started sleeping with him after the wedding," I admit. "And then...I started sleeping *with* him. I moved into his bedroom. It felt like we were building a life together. He brought the twins to the house for Christmas for me. And I wanted to keep them forever. I wanted what was happening to be real, Flip. I wanted those kids to be ours. I wanted Meems to be mine, too. I wanted to be loved, and love back and not have it all taken away." I break down again, tears rolling down my cheeks, dropping onto his shirt and my hands. "But he was so cruel. So needlessly, painfully cruel. And it hurts so much, because I know he's a good person, and I know he feels the same way about me as I do about him. He just can't admit it. He ruined it all out of fear, and I'm in pieces all over again, afraid I'll never be able to put myself back together."

Flip wraps his arms around me and rocks me, like I'm a child and he's the parent I never had, but always wanted. We wear so many hats for each other—best friend, mother, father, confidant, champion, therapist, cheerleader, ass-kicker.

"Tell me I won't feel like this forever," I cry. "Tell me it won't hurt like this for the rest of my life."

"It won't feel like this forever." He kisses the top of my head. "But it will hurt for a while—at least until he gets his head out of his ass. And maybe even for a while after that."

"What if he doesn't get his head out of his ass? I feel so stupid for falling in love."

Flip stops rocking. "For one, you're not stupid, Dred. You're one of the smartest people I know, so be nice to my best friend or else."

I huff a laugh and give him a look. "I fell for your nemesis."

"I hate that he's hurt you. I hate that he's actually a nice guy behind all the bullshit. I hate that his fear reaction is to be cruel. And I hate that I might end up breaking his face because he's too much of a numpty to own his feelings for you. But of course you fell for the guy everyone loves to tear down who also just wants to make his grandma happy. He did everything in his power to try to make you happy, too. We all saw it. *I* saw it. It would be hard not to like him for that." He shrugs. "Plus you have wicked chemistry."

"So I'm not losing my mind? He has feelings for me?"

Flip nods. "Like you said, he just doesn't know how to handle them, and he's being an idiot."

"I'm sorry I didn't ask for help," I whisper.

"Me too, but I understand why you didn't." He wraps his arm around my shoulder and squeezes me. "I wish my shit hadn't gotten in the way of that. Then maybe your heart wouldn't be broken."

"I guess you and I get to be divorcees together, huh?" I joke.

He huffs a humorless laugh. "There's some real irony here, isn't there? I married Fiona in secret, thinking we would spend our lives together, and all she wanted was the money. You and Connor got married based on a contract but ended up falling for real."

"And here we both are."

"Here we both are," he agrees.

Flip married his high school sweetheart in his last semester of university. He was headed for the pros after graduation. They'd dated in high school and had broken up when they went to different universities, but they'd reconnected in their final year. He loved her and wanted to spend the rest of his life with her.

They'd kept their marriage a secret, not wanting their parents to talk them into waiting until they'd graduated. And then a few months in, Flip realized she was only in it for the lifestyle it would afford her. It was an expensive, painful lesson—one he learned on his own. I'm the only person who knows. Not even Tristan or his sister are aware that he was married, or that he basically handed Fiona his first year's salary to get her out of his life.

"I want a family, Flip."

"I'm your family."

"I want kids, though. I love being an aunty to Callie and Fee, and to Lexi and Roman's little one who will be here soon, and all the other Terror babies that are yet to come. But I want my own kids. They don't have to be biologically mine. I wanted to keep the twins so badly at Christmas. For a moment I imagined I could." I believed Connor and I could. "But what if I'm too broken to be good for them?"

"You're not. You're an incredible, resilient, amazing person, and you have so much love to give," he assures me.

"I also have actual savings now. I donated some of it to the library and a few charities, but most of the money is still there." It's socked away into investments and GICs because I didn't know what else to do with it.

"We can talk to Rix," Flip says. "She'll help you with the financial side."

"I started the foster parent application process last year. I didn't have the finances to support it then, but I do now. I know Victor and Everly will age out in the next few years, but I could still love them. I could be their soft place to land. I can give them a home they can always come back to."

Flip hugs me. "You would be great for them. Tell me how I can help, and I'll do everything in my power to make this happen for you."

CHAPTER 47
CONNOR

I'd gotten used to feeling like part of the team, but now I'm back where I started when I first joined the Terror. On the outs. The problem.

Madden has been firing eyeball daggers at me the entire practice. Even Stiles and Bright, who usually don't take sides, are stonewalling me. Coach Vander Zee seems to think my on-ice issues have everything to do with the Grace family scandal that's making headlines. My mother is on the verge of a nervous breakdown and has been staying with Portia and Bryson. Isabelle has gone into hiding and refuses to leave the house. I wish I was less surprised by the whole thing. It's not as high on my radar as it should be, though, because my own life is in shambles. My teammates know, but other than Meems, my family is unaware.

Even Romero is pissed. "You're your own worst enemy, man," he grumbles as we head to the locker room after a messy practice.

"I know." Meems spelled that out for me yesterday, and I've had the past twenty-four hours to think about how right she is.

"You need to figure your shit out," Ryker adds.

"I know."

Ryker sighs and shakes his head.

He and Romero are the only two people on the team still talking to me, and nothing they have to say is kind. It's also not untrue.

I keep my mouth shut as we strip out of our gear. Coach Vander Zee comes in and reads us the riot act, then asks to see me in his office. I nod and close my eyes a moment. If I get traded again, it'll be my own damn fault. And it'll mean I won't be close to Meems anymore. But if I end up on the other side of the country, Mildred won't have to deal with me, and maybe that would be better for her.

I'm still sitting on the bench, spinning worst-case scenarios and hating myself, when Madden appears in my peripheral vision. We're both in boxer briefs. The rest of the team is in the showers.

"You're a fucking asshole," he informs me.

"Yup."

"I know what you did for Tristan and Rix at their wedding."

I shrug. "My family owns half the hotels in Aruba. If I hadn't done it, I would have been an even bigger asshole than I already am."

Flip crosses his arms. "I mean with his mother."

That gets my attention. "He wasn't supposed to tell anyone about that."

"Well, he told me, and Dred knows, too. That was an amazing thing to do, you fucking dickbag."

"The wedding would have been ruined otherwise." I scrub a hand down my face. "I could have done the same thing for Mildred, you know. I could have just stepped in and paid off the debt for her, no questions asked."

"She wouldn't have accepted the money."

"But I could have fixed the entire problem without her even realizing I'd done it. I could have made it go away like that." I snap my fingers. "But I didn't. I locked her into a contract. I made her *mine*."

Flip hauls off and punches me in the face. Like I wanted him to. I see stars, and the ache is immediate and vicious.

"You should do that again," I goad. "It'll make you feel better."

"Push my buttons all you want." He shakes out his hand. "But the only reason you're doing it is because you hate yourself, and you want someone else to take away the emotional hurt you've caused by distracting you with physical pain. You locked Dred into a contract because you wanted her. Not to piss me off —although I'm sure that gave you a little thrill—but because you actually liked her, and it was the most logical way in your messed-up brain to have her. Man the fuck up, Connor. Take some responsibility for yourself." His eyes are on fire, and he looks particularly wrathful. "You broke my best friend's heart. I know you've got your fair share of issues, and your family is a mess right now, but what you did to Dred is un-fucking-forgivable."

My stomach bottoms out with that statement. "She's better off without me."

He sneers at me. "What the fuck is wrong with you?"

So many things. "Mildred is kind and good and all the things I'm not. She'll get sick of me and my messes. I'm not good enough for her, and I sure as fuck don't deserve her. Especially not her heart."

Flip's lip curls, and his expression shifts to irritation. "First of all, everything you've done, however convoluted and backwards, says something completely different. Secondly, you don't get to decide who my best friend deserves to love or what choices she makes."

I frown. Of all the reactions he could have, this is the last one I expected. More shots to the face, yes, but not him defending her feelings for me.

"Don't be a fucking idiot, Connor. Dred is loyal to the core and the most amazing person. You want her back? Figure out a way to undo the damage you did when you decided shredding her heart was the best way to keep your own safe. She has been hurt by so many people." All his anger turns to anguish. He takes a moment to center himself. "By the people who were supposed to keep her safe, who were supposed to love her the most. And despite all the shit she's endured, she is still one of the best people I know. Own your stupidity, and find a way to take yourself off that list."

He leaves me sitting on the bench, eviscerated.

But he's right, about all of it. And I added myself to the list of people who have hurt her. I need to fix that—to prove to her and to myself that I'm nothing like my father. That I can love her the way she deserves. That I can take care of her heart, if she's willing to give me a second chance.

I wait until the rest of the team is out of the showers before I step in. When I'm done, I head up to see Coach Vander Zee. He's alone in his office when I arrive. He looks tired.

"Have a seat, Connor."

I take the chair across from him.

He tents his hands, pointer fingers touching. "How are you?"

"I've been better."

He squints, eyes going to my jaw. I know from the mirror in the locker room that it's already turning purple. "What happened to your face?"

"Just clumsy."

He arches a brow. "That's the story you're going with?"

"Yup."

He sighs. "The issue with your family must be stressful on top of everything else."

I shrug. "I have bigger problems."

"I heard that things aren't so good at home."

"From Coach Forrest-Hammer?"

"Yeah."

"Did she happen to mention how Mildred is doing?" I ask.

"That's a conversation you should probably have with Lexi, or possibly your wife," he offers. "I don't know the story, and I don't need to, but if you need time off the ice to sort out your personal issues, we can arrange that."

"I don't know that time off will fix this," I admit. It certainly won't make things with my teammates better.

"You've had a lot thrown at you this season." He doesn't elaborate. Just lets it hang there.

"Yeah," I agree. *But I made my own bed.*

He sighs. "Look, Connor, you're an excellent player—better than your stats suggest. We brought you to this team because we see the potential in you, and up until last week, this season has been the best of your career. The pressure can be intense, especially when you have conflict coming at you from all sides. You worked your ass off to get here, just like the rest of these boys. I know you've felt the need to prove yourself, not just to the team, but to everyone else, too. I don't envy your position, or what you deal with off the ice. But when shit goes sideways, it's easy to get caught in the spiral and let it pull you down. If someone offers you a hand, take it, because it can be the difference between staying in the hole you dug or finding a way out."

I nod. "You're right. I know you're right. I'm trying to figure it out."

"Just take the time, if you need it."

"Thanks, Coach. I'll let you know, okay?"

"Okay. Rest up. We've got a big game tomorrow."

I leave his office and head down the hall to Lexi's. My palms are sweaty by the time I knock on her open door.

She looks up from her computer screen, but doesn't speak.

"Can I talk to you?"

She motions to the chair across from her.

"As Lexi and not my coach," I clarify.

She nods.

I cross the room and take the offered seat. "Have you talked to Mildred?"

"Yes."

"How is she?"

She crosses her arms. "How do you think she is?"

I drop my head, focusing on my wedding band. "I really messed this up."

"In full Connor form, you absolutely did." Lexi rubs her belly. "What is it that you're trying to ask?"

"I don't know. I just...I want to know if she's okay."

"Are you okay?"

"No."

"Then what would make you think she is?" She shifts in her chair, like she's struggling to get comfortable. She's due soon, so I imagine there isn't a whole lot of room left for that kid or her internal organs. "You can't mine me for information about Dred," she says after a moment. "She is my best friend, and I have to protect her and keep her confidence. I'm in a unique position in that I know the details of your arrangement. I also know that the parameters changed drastically over the past several months. You had choices, Connor, ones that could have had a very different result. I think you need to ask yourself why you chose to hurt someone you love in this way, instead of being honest about your feelings." The furrow in her brow deepens, and she holds up a hand.

I jump out of my chair. "Are *you* okay?"

"Yeah, I just...I had Braxton Hicks earlier in the week. It's probably the same thing again."

"Shit. I'm stressing you out."

She shakes her head. "I'm fine. I'm just really pregnant."

"Why don't I drive you home?"

She grimaces and rubs her belly.

"Please, Lexi. Let me do this for you."

"Yeah, okay. That would be good." She pushes herself to standing. "Let me just get my stuff together."

I help Lexi with her things and walk her to the elevator. I'm struck by the fact that these people who love Mildred and have her best interest at heart aren't shutting me out the way I did her. And they're also not pouncing on my weakness the way my father would. Instead they're reaching to pull me out of the hole I dug. And doesn't that tell me everything I need to know about the woman I married? She is loved and beloved, and she and everyone around her want to show me I can be too. This is a once-in-a-lifetime gift, and it's my turn to step up and prove that I deserve it.

When the elevator arrives at our floor, Romero and Ryker step out.

"Everything okay?" Romero asks, putting his hand over the sensor to keep the doors from closing.

"Yeah, just Braxton Hicks." Lexi rubs her belly like she's trying to make a genie appear. "Connor's driving me home."

"You want one of us to follow in your car?" Romero offers.

"It's fine. I'll come back and get it once Lexi is settled, but thanks." I follow Lexi into the elevator.

"Message if you need any help," Romero says.

"Thanks, man." I give him a chin tip and press the button for the parking garage.

The doors slide closed, and Lexi leans against the railing. "The rest of the team will come around."

"I'm used to being on the outs."

Her eyes narrow on my jaw. "What happened to your face?"

"Flip and I had a discussion."

"With your fists?"

"I deserved it."

She sighs and continues rubbing her belly. "I really hope this doesn't send you back to last-season-style conflict."

"He's pissed that I've messed up my life and his best friend's, but his focus is on the team."

She grimaces and grips the rail.

"Let's not talk about this. I feel like it's causing you unnecessary stress. Are you sure you don't want me to take you to the hospital?"

She shakes her head. "My water hasn't even broken. I'm better off at home. Thanks, though."

We walk out to her car, and I get her settled in the passenger seat for the drive to her and Roman's place. Once she's upstairs, I make sure she's comfortable. "You sure you don't want me to stick around until Roman gets home?" I ask.

"He'll be home in an hour. I'm just going to clean the cupboards or something."

"Shouldn't you be resting?"

She shrugs. "I feel better when I'm moving around. Thanks for the ride, though."

"No problem." I open the door.

"Connor."

I look back over my shoulder.

"The first step to cleaning up the mess you made is to reach out to Dred."

"I know."

I need to prove to myself and Mildred that I will never hurt her like this again. That I won't let my fears get in the way of my love for her.

CHAPTER 48
DRED

"Connor's here." Everly's nails are digging into my arm. She's been halfway in my lap since we arrived at the hospital over an hour ago. Apparently Connor drove Lexi home sometime after practice, and a couple hours later she realized her Braxton-Hicks contractions were actual labor.

I offered to drop Everly and Victor off at the group home—explaining that babies come in their own time and we'd likely be hanging around the hospital for a lot of hours—but they said they'd rather be with me, so here we are. I have a feeling they wanted to come partly because they hoped Connor would show up.

Since leaving Connor, I've been surrounded by my friends—particularly Roman, Lexi, and Callie, who have very much become my family too—and the twins have been like shadows. In my downtime, I've been fully immersed in gala preparation and working towards getting myself on the foster parent list. Thankfully those two things have kept me preoccupied. I haven't told Everly and Victor yet, because I don't want to set them up for disappointment if it doesn't pan out, but my happiness eggs are fully in this basket.

There's no adequate way to prepare for the way it feels to see

Connor in three dimensions. I'm sad and angry that he can't own his feelings. My heart aches with the loss and races with longing. I wish I could magically erase everything that's happened between us since Christmas, when the best news for Meems signaled the beginning of the end for us.

Callie stands to rush over to say hi to Connor, but then turns back to me, which breaks my already shattered heart even more. She's seen me crying over Connor. Now she doesn't know what to think. But I nod to her, and she runs the rest of the way to him.

He opens his arms, and she throws hers around him.

"Why isn't Callie mad at him?" Everly rubs her face on my arm, like a cat looking for comfort.

"They have a different relationship."

"Does it make you upset that she's hugging him?" There's real longing in her voice that matches what's in my heart.

"No, it doesn't make me upset." He's always felt like an island. I'd rather not contribute to that. "You should go talk to him."

"Why doesn't he come over here and talk to you?" She presses her cheek harder against my arm.

"He probably wants to be respectful." That's easier to swallow than him truly being incapable of doing so. "Lexi is my friend, but Connor is also friends with the team and Roman and Lexi," I explain. "It's complicated for us, but it doesn't have to be complicated for you."

"Why can't things just go back to the way they were?"

"I wish it was that simple, sweetheart." I lean my cheek against the top of her head. "Go say hi. He's been asking about you."

"He has?"

"Yup. He asked Lexi how you're doing, so now you can tell him yourself."

"I'm mad at him, though."

"You can be upset and still want to talk to him."

She rolls her bottom lip between her teeth. "Will you be upset?"

"No, not at all. It would make me feel better if you went over there, actually, because I know you're missing him and he's missing you, and there's no need to keep feeling that way when you're both right here."

"Okay." She drags herself out of the chair, but looks over her shoulder at me twice as she crosses to him.

Victor watches her from the other side of the waiting room where he's playing cards with Dallas and Flip. He'll be less likely to approach Connor out of loyalty to me.

All of Lexi's closest people, who are also the ones most upset with Connor, are here. It says a lot that he's willing to brave the angry masses to show his face.

Rix drops into the chair next to mine. "How you doing?"

"My heart is pretty beat up," I admit.

"Have you talked at all?"

I shake my head.

"Maybe today should be the day."

"Maybe." My chest constricts as Everly's hands start flailing while she explains something to Connor.

Victor is the stoic one who keeps his emotions on lock, while Everly lets all of hers out. Everly feels very much like her parents have broken up, and it's the same for me. I turned four pieces into a whole in my head, and I'm drifting between sad and angry at the loss.

"I just don't get why you haven't talked! How can you solve anything if you don't? You can't make me feel like I finally have a family and then take it all away! It's not fair!" Everly bursts into tears, and Connor wraps his arms around her.

She sags into him, sobbing against his chest. My poor glued-together heart threatens to turn into pieces again. Connor glances at me over her shoulder and the sadness in his eyes almost does me in.

He holds her while she cries.

Like a father would.

Like my partner would.

Like the man I fell in love with would.

I ache with the desire to go to them, to comfort her, too. But they need this moment, where she falls apart, and he shows her he cares. I want our feelings for each other to be big enough to get past this, but I also need him to see what happens when he shuts out the people who love him. The consequences are real, and vast and painful.

I need him to find the place where he's ready to own the hurt he caused. Maybe seeing the impact on Everly—a girl without a family, who for a moment in time believed maybe she could have one—will help give him the clarity he needs.

I excuse myself to the bathroom, because I'm on the verge of tears. When I come out, Everly drapes herself over my back like a weighted human blanket. "I miss him."

"Me too."

"He misses us, too. He misses you."

When I look up, Connor moves toward us, and his eyes find mine. I see the regret written all over his gorgeous, forlorn face. His hand lifts, and for a moment I think he'll reach out and touch me. Ground me. Ease the ache in my heart. But he doesn't.

I wish love didn't come with thorns.

Roman appears in the doorway, and all eyes move to him. His wide smile tells us the most important thing. Lexi and Roman are parents.

"We have a brand-new baby girl!" he announces.

Hammer is the first to hug him, and then everyone converges, smiling and laughing and congratulating. It's a beautiful moment, and my heart fills with happiness for him and Lexi and her sisters. They deserve this opportunity to feel whole.

But the piece of me that longs for my own family aches, and I wonder if I'll ever have a heart full of my own happiness, and not just joy for the people around me.

CHAPTER 49
CONNOR

I'm kicking myself for not pulling Mildred aside at the hospital when I had the chance a few days ago. But I won't waste another opportunity. Tonight is the library fundraising gala, organized with the help of Hemi and Hammer, to support Toronto Central's community programs. Meems is my date.

Tristan steps up beside me as I grab Meems a ginger ale from the bar. "How you doing, man?"

"Okay. You?"

He knows the story behind me and Mildred now. The whole group does. There's less animosity from my team and a lot more pity. I'm not sure which I like less.

"I'm good." He surveys the wall of silent auction items, half of them donated by me and Meems. "This is quite the event."

"It should keep the library programs running for the foreseeable future."

My plan is to make sure Mildred never has to write another grant proposal. Meems was livid when she discovered my father had pulled the funding she'd set up years ago. She was also beyond enraged when she found out he'd been cheating on my mother. She's feeling better since we fixed the library funding, but I don't know what will repair things for my father.

"Dred does amazing things for her community," Tristan says.

"She does."

After a beat of silence he adds, "I'm sorry I told Flip about what you did at my wedding, but I'm also not sorry."

"It's okay. It's not fair that I asked you to keep that secret for me."

He shrugs. "We're all keeping secrets. You don't have to keep hiding the fact that you're a good guy, Connor. You can own it."

"Am I, though? I could have just made Mildred's problem go away like I did yours."

He sighs. "How would that have worked, though? She wouldn't have accepted it as a gift. It's not how she operates. You know that. You knew that from the start, though, didn't you? After all the time you spent with her at Callie's games."

"Yeah." I sigh. "She's an easy person to care about."

"Yeah." He looks across the room. "Isn't that the same woman Quinn brought to your wedding?"

I stiffen.

"Sorry, man." He claps me on the shoulder, expression shifting to chagrin. "I didn't mean to pour salt on that wound."

"It's okay. It's my fault it's bleeding. And yeah, that's Lovey Butterson. They've been friends since childhood."

He nods. "I remember her being around when we were at the Hockey Academy. They don't really give me the friends vibe, though."

"Yeah, I agree with you there, but maybe they're not ready to own it." Like how I wasn't ready to own my feelings for Mildred. "Especially with how close their families are."

"I know how complicated that can be."

"It worked out for you, though." I rub the back of my neck as my gaze catches on my wife. "Who knows, maybe I'll be able to dig myself out of the hole I made, too."

Mildred looks stunning in the wine-colored dress she wore to her bridal shower. And I love that she's wearing it again. This is a rebellion of epic proportions as far as my family is concerned.

She's across the room, surrounded by her friends, talking to Meems. Mildred is smiling, but she looks tired. I wonder if she's having the same problem sleeping that I am. For a few months, the away games were manageable because I knew I'd be able to wrap myself around her when I got home. Now her absence in our bed has made sleep elusive. Grace Manor only feels like home when she's in it.

"What the fuck?" Tristan mutters, pulling me out of my head and back to the present.

"What's wrong?"

"Did you know your parents were coming?"

"I wasn't aware." Although I haven't been on speaking terms with my father. I kind of thought my mother wasn't either.

Yet sure enough, my parents are standing together near the entrance. My father looks polished and put together, as if unaffected by the relentless bad press of the past several days. On the surface, my mother also seems put together, but I know this has been hard on her.

My sisters are the ones my mother leans on when she needs support, but I sent a fruit bouquet and her in-home massage therapist to Portia's last week when she was staying there so my mother would know I was on her side. She called me a few days ago and broke down, apologizing for...everything. It doesn't fix anything for either of us, but at least we're both acknowledging that even when shit goes sideways, we're still family.

"I'll be back," I tell Tristan.

"We've got yours," he says.

I cross the room, heading for the man who has always made me feel like less-than so he can feel bigger. I'm done making my own life more difficult. I don't have to create fights where there are none.

My mother looks appropriately nervous at my approach. I lean in and kiss her cheek. She doesn't need me to tear her down more than my father already has. I turn to him and offer a placid smile. "I hope you're here to offer support and not stir shit up since you don't always deem this library worthy of funding."

He rolls his shoulders back. "Your mother thought it would be good press for us to attend, that it might help repair some of the damage that's been done."

"Don't you mean the damage *you've* done?"

His jaw works. "You don't know what you're talking about."

"The whole world knows what I'm talking about. At least own the fact that you messed up instead of trying to gaslight everyone into believing whatever fiction you've created in your head. You didn't think about anyone but yourself. You *never* think about anyone but yourself." I stop myself and lower my voice, because the last thing my mother needs is more people talking. "Because if you did, you would see how unbelievably lucky you are to have someone who is willing to stand at your side after you've disgraced not only your name, but your entire family. How does it feel to be the embarrassment instead of the embarrassed?"

"I made one mistake—"

"You mean on top of this one?" I tap my chest.

"You've made your point, Connor."

"Have I, though? It's not everyone you've affected that you're worried about. It's just how you appear. You don't care if your daughters can't leave the house without being heckled. You don't give a shit that you broke my mother's heart, or that you went out of your way to make my wife feel like trash. I spent my entire childhood seeking your approval. I don't want it or need it anymore, especially not after your hypocrisy and the way you so carelessly humiliated our family."

Mildred and Hemi move to the stage, seeking the audience's attention so they can announce the winners of the silent auction. Meems has found her way over to us. She steps in to kiss my mother on the cheek, but doesn't greet my father with the same affection. He's lucky she doesn't stomp on his foot. I know she'd like to.

I move to stand between my mother and Meems, bending down to whisper an apology for not bringing her something to drink, although it looks like someone else took care of it.

"The handsome one with hands the size of baseball mitts brought this to me." She squeezes my arm. "Everything okay?"

"Just fine," I promise and focus my attention on my wife. I haven't spoken to her since I broke both of our hearts, apart from a brief and tense hello at the hospital when Lexi gave birth to baby Ariel.

Hemi starts by thanking everyone for attending, and then the silent-auction items are claimed by their winners, most of which happen to be my teammates. Mildred is definitely on the edge of emotion as the total amount raised keeps growing, and then it finally reaches two million dollars.

Her voice wavers as she adjusts the mic and thanks everyone for their generous contributions.

I glance down at Meems with an arched brow.

"Whatever you're thinking, you should do it," she whispers.

I smirk and raise my hand, calling out, "My family would like to make an additional donation!" I wink at my father and head for the stage.

Mildred looks nervous. This is appropriate considering what she knows about my family dynamics.

Hemi gives me a look that tells me if I pull an asshole move, every single horrible promo op will be mine until the end of my time with the Terror.

My mother looks terrified, and my father looks like he wants to bury me. But Meems nods her approval. She and Mildred are the only ones who matter.

"I promise this will be good," I assure Hemi when I reach the stage. She gives me the smallest of nods.

I turn to my wife. "You look beautiful."

"What are you doing?" Mildred says through a tense smile and clenched teeth.

"Fixing the things I can for the people I care about." I turn to the mic and raise a hand. "Hi, everyone."

A confused murmur runs through the crowd. Someone takes a photo. Several phones rise, and the media covering the event move in. "A round of applause for Wilhelmina Reddi-Grinst, Aurora Hammerstein, and Mildred Grace for their hand in organizing this spectacular event." I clap, and everyone joins in. "And to all the incredible donors and sponsors who have helped raise two million dollars in support of Toronto Central Library's community programming."

More clapping follows.

"On behalf of my parents and my grandmother, the Grace family would like to make a donation in Mildred's name."

A collective gasp runs through the room and is echoed by my wife.

"Mildred has opened my eyes to the importance of library programming and free access to knowledge. My grandmother has always championed libraries, and in her honor we would like to match the funds raised tonight and double our donation, and we will continue to do so on an annual basis to ensure that these programs are able to continue indefinitely." I turn to my parents. "Mom, Dad, and Meems, Mildred and I are so unbelievably grateful for your generosity. Thank you for supporting us."

Mildred looks shocked, and my dad looks like he might burst into flames of rage.

But I've just secured funding for every program Mildred could possibly dream up, and I've spun a beautiful new lie that paints my family in a positive light. Now maybe my sisters will be able to leave the house without sunglasses before the next millennium.

"Thank you so much," Mildred whispers into the mic.

My mother claps enthusiastically, her eyes full of emotion as she calls out, "We're so happy we can support you both."

Hemi steps in and takes over, and I reluctantly leave the stage and my wife.

Everyone claps and cheers as Hemi wraps up the auction.

My father leans in, speaking through gritted teeth, "How dare you—"

"How dare I make you look good? How shameful am I now that I've saved your reputation and shone a positive light back on our family?" His mouth opens, but nothing comes out. "Don't worry, though, I didn't do it for you. I did it for my mother and sisters." I clap him on the shoulder. "You're welcome."

CHAPTER 50
DRED

It takes another half an hour before Connor can get back to me through the throng of photographers and excited library staff. He looks beautiful, regal, uncertain, and hopeful. Meems is on his arm.

"Hi, Mildred." My name from his lips makes my heart ache.

"Hi, Connor." So much has changed since Connor proposed that contract—my life upended, I lived a fairy tale, my heart has been broken, and my resilience tested. "Hi, Meems."

"My sweet girl." She wraps her arms around me and gives me the kind of hug that makes me want to weep.

"Thank you for that generous donation."

"It was all Connor." She winks. "I'm heading home."

"Should I walk you out?" Connor asks.

"Absolutely not." She holds our hands. "You two need to talk." She kisses me on the cheek, then does the same with Connor. Dallas swoops in to escort her to her car, where a driver should be waiting.

Connor tugs at the collar of his shirt. "I promise I didn't orchestrate that."

"Meems does what she wants," I reply. "And that was quite the amazing contribution you made on behalf of your family."

397

"I want your programs to run without you having to spend all your spare time writing proposals, and I want my mother and sisters to have peace, and Meems to be able to focus on her health instead of family drama."

"What about what you want?"

"I'm working on that." He clears his throat and tucks his hand in his pocket. "I'd love to talk. I understand if now isn't the best time, or maybe you need more time, or maybe you'll never be ready to talk… But, uh, if you find you are, I would love to apologize." He swallows. "And tell you how I feel about you."

I don't want to hand my heart over just to have it battered again, but I can't ignore the glimmer of hope this offers. And anyway, I can't move forward if we don't deal with the fallout. "We can talk."

Hope softens his features. "Now? Or would later be better?"

"We can talk now." I'd rather do it here, on my turf, where my friends are close and so are his teammates in case I need someone's shoulder to sob on.

He follows me into the hall. I poke my head into one of the storage rooms. There are empty boxes and supplies everywhere, but it's private and we won't be interrupted, so I usher him inside.

He glances around. There's nowhere to sit, and we can't really give each other much space.

He rubs the back of his neck. "I'm so sorry."

I cross my arms and wait, because I need to hear *what* he's sorry for.

"I was horrible to you."

"You absolutely were," I agree.

"You didn't deserve to be treated that way."

"I didn't."

"There is no excuse for how cruel I was, no reason that could ever justify why I shut you out the way I did. But I'll try to explain." He takes a deep breath. "I self-sabotaged out of fear, and I had no right to take those fears out on you. You've been nothing but kind, and soft, and empathetic, and I didn't meet you halfway. I didn't meet you at all, and I wish so badly that I could take it all back, but I can't. I can only tell you that I see what I did and the hurt it's caused you, and if you let me, I will spend the rest of my life making up for it."

I hug myself, my emotions on the edge of unraveling. I want to believe what he's saying, but I'm terrified to put my faith in him, in us.

"How can I trust that you won't just shut down on me like that again? What happens when there's another situation with your family?" *Or heaven forbid, the day we actually lose Meems.* "I can't be on the outside of your spiral, Connor. I can't give my heart to you if you'll keep mistreating it."

He nods, throat bobbing. "I see what's been done to you, and what I did to you, and I promise that I will never let my self-loathing take over my love for you again. Because that's exactly what I let happen. I didn't put us first the way I should have. I can't undo the past, but I love you, Mildred, more than I ever thought possible. And I will never make you feel unwanted again."

Tears rise, cresting on a wave of joy and hope and deep uncertainty. I want those words to be enough, but I need him to live that and not just tell me. And that will take time.

"You pressed your fingers into a wound I've carried with me my entire life. You cannot do something like that to me ever again. I won't accept it. I won't allow it, and I won't stay for someone who uses my weaknesses against me, unintentionally or not. I don't want a husband who is cruel. I'd rather be alone."

Shame washes over his face, along with deep sadness and heartbreaking acknowledgment. He's owning this. All of it. "You deserve to feel cherished every day, Mildred. I know how fortunate I am to be able to love you, and if you give me a chance, I promise I will never risk losing you or take your amazing heart for granted again."

Connor pushes his sleeve up and peels several bracelets from his wrist. He skims the back of my hand and I flip my palm over as fragile hope blossoms in my chest. He's speaking my language, showing me with actions that he understands his error as he places the first one in my palm, then the next and the next.

I'm sorry.

I love you.

I miss you.

I finger the delicate beads, my chest aching even as small pieces of my heart start to mend. "I want the best of you, Connor. I see everything you have to give." The way he's been showing up for the people he cares about, being there for Everly at Ariel's birth, standing up to his father tonight, finding a way to make things better instead of giving in to the worst side of himself—those are acts of selflessness, and that's the man I fell for. "I just want *you*. But you have to give me all of you, not just pieces. And not just sometimes."

He rubs the back of his neck and drops his head. "I didn't want you to see all the bad parts."

"There are no bad parts." I move closer and tuck a finger under his chin so his steel eyes meet mine. He's so forlorn. The fallen prince, used to being told he's not good enough. "But I deserve the man who gives because it's the right thing to do, and who will do anything to make the people he loves happy, because it makes you happy too. That's who I fell in love with."

He curves his fingers around mine. "I want to be the man you play board games with, who reads to you while you're in the tub, who you wake up beside every day, and spend your holidays with. I just want the chance to show you I can be the husband and partner you deserve."

I want this. I want him. I want the life I saw unfolding before fear got in the way. But I'm going to be cautious.

"Why don't we start with a date?"

CHAPTER 51
CONNOR

I've come full circle as I knock on my wife's apartment door—the one I made hers as a wedding gift. I'm hoping to move her back home sooner rather than later, but first...

The door opens, and my aching heart feels suddenly whole again. Mildred is wearing jeans and a T-shirt—I told her we were going casual tonight—her hair hangs loose around her shoulders, and I can see my reflection in her glasses. I look like the love-sick fool I am.

I rub the back of my neck because I don't know what else to do with my hands. "Hey."

She smiles up at me, warm and welcoming and perfect. "Hi. Want to come in for a minute?" She steps back, giving me room to enter her apartment. "I just need to feed Dewey, and then we can go."

"Can I hug you first?" I ask.

Her expression softens. "Yeah. I'd love that."

She opens her arms and steps forward. I wrap my arms around her and drop my head, nosing my way through her hair so I can get to her neck. "I've missed you." Her strawberry-and-vanilla scent blankets me in a wave of hope and comfort.

She runs a soothing hand down my back. "I've missed you, too."

All the broken parts of me seem to mend with her closeness and that admission.

Eventually she releases me, and I follow her to Dewey's enclosure. "Can I say hi to him, too?"

"Of course." She carefully retrieves him—this cage is much smaller than the one still at the manor—and our fingers brush as she passes him to me.

"It's been hard to sleep without the sound of him rustling around," I admit as I rub his belly.

"Once you get used to it, it's tough to get unused to." Mildred nods and scratches the top of his head.

He makes his snuffling sound and starts crawling up my chest while Mildred prepares him a snack of fresh fruit and mealworms.

"It's been hard to sleep without *you* next to me," I add.

She nods and smiles. "It's been the same for me."

Hopefully, if today goes well, the restlessness will end for both of us.

My gaze catches on the paperwork scattered across the kitchen table. "You aren't still working on program proposals, are you?"

"No." She sets the food in Dewey's cage. "I moved forward with my foster parent application."

"For Everly and Victor?"

She nods. "I want them to have a real home."

I smile. "I looked into it after Christmas, to see what was involved."

Mildred's eyes flare with surprise. "You did?"

"Yeah, but Meems's surgery distracted me. I started the paperwork last week, after the library gala." I set Dewey back in his enclosure. After Mildred said yes to a date, I wanted to be prepared for any possible outcome, particularly the best one.

"Seriously?" Mildred's eyes fill with tears.

I nod. "I didn't want to take them back after Christmas."

"Me either." She settles her hand against my cheek, exhaling an unsteady breath. "But one step at a time. Take me on a date before we start talking about fostering teenagers."

"Okay, darling." I turn my head and kiss her palm. "I have something for you." Many somethings, but one at a time. I roll the too small bracelet off my wrist and onto hers, where all the other ones I've given her live now.

She smiles and runs her fingers over the beads that read *Connor + Mildred + First Date*. "I love that you're commemorating our special moments."

She kisses my cheek, and then we head to the front door where she puts on her winter boots, and I help her into her jacket. The door across the way swings open when we leave her apartment, and Flip pokes his head out.

He arches a knowing brow. "Glad you got your head out of your ass."

"Me, too," I agree.

"Nice move at the gala the other night."

I tip my head in acknowledgment. "It felt right."

Flip nods his approval. "Treat my best friend like the precious gem she is."

"I promise I will."

"Good. I wouldn't want to have to punch you in the face again." He disappears inside his apartment.

"You two seem okay," Mildred observes. "Apart from him punching you in the face."

"That had been a long time coming, and I deserved it." For what I did back at the Hockey Academy and what I did to the woman standing beside me.

We take the elevator to the lobby and step out into the cold winter afternoon. Mildred huddles into her jacket as a gust of wind ruffles her hair.

I help her into the car before I round the hood and take my

place behind the wheel. "Would you like me to tell you where we're headed?"

"Is it outside of the city?"

"No, it's fairly close." I shift the car into gear.

"Then no, you can surprise me." She rests her arm on the center console.

That feels like a gift. I cover her hand with mine. "Thank you for saying yes to a date."

"It would have hurt too much to say no." She flips her hand so we're palm to palm. "How is your family? How are Isabelle and Portia?"

"My sisters are okay. This thing with my father really shattered the façade for Isabelle. She's tired of playing her role. I think my mother is, too."

"Would she ever leave?" Mildred asks. "Would any of them?"

"I don't know. Probably not my mother. But maybe Izzy." She's struggled the most with the betrayal. "She's young, and there's so much life left for her to live. I don't think she wants to spend it being unhappy."

"She has too big a heart," Mildred agrees. "How do you feel about all of that?"

"I expected to feel more vindication. I've spent my whole life being the family embarrassment, but maybe I was just a convenient shield for my father. If everyone was always looking at me, they wouldn't be focused on him. Mostly I'm sad for my mother and sisters and Meems and the way this has affected them. The donation to the library has at least helped smooth things in the eyes of the media. And my mother's commitment to upholding the Grace family name is both impressive and an imprisonment."

"I'm really proud of the way you flipped the script on your father," Mildred says. "So was Meems."

"She's been pretty pissed at me."

Mildred smiles. "I know. We talk every day. She told me not

to fold too quickly."

I laugh. "Meems would not want to make this easy for me, considering how hard I made it for myself."

"I think you learned the lesson," Mildred says wryly.

"I'm making a personal vow to only learn these lessons once from now on." I rub my thumb over her knuckles, so grateful to have her close again. "How are Everly and Victor? I've been messaging them, but sometimes Victor is hard to get a read on."

"They're excited about this date. I think Everly is hopeful, and Victor is more cautious. They've been let down a lot."

The wash of guilt makes my heart clench. "I'm sorry I contributed to that."

"They understand that you were under a lot of stress."

"Doesn't excuse my inability to see how it affected anyone but me." The impact of all the hurt I caused has been sobering.

"Stop beating yourself up over things we can't change, Connor." She squeezes my hand. "We're here and moving forward. They're resilient, and so are we. We wouldn't have gotten ourselves into this in the first place if we weren't."

I park in a public lot and guide her down the street. It's a busy afternoon, with people out shopping despite the biting cold. Mildred stays close, hugging my arm and tucking her chin into the collar of her coat.

"Here we are." I hold the door open and usher her in.

Her glasses fog up immediately. She takes them off and looks around, a smile curving her mouth. "A bookstore. It's like you know me."

"Not just any bookstore." I take her glasses and use a cleaning cloth to rub away the moisture before I carefully set them back in place. "The best bookstore."

She looks around, eyes widening in surprise. "Oh wow."

"They just opened this week."

It's like walking into a storybook. Archways made of old library books frame each aisle. "It's romance focused, and for every three books purchased, one is donated to a charity organization of your choice."

"This is incredible."

"Shall we browse?"

"Please." I grab a book basket, and Mildred links her arm through mine.

She leads me down the romantasy aisle, and we scour the shelves of new and gently used books. She points out favorite authors and favorite titles, noting the ones she thinks I would like and adding books to her basket as we go.

We spend two hours browsing, picking for her, Everly, Victor, and Meems before we grab coffees and settle into one of the plush couches. Mildred nestles into my side while we read one of the books she selected together, like we often used to do in the library at home.

I press my lips against her temple, comforted by the weight and warmth of her against me. "I missed having you close."

She looks up, eyes meeting mine. "I missed everything about you."

My gaze drops to her mouth.

"You shouldn't look at me like that when we're in public," she whispers.

"Then you and your lips should try to be less audaciously tempting, darling."

"Still such a villain…" She laughs.

"Still such a beautiful menace," I note.

She licks her lips, voice barely carrying across the space between us. "You should make a scene."

"A big or little one?"

She holds her fingers apart the tiniest bit. "Just a little one. I want to come here again."

I tuck my finger under her chin and bend until my lips almost touch hers. "I can't express how devastated I was when I thought I might never have the chance to make another memory like this with you." I brush my lips over hers. "I promise to give you the best versions of me, and to put that cruel part of me to rest. He'll be buried for good now."

Her palm rests against my cheek, her eyes warm with approval. "There's my sweet villain."

I slide another bracelet with the name of the bookstore and today's date onto her wrist. We stay snuggled together on the couch in the bookstore for another half an hour, and then I take her to the Pancake House for something to eat, because she loves it there. She orders the strawberries-and-cream pancakes, and I settle on bacon and eggs. As I slide yet another bracelet with the Pancake House on it, along with the date, the pieces of my heart slowly knit themselves back together.

"A bookstore and the Pancake House is my idea of the perfect date." Mildred sighs as she pushes her plate away. The strawberries and the whipped cream are gone, but she only made it through one pancake. Priorities.

"I hoped you would love it."

She reaches across the table, flipping her palm up. "Thank you for knowing me."

I drag my fingers over hers. "I want this date to be about all the things that make you happy." We've both had enough of dressing up and being put on display these past few months. "And I have one more surprise in store for you."

"I'm not sure how you'll top this, but I'm excited for whatever is up your sleeve."

I pay for dinner, and we leave the diner and drive to the next stop.

Her eyes widen as she takes in the sign above the venue. "Pierce the Veil are playing? How did I not know this?"

"You've had a busy few months." I pull up to the valet.

She grabs my arm. "You got us tickets?"

"I got us tickets," I confirm as I put the car in park. "Stay right here for a moment, please."

"Yes. Okay. Yes. Oh my gosh. I'm so excited. Wait!" She stops me before I can open the driver's side door. "Come here."

Mildred pulls me to her and suddenly my whole world is strawberry shampoo and soft, warm lips I can't ever get enough of. My existence aligns with that kiss. I would live in this moment for eternity if I could, here where I feel claimed again.

But we have a concert to attend, so after a moment, I gently pry my lips from hers. "Hopefully to be continued."

"Definitely, yes."

I jog around the car to help her out, and we head inside. Mildred's excitement is infectious as we enter the music hall and the attendant scans our tickets.

"Follow the signs to pick up your backstage passes." He points to the arrows above our heads.

"Backstage passes?" My wife clings to my arm, eyes wide. "This is unreal."

I press my lips to her temple. "I'm glad it makes you happy."

"*You* make me happy."

"When I'm not being awful, anyway."

She kisses my cheek. "Your feelings were on fire, and I didn't let you get away with it."

"I'm glad you didn't, and I've learned my lesson." I slide yet another bracelet on her wrist, smiling at the collection of memories we've made tonight.

We pick up our backstage passes and head to our front-row seats. Mildred spends the next two hours belting out lyrics and kissing my jaw, neck, and cheek. Her joy is everything I needed today, and I vow all over again to do everything in my power to keep her happy, and to treat her with the love and respect she deserves, even when everything in me is hurting and raw and angry.

After the concert, we're ushered to the private room with all the other backstage pass holders.

"Connor Grace!" the lead singer shouts as the rest of the band follows him into the room. "I thought they were bullshitting when they said you had backstage passes!"

He comes over to us, taking my hand in his. "You're having a killer season."

"It's been a good one," I agree.

"Can I get a photo?" he asks.

"Absolutely, as long as my wife can get a picture with you and the band."

Mildred is practically glowing.

"Shit, yeah, of course." He turns to Mildred and extends his hand. "Hi. It's nice to meet you."

"You too." Her smile lights up the entire room.

The lead singer looks around, like he's finally cluing in that we're not the only people in the room. "Hey, all!" He waves, then points to me. "This is Connor Grace, hockey legend."

"The original villain," Mildred says cheekily.

We take photos with the band, and a few of the other backstage pass holders request photos with me. Mildred is absolutely beaming as the band makes their rounds, giving everyone some attention.

"I have something special for them to sign." I pull a small hardbound book from my pocket and pass it to her.

"What is this?" She runs her hand over the cover and flips it open. Her mouth drops open. "A book of their lyrics? Where did you get this?"

I want to bottle the wonder in her eyes and carry it with me always.

"I had it bound for you. It's one of a kind," I explain. "Fee helped me with it." She's a crafty one.

"This is unbelievable." She throws her arms around my neck. "You're unbelievable."

I fold her into my embrace and revel in how good it feels to make her smile.

Mildred is buzzing on the drive home, the signed book of lyrics hugged to her chest. "This is the coolest, most thoughtful date I've ever been on."

"I'm glad." I needed her to know I pay attention, and not just because her happiness was tied to Meems, but because her joy is my joy.

I pull into the temporary parking spot at the front of her building. I don't want tonight to end. I don't want to go home, where she isn't, and wake up alone.

Mildred slides her fingers between mine and curls them around my hand. "You should park in the underground and come up."

My lack of honesty is what tore us apart. I won't let it happen again. "I want you to come home."

She lifts my hand so my palm rests against her cheek. "I want that, too."

"So let's go."

"Dewey is in my apartment, and I have to work in the morning, so I won't be able to come back and feed him."

"Flip could do it, or I could stop by before or after practice and pick him up."

"Either of those are possibilities."

I hear the *but* in her voice. "We can just go up and get him now," I suggest.

She turns her head and kisses my palm. "If we go up, we're not leaving until morning."

"Hmm..." I nod slowly. "You do have a point."

"And we're here now. The house is another half-hour drive—twenty minutes if you break laws and run lights."

"Breaking laws seems like the opposite of ideal," I muse.

"Mm... Right." She shakes her head and gently bites the fleshy part of my palm. "However unconventional, this is where we started. I want this night with you in *my* bed, so I always have that memory."

CHAPTER 52
DRED

The moment we're inside my apartment, I try to pull Connor's mouth to mine.

"We should probably take our shoes off so we don't track snow and salt through the apartment," he mumbles around my tongue.

"Why so responsible?"

"Just thinking about the things that irk you, like wet socks."

"I really do loathe wet socks."

"I'll always look out for what's best for you, even if it means delaying your gratification to save your irritation." He drops to one knee on the mat and tugs the zipper down on the back of my boots.

He holds the heel, and I brace a hand on his shoulder so I can step out of them one at a time. "So thoughtful."

"Just trying to be what you deserve, darling."

While Connor loosens his own laces, I run my fingers through his silky, dark hair. I've missed him, especially this part—the soft version of Connor who wants to take care of me and values my happiness. He was always there. It just took us a little time to bring him to the surface and keep him there.

"Every time you showed up for one of Callie's hockey games

and sat next to me, every time you opened your arms and heart for that little girl and gave her all the best parts of you, my heart opened a little more for you. I saw you."

"I want to be that for you." Connor wraps his arms around me, and I sink into the embrace.

I rest my cheek against his chest, feeling his heart beating. "I want you to be that person for you, too."

His fingers trail up my arms. "Thank you for giving me another chance." He cups my face in his warm palms.

My stomach flutters with anticipation, and I tip my head up, waiting.

Connor lowers his mouth to mine. This kiss is a promise of what the future can hold: a life full of love, and warmth, and happiness.

I take his hand and guide him through my apartment to my bedroom.

It's simply furnished with a double bed, nightstand, dresser, and full-length mirror. It's nothing like my opulent bedroom at Grace Manor, or the one I shared with Connor after the wedding and will be happy to return to, but this space is full of memories.

It's more than just a gift from my grandmother, a piece of my history, and a link to the woman I'll never know. It gave me the family I have now, including the man beside me.

He moves behind me, wrapping his arms around my waist. He inhales deeply and exhales on a sigh. "It's so perfectly you." He drops his head, pressing his cheek against my neck. "It smells like you."

He adds another bracelet to my wrist that reads *Connor's Little Menace*. Each one represents another piece of us, a collection of memories for me to treasure.

I turn in his arms, linking my fingers behind his neck. He dips down to kiss me gently. There's a relief in being touched by him—the feel of his lips on mine, his hands in my hair. We undress slowly, taking our time, mouths exploring each newly exposed inch of skin as we bare ourselves for each other.

Connor pulls the comforter down and lifts me onto the bed, then stretches out next to me. He takes up most of the space with his massive frame, and I love it. His erection nudges my hip as he traces the dip at my collarbones with a single finger. Need and desire swim in his eyes, but it's accompanied by so many other emotions, I could drown in them.

"How would you like me to love you, darling? Am I allowed to take my time, or are you feeling too impatient?"

I skim the curve of his bottom lip with gentle fingers. "I suppose it depends on how villainous you're feeling."

He rolls over on top of me, legs bracketing mine as he props himself on one elbow and trickles his fingers slowly along my neck, over my breast, skimming my nipple before drifting lower. "Scale of one to ten?" His voice is all gravel.

"I think you're already at an eleven?"

"Maybe even a twelve." He sucks my bottom lip.

I hook my leg over his as he presses into my hot sex and his erection slides over my stomach. "That's quite the evil mood."

"You want it to be memorable, remember?" He shifts, one thigh settling between mine, and his lips find the edge of my jaw. "Close your eyes for me, please."

"I want to see you," I admit.

"In a bit." He lifts his head, steel eyes meeting mine. "I want your sweet moans of surprise filling the room. I missed them."

"Kiss me first?" I ask.

"Of course, darling."

My eyes flutter closed as he slants his mouth over mine, tongue soft, each stroke light and languid. I want more of his weight on me, more of his skin pressed against mine. I try to pull him down, rub myself against his thigh, but it's not enough. And of course he knows it.

He breaks the kiss and presses his lips against each eyelid—a reminder to keep them closed—and the most delicious torment begins. Soft lips on my skin, fingers trailing, thigh pressing against me, the head of his cock wet against my stomach.

He works his way down my body, so soft and sweet until he shocks me with a sharp press of teeth. I shove my hands in his hair and gasp, then moan when he follows with intense suction and featherlight fingers brushing along the top of my thigh.

"So mean," I groan.

"The meanest," he agrees, his lips dancing lightly over the skin below my navel.

He shifts and presses my thighs open, his deep groan making the muscles below my waist clench. I open my eyes as his palms smooth up the inside of my thighs, his face a mask of dark desire.

His gaze lifts to mine. "Such a pretty, soft cunt." His thumbs brush over sensitive skin. My whimper curls his lip in satisfaction. "Should I fuck you with my fingers first, darling?" He eases a single one inside, stroking the place that makes me moan before he withdraws.

He sucks his finger clean on a deep groan. "I think I'm hungry." Connor's lust-darkened eyes stay fixed on mine as he drops his head and licks up the length of me, laving my clit before he swirls his tongue .

I can't take my eyes off him as he devours me. Needy, wet sounds fill the room.

He adjusts our position, dragging me down the bed until I can see our reflection in the full-length mirror.

I slide my fingers into his hair, gripping the strands. "Such a wicked mouth."

"Such a sweet, tempting cunt." He loops his arms around my thighs and holds me open, fucking me with his tongue, lapping at me, sucking and biting, keeping me on the edge, and just as I'm about to tip over, he blankets me with his body and fills me in one smooth stroke.

And I come, body shaking, his name breathed across my lips. He presses me into the mattress, the weight of him the only thing tethering me to Earth. "I missed you so much."

Nothing compares to being connected to him like this, and now that I have him back, I don't ever want to let him go again.

"I know. I'm sorry. I missed you, too. I'll never do that to us again." He frames my face with his palms. "I love you."

"Say it again," I whisper.

He rolls his hips. "I love you." Soft brush of lips. "Endlessly."

"I love you, too," I murmur.

Each time he whispers those words, they heal the fractures in my heart. He's mine, and I'm his.

I come again in crashing waves of bliss, and Connor comes with me, both of us full of love and hope, and the possibilities of the future.

We lie there for long minutes, Connor's weight a comfort on top of me as he kisses my lips and cheeks and jaw.

I run my nails down the back of his neck. "You know, the sheets at home are a lot nicer."

He grins down at me. "The bed is roomier, too."

"We hardly need a king when you're always trying to turn me into your blanket."

"I'm not the only one who's a fan of cuddles." He kisses my nose.

"Mm... I miss coffee by the fireplace."

"And your library."

"That, too," I agree. "And Dewey misses his luxury condo."

"Tomorrow we'll move you two back home, then?" There's a hopeful lilt in his voice.

"Yes, please."

CHAPTER 53
CONNOR

"Pull your sleeves down!" Mildred's tone is chastising as she tugs the black fabric until my tattoos and my bracelet proclaiming me as *Mildred's Sweet Villain* are hidden. "The arm porn is too much for these women. Have a heart."

"See you next week!" A pair of young moms waves at us as they leave the mom-and-tots circle at the library.

"Bye, girls! Don't forget to grab a onesie and extra snacks on the way out!" Mildred calls after them.

"The number of moms has doubled since Connor started showing up," Everly observes, draping herself over Mildred like a cape. "Are we going now?"

"Right after we clean up." Mildred pats her hand. "Go help your brother."

Everly flits over to Victor, who's already put most of the chairs away. Mildred watches them with a smile.

I kiss her temple. "Soon."

She looks up and I drop a kiss on her lips. "I know. I'm just impatient."

Since Mildred moved back home with Dewey a few weeks ago, we've been working to push through the paperwork to become foster parents. We want Victor and Everly to have a place they can call home, and we want it to be with us.

We finish tidying, collect Meems, who's been happily snuggling one of the babies, and drive over to the arena. Callie's team is in first place and heading for a championship tournament.

Fifteen minutes later we park and head inside. The girls link arms, and Victor hangs back with me, wearing a pleased smile.

"Everything good?" I ask.

"Yeah, everything is great. Everly is the happiest she's ever been," he notes.

"She seems more settled these days," I agree.

"She is. She's doing a lot better in school. She's not really getting in trouble."

"I feel that. I'm a better hockey player thanks to Mildred, and more settled too."

"She has that effect on people." Victor nods.

I want to tell him that soon we'll be able to make this sense of security permanent, that we'll be able to give him the stability and love he craves and deserves. But I can't yet. We're almost there, and we want to wait until all the paperwork is complete.

We join Lexi, Fee, and her best friend, Cammie, in the stands. Everly flops into a seat and pulls Victor down beside her.

"Perfect timing!" Lexi cradles baby Ariel to her chest. "They've almost finished warmups."

"Look at that sweet face." Mildred slides into the seat next to her and rests her cheek on Lexi's shoulder. "You're pretty too, Lexi."

Lexi laughs. "Do you want to hold her?"

"I would absolutely love to hold this sweet, tiny nugget of adorableness."

Lexi passes Ariel to my wife, who coos at her.

Roman, who was talking to one of the coaches, comes over and wedges himself into the seat next to mine—they aren't built for guys over six three—with a smirk.

"You gonna be next on the baby brigade?"

"Calm down, bro. We have to see some kids off to college first," I murmur.

Understanding and compassion lights up his face, and he drops his voice to a whisper. "You get everything finalized?"

"We're close." Roman and Lexi have been helpful on this journey since Lexi is the legal guardian of her sisters, and Roman formally adopted them last fall. Now they're officially his.

Everly's head appears between mine and Mildred's. "Fee and Cammie are going to the concession stand."

I pull a twenty out of my wallet and pass it over my shoulder. "Please bring me the change, if there is any."

"Thank you!" She kisses us both on the cheek and disappears.

Callie skates past, waving at us as she heads for her net, but then she circles back and stops in front of Victor. He smiles and taps the glass with his fist.

"How have I been so easily replaced?" I mutter.

Mildred grins and kisses my cheek as Callie skates away, pulling out some figure skating moves as she goes.

"She's the only girl who ever loved me without even knowing me," I lament.

"You'll get over it." Mildred nudges my shoulder. "Here, hold this adorable baby."

I put out my arms.

"Push your sleeves up first, though."

I do as my wife asks, then take Ariel into the crook of my elbow.

"Ahh, there's the magic…" Mildred snaps several pictures, her eyes sparking with heat and full of promise.

I see our entire life writing itself for us; a home full of love and family, kids and grandkids and Terror reunions. I want it all. And I want it with Mildred at my side.

CHAPTER 54
DRED

"I'm so excited!" Everly is bouncing around us like Tigger with springs in her feet.

"Keep your eyes closed," Connor tells me.

"Your giant hands are covering my whole face," I assure him. "I can see nothing."

"You love my giant hands," he murmurs.

"Not in front of the children." I elbow my husband in the ribs.

"Victor, can you get the door, please?" Connor asks.

"On it."

A door opens. Based on the smell, we're in the garage.

"Are you ready?" Connor asks.

"Show her, show her, show her!" Everly claps.

Connor drops his hands.

"Happy birthday!" the three of them shout.

In the middle of the garage filled with outrageously expensive cars is... "Betty?"

"It's Betty!" Everly gazelle leaps across the expansive space and jazz hands her way around my car.

"I thought maybe she went to the car graveyard." When Connor handed me the keys to one of his cars and told me it was mine until further notice, I wasn't totally convinced Betty would make it out of her makeover.

"I would never." Connor looks aghast.

I arch a brow.

"Okay. I would, but I know how much you love Betty." He takes my hand and pulls me over to my car.

"She looks brand-new," I marvel. No rust. No missing side mirror.

"That's because she pretty much is," Everly says. "I helped pick out the fabric for the driver's seat." She opens the door. "Ta-da!"

My seat is covered in a strawberry pattern. The entire interior is brand-new—everything is brand-new.

Connor rubs his hands along his thighs. "Do you like it?"

"I love it!" I throw my arms around him. "Betty was a piece of shit. I can't even imagine how much it cost to do this."

"Your happiness is invaluable." He passes me the fob. "Everything has been updated, so it runs like a new car, even though it's still Betty. Why don't we take it for a spin over to the Watering Hole?"

Everly climbs into the back seat. "Get in! Let's go!"

Victor climbs in beside her, and I slide into the driver's seat. Connor is comically large in this small four-seater. The engine purrs to life, and I drive my new-old car to the Watering Hole, the Terror's favorite local pub.

Everly and Victor join Fee, Callie, and Tally, and we settle in with our friends—because of course they're here. Connor has once again made sure I'm surrounded by love and the family I made for myself. I couldn't ask for a better birthday celebration.

Afternoon slides into evening. I've definitely had far too many margaritas, so I ask Connor to get me a virgin drink. I don't want to end up spending tomorrow in bed for all the wrong reasons. Flip puts his arm around my shoulder and gives me a side hug.

"Happy birthday, bestie."

"Thanks for the very ostentatious but hugely appreciated gift." Flip bought me a deluxe set of all of my favorite board games, designed to look like books. "I can't wait to put them on my shelves."

"I'm sure you also can't wait to kick my ass at all of them."

"Also that," I agree.

He glances over at the dart boards where Victor is currently dominating—of course it's something he's randomly good at—and the girls are laughing and cheering him on. Callie stares at him with adoration.

Tally excuses herself to the bathroom, and Flip's eyes follow her. "I'm hammered," he announces.

"You are." He's bleary-eyed, a state he rarely gets into these days. "But you don't have a game for a couple of days, so you're allowed to have a good time on my birthday."

"I probably won't remember this tomorrow."

"Probably not."

"If Tally wasn't my coach's daughter, I'd do anything—"

"Shots for the birthday girl!" Dallas does some ridiculous hip shimmy as he dances his way over to us.

"Shots are never a good idea," Flip and I say at the same time.

"These are ninety percent juice. I made sure of it," Hemi says from behind Dallas.

He passes them out.

Hemi leans in and whispers, "They're all juice. No one needs the hangover."

We shoot them, and Flip gets pulled away by the guys, so he never finishes that sentence. But I already know what he was going to say.

Victor has the honor of driving us home at the end of the night, with a ninety percent-sober Connor in the passenger seat, and me and Everly cuddled in the back.

When we arrive home, I fully expect everyone to go straight upstairs, but Connor suggests a quick stop in the kitchen for a snack before bed. It's not the worst idea. I could use some water and maybe a slice of leftover strawberry cream cake.

"There's one more gift," Connor whispers as Everly and Victor rush ahead of us.

"Because Betty and a night out with my friends isn't enough?" I squeeze his arm.

"I had to save the best for last."

When we reach the kitchen there's already a fruit and dessert platter set out for us, along with plates and cutlery and birthday napkins. On top of one plate is a large white envelope with my name written in Connor's neat cursive.

"Oooh! What else did you get Dred?" Everly slides into one of the seats and starts loading her plate with fruit.

I give Connor a quizzical look.

He tips his chin. "Don't keep us all waiting."

Victor takes the seat next to his sister, and Connor and I take the ones across from them.

I open the envelope and peek inside, then glance at my husband. "They finally came through?"

His smile is soft and warm and full of joy.

My hands shake as I pull the documents out. "Oh! Oh my gosh." It's not just the paperwork approving us as foster parents. It's also the paperwork to foster Everly and Victor. All that's missing is my signature. My bottom lip trembles, tears threatening to spill over. "Oh, Connor."

He wraps his arm around my shoulder.

Everly and Victor's eyes are wide with worry. "What is it? Why are you crying?"

"They're not sad tears, they're happy tears," I rush to explain.

"Oh." Everly's shoulders relax. "What did Connor get you? Another car?"

I shake my head. "A family."

Victor frowns. Everly tips her head.

Connor kisses my temple. I'm too choked up to explain.

"We've been working on securing our paperwork to become foster parents," he explains. "And it finally came through."

Everly's gaze darts between us, wide with shock. Victor is still beside her.

"We want to foster you," I choke out. "Both of you."

Everly and Victor look at each other and then us.

"Seriously?" Victor whispers. "You want us?"

I nod. "More than anything."

"We want this to be your home," Connor says gently. "We want to be a family."

"Your family," I add. "If you want us."

"We want you," Everly blurts, then looks to her brother. "Right?"

Victor nods. "Yes. We want to be yours."

He and I burst into tears at the same time, and then the four of us are on our feet, converging into a hug, Connor's arms enveloping all of us.

There is no gift that can top this.

I have everything I need. An adoring husband, two beautiful teens I get to help move through the world with love and the support of my partner, an amazing Meems who gets to be a great-grandmother, and a found family who always have my back.

I tip my head up to find my husband gazing down at me with love. "Best birthday ever."

EPILOGUE
CONNOR

"Everly, please put your phone down and finish your breakfast," I say for the tenth time.

"My hair is doing something weird." She slides her phone back in her pocket, though, before I can confiscate it.

"Your hair looks great," Mildred assures her.

"You look beautiful as always," Meems confirms.

"Thanks, Meems." Everly nuzzles Meems's arm like a happy cat. "You're beautiful, too."

"Thanks, sweetheart." Meems kisses the top of her head.

Meems is just as taken with the twins as Mildred and I are.

"I'm too nervous to eat," Everly declares. Then she douses her pancakes in two liters of maple syrup and takes a bite anyway. She chews and pushes her plate away. "I'll eat these as a snack later."

"Can I do the same?" Victor asks. Normally he's like a vacuum cleaner with the way he hoovers up food, but today his plate is still half full.

"I'll throw some snacks in my bag," Mildred offers.

"And we're having a celebratory lunch after anyway," I remind them, adjusting my tie.

Mildred pushes her chair back and stands, moving toward

me. Her hands settle on my chest, grounding me. "You a little nervous, too?" she asks.

"Excited mostly. I just can't wait to make it official." The twins have been with us for the past six months. As soon as they moved in, Mildred and I started the process of formally adopting them. We want them forever. Today we're signing the adoption papers.

"Me either." She pushes up on her toes, and I bend to accept the kiss.

"Arms out everyone!" Meems declares.

We all extend one to the centre of the table, palm up and she drops a new bracelet into each of our palms.

"Oooh! These ones are flashy!" Everly's eyes are lit up with joy.

"That's because they're special." Meems winks.

Each one has *Grace Family* in gold lettered beads, followed by each of our names.

In just a couple of hours, Victor and Everly will be ours. We'll be our own little family, not just in our hearts, but on paper, too. For the first time in my life, I truly belong to someone.

Every time I sat next to Mildred at a hockey game, every smile she graced me with, every word she spoke—wrapped themselves around my heart.

I thought I was helping her and getting what I wanted in the process, but then she gave me her heart. And claimed mine.

I'm her sweet villain and she's my little menace.

We belong to each other until the end of forever.

And that might just be long enough.

Need More Connor and Dred?
Subscribe for instant access to a bonus scene:

ABOUT THE AUTHOR HELENA HUNTING

NYT and USA Today bestselling author, Helena Hunting lives on the outskirts of Toronto with her amazing family and her adorable kitty, who thinks the best place to sleep is her keyboard. Helena writes everything from emotional contemporary romance to romantic comedies that will have you laughing until you cry. If you're looking for a tearjerker, you can find her angsty side under H. Hunting.

OTHER TITLES BY HELENA HUNTING

THE TORONTO TERROR SERIES

If You Hate Me

If You Want Me

If You Need Me

If You Love Me

If You Claim Me

If You Keep Me (Coming March 2026)

I Could Be Yours

TILTON UNIVERSITY SERIES

Chase Lovett Wants Me

THE PUCKED SERIES

Pucked (Pucked #1)

Pucked Up (Pucked #2)

Pucked Over (Pucked #3)

Forever Pucked (Pucked #4)

Pucked Under (Pucked #5)

Pucked Off (Pucked #6)

Pucked Love (Pucked #7)

AREA 51: Deleted Scenes & Outtakes

Get Inked

Pucks & Penalties

Where it Begins

ALL IN SERIES

A Lie for a Lie

A Favor for a Favor

A Secret for a Secret

A Kiss for a Kiss

LIES, HEARTS & TRUTHS SERIES

Little Lies

Bitter Sweet Heart

Shattered Truths

SHACKING UP SERIES

Shacking Up

Getting Down (Novella)

Hooking Up

I Flipping Love You

Making Up

Handle with Care

SPARK SISTERS SERIES

When Sparks Fly

Starry-Eyed Love

Make A Wish

LAKESIDE SERIES

Love Next Door

Love on the Lake

THE CLIPPED WINGS SERIES

Cupcakes and Ink

Clipped Wings

Between the Cracks

Inked Armor

Cracks in the Armor

Fractures in Ink

STANDALONE NOVELS

The Librarian Principle

Felony Ever After

Before You Ghost (with Debra Anastasia)

FOREVER ROMANCE STANDALONES

The Good Luck Charm

Meet Cute

Kiss my Cupcake

A Love Catastrophe